War.

Decades after the End, which caused the majority of mankind to vanish in a single moment, civilisation is in danger of crumbling forever. Fires line the horizon, distant screams ring out from every direction, and a blanket of shadow has descended over all of England.

New Canterbury and Canary Wharf, the last bastions of the Old World, are cut off and surrounded. An army marching from the North, and a supernatural struggle between good and evil, threaten the survival of everyone.

Norman Creek and the mission of New Canterbury must overcome their demons and lead the resistance against the encroaching hordes. Outnumbered, outgunned and alone, they must fight to keep the Old World alive, as the last war of humanity begins.

**Join My List to keep up with new releases:**
**http://eepurl.com/V4niL**

# THE RUIN SAGA

## VOLUME III: FRAY

Harry Manners

# PART 5

# THE CENTRE CANNOT HOLD

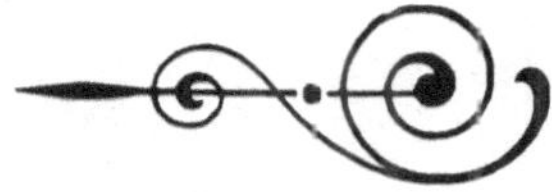

A person often meets his destiny on the road he took to avoid it.

— **Jean de La Fontaine**

The belief in a supernatural source of evil is not necessary; men alone are quite capable of every wickedness.

— **Joseph Conrad**

# PROLOGUE

One minute before the world ended, Lucy Callaghan got ice cream.

"Thanks, Mum!" She beamed, skipping from the parlour and licking the cone as she went.

Her mother grunted at the counter, fussing with her handbag.

St Pancras International glittered before them, more glass-domed jewel than rail hub, buzzing with London's business elite, gawking tourists, coffee-slurping office drones, and bopping teens on their merry way to untold mischiefs. High-end chain stores lined the interior of a space the size of a cathedral, leading away towards the London Underground. Lucy waited as her mother paid for tickets, licking her ice cream cone, resisting the urge to look at the handbags in Gucci. She liked grown-up things. She was getting older now, almost seven.

She knew better than to ask as Mum said there were going to be a lot of connecting trains today and they were on a tight schedule. But Lucy also suspected the ice cream was an attempt to barter for good behaviour. It was a long way to Manchester. Lucy could make life hell.

Underneath her enjoyment of the creamy goodness, a small part of her—the treacherous *grown-up* part of her that liked handbags—realised that there was no room for pushing Mum today. Times were tough, Mum said, and that meant they had to move again.

She had told Lucy only last week. Lucy had tried screaming, then crying, then sulking. That hadn't done it. That never did it.

Mum said they had to go where the jobs were. Lucy thought that was pretty dumb. Some of her friends' mothers lived *on the dole*. She wasn't quite sure what that meant, but she knew it meant getting money for not doing very much. She got in trouble when she said that. Mum said she didn't take charity. *We'll eat out of bins before I take money without earning it*, she said.

Lucy had almost argued, but Mum had given her one of her patented *don't start* looks.

Their apartment had thinned of furniture and ornaments of late. Lucy didn't like watching lamps or piles of CDs go missing, especially when all Mum could talk about were the *hot meals* they ate later in the day. Eventually they had run out of things and had to snuggle on a single mattress on the floor. Then a smelly bald man had come around and said they couldn't *doss around for free* anymore, and he wanted them gone.

That was yesterday. Lucy was scared the man would come again, but this morning Mum had packed a bag of what they had left and marched Lucy to the train station.

She had made Lucy wear her best red dress and plastered her own face in makeup. She said she had an interview for a job.

Lucy complained she didn't want to go. Why couldn't Mum get a babysitter?

"The same reason we don't have a manservant and a Rolls," Mum had muttered, giving a harsh bark that didn't sound anything like a real laugh.

Lucy didn't get it. She didn't get a lot of things right now. But she did know there wasn't any money since Dad left. Definitely not money spare for ice cream.

A distant disquiet throbbed in her belly. If she had been older, she might have recognised guilt.

Instead she took another bite of her cone, and the feeling went away.

Her mother walked around her with a heavy puff and leaned against the wall. Already her hair was ruffled into a mousy bird's-nest, and her lipstick had lost its sheen from ceaseless nibbling.

"Good?"

"Yeah," Lucy said. She wasn't really listening, watching the world pass by.

"Good. Good. Enjoy it, baby."

Lucy stopped licking. There was something strange in her mother's voice. "What's wrong?"

For a moment her mother seemed on the verge of saying something, her lips pale under all that lipstick. Lucy didn't remember ever seeing her look so tired. Then her lips came back together, and she ran her hand along Lucy's neck, stroking her hair.

In the midst of commuter bedlam, they smiled at one another, and a strange ache touched Lucy's throat.

Life was funny, Lucy decided. Often it hurt, and you didn't know why.

But it was okay. In that moment, she had Mum, and she had ice cream.

Nearby, a young mother played a ditty on one of the pianos dotted around the station. Her chubby baby kicked his little booties in his pram beside her, gurgling happily.

Lucy and her mother watched the woman's fingers dance across the keys with featherlike grace, and the world flexed in their wake.

"We'll survive," Lucy's mother said and squeezed her neck.

Lucy had just decided to be brave on the train to Manchester—brave for Mum—when everybody around her doubled over and screamed.

A moment later, all was dark and painful. Nerves crackled, muscles contorted. Lucy was suddenly utterly lost and alone. So things remained for countless years, years of toil and suffering, along with seven billion other lost souls amid endless darkness.

*

The station jarred to a halt, and every clock and wristwatch stopped at precisely 08:15. The shock front, a silver wave propagating at the speed of light, passed through space, metal, and flesh alike, taking every human being with it in as many puffs of diaphanous mist.

All across the world, that same pulse brought each person a moment's chill in their bones as the echo of doom rattled in their ears. Then it was over. Suddenly, totally, over.

Like a sieve through a fish pond, the End stripped humanity from the earth. Somewhere amidst the turbulent firmament, spinning end over end, a lone ice cream cone splashed down upon a tiny, crumpled, red dress.

This was the way the world ended.

*

A second later, two figures exploded into being from the dissipating mist, one sauntering and the other sprawling.

Fol skidded across the tiled floor, beaten and torn. All around him, far beyond this place and yet right beside it, a thousand strings holding the fabric of things in place stretched, pinged free, and began a long process of unravelling.

Despite the terrible knowledge that one false move could bring his long life to an unceremonious and ugly end, a thought took flight in his mind like a trapped moth: to feel again, to know pain. Such was to be alive. Bleeding from a barrage of blows both physical and beyond, he screamed, "Son of a bitch, whore!"

The mist cleaved in the wake of the hulking behemoth in pursuit. Heavy footfalls boomed under the high roof, coupled with a laughter that could have wilted flowers upon their stalks. Wreathed in golden plate armour, shining with the reflections of *other places*, a creature seven feet tall and with skin the colour and texture of volcanic ash stalked towards him. A curdled, guttural voice welled up from deep in its chest: "Highcourt is fallen, Jester."

Fol spat at the great lumbering thing and launched himself from the floor in a shower of curses.

His face met a fist brought up almost casually, swatting him aside. Bright lights and ringing erupted in his head. Skittering into a pile against the base of a pillar, he wiped blood from his lip, transfixed by it in all its vivid glory.

He felt them—all of those abducted to the void to labour, under incredible strain, forever tortured. The others had winked out like candles in a deluge. None but he remained to share the pain. Every fibre cried out, shuddering on the brink of shattering.

The pain of the seven billion Vanished souls coursed through his flesh.

Mountains had eroded and oceans boiled in the course of his life. Countless empires had risen and crumbled. Untold atrocities had passed in that time, but none so great as this. None so heinous. Upon the tiled floor, lying atop a little red dress covered with melted ice cream, Fol wept.

The thing before him opened its mouth yet wider and roared with laughter, a footlong chin bobbing under a mouthful of needle-like teeth. "This world is ours."

Fol shook his head, looking once more at the blood on his fingertips. To know eons without number in prosperity and dignity, watch the Web of All Where pass by with its tides of mortal lives—then to bleed one's own blood.

So grand had the dominion of Highcourt become that they had grown lazy and decadent. And now it was all gone.

*Great Weaver, forgive me. I have doomed us*, Fol thought.

But then from the firmament, knowing, delivered by an unseen hand—one far beyond the gold-plated tadpole who had stood mocking him a moment before. One far beyond.

*It's not over. Maybe, maybe I can fix it.*

He saw glimpses of a long road ahead, one that stretched clear across All Where. It would mean pain, death, and misery, and the road might be never-ending. But somewhere out there waited a few who might undo these wrongs.

*Creatures of destiny*, he thought. *The Frost didn't take them all. There are survivors. It's not over.*

*It's not.*

"You have no idea what you've done," he breathed, crouched on the floor.

Another laugh, one that shook the foundations of the station. All around them, the echo festered and took on life of its own, lingering to spite the myriad piles of suits and loafers, trousers, briefcases, smartphones, pacemakers, and necklaces littered every which way—a carpet of possessions over a world scraped clean, sanitised in the wake of coming darkness.

"This world falls, and the rest will follow. It is inevitable; soon the master will be free." The golden creature turned its gaze upon Fol. "I can't thank you enough for all you've done."

Fol searched inwardly for somebody, anybody, but found only silence. Only moments ago he had battled alongside the others in Highcourt's crumbling halls; the air had been filled with the war cries of scores of battles across the cosmos. Now, in the vast reaches of space, nothing. All Where reeled from the blast, its guardians in tatters. Nobody was coming to save him.

Fol's lips quivered. The agony of seven billion, for a brief searing moment, faded in the wake of overwhelming guilt.

*I did this. For all this time, our gates stood against the night, and in the end, it was the Jester who brought down the Kingdom of Highcourt.*

A piece of him died then, a secret part deep in the well of his being. Something vital and good. In its place, tainted and broken, a tar-like treacle flowed and took root.

He gritted his teeth, snarling. "You tricked me."

A long-nailed finger thrust into the air. "Ah, *tsk tsk*. We must tell no lies."

"You tricked me!"

"Rule number one of any con artist, master Jester." Each word came with a single booming footfall, hammering nails into Fol's chest. "Nobody can scam a mark who isn't greedy."

A tiny groan escaped Fol's throat.

*I betrayed them. Betrayed them all.*

"I can fix this," he gasped. "I can fix it. We'll stop you."

"There is no *we*. You, great and righteous fool of the great courts upon high, are the last." The thing swept down from its towering stature such that its snarling countenance was but an inch from Fol's face. Breath rank with rotted meat wafted from the fetid jaws. "You are alone."

Fol shook his head. "No, no. They still live."

This time, not a laugh, but a disgusted snarl. "Your *creatures of destiny* can't help you now. They don't even know what they are themselves."

"They will once I find them and bring them together. Once you're back in your hole, we'll put this right."

"The road is longer than you can imagine, fool."

"Lucky I've got no strings attached now." They stared at one another a long moment. "Unless you'd rather kill me now and be done with it?"

The creature grinned. "Better to watch you squirm like a maggot, Jester. Better to watch you fall."

They glowered at one another, inches apart, until it seemed time itself had stopped and they had turned to stone.

Then a clatter rang out from behind them as something moved alone under the station's ceiling. Another voice spoke inside Fol's head.

*Even if you succeed, you will be beaten. Some things cannot be undone—*

The dark thing now alive in Fol's heart twitched.

*—and your long quest will cost you, cost all of you. I wonder if, in the end, you'll wish you had let it all tumble down.*

Fol bit down on his tongue. He would do whatever it took.

"One of these days I'm going to carve their names on

your body," Fol said. "All their names."

The thing faded before his eyes, a floating smile from an impossible creature only half there, quickly blurring to mere echo and tricks of the light. "*Happy hunting, Jester.*"

Then Fol was alone.

*Not quite alone*, he thought, watching a man stumble from the London Underground escalators. His eyes round as fog lights, suit rumpled and tear-stained, he staggered like an infant taking its first steps. He looked around at the station, which lay unharmed and yet gutted, there and yet a ghost of itself, his mouth agape in a wide O. When he tripped in a slick of melted ice cream and fell upon the tiny red dress, he screamed.

He screamed like he would never stop.

Fol looked away. These creatures were so blind to reality, so short-lived and frail. But they were bright, so very bright, shooting stars that blotted out all else. He couldn't let them fade into nothing. He wouldn't betray them as well.

The road before him was long, so long. From here darkness would only spread, and so few stood a chance of stalling it. But they were out there. He felt them, felt them well. Some were close, some far—so, so *far*—but he felt them all. The first was a mere step away from here, and with an internal flex he pushed his sight outwards into this world and saw fog-cloaked moorland, a sign that read *Radden Moor*. A young blond man upon a hillside, a screaming baby in a cottage crib.

It was time to pay them a visit.

Fol stood on shaky legs and watched the stumbling

survivor from behind the pillar. All over the world, they would be the same as this. Alone and afraid. All their lives, these chosen few would struggle against a world winding down and going threadbare, fighting against the darkness. And if they failed, the consequences would seal the fate of every creature in All Where. Because what happened once could always happen again.

The Web took no sides.

Feeling his way across a land now strewn with jewellery and hunks of primitive electronic gadgetry, he found what he was looking for: the trail's first breadcrumb. Fol stepped daintily from the station across a few hundred miles and landed upon a suburban street corner. Close by, a fire raged amongst a pile of crushed vehicles. Across the street, a young man was calling for help, bent over a smoking body.

Fol stared as the young man looked up at him and bellowed for help.

*So this is the one*, he thought. *One to watch. One who could start us on our journey.* A black mark blighted Fol's mind's eye. *Or send us all to hell.*

It would take time for everything to fall into place. Meanwhile, there was much to do.

Fol glimpsed another somewhere close by, just beyond his sight, and knew he had found the first creature of destiny: a chubby baby with big, bright emerald eyes.

Satisfied, he stepped away from the street corner, leaving the blond young man screaming upon the pavement, and landed back in the station. The suited commuter was still waddling back and forth among the piles of clothing across

St Pancras, warbling and gasping.

Fol ignored him and approached a piano, beside which an empty pram lay adorned with tiny, empty baby booties.

Smiling to himself, he rested his fingers on the keys and started playing a tune from another world. "It begins," he said.

1

"Last again, loser!" Bud cried from the ash pit.

Evian scowled, traipsing through what had once been the vegetable patch, trampling a few remaining tomato plants. "No fair, you always leave me behind."

"One day we really will leave you if you're not careful," called Pepper from somewhere nearby. Her jeering laugh cut like glass.

Evian suppressed another scowl.

"You sleep in like we was lords," Bud said, tossing aside the charred remains of a hair comb, crouched on his haunches in the burned-out living space, waiting for Pepper to probe the rest of the house. He was starting to get fur on his face like older boys, too tall to fit through the tight crawlspaces where the good treasure tended to hide. He looked good, and he knew it—but she wasn't going to tell him that. He was getting so lazy that his chiselled jaw was losing some of its charm.

He would expect a fair share of the loot, of course, even if Evian and Pepper did all the scrambling around the hot cinders themselves.

Evian stepped carefully over the still-smoking outer wall, no more than a strip of foundation sticking a few inches out of the ground. Everything was still warm, a dry kind of heat that came only from intense fire, filling the air with a clinging acidity that etched the back of her throat. She wrinkled her nose. "What's that smell?"

Bud grunted, his gaze locked fast on a small pile of debris he'd collected, filtering through it. A shadow crossed his expression.

"What is it?" She waved a hand in front of her nose, kicking idly at a blackened table leg. "Smells pretty good. Like bacon."

"Evian."

"I could go for some bacon right now. We haven't had meat in so long."

It had been a rough year. To even speak of bacon would have been heresy a short while ago when the meekest scraps of food had all but vanished. People had died, a lot of people. Even the lords of the North had starved.

A year ago, the Pepsi Squad had been over two dozen strong, Robin Hoods of the wilds, robbing from the lords and giving to those in need—and seeing as they were all orphans, who could have been more in need than themselves? Times had never been easy, and when food ran short they were the first to struggle, but they had had each other.

Then the food ran out completely.

Sunny D, Horlicks, Sprite, even Bovril. All gone now… It had been just the three of them since winter's end.

"Seriously, where is it? You found breakfast, and you're hiding it from me," Evian said.

The shadow on Bud's face deepened. "Evian…"

She whirled, stomach gurgling. "Stop holding out. I saw the barn on my way in. They had pigs. So, bacon. Gimme!"

A half-cindered book tumbled from Bud's hand. "Evian, bloody hell, would you *think* for a moment!" he yelled.

Evian flinched. Bud never yelled. "What's up with you?"

He just stared, his eyes big and round and—yes— tearful. Beaten into action, Evian's mind turned anew to the burned-out house around her.

Just like all the others. They littered the landscape like tiny beacons, any free-standing inhabited structure for all the miles in the Pepsi Squad's territory—and probably much farther beyond. A few days ago people had just showed up, swept through this place on their way north, and set fire to everything in their path. Thin, broken, mean-looking people, marching under the flag of a white bird.

The highwaymen and lords of the North had squabbled over this land since long before any of them were born. Evian would be fifteen soon—she wasn't quite sure when, but soon—and she had never seen anything that could match them. This land belonged to them.

No longer. They had been extinguished, exterminated like a pack of wild dogs, in a single day of bloodshed.

Evian didn't understand it. Didn't care to. They'd got more loot out of it over the past few days than the previous six months combined.

She realised now, staring around, that she had forgotten.

So busy had she been hauling away all she could, thinking only of what they could trade for, of who they could become if they stockpiled enough—the new lords of the North! People would come scrabbling to them instead of the other way around. She had forgotten what these burned-out husks really were. Homes. People's homes.

These things had been precious to people. These were their walls, their food, their books. All set ablaze in a great string of conflagrations that had lit up the whole valley. Her nose wrinkled again, but this time it brought not hunger, but horror.

*The smell of burned meat…*

A hand flew to her mouth. She turned away, uttering an unladylike *urgh!* and vomited bile into the ash. It sizzled at her feet, cooking off and rising up into her face, eliciting a further bout of retching. It didn't stop until she was on her knees, wiping her mouth with the back of her hand. She looked sheepishly at Bud, but he didn't laugh or sneer, just offered a sympathetic blink and went back to sifting through the junk.

"Where's Doc?" Evian muttered.

"Here," called Pepper, screened from view by the chimney stack, the only piece of the burned-out house still standing. "This place is a dud. There's nothing that's not melted but a few cookbooks and pots. Nothing to actually cook," she added bitterly.

"Let's move on. The next one will be better," Bud said, rising from his haunches.

"I haven't looked!"

"Trust me, there's nothing."

"Nothing," Pepper confirmed.

Evian pouted. "Fine. Let's go."

Bud looked over the marred paperback in his hands, wrinkled and blackened with the heat, and cast it aside on the table. He filled his pockets with a few salvageable odds and ends—nothing worth trading, the kind of useless trinkets only boys liked: a large silver coin, string, and a few stained playing cards. He gave Evian a brave smile. "We're doing good. We just have to keep going; soon enough we'll be back on our feet. You'll see. We'll be rich as any king of the Old World before long—"

A section of the chimney stack crumbled as Pepper burst over a pile of rubble, seeming almost to cleave right through it from sheer panic. Her stout body radiated alarm, and her eyes were enormous in her head. A strangled "*Ack!*" escaped her throat as she collided with them, and the trio spilled across the floor. Before they hit the ground, she was shushing them viciously, clamping her ashy fingers over their mouths hard enough to split Evian's lip.

Suddenly a great weight seemed to have fallen over the house, an oppressive silence only enhanced by the distant crackling of remnant embers somewhere in the cellar.

Evian struggled, but Pepper held fast, tears spilling from her eyes.

Bud managed to shake her off. She feinted as though daring him to make a sound, but he held up his hands, one warding hand out in front of him, the other held to his lips to show he understood.

Pepper bared her teeth, fists bunched, snot dribbling over her lips. Her eyes darted in their sockets as she inched back towards the walls.

*What?* He mouthed.

Her lips retracted completely, the snarling leer of a cornered dog. *THEM!*

Evian's stomach imploded to the size of a grape, pouring liquid fear into her abdomen. "Oh no," she squeaked.

"*Shhh!*" Pepper abandoned silencing them and pressed against the nearest wall, huddling into a shuddering ball.

Evian cast a desperate glance at Bud, her mouth ajar. Tears stung her eyes.

She could usually see all his clever plans flitting behind his eyes. Bud always had a plan. But right now, there was nothing in those soft brown eyes but blankness.

He took her hand and pulled her against the wall alongside Pepper where they cowered in unthinking, shuddering fugue.

*No. They can't be back. They can't. They left. They went away. There's nobody left to burn. They're all gone.*

Her heart leapt.

*Except us.*

The silence deepened yet again, clawing at her ears. After a moment she realised it hadn't deepened but only been contrasted by a new noise, one rising from silence like a leviathan from the deep.

Somewhere out there, beyond the blackened walls, many footfalls upon muddied ground. A great many.

Evian pressed tighter against the remains of the Pepsi

Squad, and they cowered together in a ball of tears and nerves as the sound grew louder, rising above the dying flames and the trickling breeze. For a few odd hanging seconds it seemed it could grow no louder, then metamorphosed into a rumble that shook out showers of ash from the wall. The earth throbbed to the marching beat.

*It can't be. It can't. There aren't that many people in all the world.*

In defiance of her, the rumble grew louder still. The house seemed ready to crumble to so much sand.

Bud trembled against her skin. Even a minute ago she would have given anything to have him against her like this. Now she only hoped he didn't wet his pants.

"Look!" Pepper squeaked. She pointed a shaking finger out through the denuded window frame beside them, past the barn and across the valley.

The grey morning, dark and lifeless under lacklustre clouds, had been stained by a dark cap upon the hilltops. Evian watched the wilted grass become smothered by the first lapping waves of some dark encroaching ocean, thrusting its fingers over the horizon. Spilling down into the valley to the rhythm of the marching beat underfoot, the smudge resolved into something that took Evian's thundering heart and stopped it entirely.

A carpet of people marching south. All armed with blades, with guns, with long poles trailing a symbol she had hoped never to see again: a white bird painted with four aggressive slashes; round body, two wings, and a bulbous head. The sigil of a pigeon.

Something clicked in Evian's head; a primal will to survive that overcame the numbness steeling through her conscious mind.

She crawled from the huddle, dragging the others in her wake. Bud and Pepper hissed and yelped, but she sent a blazing glare over her shoulder, and they fell silent, yielding to her. She yanked them until the three of them pressed against the legs of the dining table. She nodded to the chimney stack where a small hollow lay exposed, where the fire had partially eaten through to the wall space.

The dark stain upon the land grew closer, stretching from horizon to horizon.

*Oh my God. So many people. So many!*

They had to get to the crawlspace. If they were found, three little piggies in their house all fallen down…

A shiver ran through her, and her skin crawled with a foreign chill.

Evian counted down on her fingers, mouthing: *Three, two, one, now!*

Grimacing, the three of them half crawled, half tumbled over the smouldering floorboards. A breeze had picked up from nothing, rustling Evian's hair, tugging at her as though a vanguard of the coming leagues. How could so light a touch of air upon her skin bring such a strong urge to throw back her head and scream?

Pepper reached the crawlspace and scurried inside, hissing and cursing, and Bud followed close behind. Pepper, so small and lithe, managed to squeeze herself into a cranny only inches wide. But Bud's body, thick with freshly-blossomed muscle, took up almost all the remaining space. On any other occasion, Evian would have said she would never fit.

*Not today. I'm getting in there.*

She vaulted in after them, ignoring gasps of pain and the crushing embrace of the walls around cramped ankles and bent limbs.

A strange, distant part of her mind flashed up a memory of an Old World book she had seen once: an encyclopaedia of animals out there in the world. She had loved the water animals the best. And her favourite of all had been the strangest: the octopus, eight-legged and boneless and so wonderfully *weird*. They could squeeze their entire bodies into milk bottles to get at their food.

They probably looked like that now. Three human beings, bottled inside a chimney.

And yet, even in here, the wind persisted—there was no space between them for air to flow, yet the wind blew.

Despite the growing rumble, amplified by the hollowness of the chimneys above their heads, Evian frowned.

It wasn't a wind. Not really. It was something else: a caress, so gentle and cold that she thought her arm might become covered with tiny snowflakes.

"What's happening?" Pepper hissed from the chaos of bodies.

"It's so cold. There are embers under us. We should be boiling." Bud breathed.

"Shh!" Evian said.

The three of them grew silent, their breathing terrifyingly loud, reverberating in the enclosed space. From here, all they could see was a small window of the house before them, facing southward—shielding them from view, but also blocking their line of sight of what approached.

Outside, the rumble grew still, and the army marched ever southward. Wide-eyed and shaking, they waited as the cold grew only stronger, seeming to intensify at the same rate as the footsteps' volume—almost as though the army brought with it a halo of otherworldly chill.

Evian died a small death when shadow first splashed over the garden path. A single human profile that immediately became several, then many, then smothered into an amorphous undulating wave heading towards the barn. The cold seemed to steel into the chimney with bony fingers and grip her by the throat when the marching men and women began to pass. A single mass of starved bodies, sticklike and angular, shuffling forth over the land, their faces fallen and mute.

Like a river the army flowed around the burned-out ruin, spilling into sight from both sides and passing on. Evian kept her hands clamped over Bud's mouth, and Pepper kept hers over Evian's. Her skin thrummed with cold so intense, she was sure it would flay her alive.

Then footsteps separate from the marching beat, deeper and closer. Somebody had passed through the house's fallen walls, moving over the floorboards to their left. Evian bit her lip hard to staunch a scream. Bud and Pepper had become stiff as the chimney's bricks.

Three men stepped into sight, looking around at the charred remains of the living room, a mere six feet from the chimney. One was wolfish and round-shouldered, another young and limping. They paused a few moments to look at the remains, then moved on, stepping over the walls and following the army south, as though shepherds following their flock. The last man, however, remained. Tall, covered in an oilskin duster, he stood before the dining table, facing away from them. Upon his shoulders, two pigeons bobbed and cooed. The birds stared directly at Evian, and for a horrific moment her mind tortured her with a mental image of the birds leaning into the man's ears and whispering, *There. Over there.*

Instead, the man held his arm out to the side, his gaze fixed on the book in his hand. The half-burned paperback Bud had cast aside.

The pigeons cooed contemplatively upon the man's shoulders.

He was so close that even from their hiding place, Evian could read the title: *Alice in Wonderland.*

The following moment could have stretched on for years, thrumming with something *more*. The biting cold screamed down upon Evian's skin, and in her peripheral vision she realised that snowflakes really *were* forming on her skin, blossoming upon her forearms' fluffy down.

Struggling for breath, she watched the man turn to face the chimney, his eyes still on the book.

*His face. His face... Where is his face?*

She glimpsed bone and exposed muscle, a terrible mask

of beauty spoilt. Above cheeks half-missing, through which exposed molars peeped, a pair of bright green eyes moved over the book. Eyes intelligent and sparking with intent and rage.

Evian knew she would never forget that stare, one broken and twisted, lost between life and death.

The man with the emerald eyes took the book gently in both hands, held it there before him a moment, then with sudden violence tore it in half. The pages fluttered down like so many feathers, twirling amidst the snowflakes raining upon the ashy floor.

# II

Norman Creek chased a ghost through the forest.

Little Billy Peyton's shadow flitted between the trees far ahead, wisps of flaming red hair and pale Irish skin amongst the branches. Despite his calls for her to slow down, she kept her relentless pace, giving no indication she'd heard. Cursing and praying he didn't get lost out here in the ancient foggy woodlands, hundreds of miles from home, Norman plunged onwards.

His lungs burned from running, and fog pressed in close all around. Gnarled branches loomed from the white blanket so fast that he relied on instinct to dodge them, ducking and wheeling on the balls of his feet. His head throbbed to the beat of a single looping thought: *This is stupid, this is stupid, this is stupid.*

One false step from any of them would result in a broken ankle. But there was no slowing. No time to think. Not when the stakes were so high.

Robert, Lucian, and Richard pursued a few paces behind. Of the two dozen who had set out from New Canterbury to this strange place in England's far north, only the four of them remained. The others lay in pools of blood, back upon the clifftop from which they had just descended.

With every blink, Norman saw their blank staring faces in his mind's eye. Cut down by James Chadwick, the architect of all their strife, the man with merciless emerald eyes. Their enemy. Their brother.

*Stop that,* he scolded himself. *You can't help them now. The others still need us. Keep your head.*

If he let himself wander, everything that remained of the Old World would vanish forever. Right now an army marched to erase New Canterbury and the Alliance of the South from the face of the Earth. And once that happened, there was no going back. The world as they knew it would plunge unheeding into a new dark age. Everything they had worked for would be lost.

"Keep your bloody hands to yourself." Lucian scowled behind him. The vicious grey-haired little man sounded fit to tear the world a new orifice and forget his weeks of starving and slaving away as James's prisoner.

"You're stumbling. You can barely stand," Richard grunted.

"I'm fine!"

"Keep your damn feet up then, you knackered old goat!"

Despite apocalyptic stakes and the bloodbath from which they had just emerged, Norman grinned. To think that Richard, a scrawny little bookworm, would ever square off against Lucian McKay.

He had changed. Watching your master die in front of you could have that effect.

It had been two hours since the man who perhaps had been the world's last scholar, John DeGray, had been gunned down along with the others. Richard, his apprentice, had been right beside him. His face still bore dried flakes of his blood.

Neither of them were meant for this world. They belonged to the Old World, a place of knowledge and relative civility. Not today's world, a place of tooth and claw. A land of survivors.

Robert Strong's deep no-nonsense voice followed them all through the trees from the rear. "The more you two talk, the slower you move. Now shut it before I smash both your heads together."

A moment's silence reigned, and Norman felt the old forest press in on them from all sides. He realised just how alone they were out here. With James's army departed, for all they knew, they could be the only people for dozens of miles in any direction. And this was no ordinary place.

Radden Moor, cloaked in its veil of wandering fog, heath-clad and barren and iron-skied, was a special place.

Something told him that if they became separated in these woods, they would never be reunited, not even if they passed within ten feet of each other. The forest would consume them.

"Billy, wait!" Norman called.

Her distant voice echoed from up ahead. "No time."

"We'll lose you!"

"Then move faster."

"The fog's too thick. If I lose you…"

"You'll find me. I feel you." He could no longer see her save for the dimmest flicker of shadow through the creeping fog. Her disembodied voice crept through the branches. "Don't you feel me?"

He didn't answer, didn't need to.

"How much farther?" Robert bellowed.

Billy's voice again, sounding even farther away, terrifyingly faint. "Almost there."

*How can the kid be so calm? Calmer than four grown men? She can't be more than nine or ten years old.*

Because kids still had that magic spark alight inside them. The willingness to look into the abyss, see monsters and vampires born of imagination, and keep going anyway. This kid in particular had something extra too. A certain brightness, like she had been spliced into the world from a place where the sun was brighter.

Even from back here he could feel her presence, the intimate proximity of somebody standing only inches away.

*If I'm going to get through this, I'm going to have to try relighting my own spark. Gotta keep moving, Norm, and don't look down. It's a long fall to crazy town from up here.*

Lucian grunted behind Norman. "'Almost there.' Wherever the hell that is. Anybody notice we're going the wrong way?"

"Norman, he's right. What are we doing out here?" Richard panted. "James went south. Home is south. We have to beat them back. We have to warn them."

Robert said nothing, yet his reticence seemed loudest of all. There was more than home waiting for him back there, more than their duty to the mission of New Canterbury. He and Sarah Strong had wed the minute before they had departed for this place. Now a bloodthirsty army of ten thousand stood between them.

Their collective gaze needled the back of Norman's neck like cat's claws.

*A few weeks ago I would have crumbled. Robert or Lucian would be in the lead, and I'd be following them every step of the way. Now…*

Now it seemed he saw farther than his eyes' field of view, felt the soil underfoot through the soles of his shoes.

Something had awoken in him.

*Don't call it destiny. People have pushed that on you since the cradle.*

*Then what is it?*

He answered himself, an unyielding plaintive voice from the root of his mind: *I'm awake now. I know what I have to do.*

He didn't know how. He just knew. And so he said nothing at all, just kept running.

Behind him, they followed and said nothing more.

Heart pounding, legs begging for mercy, Norman threw himself over logs and under overhanging branches, narrowly missing losing an eye more times than he dared count. All the while a strange sonar inside his head pinged, picking out the Irish girl streaking ahead, homing in on something.

Exactly what, he didn't bother to guess. Reality was stranger than fiction.

*It sure is now, anyway.*

Then light. With a grunt Norman flung a hand up over his shoulder, praying the others were close enough to see it through the fog, and ground his heels into the ground. Billy had stopped dead, and as he skidded to a halt, he realised they had reached the edge of the forest.

He ignored Lucian cursing Richard and stepped from the treeline onto a vast stretch of heathland. As his eyes adjusted, light that had moments before seemed blinding and radiant faded to its true nature: dank and lifeless, painting the world in metallic hue—the antithesis of summer's golden glow; an anti-glow, such that even Billy Peyton's youthful rouged cheeks seemed sallow and aged.

She stood beside him, ankle deep in heather, looking out over Radden Moor. Miles away, a ridge of mountains fenced in the landscape, snow-capped, gnarled, and knobbly like some old crone's arthritic knuckles. A few towns and villages dotted the heath here and there, Victorian and slate-roofed, askew and ramshackle and grey.

"I can't imagine what it was like before the End," he said.

"I can't imagine anything from Before," Billy said flatly. "Daddy always said there was no Before. Just us from the beginning of time."

Norman looked at her, searching for a smile. He saw none. She wasn't kidding.

*Is that what we've come to? She knows nothing of the Old World?*

He knew that many out in the wilds thought as much.

But to hear it in person, from one so young and bright…

That was what awaited them all and their children if they failed now. The lords of the North had ravaged most of the country since the End. New Canterbury and the Alliance were the only things keeping civilisation's flame alive in the farthest south. It would all go away if they didn't stop the marching horde.

Billy walked slowly through the heather, finding safe footings invisible to Norman. He followed her exact paces, unthinking, trusting, motioning over his shoulder for the others to follow. For a time they moved in single file, a desperate plodding crawl, five lonely figures upon a landscape that seemed set to engulf them through its sheer enormity. Icy wind tugged at his clothes, ripping his hair, cold that he knew somehow had nothing to do with temperature.

The same cold nestling in his chest, the cold that had infiltrated his nerves and bones as soon as he stepped foot in this place. Infecting him, taunting him.

Far away, several threads of diaphanous milky figures milled to and fro across the moorland, going about businesses of the distant past: Echoes of the Old World that had plagued him since all this had started. They were everywhere here in Radden. Any notion of them being figments of his deranged imagination vanished now, for he caught Billy's eyes glance in their direction.

"You feel it too, don't you? You see them," Billy said, up ahead.

Norman blinked. Waited.

"You feel it."

"What is it?" he said.

"What's what?" Lucian hissed.

They both ignored him.

"I don't know. I don't know a lot of anything."

"But you see them? They're from Before. I know they are. I've seen their—"

*Phones*, he thought. *I've seen them carrying telephones. Wearing suits.*

She seemed to sense his thoughts. "I saw a flying machine. Just like them. There, but not." She glanced at him over her shoulder, furtively searching. "Were there flying machines, Before?"

"Yes."

She turned solemnly away. "I see them everywhere here."

"Does it… does it hurt you too? The cold?"

"Yes. And no. Both."

"Why here?"

"Some places are special, Norm. The Panda Man told me."

Norman didn't bother enquiring any further. Some things were just too crazy.

Silence reigned over the group a moment, bar the banshee wail of the wind.

"When all this is over, you're both going straight into a pair of straitjackets," Lucian said dourly.

They pressed on like that until the weight of all those hanging on their success or failure grew too much. "Billy, we can't keep walking out here. Every minute we waste means they get closer," Norman said. "…Billy!"

She came to a stop, seemingly in a daze, hunch-backed and swaying, rising and falling with breaths that seemed too deep for her little lungs. "We're here," she said.

Norman paused and looked around. The others came up to stand beside him, and as one, they stared about. They stood, quite literally, in the middle of nowhere: on all sides lay at least half a mile of barren unbroken heather. Not even a single rock or tree or free-standing structure lay in sight.

Except for the ragged hole directly before them. A gap in the soil that dropped into a gently sloping tunnel, big enough for a grown man to descend at a crouch. For all the world, it looked like the entrance to an enormous warren.

"What's this?" Norman said.

"I don't know," Billy said. She blinked rapidly, as though confused as to why they were here. But there was no hesitation in her voice. "We have to go down."

A silent thud landed in Norman's chest.

"This can't be happening," Richard said, his peaky face whitening further. "Are we really thinking of going through with this? Time is slipping away, real time. I can't… I can't believe we're doing this. This can't be real. It's… it's crazy."

"There's a lot of that going around right now," Norman said absently.

*Let's not mention that I could barely walk when we left home, nursing a few broken ribs and some heavy psychological baggage. Now I feel like I could run a million miles and face a dragon. It's this—*

"It's this place," Billy Peyton said, unblinking. She addressed them all, but her gaze lingered on Norman a moment too long, beaming a certain knowing intensity. "The rules are different."

Norman blinked, stunned. The very same words had been on the tip of his tongue.

He shook off a mental echo of what she had showed him. They had seen one another in their dreams before ever meeting. Putting that particular insanity aside, he also knew she had guided him to something far worse: a dark place where he could have never gone to without her, a place of suffering and pain and eternal labour—a place populated by billions of screaming, slaving people. People who had once lived and breathed and walked this Earth before—

Before the End.

He shivered.

"Norman, I'm with you to the last," Robert said, leaning down to Norman's ear, his stature dwarfing them all. His hand wrapped around Norman's arm, and for a moment Norman's sense of power was punctured by the gaze of the enormous man beside him—a man ready to tear people limb from limb to get back home. "I'm not going to ask questions. I don't care. I just need to know that we're going to get home, and that we'll get there before Chadwick." His eyes drilled deep down into Norman's skull, X-raying him to the minutest detail. "Are you sure about this, Norman?"

Norman felt his old self, who had shirked leadership and responsibility, drag his shoulders towards a hunch, urging him to cower. Even now, after all they'd been through, it took everything he had to look Robert in the eye and say, "I'm sure. This is the way. We will make it back in time."

"Your word on it, Creek."

Norman gripped Robert's arm in turn, his hand reaching only halfway around Robert's bicep. "I promise."

Robert stared a moment longer, then released him.

Norman turned to the others. The sight of their filthy sweat-stained faces—especially Lucian's, who had for all his life seemed an indefatigable bough of strength, now hanging emaciated and sallow-eyed, half-propped by Richard behind him—stalled Norman for a moment. In that bleak second, his will thrummed and threatened to falter.

*Weak, we're so weak. Four idiots running around in the woods, trying to save the world. And how? By following a freaky little magic girl down a rabbit hole.*

He steeled himself and said, "Do you trust me?"

Lucian watched him carefully, an appraising look lighter than Robert's penetrating stare, yet it sent Norman's flesh crawling. Lucian wasn't just searching for a lie or weakness; he was seeing him anew. Lucian knew the old Norman was still there and saw it as well as he saw Norman now.

Somehow, that made it all the more raw when the tiniest amusement glimmered on his rugged old cheeks. "For my bloody sins."

Norman turned to Richard. The young apprentice was looking at Billy, who had pulled out a ragged piece of cloth, rolled up into a scroll. Like her, it seemed too bright, as if it didn't quite belong in the world.

She unravelled it, revealing strange pictographs and a winding path between them: an archway, a dilapidated shack, stone ruins, the weathered mountaintops that were unmistakably those upon Radden Moor's horizon, and finally a round black smudge. The rabbit hole.

Billy put the map away without a word.

Richard mouthed wordlessly, silently cursing with a roll of his eyes, then shrugged. "Fine. Whatever. Who needs sanity, anyway?"

"Hold on to that attitude, kid," Lucian said as they gathered around the hole. "Looks like you'll need it."

Norman and Billy crouched around the lip of the hole. "Down then?" he said.

She nodded, the fatalistic grimness of someone decades older. Without a word, she leapt down into darkness.

Norman stared stupidly after her, then something tugged in the base of his gut. The painful chill in his chest twitched as though alive, tugging him down into the ground.

"All righty then…," he muttered. Clearing his throat, he bounded on the balls of his feet, cursed, then jumped into the hole.

The tunnel floor lay a mere four feet down, yet it felt like he fell for several seconds. By the time his feet touched ground, the air had altogether changed. From bare and stripped of life, robbed of scent and volume by the eerie moors, it became warmer and redolent of decay—not unpleasant, but peaty and rich.

He rolled clear of the opening, his face screwed up in

anticipation of stabbing pain from his ribs.

*Even a few hours ago I'd be screaming right now.*

Instead he felt nothing bar the creak of the soil compacting under his weight. He came to a stop after he was sure he was clear of the hole, then waved his hands around in the pitch darkness.

"Billy?"

To his left: "Here."

*She sounds a hell of a lot calmer than me.*

She also sounded too far away. Not because her voice was faint, but because he felt as though in the presence of another; one much closer.

And not just a single presence. For an awful moment his mind conjured an image of an encircling ring of figures, mere inches from his face, bestial and muscular, blowing hot stinking breath onto his skin. Things not quite human.

Billy gave a grunt from somewhere up ahead, and a *click* rang out. A flame blossomed and threw her cherub-like face into harsh relief, an illuminated head bobbing amidst total darkness.

"There are torches," she said. She waved a match in her hand. "Grandpa's magic."

Norman tried not to wonder how she sensed his questioning stare. There was no way she could see his face.

"Uh huh," he said. His eyes searched the corners of their sockets, looking for a mouthful of needle-like teeth, fur. Maybe horns.

Because in the brief instant when Billy had lighted the torch in her hand, they hadn't been conjurations of his imagination. They *had* been right in front of him.

"What's wrong?" Billy came closer, watching him carefully. Even at half his height, she seemed infinitely stronger, braced against the dark.

"It's just… I thought I saw something," he said lamely, feeling only more foolish as Lucian landed in the tunnel behind him and clapped his hands to receive the few weapons they had managed to salvage from the abandoned camp.

Billy turned to face the tunnel ahead, a gaping maw stretching on to infinity. Darkness seemed to come too soon, sucking the light up a mere ten feet ahead of them and veiling what lay ahead. "Everything is funny, now. You get used to it."

Norman cleared his throat. "You're just a kid," he muttered, shaking his head. "You don't seem scared."

She blinked and turned slowly to him as Robert's hulking form came whomping down beside them, his heels sinking a quarter inch into the mud. Billy's gaze had become aglitter with hurt and confusion. "I'm so afraid," she uttered, so quiet he wondered if she had spoken at all. "I've been afraid for so long I forgot what it was like before." He caught a glimpse of the little girl under all that callous, and his heart wrenched until he thought it might break in half.

*Good thing Allie's not here*, he thought. *She'd squeeze the munchkin to death.*

Then his heart did the impossible and wrenched a little more as Allie's face danced before his mind's eye. She was still back there, waiting with the others. He had left her to come here—because it was what he had had to do. In some book she would be the maiden locked up in a white tower, her hand held to her forehead, upon the brink of fainting and devotedly awaiting his return.

If Allie could have seen that mental image, she'd have busted a gut laughing. Then kicked his arse for being a pig.

A few weeks ago they had been little more than strangers. The famine, the army, all this freakery and the threat of imminent doom, had brought them clinging together. And yet she had done what he couldn't. If it hadn't been for her, he might have stayed back home, cowered with the others as the fires grew closer, and all their friends fell silent. But she had been there, had damn near kicked him onto his horse.

He put a hand to his brow and squeezed. "I'm sorry," he said. "I am."

Billy shrugged. "It's okay."

"You lost people." It wasn't a question.

She waited until Richard pounded down beside them, then set off down into the tunnel. "Everyone," she said.

Norman Creek glanced at the others close behind him, their eyes huge and white and staring.

"Who's down here?" Richard said.

"Stop your yammering," Lucian grated. "Ain't nobody but us."

"I felt something just now. Bats?"

"No," Robert said. "No guano."

"What then?" Richard cried.

Lucian bared his teeth, which lit up in reflection as white as his eyes. "Your imagination, sweet pea."

"Shut up, Lucian."

They set off after Billy.

"You still don't think I can do this, do you?" Richard said.

"No."

Richard was silent a moment. Then he said, low and hurting, "You'll see."

"Quiet," Norman whispered.

To his distant surprise, they fell silent immediately.

*They sense it too.*

*It? Or them?*

The four men hurried to catch up, lest the sucking darkness consume them again.

They all moved awkwardly, especially Robert, their backs bent and backsides thrusting out behind them, shuffling at a half crouch along the rough-hewn walls of the warren. Billy's head fell short a full foot of the ceiling and walked unheeded, striding with inhuman lack of fear. Norman noticed a paring knife held in her grip, not thrust out before her against the darkness, but there, ready.

*Who is this kid?* he thought. *What could have happened that messed her up this bad?*

His mind turned to the kids back in New Canterbury whom he had schooled. It had been one of the few things he had really enjoyed; none of the kids had expected anything of him. Those children were the first in forty years to be brought up in the safe embrace of community, sheltered by the Alliance from the naked hostility of the wilds.

*What will they think when James and his army show up? When the city is surrounded by ten thousand people looking to kill them and their families? They don't know what things are really like out there. And that's where we went wrong: we all forgot. That's why we're in this mess.*

*Will the kids sense danger? Even when the burning and killing starts, will they even run?*

The thought spurred him to settle a mere step behind Billy. No matter what kind of airy-faerie weirdness they had to endure, he would get back there. Even if only to die alongside them.

The tunnel walls hardened as they descended the gentle gradient. Overhanging tendrils of milky plant roots withdrew, crumbling soil grew compacted and gravelly, and eventually became solid stone, black as obsidian. By Billy's light they soon passed yet more torches. Taking one each and feeding off Billy's flame, they soon had enough light to push back the darkness.

A little of the gnawing unease receded, fingers of shadow withdrawing from Norman's flesh and cowering back beyond the halo of their bubble of orange flame, just out of sight. Yet for all the flame's warmth and the hot stale air down here, the chill nestled in his chest refused to thaw one degree. Instead it grew only stronger with every step they descended, extending down his arms, to the very tips of his fingers.

All trace of earth vanished and rock took over entirely.

The clacking of their footsteps receded away into nothing, consumed by the darkness along with the light.

Norman abandoned all pretence about grown-ups not believing in monsters. Though he might not have seen them, he felt them out there, drawn to them like moths to a flame, old and strange things waking, semi-conscious, from long slumber to watch them pass by. All the while, they chattered to one another, in tongues inaudible to human ears.

Norman jerked in fright when a sharp whistle rang out behind him.

He whirled to see Richard blowing air between his teeth, frozen in a forty-five-degree list to his right. He ignored almost falling when Robert's bulk collided with him, his lips peeling back.

Something painted the wall, colour and form plastered over the rough surface of the black rock. Norman squinted and together they leaned in, heads almost pressing together. By their combined light, Norman made out a pair of stick figures drawn in chalk. The eight-legged form of a black spider hanging from a swinging bob—

A raging thought rocketed through Norman's head like a siren: *Pendulum.*

—and below it, wrapped in chains, the winged form of an angel. No halo, but an angel.

Norman span in a circle, pressing his torch flush against the ceiling. Jumping and animated by shadow, he caught sight of dozens of similar figures strung out along the length of the tunnel.

Silhouettes of humanoid forms. Great courts of robed figures, feasting on strange creatures, cheering on fools who danced and capered in their midst. Great armies clashing before castles and fiery chasms. Titans laying waste to Lilliputian micro-cities. Stick figures in death duels, their faces frozen in unending screams of rage and pain.

They were everywhere.

"Well, that's just bloody terrifying," Lucian growled.

"Just like the hieroglyphics in the great pyramids," Richard muttered, his voice threaded with academic fascination.

*You can take the nerd out of the classroom...* Norman thought idly, then noticed Billy standing ahead of them, waiting, her eyes expressionless.

"Don't stop," she said.

They ceased inspecting the pictographs and turned to her.

"Don't ever stop. You'll start asking questions." An irritated hitch infected her lip. "And questions always lead to more questions."

She turned and left them behind once again, not even glancing at the cave drawings as she descended still farther into the earth.

Norman decided that was as good advice as any. No more questions. Just get it done.

They followed the little Irish girl down for another few minutes until Norman began to wonder how deep the tunnel could possibly go. When forks began to appear, leading off into the darkness like a branching artery, his feet screamed for him to stop.

*If we get lost, we'll never get out. Not if we keep going. Once the torches go out…*

But he kept walking. They all kept walking. Billy's unhesitating advance drew him on. She didn't even seem to notice the forks in her path, oblivious to the catacombs under Radden Moor.

Norman was getting a feel for the connection between them now. Not telepathy nor any other kind of archetypal *power* of Old World fantasy. It was altogether subtler, a kind of empathy. He couldn't read her mind any more than he could have moved objects with his thoughts, but he felt her unflinching certainty, coupled with her undercurrent of eternal bafflement.

She knew the way but had no idea how she knew. She trusted as he trusted.

They walked in silence, half-choked by air that might not have stirred for centuries, until at last the roof sloped upwards and the men could walk unimpeded. Things seemed to grow fresher, the dark more diffuse. The inaudible chattering in the shadows receded, and the paintings were replaced instead by symbols, or letters— perhaps runes, all painted in vibrant colours. Nothing Norman recognised, nor any picture of ancients' artistic perfection, but instead the sprawling finger-paint splashes of some manic child.

Norman blew a long sigh, surprised by a dizzy spell. He felt as though some great pressure had just lifted off his shoulders, one he had been unaware of carrying. They had passed through something not meant for them and come out the other side.

Norman got his biggest fright yet when Billy stopped in her tracks.

"What?" he said, unnerved by how thin his voice sounded. "What is it?"

"Get back if there's somebody, kid," Lucian said. "Get behind us."

"No." Billy sounded unsure for a moment, a little distant. Then she cocked her head, turning her ear toward the ceiling.

Robert made to speak, but she held up a finger sharply.

They fell silent and still and waited. They shared uncertain glances, their hands braced upon the butts of their precious few guns.

Then Norman heard it: music.

Billy turned on her heel to face them and rolled her eyes. "It's just the Panda Man," she said. "He's silly."

Then she made off again, striding with purpose, sighing as though a mother on her way to the certain mess of some petulant child.

"What is that?" Norman said. It was no instrument he could recognise, over which sang a young man's voice in an accent he couldn't place, backed by strange electronic screeches and thrums.

It was like nothing he'd ever heard.

"Is that what I think it is?" Robert muttered. "I was five when the End hit, but…"

"Yes," Lucian said. "Yes, it is." A queer grin had spread

onto his cheeks. It was strange to see Lucian smile at any time, but this wasn't even a smile, not quite. It was the face of somebody dredging up something from a place in their mind so hidden and buried that it pushed all their faculties aside as it surfaced. "Never thought I'd hear that again."

Then he started laughing, a horrible grating sound that loaned his eyes a half-crazed sheen.

"What?" Richard said. "What is it?"

"That," Lucian said, his gaze lost somewhere in distant memories of the Old World, "is Jimi Hendrix."

*

The tunnel brightened as they made their way. Billy had disappeared ahead, striding off into the darkness, unheeding. Norman hissed her name a few times, but she didn't stop. Only the receding clack of her footsteps told him she hadn't simply become one with the void.

The music grew louder with each step.

*What kind of music is that, anyway? It sounds like… It's actually pretty good,* Norman thought.

"This… Hendricks, he was a musician Before?" Richard said.

"Hendrix, with an X," Lucian whispered. "Before even Agatha's time. The old Old World." He gave an odd grunt. "Crap. My dad used to love this song."

"Quiet," Robert said. "There's light up ahead."

He was right. Norman inched forwards, a rusty pistol raised. He had found it amongst the deflated remains of the camp James had vacated; it had most probably only been left because of its poor condition. He doubted it would ever fire.

But it was all they had.

Torn between chasing Billy and approaching stealthily, he executed an absurd tiptoed crab-march, advancing with the others bunched up right behind him. The light grew brighter in step with the music until the shadow had all but vanished and Norman's ears throbbed to the tune's beat. The tunnel bent at ninety degrees directly ahead; beyond that, he sensed open space, and something else.

Billy was nowhere in sight. She had already turned the corner.

"Damn it," Norman said. If he stopped now, he would only find excuses to keep stalling.

He glanced over his shoulder. "Ready?"

The others looked anything but, yet they nodded as one, their own unreliable firearms at the ready.

Norman took a deep breath, over a hundred feet underground with the voice of an Old World rock star drumming in his ears, and stepped around the corner.

At once, the pistol dropped to his side. Billy stood only a few paces ahead, turned half to him and half to the small cavern that lay spread out before them. She gave a small, wry smile and nodded as though to say *It's okay. He's with me.*

That certain *he* stood close to the opposite wall of the rotunda-like cavern. A wiry man jigged back and forth, his back to them, a tall figure with jagged jet-black hair that seemed to defy gravity. Light-footed and animated, he hopped to and fro to the beat. With a theatrical twirl he turned around to face them, revealing alabaster skin, a beautiful young face, and a pair of glowering eyes—the hungry eyes of a man one step removed from humanity. Limber as a newborn, he bounced over the obsidian floor, by the light of a roaring fire at the cavern's edge, his bottom lip wedged between his incisors. All the while, he jammed away at an imaginary guitar.

"Who's this idiot?" Lucian grunted.

"Looks pale. His eyes… What's wrong with him?" Richard said.

Robert said nothing but moved to stand a little in front of Billy, eyes wary in his boulder-like head.

Norman noted their reactions only subconsciously. His vision had narrowed down to total blackness bar the dancing figure before them; one he recognised as the man who had appeared in his dreams. Dreams of a city, a storm; the night he lost his parents and received the scar upon his head. The man with dark streaks under his eyes. "You," he muttered.

Mr Hendrix's voice faded, going out on a long hanging vocal, and the man dropped to his knees, strumming his imaginary guitar, his eyes closed in bliss and his head bobbing. On the final violent note he gave an equally violent jerk, using its momentum to ascend to his feet and spread his arms. "Man, that boy could sing!" he cried.

His voice died down in a cascade of returning echoes from the myriad tunnel forks, descending into a ringing silence so loud Norman thought he might have gone deaf.

Then the man with the dark streaks under his eyes laughed, cutting through Norman to the cold in his chest, which shivered like a well-trained pet. "Friends, welcome," the man cried. He turned to Billy and gave a small, ironic bow. "Madam."

Billy stared at him with eyes like shards of ice. "Don't play games," she said.

He regarded her a moment, still half-bent. His eyes flicked away from Billy to the rest of them. A hint of amusement lurked behind his wolfish gaze. "She's a card, isn't she?"

None of them replied.

"Billy?" Norman said without taking his gaze away from their host.

"This is the Panda Man," she said.

The man's lip curled a tad, a chink in his polished exterior.

Norman frowned, this time looking at Billy. She shrugged in reply, running her fingers under her own eyes to signify the streaks.

Behind Norman, Richard laughed, the high unstable twitter of a man who accepts what he sees on the express understanding that he stands at insanity's door.

The stranger cleared his throat. "My name is Fol, of Highcourt," he said. "I come at the behest of some rather powerful characters."

Norman sensed the others stiffen. Lucian's hand locked around his upper arm. Hammers being cocked back flashed on the edge of audibility. Norman turned his head a little, shook it minutely, and after a pause the hand fell away. "Just wait, let's hear him out," he muttered.

The man waited politely, then straightened and gestured to the fireside where enough chairs for them—exactly the right number—sat arranged around a partner's desk. How anybody could have lumbered the great slab of mahogany down through the tunnel was anybody's guess. Emblazoned upon it, cast-iron and ancient, was the seal of a swinging pendulum.

Fol, of Highcourt, waggled his eyebrows. "Please, won't you join me for a little chinwag? I think some answers are long overdue."

# III

New Canterbury lay in shadow. High above, pigeons wheeled in flocks belittling anything the city's inhabitants had ever seen—since the day of the End when the skies had been thick with every winged being. Circling the city in undulating formation, the birds were joined by yet more from all directions. Throbbing and wheeling, the flock cast dancing shadows down onto one of the last standing cities of the Old World. Below, many of its people watched, mesmerised, from their rooftop hides; others kept their eyes resolutely on the ground, their faces drawn into masks of doom.

Sarah Strong spied them all, perched atop her house's roof, curled like a gargoyle with one hand clutching the open window frame.

A distant remnant of her old self, from before all this—the gawky librarian who had laid down for everything and hid from the world behind her books—gibed, *You must look like Quasimodo, hunched up here. Who the hell do you think you are? They look to you? You're nobody. You can't do this.*

She silenced the voice with a shrug of her shoulders as

though shaking off a fly. "Shut up," she muttered under her breath and returned to scanning the city.

The cathedral with all its myriad intricate spires stood to her right, a paragon of Old World might, buzzing with half the city's populace. Anybody who couldn't fight had by now either barricaded themselves into their homes like shivering gophers, or they had fled to their place of worship.

Elder Agatha had taken in hundreds who had seldom visited a pew all their lives. She had defied all expectations by emerging from the depths of dementia. Nobody had expected to see her alert again after Christmas when the famine had hit its peak. But the surge of people crawling through her doors had rallied her.

Sarah thanked her for that, even if her guts twisted at its necessity. Those who had gone north to find help had done so over a week ago. Too long.

The birds had circled overhead for the past few days, and a definite sense of finality had come with them. They all knew something was coming—and that their only real hope was to throw everything they had at whatever appeared in their midst. Nobody was stupid enough to suggest they could win. But if even some of them were going to survive this, they had to fight.

"Bastards," she muttered, watching yet more able-bodied people retreat from the pigeons into the cathedral.

Two voices warred behind her eyes:

*A few days ago you would have been down there with them.*
*But I'm not. I'm here. I'm making a stand.*
*Not everyone can fight. Not everybody wants to.*

*There's no room for that in this world. We fight or we die. Some prefer death.*

*Then that's exactly what they'll get.*

She pulled her gaze away from the cathedral and turned to the street to her left. Some semblance of relief came to her as she watched a group of militia heave on a rope looped around a pulley, lifting a motor car into the air. A few beefy men guided the floating chassis out over a barricade already two cars deep. Across the entire northern edge of the portion of the city they occupied, other pockets of militia completed similar blockades.

*My militia*, she reminded herself.

It caught her off-kilter: that she, of all people, could have mustered a guerrilla army in a matter of weeks. It was absurd, and for a moment that very fact sliced a chunk off her confidence, leaving a small hole through which doubt came rushing in like the tide.

*What if I'm the wrong one? What if I'm just giving them false hope?*

A small, younger voice from much deeper down: *What if I can't be brave when the time comes?*

She waited for that other, calloused voice to reply. None came.

She forced herself not to chew her lip.

"They moved fast."

Sarah whirled whip-like, drawing her pistol from her belt and training it upon the newcomer. It was clumsy and unpolished—she hadn't so much as held a gun a few weeks ago—but all the intent was there; every mote of willpower trained upon pulling that trigger.

Heather's long equine features had contorted into a blank-faced stare. Her hands rose up slowly, her fingers waggling. "Don't shoot, sheriff, it's just the deputy."

Sarah lowered the gun slowly. "You don't want to be my deputy," she said.

"Too late for that now, isn't it?"

"It's not too late to go down there." She nodded to the cathedral.

Heather spread herself into the window frame, bracing her hands upon the sill and leaning out. Her face darkened. "You think I'd do that? Back out on you now?"

"I wouldn't blame you."

"Bollocks, you wouldn't. Those people are just sticking their heads in the sand."

"Maybe, but I know you wouldn't be one of them. Agatha's doing good work down there. Those people need… something to keep them together. They look to you."

"I haven't worked the clinic in days."

"Doesn't matter. People trust doctor's orders." She looked to Heather's drawn, exhausted face, and with some effort, laid a hand on her arm. "You could help them through this."

Heather snorted. "While the bullets fly and everybody else dies for me? No thanks."

Sarah caught her retort between her teeth, just: *You're not the right person for this. War's no place for a healer.*

*Look who's bloody talking!* she thought.

A fit of giggles rolled through her, unstoppable and gut-busting. It took all her willpower to stifle it, but still a snort escaped her nostrils.

She felt Heather's eyes on her and kept her gaze resolutely on the barricade forming below. Still she could feel the pressure of that stare. She sighed and smiled—her cheeks stretched and complained at the contortion. It had been a long time since her last smile. "I'm glad you're here."

The ghost of an appreciative glint flashed behind Heather's eyes. "Ew, girly gushing."

They settled into companionable silence for a while. Inevitably, their gazes fell upon the pigeons wheeling overhead. There was no ignoring them nor the undulating patterns, the eerie strictness with which the flock adhered to the city's border. Like a bullseye.

*Here be lambs, ripe for the slaughter.*

"They're coming, aren't they?" Heather said.

Sarah didn't reply for a while. She felt sure the image of those flocks would be forever burned into her retinas.

Wrenching her gaze away, she turned to the treeline at the city's edge. A moment of terror bolted through her when she saw leagues of figures racing across the fields towards them. But it was just the shadow of the birds upon the crop-heads.

She drew a long sigh. "Funny, isn't it? I think we all feel it."

They were out there, somewhere. Marching.

A hand wandered into her peripheral vision. She resisted at first, tightening her jaw—knowing she had to stay strong until the end—but of its own volition, her hand wandered down to Heather's and gripped it. Coupled like that, they hung there in the window and watched the city prepare for its last stand.

"We'll be fine." Her own words fell flat on her ears, but she said them nonetheless.

"How can you say that?"

"Because. They're still out there, and they're coming back."

Robert and the others. She felt them in her gut just as strongly as she felt the marching footsteps of their would-be destroyers.

*The radio message from the north might have come through. If they found the Scots' ambassadors, perhaps they'll bring back help. Perhaps we could put up a real fight. And maybe, maybe, we can win.*

Maybe.

Either way, Robert *was* out there. And he *was* coming back. Whether it was in paradise or amidst blasted rubble, they were having their damn honeymoon.

Heather gave her hand an extra squeeze as though sensing the internal struggle, and Sarah gave one in return. They returned to watching the city, and this time Sarah ignored the birds, focusing instead on the militia's efforts. There was no chance they would ever really be prepared, but they were making progress.

And that was something.

Her gaze wandered back over the fields, and this time she saw only the pigeons' shadows. She didn't see the people wandering across the field until the clouds shifted and a sunbeam poured momentarily down upon the land, lifting the shadows clear. There were people everywhere, walking through the young crops towards the city.

Sarah tensed, on the verge of launching herself through the window to sound the alarm. Heather gripped her hard, keeping her in place. "No, wait. Look!"

Sarah looked again more carefully, taking in the slow plodding pace of those in the fields, strung out in a long ant trail, wandering, uncoordinated. She hadn't seen them because they moved so slowly, and they were so scattered. Scattered but plentiful: dozens, maybe hundreds. There was nothing hostile about them, nothing predatory.

Instead, their approach spoke of the dull death march of cats who crawl to a place of comfort before they lie down to die.

They were heading for Alexander's house.

# IV

"Are you sure about him?" Norman muttered to Billy as they sat before the desk.

He kept his gaze fixed on the pale-faced man, sensing the others keeping their hands on the butts of their pistols. One false move, and they'd blow him away.

That would be bad. Suspect or not, Norman knew the man was important—probably their only chance of getting back home in time.

"No," Billy said, not without a hint of venom, "but he's not one of them."

"Them?"

"The Bad Men. He's on our side."

*What side would that be?*

"Uh huh." He paused, no more comforted, hovering an inch above his seat. He flinched when Billy's fingers alighted on his hand. "Trust me," she whispered.

Norman blinked. He didn't know this girl, had met her perhaps three hours before.

*I do know her. I've seen her. And through her, I've seen other things.*

He suppressed a vague shudder and turned his eyes once more on the pale man. "Fine, we're sitting," he said.

The man, himself seated behind the desk, kicked his heels up onto the mahogany top. Mercurial, hard to read, his features shifted ceaselessly between extremes of sorrow and mischievous delight. He ran a hand through his hair, which didn't yield an inch. The jagged spikes were no feature of styling but instead almost part of his skull; a jagged tear where some protuberance had been torn away—

"Spill it," Lucian grunted. "I've had enough of this macabre goop. We got one mission here: get home."

The man spread his hands in placation. "Like I said, I think a few answers are in order."

"I don't need any bloody answers. The time for talk is past."

"On the contrary, talk is the flavour of the moment!"

Robert seemed to pop some spigot of self-control. "Lucian's right. We don't have time for this, Norman." He nodded to the desk. "This stinks, and I can't get distracted now. They all need us."

Norman cut Richard off before he could join in. "*Just…* wait."

"Norm—" Lucian hissed.

"I said, wait." Staring down Lucian was like playing chicken with a charging horse, but Norman refused to give in.

The silverback's jaw tightened, but he nodded and sat back.

"Your name was…," Norman said, rounding on the desk.

The stranger tipped his head, acquiescing. "Fol, of Highcourt."

Norman made to introduce them in turn, but Fol waved a dismissive hand. "Not necessary." A smile crept into the corners of his mouth. "I know."

*Of course you do. You've been watching me for a while, haven't you? Maybe you've been watching us all.*

"Fine, Mr Fol. I'm going to make this really clear. Whatever's going on, whatever you've got planned, forget it. We're not interested. Billy says you know a way to get us home. I'm going to take a chance, because I can't see any other way. But if this is some kind of trick, I promise on behalf of every man, woman, and child still free in this world"—their eyes locked in sizzling stalemate—"I'll kill you."

Fol's light and easy smile drooped into a stony glare with jarring rapidity. "Good," he said. "I hope you mean that."

Norman blinked despite himself. "Why?"

"Because you people are among but a handful who can stop what's coming."

"That's why we're trying to get home," Richard said. "If the Alliance falls, everything of the Old World we're keeping alive will disintegrate, and the whole country will slide—"

Fol waved a hand. "I'm afraid you don't understand. I'm not talking about a mere descent into anarchy. Empires rise and fall, civilisation comes and goes; such is the way of mortals. I'd never be concerned with natural order." He stood slowly and leaned over the table. "I'm afraid that none of you, for all your threats and concern for your friends, are anywhere near scared enough. If you had known before now what the stakes really were, you'd have had me against the wall with a gun in my mouth the moment you laid eyes on me."

"Don't tempt me," Lucian growled. "We said no more gab. Get to the bloody point!"

"It's not something that I can just explain. To really understand, I'll have to show you." With that, he gestured for them to rise, nodding to the crest of the pendulum upon the table. "Come closer and put your hands here."

Norman had no intention of moving. All this reeked of some gigantic waste of time; a red herring leading down some cosmic avenue of freakery, one that would leave everyone back home to die.

Billy stood without a word, stepped lightly over to the desk, and with a glance of contempt in Fol's direction, laid her hand on the crest. The brass glyph dwarfed her, making her rosy fingers seem so very tiny and delicate.

*She asked me to trust her. But can I really trust the fate of us all to some mystic trip?*

Norman had no idea what he believed until he found himself standing to join Billy by the desk. He glanced at her, and any doubt ebbed under her long-suffering stare. He gave her a wink and turned to the others.

He wasn't going to force them. He had chosen, but he wasn't going to force this on them. If they were going in pursuit of insanity, they all had to jump together, or they wouldn't go.

Robert was first to stand, a blazing look of mixed warning and gratitude emanating from his rounded head.

Norman knew what that meant: if they succeeded, it would be Norman who had led them to victory; but if they failed… it would be Sarah's blood on his hands.

*No, that won't happen. We won't let it.*

Still, the mental images flashed before his eyes, an unending cascade: bullets, running feet, the quaint cobbles of New Canterbury splashed with blood.

Richard came next, shaking his head. Every step of the way, he muttered, "This is mental. Mental."

Everyone, Fol included, waited for Lucian to make his choice. He glowered at the ground when he finally rose, not meeting a single eye until his hairy digits slapped down onto the crest, then locked onto Fol. "Like the boy said," he glowered, "if this is a trick, you die."

Fol gave a small bow, his stony look having once again blossomed into a light-hearted, almost facetious grin. "Understood. Now, shall we?"

The next moment, the cavern was gone, and Norman almost screamed for darkness rushed in on all sides, and he was flying. He endured a nauseating sensation of falling, but in no direction his internal compass could parse; some other flavour of *sideways* that boggled the mind. A brief instant of pain followed as the chill in his chest rushed out, pain and cold so intense he felt he might shatter, and then his entire body folded up through impossible angles like an origami swan.

Then darkness again, and the other five were before him

again. They all hovered amidst nothing. Just nothing. At first he thought a black canvas had replaced the world. Then he looked down what seemed a hundred feet at least, and he saw them.

*Them.*

His heart stopped. The sight was a horror to outstrip all others, but it wasn't the sheer oddity of what he was seeing: it was that he had seen it before with Billy. In his dreams.

"Oh my God," Richard said, his voice infantile and on the verge of tears.

*There are so many of them. So many...*

The floor of the strange other place undulated in constant motion, its colour a rusted palette ranging between chalk and charcoal.

People. Endless, screaming, flailing people. A carpet of human beings without end, stretching away into infinity in all directions. Blindly pressed together amongst the accumulated filth of decades, starving and agonised, yet without death; crushed face-to-face, yet entirely alone in their own personal hell.

"Is that...?" Richard stammered.

"The Vanished," Billy said. "The people from Before."

"Trick." Lucian's voice had lost its gravelly edge and seemed on the brink of snapping. "It's a trick. I'll... I'll kill you. I said no tricks." He made a loose grab for Fol, but there was no fight left in him as though he had taken twenty rounds in a boxing ring.

Fol's voice was gentle. "It's no trick. Nobody should ever have to see this." A brief pause. "But you'd never believe me otherwise.”

“It can’t be,” Richard said. His voice had devolved entirely to that of a child’s, his eyes wide and staring.

“It is,” Fol said.

Richard swallowed sharply.

Norman and Billy said nothing more. It seemed outrageous and almost funny, but the truth was the two of them had seen this enough. It was horrific, gut-wrenching, sure to haunt their dreams for the rest of their lives. But he didn’t disbelieve it one iota.

Before them writhed the last generation of the Old World, brought to this torturous purgatory.

Robert swept a long stare over the carpet of Vanished, then calmly turned back to Fol. “Tell us,” he said.

Norman’s throat tightened. Somehow, seeing the determination in those frank chocolate eyes hurt more than the sight of billions of screaming innocents.

*He’s getting home even if he has to punch through the devil himself.*

Richard, however, had started mewling. His hands reached up to his head, and he curled into a ball, not falling in this place without gravity, only turning in free fall, scrunched into a jittering foetal position. Tears dropped from his chin. “No, this can’t be happening. No, no, no, no…”

“I-I…” Lucian scowled. “This… No. This isn’t real.”

“It is real,” Fol said. “I promise you.”

“No, this is the same trick as before,” Lucian cried. His eyes grew wilder with each word. “It was you, wasn’t it?

You'll never get me with your mumbo jumbo, not like you got him."

*Him? Don't crack on me now, Lucian. Don't you dare,* Norman thought desperately.

Fol sighed. Suddenly his facetious gleam had punctured yet again. An ancient fatigue shone through for an instant, and Norman's skin rippled with some extra perception, one he had only before received from Billy.

*He's been waiting. Waiting for so long for this moment. For us.*

"You have to listen to me," he said quietly.

Lucian made another weak grab for him. "You won't take any of us. You've already taken him away from me. I won't let you do it again!"

Norman's lips parted in shock for there were tears in Lucian's eyes. Never, in all his life, had he seen Lucian shed a tear.

"Listen. Listen, now," Fol said, his face draining of any remaining colour.

"No, no, no!" Richard wept without end.

"Lucian, stop," Robert said. "There's no time."

"Please listen to me..." Fol uttered.

"I won't be taken; I'll fight you. I'll kill you, you son of a bitch!" Lucian barked.

"No, no, no, no..."

"You took my brother, but you won't take me!"

"ENOUGH!" Fol's voice tore through them as though they were made of paper, a searing intensity so great he seemed ten times as large. For a brief moment looking at him was unbearable, like staring into the sun, and Norman glimpsed something else superimposed in Fol's place: something elemental, beyond his comprehension. "I have waited too long for the time to be right. You people will listen to me now, or our last chance is gone. *YOU WILL LISTEN!*" His voice rose to a stentorian rumble, silencing any remnant retorts.

They all watched, waiting, hanging absurdly in mid-air. Norman had time, before the man of Highcourt spoke again, for a single errant thought:

*This is just so bloody weird. Why couldn't I have just taken a bullet to the head instead?*

"I told you that you didn't know the stakes. Now you do," Fol said. He gestured to the millions—perhaps billions—of screaming people below. His shoulders rose and fell as he took long, slow breaths. Some great unseen fire, one that could have destroyed them all in a flash, slowly died down. He sighed. "I need you to understand. So…" Astonishingly, a thin smile graced his face. "I have to tell you a little story."

This time, none of them interrupted. Instead, they all turned to the Vanished as though some secret magnetism drew their gaze. Fol's voice washed over them in dulcet waves.

"In the beginning, there were two. Both were wise and fair, servants of the creator: the Pendulum that must always swing, from which pour the threads that bind our universe together. One, the Great Weaver, would for all time hang from these threads and fashion the body of reality, breathe life into the stars and oceans, creatures and lives of men. The other, the Angelic One, would watch over them, guide the ultimate fate of all towards becoming one with themselves and the Pendulum. Thus, together, they would bring the cosmos towards greatness and peace.

"This was the bargain set before them. An eternity of servitude in exchange for the knowledge that they would embody the true definition of divinity. So the Great Weaver fashioned a cosmos of myriad worlds of untold number and variety; all beside one another, yet apart, joined by threads unseen to all but a handful of Guardians, whom the Weaver charged with maintaining its creations.

"The Angelic One guided creatures great and small to their respective destinies, fortunes, and deaths. Those great and meek it nurtured to the heights of enlightenment, and across the Web the Weaver and the Angelic One were worshipped. For a time beyond timelessness, a goodness lasted as undying as the stars they had birthed. All was fair in the new realm of All Where.

"But all things come to an end. While the Angelic One guided the powerful and strong, it saw the Weaver was but a limit to its own power. All Where would forever risk ultimate ruin should the Weaver falter. So the Angelic One set out to take the Pendulum's charge for itself, and itself alone.

"The Battle of the Elementals raged beyond the perception of mortals, yet in the Solstice Scrolls, passages speak of galaxies shattering, flinging billions of worlds into darkness, forever lost to the coldness of space. Stars dimmed in sequence as warring shadows passed by, two figures locked in desperate struggle; one manlike and winged, the other eight-legged and many-eyed. Entropy reigned supreme, sicknesses ran rife, and across the near-infinite worlds of All Where, rivers ran red with blood.

"In the end, when the dust settled, the Angelic One lay defeated. There was no demoting it, no destroying it, for the bargain had been struck: to break it would bring All Where to catastrophic collapse. The Great Weaver had but one choice: imprisonment. The darkest, most inescapable prison in all reckoning."

Norman blinked, looking at the writhing carpet of the Vanished afresh.

*It's this place. This is that prison.*

"Yes," Fol said. "Yes, it is this place."

Norman started, but let it pass. No doubt the same thought had passed through all their heads.

But still, still. Billy had surely read his mind at least once. It wasn't absurd that Fol had done the same.

*Nothing's absurd anymore…*

"The Great Weaver gathered its Guardians, and together they cast the Angelic One to this place. To ensure it remained, they forever placed it in chains: the charge of maintaining the Pendulum's swing. The task destroyed every Guardian but the Weaver itself, great beings the like of which would never pass this way again. Yet the job was done, and the Angelic One slaved alone, lost and trapped.

"That, friends, is the origin of all that is, was, and will ever be. The story of the Web of All Where."

A long, long silence followed.

"Uh… uh," Lucian said at last.

Norman tore his gaze from the Vanished with enormous effort. "What happened? If this is that prison, why are all these people here? Where's the Angel?"

Fol flinched. "It may be called the Angelic One in the origin scrolls, but whatever it is, it is no angel."

Norman waited.

Fol went on. "All things come to an end. *All things*. For another age, All Where has endured; a shadow of its golden years, but fair. I hail from Highcourt, home to those who follow the ways of the old Guardians."

Richard, who had finally unravelled from his foetal ball, shook his head wearily, his face red and tear-stained. "I don't understand."

"I don't expect you to. The world is a strange place."

"It can't be true. It's just illogical. This is the stuff of fantasy." He looked around at the rest of them. "Think about it. It's just as likely all this is the raving delusion of any one of us."

"Don't, my head's spinning enough!" Lucian spat.

"But that's the truth. There's no way for us to know." He looked sheepish, ready to recoil from Fol, but defiant.

Fol shrugged. "There's no arguing. But how is that different from any day you have lived your lives? Your world ended. Billions of people vanished. Does that sound logical to you?"

Silence.

Billy hadn't turned away from the Vanished. Norman

touched her shoulder. "Are you okay?"

She blinked, long and slow. "Daddy and Ma might be down there with Grandpa," she said quietly.

"No. They're dead. And dead is dead," Fol said shortly. Then he added with a touch of softness, "They're safe from this place."

"Fine," Richard said. "Fine. If this place, this Highcourt, has power, how could you let this happen?"

Fol's face slowly fell, his jowls sinking—the face of an aged and frail man; translucent skin around milky eyes. "My home is gone. Highcourt fell, just before... before"—he gestured to the Vanished—"everything changed."

A beat of silence.

Then Robert said, "I don't care. I don't. None of this has anything to do with us. It doesn't matter what brought the End. All we need to know is how to get home. If you can get us there, do it."

"It does matter," Fol muttered. "It may be the only thing that still matters."

"We're waiting," Lucian said.

Fol's mouth worked as though searching for the right words, then he said, "Frost."

"Frost?" Norman said.

He nodded. His gaze lingered on Lucian and Robert. "You lived before the End?"

They nodded.

"Then you felt it, didn't you? The moment they all went away: the pain, the cold, like you could never be warm again, would never see anything but darkness."

Their faces paled. Norman wasn't sure whether he felt what they felt through empathy or in his own chest: a nugget of that very same cold nestled there, as much a part of him as his beating heart. He swallowed. "What is it?"

"It is life, and death, a conduit and an entity all of its own. It is the stuff that drives All Where, the threads of the Pendulum incarnate."

"And?" Robert urged.

Norman spoke without thinking. "And it's coming back."

They all turned to him.

"I've felt it. It's shown me things." From nowhere Billy's fingers gripped his, and he squeezed them tight. "Before we left home, I could barely stand. Now… Now I feel it inside me, driving me like I'm some wind-up clock. It was all over Radden. It's spreading, isn't it?"

Fol stared for what seemed an age. "Yes."

"And if it spreads too far?"

Fol gestured to the dark place beneath them. "Then this place will consume all that remains of your world, and the End will at last be total."

"The End will come again?"

"The End will come again." Fol nodded. "And this time, there will be no survivors."

"Why? Why now?" Lucian grated. "After all this bloody time?"

"Even trapped slaving under such incredible strain, the Angelic One can never be silenced. Its influence is built into everything spun. While we have slaved to keep the balance, it has whispered into the dark, and the things that lurk there have gone over to its will. There may be an army marching on your home, but there is one so much grander and more terrifying out there, set against us all. They swept Highcourt aside in a single day." A twisted grin spread over his face, threaded with sick malice. "We grew blind, weak, and ignorant. We dared to believe things had settled and that the Web had found its peace. We were so wrong. Now they're all gone. Without Highcourt, they can tear it all down, break the bonds that tie worlds together, and deal the final blow that will bring All Where to an apocalypse upon every level of existence."

"Why?" Norman said.

"Once the playing field is levelled, the Pendulum's swing may stop, and the Angelic One will be unburdened… free. Whichever universe it plans to spawn, be thankful you'd be long dead before it started."

"How is that related to our world? Why take us if there are so many worlds?"

"Because yours is one of a few that lie at the nodes of all the connected strings. Like a handful of balloons: cut the central string, and they all fly apart, drifting forever away to die alone. Wiping your world clean got the ball rolling. Now decay eats at every corner of All Where."

"And them?" Norman motioned to the Vanished.

"They have taken the burden. Some of it, anyway. They labour under the Pendulum's swing. The Angelic One is still bound to this place, but without the strain, without its shackles, it grows more powerful. Soon its shadow will spill from this place, weaving its fingers into every fragile mind and tortured soul. And when that happens, the last great war will begin. One we could never win."

"So we stop this, stop the Frost, and what? We stop the Angel—whatever it is?"

"We stall it, maybe. For a while. The rest comes later." He glanced at Billy. "But if we fail now, it'll all coming crashing down. This isn't the first time I've tried to put things right. The first time, I failed. I forgot how… fragile, you creatures can be. In fact, I made things a hell of a lot worse." Fol winked, ever mercurial, now even grinning. "Sorry, folks, but you're my do-over."

Norman cut his hand through the air. "The others are right. This doesn't help us. We don't need to know. The End is past. Our friends need us now—"

Fol held up a hand. "I needed you to know all that so that you can understand *why* this is so important. The End will come again, but there is no magic doomsday button, no horde of monsters to burst from the ground and drag you down. It will come from inside you all, from your own fears, from want of hope. If this army destroys your home, you won't just lose your friends; it will be the spark upon the kindling. The End will wash over the whole world."

"What about them down there?"

The spark in Fol's smile flickered. "You can't help them." Again, he seemed to have eyes only for Billy, who still stared down into the writhing masses, her back to them all. "But maybe you can help yourselves."

Norman nodded slowly. "Now we know."

Fol seemed pleased. "Now you know. Time to get going."

Norman glanced between Fol and Billy, then cleared his throat. "She's special, isn't she?"

Fol said nothing, his eyes glittering.

"Can she save them?"

A long measured pause. "Maybe. One day."

Norman touched Billy's shoulder. "Billy, it's time," he said. "We have to go."

"I know." She sounded far, far away. "They're out there, you know, Norm. The others. I can feel them."

"Uh huh, that's great," Norman said, turning her around to face him. "But we have to go. Are you with me?"

Her eyes remained glazed for a moment, but then she seemed to return to him from a great distance. "Yes."

"Good. Let's go then," he said to Fol.

Lucian wheezed, "If you really can work up some magic voodoo to get us back."

"I can get you close enough. Maybe."

"We'll take it. Show-and-tell's over." Robert's voice was dead, unyielding. "We're going now, or you lose your spine."

Fol's inveterate grin sharpened. "I like you." He held out his hands. "Group huddle!" he cried, giving a little titter.

Norman offered Billy a weak smile. With what seemed enormous effort, she returned the sentiment.

"What the hell's the matter with you?" Lucian growled as he floated closer, linking hands with Norman and Richard. "You got a screw loose? How can you laugh at a time like this?"

"Because," Fol said, winking, "back home, I was the Jester. Let one hell of an old fella tell you: most times, laughter is all we have."

Then Norman tumbled through space again, turning backwards through the same impossible angles, leaving the dark prison and the Vanished behind, a long wailing echo ringing in his ears.

V

The spiky-haired woman gripped the rakish young man by the shoulder so hard he grunted. "Shh, they'll hear you!"

"Nobody's listening. You know I'm tellin' the truth," he said.

"I said shut up!"

He threw her off. "What's the plan once we're through? Say we burn everything there is to be burned, what then? What's the point?"

"Gettin' even. They starved us out of house and home and left us to die."

He beat her across the mouth. "Don't be a damn fool, woman!"

She cried out and slapped him back. The two of them sneered at one another, half-crouched like cats in the dying afternoon light. "Don't you fuckin' touch me."

"I just trying to beat some sense into you. I want to get even as much as anyone, but I didn't sign up for this. This is just bloody murder. They're going to destroy everything they touch and they won't stop until there's nothing left to torch but themselves."

"Don't be stupid."

"I'm tellin' you, we'll turn on each other when the last of the Alliance folk are in the ground."

The woman said nothing.

Charlie watched from behind the rocky bluff where his campfire flickered. He cringed inwardly.

*Why do the damn fools have to have their little secret meeting here?*

If only they knew the lion's den lay a few feet away.

The two idiots had crept away quietly for their little collusion. On Charlie's right, through a thin screening of trees, the main encampment lay sprawled across a square mile of open prairie. Thin tendrils of smoke trailed skywards from enough campfires to boggle his mind, even now. He had grown up with only his father for company. The towns they had visited had numbered in the dozens at most.

He would never get used to these numbers: thousands, all looking for blood.

Over a day, they had been marching. The land had been scoured clean on their way to rendezvous in Radden Moor. Anybody left had either taken up and scattered, been cut down where they stood, or been absorbed into the marching ranks.

*We're all broken. Some of these people were highwaymen and bandits, but most of them might have broken bread with strangers not long ago. Now look at them. They're so thirsty for blood they're a hair's breadth from taking chunks out of one another.*

The weak were being left in the army's dust, sloughed off like dead skin. It was almost as though the army was an organism unto itself, a relentless carnivore bent on mindless killing, growing ever more terrible as those with conscience were stripped away, leaving only the true killers to carry on.

The arguing pair had already sealed their fate. Presently, Jason crept from the fireside, his wolfish chops greasy with juices from the squirrel he had been devouring. His long curved knife was already unsheathed and ready.

The man implored the woman, wringing his hands. "Let's just go now."

She hissed into his face, mere inches from his nose. "I buried a husband by the road. My two boys. Am I just supposed to forget about them? I won't let them get away with what they've done. They think they're better than all of us, that they can take what they want, that protecting rubbish from before the End is more important than us right here and now. They all deserve to die!"

The man's voice broke. "I don't want to kill anymore, Kelly. I just wanna go home."

She said nothing.

Charlie looked to the green-eyed figure sat across the fire from him, the face thankfully veiled by a balaclava. A pigeon rested on his shoulder, and he fed it breadcrumbs with pensive tenderness. He didn't glance up at Jason.

"James," Charlie said. "They're just idiots."

James Chadwick said nothing, just kept feeding his pigeon one breadcrumb at a time.

"Flog them, cut them, beat them bloody, and leave them

as an example."

James stroked the bird's head with his index finger, and it gave a contented little coo in response.

Charlie glanced to Jason, now only feet away from the woman. She had her back to him. The fronds would screen him entirely from view. Not that they would have stood a chance if he had been in full view.

"They don't have to die," Charlie said.

James let the remaining breadcrumbs fall to the dirt and looked at the scene playing out behind the bluff. Nothing registered in his eyes, not a glimmer of joy nor note of interest.

"If I have to punch you out and drag you, you're coming with me, you stupid bitch," the man said. He held the woman by the hair, grunting as she clawed at his fist. "I know you don't want it to end like this."

"Let me go." She was weeping, snot dripping down her chin. "Let me go, you bastard, let me go." She collapsed onto him and sobbed, beating weakly at his chest.

Suddenly they were in a gentle embrace, the man no longer yanking her hair, but caressing it.

"They're all gone," she said.

"I know. We can't change that. All the killing, it won't change anything." He held her tight. "We have to go."

She nodded tearfully and sobbed yet again.

Jason left the fronds and stepped into view, twirling his knife with a carnivorous snarl on his face.

The man and woman closed their eyes, swaying to and fro.

Charlie glanced between James and Jason. The childish part of him that believed in good and bad, black and white, light and dark, screamed for him to call out. His own father's face floated before him, one he knew was now rotting somewhere far south of here in the forest, shot full of holes. His father's voice, a beseeching whisper: *Don't let this happen. You're a good boy, son.*

*Maybe once, Dad*, he thought.

Charlie sent no warning. He watched Jason take the last step towards the couple swaying in each other's grasp, and then he turned back to face the fire. A wet splatter rang out, followed by the briefest shrill scream.

All the while, Charlie kept his eyes on James Chadwick, who stared into the fire, each flame mirrored in the vast emptiness of those emerald eyes.

# FIRST INTERLUDE

1

"It's a strange thing, beauty. Men have spent fortunes, entire lifetimes, chasing it. Whole empires have knelt before it."

Beth Tarbuck held her breath and tried not to flinch as the knife-edge brushed her cheek.

The slurred voice tickled her ear, uttered inches behind her head. "So fragile. Just one nick of the blade, and it's gone forever."

Beth bit her lip, determined to hold Malverston's gaze. The mayor's hot stinking breath washed over her as his face drew to within an inch of hers, inhaling through furry nostrils, smelling her.

She shivered, and the blade clipped the top of her cheek, a tiny pinprick of fire under her left eye. Something warm trickled down towards her chin.

He groaned, a heady sensual noise that made her gorge rise. "I think I'll have you sit on my face tonight, girly," he whispered.

"Go suck peaches," she spat.

He laughed and drew back, his wicked eyes looking her up and down. Yet underneath his ugly veneer, she was satisfied to see the same frustration she had always seen. The kind of frustration that could only come from a lifetime of gawping at what one can't have. Every time she had looked at the rotund, old mayor, she saw a shadow of somebody else—a young gawky, snivelling weed, riddled with acne, jealous, supercilious, and mean. She could sense the rejections he had suffered in every hungry pry of his fingers; all the women who had looked down their noses at the eager, leg-humping fat boy and laughed.

"You like this, don't you?" he said, biting his lip. "I know you do. You can't help yourself, like a bitch in heat."

In his drunkenness he had grown more volatile with each swing of the bottle. Since she had been tied to the chair, he had got through a whole bottle and a half of hard liquor, and he looked as though he meant to go on. The sheer volume of the great beach ball of a man would soak up a lot of it—any ordinary man would have been stretched out on the ground by now—but everyone had a limit.

Once he passed that, there would be no room for error. Malverston was turning into a bomb before her eyes, one she knew she couldn't help but set off. She refused to lay down for him, to become a sheep and submit. Even if it meant he carved her face off and capered about wearing it like a mask, she'd kick and fight to the last breath.

Beth didn't move one inch, her face contorted into what she hoped was a disgusted grimace as Malverston's tongue snaked out and tickled her cheek.

"I know you always loved that," Malverston whispered. "Every time you lay in my bed, you pretended you didn't, but you did. Women are all the same. Pretend you don't want it, but deep down you're looking for a reason to spread 'em, especially for big, powerful men."

She tittered harshly into his face. "Like you?"

His expression flashed between surprise and confusion behind his drunken hunger. "I hold every scrap of land between here and Dorset, little girl. There's no bigger pair in all the land."

Ready, Beth licked her lips, glancing down below his belt to the pathetic protuberance stretching into view. "Oh, I'm sorry, mayor. I didn't know we were talking about raisins."

Her stared at her deadpan for a moment, then the half-filled bottle came up from out of view and collided with her temple.

Beth lurched sideways in the chair and recoiled against her restraints. The world span and for a moment she was certain she would vomit. Then she was panting, and Malverston had turned his back, pacing the room.

She gritted her teeth, fighting tears welling up behind her eyes, biting down on her lip. She screamed, "Why am I here?"

"I realised my mistake as soon as I sent you to Cain and his foolish friends. Your place is here."

"I'll never sit by your side, mayor."

"Oh, that ship has sailed." His brow darkened. "Your place is here so you can receive your just desserts. I am the mayor of Newquay's Moon, and I will not be embarrassed by some rosy-cheeked harlot."

Staggering from table to table, Malverston inspected the copious piles of trinkets given as tribute by farmers and homesteads across the Cornwall peninsula. One by one he inspected tarnished pieces of silver, precious stones, inoperable Old World curiosities, casting them aside without a care for which returned to the table or broke on the floor.

The town hall had vacated in the wake of Malverston's drunken roaring. Even his personal entourage had stepped outside to give, as the mayor himself had put it, *a spot of lover's passion*. The upper floor, in the middle of which her chair had been bolted down, consisted of a single slant-roofed room, the corners piled high with yet more trinkets and tributes. Two cases of liquor lay nearby, next to a metal table that looked disturbingly medical in origin, covered over with a length of tarp.

She looked at it all afresh and a sliver of fear arose from somewhere inside her. She had been here almost an hour, and not one sound had registered even on the edge of audibility. She had seen nothing of Newquay's Moon on her less-than-elegant return. Two days ago, she had been at the Alliance homestead, along with Malverston's goons, exiled for refusing his bed. She had hated going for her departure had been coupled with her home being turned upside down. Melanie, her sister, and her mother, who already had so little and worked so hard to scrape by, had been left with nothing.

Because of her.

But being at the homestead had meant being with James. James, who had appeared months ago from the wilds and cast the first twinkling rays of hope into her life. His green eyes, his easy smile, the stupid pigeons that hung around him all the time—she had noticed all of it, the moment he and Alex Cain had arrived to see the mayor for the first time. The look in their eyes had been one she had seldom seen except in her own, whenever she caught sight of herself in the mirror.

They had no intention of bowing to the cretin. They had a plan.

The first time she and James kissed had been in the peach groves under the cover of darkness. She had known then that she could never be without him. If she couldn't escape Malverston's clutches, she would rather die than lay in his bed, night after night, with his flabby bulk pumping impotently atop her.

When Malverston had flung her away to the homestead, despite the knowledge that she was leaving her family behind, a secret relief had nestled in her chest. Because she had been going to him, and briefly, she had dared to hope that it might be the end to her suffering. But when she had arrived, the fantasy popped. Malverston's goons, wheedling their grubby fingers into the Alliance's classrooms to learn the ways of the Old World, had taken her as their plaything. While her mind's eye had played film reels of James cutting them all down, one by one, he had left.

He left her alone with those monsters. She fought them

for an entire day while James's friends watched, their hands tied by dirty politics. Then while she slept, a bag had been thrust over her head. The next time she had seen light, she had been back in the Moon.

"Why bother sending me all that way just so that you could bring me all the way back?" she said.

Malverston turned from the table and splayed his arms as though to say, *What are you gonna do?*

"I remember what you said. You said I was all used up. What's the matter, mayor? You realise just how much you need me? That I'm the only one who's willing to stand your filth, because she had something to lose?"

He gave her a long look-over, running his tongue along his teeth under his lip. "You are used up," he muttered. "Tainted. I can see it in you. You always had spice; that was what made it worth putting up with your shit. But now…" He cocked his head to the side, and he pointed the knife at her, waggling it back and forth. "You've got that look in your eye." He waddled closer, placing each foot menacingly before the other. "It's that kid. That Chadwick."

Beth clamped her teeth together, desperate not to let anything show on her face. But she knew he'd seen her momentary shock by the glint that sparked in his eye.

"I knew it," he hissed. "That little bastard wheedled his way into my home, ate my food and drank my ale, and he thinks he can take my property from me. Oh, I know their type well, my dear. They talk of peace and rebuilding, traipsing around the country like it was theirs for the taking, treating the rest of us like we were helpless simpletons without their guidance." He spat on the floorboard at her feet. "As though they were something special. Well let me tell you something,"—he stopped before her, hips thrust out at a disgusting angle towards her face as he reached out a liquor-soaked digit to caress a dangling lock of her hair—"you are *mine*, and you always will be. No little twerp from out east is going to come and steal from George Malverston."

Beth glowered up at him. "He's going to kill you," she said. "When he does, I'm going to be there, and I'll be smiling."

Malverston grinned, a bare-toothed leer. "I suppose you think he's going to swoop in here and take you away with him."

"He's coming for you. They'll all be coming."

Her voice almost wobbled for she knew nothing about James's companions. In fact, what did she really know about him? Not much. She had never been much interested in his great mission. In fact, she hadn't wanted to know. She had only wanted him.

Would they come after her? Or would they stand back and watch for the sake of Cain's precious Alliance? That was why those snotty goons had been there at the homestead anyway: to learn the ways of the Old World, in exchange for whatever it was Cain wanted with the lands around the Moon.

*No. He will come.*

Malverston was laughing. Did he see her doubt?

"I'm counting on it!" he roared, whirling and striding

towards the covered table. He laid a hand on the tarp, caressing it, as though relishing what might lie underneath. "I have a surprise for them," he added, his voice falling to a feral growl.

Beth swallowed. "Why can't you just let us be?"

"Because a man has a right to protect his property."

"No. No, that's not it." She willed herself to shut up, sensing he was close to the edge. But she couldn't stop. That part of her that would never be a slave to him again kept her mouth running on a motor. "I know you, George. I've seen what you are."

He stilled, his back to her. The knife in his hand arced back and forth thoughtfully.

Beth relinquished control to that part of herself. She was getting to him, she could feel it. Thrusting a knife into his heart would be all that she would settle for, in the end, but this would do for now.

"You're afraid. Of him, of all of them. The Moon would turn on a drop of a hat for them if it meant they could turn you into the gutter, and you know it. You might have a chokehold on this place, but you haven't got it beaten. Now you've sent your goons to the enemy, and what, you're hoping they'll stay loyal? You're a maggot, but you're not stupid." She hurled each word at him now, injecting as much venom as she could muster. "You're just a sad, greedy little man in his fort on the hill. When you're gone, nobody will miss you, and everyone will piss on your grave on their way to the fields. That's why you're doing this now. Because if I had stayed with them, you wouldn't have anything left at all. Sooner or later, the Moon would tear you apart, or your own men would put a knife in your back."

Malverston inched around to face her, the bottle hanging limply by his side. There was fear in his eyes. Childish, volatile fear. Without a word, he took a long swing of the bottle and threw the tarp covering the cart aside.

Beth almost fainted at the sight of what lay on the table. But she wouldn't scream, she refused.

"I'll show those fools out there what happens when you cross me." He put his knife down, which now seemed a blunt and primitive piece compared to the wicked glistening things laid out upon the cart. He picked up the first of them and held it up to the light. Liquor dribbled down his chin and dripped on the floor, but he paid it no mind. He only had eyes for the shimmering blade between his fingers. His eyes flitted in their sockets from the surgery-grade edge over to her, and he grinned.

Beth's mind grew numb. She could only stare as a single weak thought echoed through her head:

*James…*

## 2

"You don't have to do this, friend. I'm just passing through." Alex spoke carefully, his hands raised, stepping slowly to one side.

"Stop moving. One more step and I'll do you," snarled the kid in front of him. Ruddy and stout with a face like a bruised piece of fruit and clothes that reeked of meat turned bad, the boy had emerged from a lean-to amidst the rubble like an eel slithering from its hole in some coral.

Alex scanned his surroundings without moving his head. They were alone so far as he could see. The kid barely looked nourished enough to hold the pigeon gun in his hands steady. But he also looked young enough and mean enough to be the kind who shot first and didn't bother asking questions. Those kinds littered the North, remnants of families shattered in endless power struggles and massacres as the lords squabbled over their fiefdoms. This little town outside Nottingham was the typical place for them to take refuge.

Alex should have been on the lookout. In the back of his mind, he realised he had been, but he had been too focused on searching for it to register.

"I'm not looking for trouble. All I want is to be on my way."

The kid's eyes trained on his pack.

Alex flicked his head over his shoulder. "There's nothing much in there, but it's yours. Token of good faith. What do you say?"

"You got a horse. I saw it. And a gun. You think I'm stupid?"

"No."

"Uh huh. Well I'm not. I'm smart. How else do you think I'm not dead like the others?"

"I'm sure you're the smartest. That's why I know you're going to do the *smart* thing, and let me leave my pack, and be on my way."

He made to step back, but the kid took a firmer grip on the pigeon gun, starting forwards. "You ain't goin' nowhere."

"Like I said, I don't have much." Alex kept his face even, but any hope of getting out of this easily was fading fast.

*He's either fresh out into the wilds, or he's lost somebody who used to protect him. Damn.*

He was pretty sure now that no matter what happened, the kid was liable to do something stupid.

"Stay there! Don't you move." The kid muttered under his breath, "I got you. I got you good. You're mine."

"That's right, you got me. Congratulations. But like I said, I'm not looking for trouble—"

"Who were you calling for?" the kid said, his eyes narrowing.

Alex closed his mouth slowly and said nothing.

The kid's face paled as his lips drew back from his gums. "I heard you. You were calling for somebody. But there's nobody here but me." His eyes widened. "That means you're crazy. You're nutty nut nuts, just like all the others. You're here to kill me—"

"I'm not here to kill you," Alex said tightly, preparing his legs to run.

*Crap.*

"Yes, you are. You're crazy! Just like the others. They all tried to kill me, so I killed them first. I got them, I got them all good!" He laughed as tears sprung into his eyes. "I got them all, *pew pew*, all gone! Just like I'm going to get you, because you're not going to get me, no, no, no, not little old me. I'm going to get you first, hehe!"

"I'm not going to hurt you!" Alex yelled, fists bunched, ready to dive. He would have one chance, assuming the kid missed.

*He might not miss.*

The kid's eyes bugged at his raised voice. "That's what they all said, but they lied. They all lied and they tried to kill me. But I got them ALL, like I'm going to get YOU." He held the gun clumsily out in front of him like a cannon. "Die, die, *die!—*"

His finger never made it to the trigger. His skull seemed to blow out above his left eyebrow, spurting the grimy brick wall beside them with crimson and gristle. The pigeon gun fell to the gravel, and the kid crumpled into a shuddering pile, jerking and twitching.

Alex dropped his hands, blinking.

Behind the kid's body, standing in the middle of the street, James Chadwick slowly lowered his rifle.

"You didn't have to kill him," Alex said, looking to the twitching carcass before him.

"He was going to shoot," James said.

Alex frowned. "He was just a kid."

James blinked. Not a trace of recognition registered on his face as though the two of them were utter strangers instead of brothers. "He was going to shoot." He shook his head, balancing his rifle upon his shoulder. "Stop following me."

He made to turn away, but Alex held out a hand. "Wait! Just... wait. Hear me out."

James rounded on him. "There's nothing to listen to. I don't want to see your face, I don't want your help, I don't want you anywhere near me."

"I'm sorry for what I did."

"You're a lot of things, Alex, but you've never been sorry, not for anything."

Alex stepped over the kid's body, desperate to hold James for a little while longer. Three days he had chased James south, away from Radden Moor, searching for him in the northern wilderness. In the endless hundreds of square miles between them and their home, finding one person had been a daunting task. His only hope had been to trust his gut. They both had to rest their horses, and Alex had most of their food. He knew James would have to scavenge from some bigger settlements on his way back.

It had paid off this once. But what had it cost him?

Almost his life.

And if he lost James now, he might never find him again. Now that James knew he was on his trail, he would probably make sure of it.

"Please, just listen to me."

"There's nothing you can say that I want to hear," James said, backing away. His face was taut and emotionless, but Alex knew he was lying. It was written into his gaze. Alex knew those eyes better than anyone; he had looked into them every day since the End when James had been but a blue-faced baby in an abandoned crib.

"You know I'd never do anything to hurt you. You know that."

"You don't care about anything but your precious mission," James spat. "That's always the way of it."

Alex kept walking, but with every step forwards he took, James took one back. "That's not true. I love you. I love all of you."

"Then why would you not tell me that Malverston took her!" James roared, all the hurt suddenly bare upon his face.

"You needed to go to Radden. I don't know why, but you had to. It was going to eat away at you until you did."

"Distract me, you mean. You wanted me focused on Newquay's Moon. You needed all your pawns in order!"

Alex sighed helplessly. "We're so close, James. So close to getting Malverston on side."

"That's all you ever think about. How much ground we can gain, how many people we can get on side. This bloody *destiny.*"

"It is our destiny!" Alex bellowed, stabbing a finger towards the ground.

James paused. "No matter what it takes, right? What's a few lives in the grand scheme of things? You figured I'd get over her, keep on trucking, and we'd be one happy family once Malverston had cut her to pieces and fed her to his dogs."

Alex bunched his fists, shaking. "We're so close," he hissed. "Don't do this."

James's lip trembled, and he gave a wordless yell. "Stay away from me. Don't look for me again."

"What are you going to do?"

James bawled, "I'm going to get her *back*, Alex!"

Then he was gone, ignoring Alex's protests. He vanished into the rubble, running on feet made agile by a lifetime in the wilds, defter than Alex's Old World clumsiness could ever match. Alex yelled himself raw looking in the following hour, but there was no sign of James. Cursing, kicking every stray stone in his path, he returned to his horse and kept on heading south.

*

When James heard Alex calling his name over the next few days, he couldn't tell on which occasions he was really hearing him, and which were merely echoes in his head.

Wrapped in his travelling blanket in upper-floor windows, his stomach growling constantly and his horse exhausted nearby, he glowered at the beast until total darkness took him, cursing it for having to rest. Every minute that slipped by was one minute more that Beth was in the clutches of that fat slimeball of a mayor.

He couldn't risk making a fire. These places had just enough food lying around for him to scrape by, but that meant they were also riddled with scavengers and hermits. That meant he was further limited to daylight hours, as he couldn't even light a lantern. As soon as the sun got low, he had to stop and hunker down until dawn.

*I'll go mad if this goes on any longer.*

The thought ran on a loop in his head, driving a thorn into his brain. His jaw ached from grating his teeth.

Alongside that thought was something all the more

maddening: an echo of the last thing he had said to Beth when he had left to ride north, when she had begged him to stay: *I will be back. They're never going to bother you again. I promise.*

Those words tortured him each time they replayed, over and over. Then when finally he thought they might have grown quiet for the night and sleep might take him, Alex's voice rose up, wandering the streets looking for him, probably waking every madman for a mile.

This was the first time they had been apart this long in all of James's life. They had read together, hunted together, learnt together. The mission of the Alliance had been born by their hands.

But the son of a bitch had just let James carry on north. He had been willing to let Beth die. James had made sacrifices all his life for the mission; he would fight for the Old World until the end of his days. But he would never sit by and let people just die. Nothing was worth that.

*He'll stop. Soon enough, he'll stop.*

But as more days passed, and the north gave way to familiar southern lands, Alex didn't stop. He kept on calling, his voice hoarse and cracked but unending, searching for James amidst the world's broken ruins.

# VI

Latif Hadad bent low in musty darkness, breath caught between his teeth. Canary Wharf, nexus of the southern Alliance, warbled beyond the walls of his workshop, but he had become deaf to it; the entirety of his attention focused on his work. He had no sense of how long he had been in preternatural gloom, hunched upon his stool. His face was inches from the HAM radio upon the workbench, which lay partially dismantled atop blueprint paper before him, teased apart with infinite delicacy, each component outlined in white and labelled. There wasn't a hell of a lot to it.

Every now and then he'd look at his meticulousness afresh, through a stranger's eyes, and snort in derision. Anybody would think he was a rank amateur, documenting such a primitive piece of Old World technology with such precision.

*I mean, bloody hell, it's just a radio. They were using these things almost a hundred and fifty years ago.*

But he hadn't left anything to chance. One wire dropped and he might break whatever fragile balance kept it working. There would be hell to pay with Lincoln if he broke the only piece of operational radio equipment in the known world.

Because the truth was they had no idea *why* this one worked. Latif had little time for hand-wavey mystical nonsense; he was loathe to listen to some of the End-day theories people touted. Alien abduction, social experiment, AI simulation gone mad, the Rapture. The nut-bags loved their little seances and get-togethers to chat about how the End had been mankind's punishment for its evils, recompense for trespasses—departing from God's path, losing itself in runaway technology, burning the rainforests, whatever.

That kind of drivel was why they were in this mess, a mantra that left sense thin on the ground. The masses of the North had lapped it up in the Early Years, spurning the Old World and its wicked ways.

So here they were, having slid to the brink of a bloody dark age, with only a few pockets in the southern Alliance to keep the wheels of civilisation spinning.

Latif grunted. "What shite," he muttered under his breath.

There was a logical explanation for everything. There always was.

There was no such thing as magic. That meant there was a good reason why this radio had picked up a signal, and not a single other had done so in forty years. He just had to find it.

*So why in all hell can't I find it?*

The others had all but given up. At first it had been a whole team of them poring over the little wooden box, tinkering with feverish excitement, certain the answers were just around the corner. But the very simplicity of the radio had been their enthusiasm's undoing. To every angle of inspection, every reference from manuals and shreds of documentation, it was standard. Nothing special, not a single screw departing from factory specs.

"You're in there somewhere," he muttered accusingly, glaring at the radio. "I'm coming for you, you little bastard. You can't hide from me."

Sighing heavily, he put the components back in place, his nimble spidery fingers moving automatically. He had done it so many times there was no conscious effort. Instead he watched his hands working, looking for a sign, some clue of something out of the ordinary. He didn't blink until the radio stood before him, whole yet again.

Nothing.

His eyes watered, his head ached.

*How long since I last slept? Doesn't matter. I'm almost there. I have to be.*

He wouldn't be beaten by a lump of wires and solder.

Sighing, he took up balls of cotton wool, stuffed them in his ears, and flicked the power switch. The room filled with an ethereal screech, a thousand nails on as many chalkboards, clawing through the wool into his skull. Frowning against the thrumming behind his forehead, squinting through eyes that had looked upon nothing else in at least twenty straight hours, he twiddled the dials.

The frequencies swept by. The same constant ring, unchanging, threaded not even by static. It was as though some great cosmic banshee broadcast its death throes across the entire spectrum.

Latif shook his head—

*Maybe it'll break if I stare enough and spill its secrets… I definitely need to get some sleep.*

—then twiddled the dial to the frequency now burned forever into his memory; one also etched in biro onto his arm and scribbled on every dog-eared piece of paper nearby. One of the others had even carved it into one of the workstations in a fit of despair.

His fingers spread away from the dial as the needle touched the sweet spot, and the wailing died immediately, replaced by something Latif would never tire of hearing: a human voice, scratchy and broken and garbled; the Scottish distress call that had been their one ray of hope.

How many times had he listened to this same looped message? He'd lost count.

But still his lips twitched into a helpless smile. The people before the End hadn't known what they had. To think somebody might be out there now, projecting their voice across half a world, to reach his ear. Thousands had succumbed to the famine this year, utterly at the mercy of the elements. They were but beasts, once again.

But this was something tangible, to show they had been greater once.

*Maybe I'm wrong. Maybe there is magic in this world.*

He listened to the whole message: the rhythm a familiar

friend. The Scots really had survived, and it seemed they had forged a similar vestige of the Old World in the far north of the British Isles. They were looking for others, for help, against a scourge laying waste to every settlement. The very same force imminent upon Canary Wharf, somewhere out there.

Norman Creek and over a dozen others had ridden north to find them, while the rest of them made ready. They had heard nothing since. And the skies grew darker.

Latif sat up straighter, shaken from his own private world, the walls of his workshop expanding out. His stomach tightened and fizzed.

It was all really happening. There were people coming to kill them. At first it had been people struggling to survive, fighting over scraps of food. Hunger drove people to do terrible things; there were no judgements to be made when it came to such desperation.

But the famine had passed. Things were getting back to normal.

Yet still they came. They burned, killed, raped, and took what slaves they would, leaving a swathe of destruction in their wake. This wasn't a fight for survival anymore. The last remnants of the Old World were being exterminated.

*That's why you're down here*, he thought. *It's all too much. And you're a tinkerer, not a fighter. There's nothing more you can do.*

Still, to think he sat here and played with his toys while what remained of their order scrabbled outside.

"This sucks," he muttered to his workshop.

His voice went unanswered. He cursed, twiddling the dial, cutting off the message. It gave way to that same unbroken screech. Latif didn't bother putting the earbuds back in, welcoming the pain, letting it wash over his tired mind and blanket out all the doubt and worry and fear.

Unthinking oblivion was better. He closed his eyes, turning the dial as the screech continued to throb and thrum. Through his hand, it seemed magnified tenfold, his entire body resonating. The strange feeling carried him off, away from the world, and his sleep-deprived mind went gladly. He floated in a dark void where there was only sensation, the air in his lungs. The waves lapped at him like water, and he floated upon them, free of all this terrible reality.

All the while his hand twiddled the dial, back and forth, back and forth, making little corrections for which there seemed no rhyme or reason.

In his half-unconscious state, he frowned.

*Am I looking for something?*

It certainly seemed so. He was tempted to shake himself out of it and get back to work, but curiosity kept him sitting with eyes closed, letting his hand run on autopilot. For a brief moment it seemed the screech itself directed him, working him like a puppet. Then the screech died again.

He released the dial as a voice once again emerged from the speakers.

*What are the chances of finding the Scots' channel blind?* he thought. *Must be muscle memory.*

Then the voice spoke again, and his eyes flew open. It

was different. Loud, jocular, and upbeat. Riddled with static and hopelessly garbled, he caught only the tone, yet there was no mistaking it: it couldn't have been further from the Scottish plea.

As though to reinforce the point, the voice rang off with a digitised *swish*, and in its place, music filtered out into the dusty old workshop.

He looked at the dial and saw it wasn't the same frequency. The needle lay fixed a few megahertz lower than the magic number scrawled on his arm.

*No. It can't be.*

Shaking, terrified he was about to destroy some miraculous fluke, he turned the dial slightly, grating his teeth this time when the screech cut in. He paused, took a breath, and turned the dial back with a prayer on his lips.

The scream died. Music again.

*God. What's happening? What did I do?*

An immediate answer from elsewhere in his mind: *Does it matter?*

Latif stumbled from the stool, his legs weak and clumsy from sitting too long. Wiping his mouth with the back of his hand, he ambled towards the door. "The old man is going to crap a goat when he hears this," he muttered.

# VII

Canary Wharf heaved with activity. The walls, over fifteen feet high and composed of reinforced concrete, had held back any would-be attackers for almost a decade. Cutting off the Isle of Dogs on one side, with the Thames flanking the other, and coupled with a contingent of armed guards upon its many catwalks, the encampment had become a fortress. Safe as any place could be after the End.

Had been. Before the siege.

"Nobody feels safe," Evelyn Fisher muttered, her smoker's lips crinkling into a pained grimace. An icicle of a woman, straight-backed and regal, with eyes that could skewer any seasoned stoic, she had shrivelled to a wisp. Wrapped in her purple shawl, which had for so long swept in her wake and served to frame her in billowing theatricality, she seemed to be wilting. She crossed her arms over her chest, gnarled fingers clutching at her shoulders as she looked through the tower's plate glass windows into the courtyard below.

Sir Oliver 'Lincoln' Farringdon could only watch, both hands planted atop his walking stick. Everything had been said, every mote of encouragement, every spin or shimmer of light poking through the dark sludge of their prospects. But it hadn't been enough. Hollowed and depleted, the stores of optimism about the camp had bled dry.

"We're all just waiting," Evelyn said.

Below, Marek Johnson barked orders at a few nursing volunteers who had erected wash basins in the path of auxiliary power lines. Stunted and muscular, his tireless figure milled back and forth without pause. There was seldom anything left to do, yet Marek had maintained an air of tautness throughout, putting on a show, keeping everybody on edge, for they would have no warning of an attack.

Lincoln bristled. Despite a combined age pushing sixteen decades, he bet he and Evelyn could take any world-weary youth.

*No. Such nonsense will not stand. We will not be beaten. I refuse to believe there's nothing to be said. And to hear dear Evie say such things, such drivel...*

Ten storeys up in One Canada Square, a great sparkling jewel that was visible for thirty miles, they could see the whole camp. The figures below moved food stores inside, erected what barricades they could, stocked piles of ammunition close to the walls. They worked tirelessly, yet every move they made and every breath they took seemed charged with hopeless lethargy.

Lincoln had seen it plenty of times in the wilds. When he, Alexander, and the others had been forging the fledgling Alliance, every other sign of habitation they had come across had been laced with it, like a sickness. Like the world was fading, winding down like a bob coming to a stop.

"I've failed them," Evelyn said hollowly. In her reflection, Lincoln watched her blink slowly as though she were in fact far, far away.

*I will not be among those our children look back on one day and say, "They were our undoing, through their inaction and cowardice. They chose not to be brave." I will not*, Lincoln thought.

"Get a good grip of yourself, woman!" he barked.

Inwardly, he prepared to cower, but he held his stance as she turned from the window. Yet all he saw was a slab of meat staring back at him, the seat of a great power vacated and bare. No fight. Just a stare.

"No," he snarled, striding forwards and throwing his walking stick aside. "I will not stand for this. Of all things, I will not *allow it!* Not you, Evie." He gripped her shoulders, shook her as he bore down upon her with all the fire he could muster. "We have to be strong. All this time we've stood against everything and built all we have, because we've stood together. Nothing has changed. We can be strong. We can. We must!"

Her eyelids fluttered. A glimmer of something stirring behind her glazed eyes.

He shook her again. "I will not let you turn your back on yourself. I can't do this alone."

She spoke as though from the bottom of a well. "There's too many, Lincoln…"

He recoiled, stung. "Evie, don't do this. Of all the

horrors of this blasted End, I will not let it take you from me as well." His voice cracked at the last word, and his frail old heart skipped a beat.

"Stop it," she muttered.

"No, I can't," he said, holding her vice-like between his fingers. He shook her still harder. The younger man in him bade him desist; they were too old for this kind of savagery. But still he shook her and, biting his lip and bearing a fit of self-hatred, he withdrew one hand and swept it sharply across her face—a face once taut and radiant with searing intent, turned pale and translucent by the long hard years. "Wake up!"

A moment passed in which he glimpsed wide eyes, awake and furious, and then stars erupted in his head, and his cheek sang with pain. His hat tumbled from his head, and the left flank of his sideburns smarted. Wheeling away from her, thrown by Evelyn's incredible wiry strength, he almost fell without his stick.

But he didn't fall. She caught him.

Now it was her hand wrapped around his, all the more vice-like. She said nothing, nor did he; the two of them merely stared at one another, and the endless times they saved one another's lives echoed between them. Then Lincoln crumpled onto her, a single gasp escaping his lips. He clutched at her shawl, and felt her fingers run through his wispy shock of white hair.

"Don't leave me, not here, not alone," he hissed. "Please."

Her voice had regained its sharp and measured edge, yet

through it a note of softness twinkled. "I'm sorry."

They remained there like that for a time, glad for the contact. Lincoln took hold of himself, rising from her chest with all the dignity he could muster.

"They're all gone, aren't they?" she said.

He drew a long sigh. "Soon," he said, "soon we will all be gone."

The survivors of the End had grown elderly, even those who had been young and fresh when the Old World departed—even Alexander.

"I can't believe it's come to this," Evelyn said. "After all we've given, the lives that were sacrificed."

"It was always going to escalate."

"But to end like this…"

"End? No, this is not the end." He took her hand and pressed it between both of his. "Our greatest achievement was always in showing just how inextinguishable the flame of civilisation really is. Even if we all fall here, somewhere and some time, there will be others. And they will know what we did here."

She gave him a thin and watery smile. "Tell me it was worth it, Oliver," she said. "Tell me I lived a good life."

He brought her hand gently to his lips. "My lady," he whispered. "There was never a better life lived."

Then it was him taking her into his arms. Clumsy rattling footsteps arrived from the depths of the tower, accompanied by exhausted panting. Lincoln didn't turn from his embrace with Evelyn as somebody arrived in the doorway behind them. From the little wheezing sounds, he recognised Latif Hadad.

*That boy knows more about machines than his fellow man. I forgot to add tact to our syllabus.*

"Yes?" he said, injecting gruffness into his voice.

"The… the…" Latif seemed utterly incapacitated.

"Spit it out, you great lump."

"We… we're picking up…"

Lincoln shot a reproachful look over his shoulder but paused when he caught sight of Latif. The boy was pale and blinking, not so much exhausted as shocked. He waited a few moments, then Latif seemed to snap somewhat from his reverie.

"We're picking up a signal."

"Yes, Mr Hadad," Lincoln said, a sinking sensation in his chest. "That was days ago. We played it before the council. I trust this is ringing bells?"

*Has the boy snapped?*

Latif blinked again, shook his head, and, incredibly, laughed. "Not this one."

Lincoln wasn't sure who tensed first, himself or Evelyn. All he knew was the next moment they were both inbound upon the pale-faced lad. He seemed to come fully to his senses as they bore down; pure and blind excitement took root. He laughed again, bunching his fists.

"I caught a signal from another frequency. Another voice. Music!"

Lincoln was halfway to casting a hand dismissively through the air when Latif took a step closer.

"*Music,* you old fools. Do you hear what I'm saying?"

*Never, ever, has he dared disrespect me in front of Evelyn. He's forgotten himself. He... he tells the truth.*

"The Blanket must be fracturing," Latif said, wringing his hands. "After all this time, it's breaking up."

"When did you last sleep? Because if you are mistaken…" Lincoln kept his tone stern, but there was no fight left in him.

*The mere mention of this, the possibilities…*

"Oliver?" Evelyn said.

Lincoln said nothing. Slowly, from somewhere he thought might have died forever inside him, a smile crept up from the darkness and tickled the corners of his mouth.

Latif laughed again. The dusty Old World office, full of computer monitors and long-forgotten files, came momentarily back from the dead like a corpse animated by an electric shock.

"Walk with us," Evelyn said. She sounded powerful, her old unstoppable self. "Say it all, and say it slow."

# VIII

Alexander Cain pushed aside the drawn curtains of his fire-lit study and cursed around a mouthful of wine.

They were everywhere now, leagues of ragged people crawling from the forest. Over the past few hours they had gathered like lobotomised farm animals upon his lawn, staring around at New Canterbury and one another; first a handful, then a couple of dozen. Now there could easily have been a hundred out there, sitting between the flower beds and garden gnomes, unpacking meagre packets of food and water and sharing them out.

Alexander stood watching them, wavering on the spot with wine dripping from his beard. When some of them looked over towards the house, he dropped the curtain back into place and turned to the fireplace. The room swam before him, a portrait of the Old World: every inch of wall-space occupied by some oil canvas or photograph, originals taken from the nation's many galleries; upon a great network of scattered trestle tables lay antique bric-a-brac from every period and culture; and around them, lining the entire back wall from edge to edge, a library of books to give even the mountains of volumes in the vaults beneath the city a run for their money.

But these books did not belong to the city. They were not meant for the furtherance of the mission. These were his books. His sanctuaries.

For so long this place had been his palace, a great bubble of trapped Old World atmosphere from which he drew his strength and solace.

Now they seemed little more than bags of pulp, slowly rotting on the shelves. Whispers of voices long vanished into the ground, their genius forever lost; the great tower of cards with which the knowledge of the Old World had been built, fallen.

Alexander wrapped the blanket tighter around his shoulders and wandered towards his armchair by the fire. Dropping heavily into it, he glowered at the leather-bound volumes as though they whispered about him, taunting and giggling between themselves.

*I shouldn't have come back. I should have stayed out there in the wilds. They'd be better off without me. Now I have a private crowd waiting for me to appear like some cult leader come to save them. Perfect.*

Alexander raised the wine bottle halfway to his lips, then sighed as he turned it in his grip to look at the label.

*Le Pin, Pomerol, 1987*

The exquisite Bordeaux had been in his private collection for at least ten years. He'd looked it up once: it had sold for over a thousand pounds per bottle. He had been saving it for the day that had for so long nestled in his imagination: their day of victory, when the Old World was reborn, the nation united in a fervour of new innovation, and Norman took his place to lead them to a new tomorrow.

He hadn't pictured this, quaffing straight from the bottle, alone and unwashed in the dark. Hiding from everyone who might look to him.

Sneering at the bottleneck as it hovered towards his lips, he took another swig, hiccoughed, and thrust it away from him. The tannin burned his nostrils as he forced it down, and he slammed his fist on the leather armrest, fury exploding from the seat of his gut.

"Why do they have to come now?" he snarled. "What do they want from me? I have nothing left to give. Why? Why would they come?"

He pulled the blanket even tighter over him, chewing his lip and sinking in the chair. "Why?" he muttered.

"'Cause you are Alexander Cain," said a brittle, voice from the doorway.

Alexander moved without thinking. Through the drunken haze, his hand plunged towards the revolver on the table beside him and waved it in the general direction of the door. He squinted through watery eyes at the figure hanging by the threshold, hunchbacked and shapeless under a simple white robe he recognised only too well.

Only a handful of elders wore those robes: the Alliance's founders. And only one remained here, besides himself.

Alexander dropped the revolver to his side, speechless, as Agatha tottered into the fire's pool of light, the flickering flames reflected in the pallor of her ancient face. Fair and serene, she had long haunted New Canterbury's streets, a benign ghost of a world departed. Right now she seemed anything but benign. Her milky cataracts moved over the room, a gaze that threatened to blister the walls if it lingered too long.

Not long ago, Agatha had been lost to the clutches of dementia, a yielding shell. For the past year, when famine had gripped the city and everyone had only waited for her to die, she had seldom recognised him at all.

*Old*, she had said, over and over, cradling his face. *You're so old.*

No longer. Presently she shook with rage. Alexander had not seen his mother in over forty years, since the morning the End had taken her away, but that morning she had glowered at him with her hands on her hips, demanding to know why he hadn't prepped for his English exam. Right now he saw her reflected in Agatha's tempestuous glare. The heat of the fire in the grate seemed to dwindle in the wake of her shadow as she looked slowly from his wine-soaked beard to the pulled curtains, then to the gun, and finally, to the bottle in his hand.

Shame climbed Alexander's throat, and he could only stare forlornly back, heavy drunken breaths whistling through his nostrils.

"Who are you?" she muttered, her lips pulling back from her teeth.

Alexander's chest fluttered, and his mouth fell ajar. He mouthed with no words to give. His shoulders slumped as he drew several heaving sighs and brought up his free hand to cover his eyes. "I've failed them, Aggie," he slurred.

He heard her footsteps come closer. When they reached only a few feet away, he made to explain himself, to somehow make her understand. Before he could sit up, the bottle was ripped from his hand, and the world went dark for an instant as her fist collided with the side of his head.

Not a slap, but a tiny-fisted punch, straight to the ear.

Shocked, Alexander watched her turn in a whirl of robes and stride back the way she'd come.

"Aggie!" he cried, dazed. "Wait. They're out there!"

"Yes, they're out there!" she stormed, turning on her heel. "More of 'em come by the minute. Why do you reckon that is, eh?" Her eye twitched, and she pointed a bony finger at him, stabbing. "'Cause of you! They come for their *messiah*! The one man everyone in this Alliance has got faith in."

He swallowed thickly and cast his gaze into the fire. "I led us here, to this. If it weren't for me, none of these people would be on death's door. They're better off without me."

"They hold by a thread, Alexander. I am doin' everything I can, but in the blink of an eye I could be gone, back to some dribbling wreck—some old biddy askin' where she is and what's for dinner." Her lips trembled under his blazing gaze, and she yelled, "What are you doin'?"

He looked to her helplessly. "I left London because I thought I would only bring the worst of it down on their heads. Then I got it into my head that my people needed me back here. But when I got here, they had more fight left in them than I did. Sarah and Allison are the ones they look to now."

"Mrs Strong and Ms Rutherford's courage aside, we will never be ready for what's coming. We need everybody, Alexander."

"Their militia is out there now, by their order. I… I don't know if I could ever have brought them to stand."

"That so?" She thrust her finger in the direction of the curtains. "So why are there people from all over the country gatherin' outside, just hoping you might show your face and give them one last shred of hope? They wait for you! They need you as much as the rest of us. Please, please, you've got to be strong."

Alexander shrugged, dropping his eyes to the carpet. "There's nothing for me to do. I have nothing left to give."

Agatha stilled. Straight-faced, she upended the bottle, emptying every drop onto the carpet. Stonily, she said, "Stay here in your cave. Don't you dare show your face until you're sober."

Then she turned and left him. The heavy mahogany door of his house—a three-storey mansion of over twenty rooms, left empty and gathering dust in the famine's wake—slammed shut with a reverberating boom that made him flinch.

He remained slouched in the chair for what seemed an age, his head smarting and his vision undulating. Once it finally settled, he stood in a fit of sobs, spinning on the spot, meaning to tear every last book from the shelves. As he turned, his arms flung limply out to the side, catching the top of one of the trestles and scattering bright, tattered packages onto the floor.

Orange and purple wrapping paper, bound in faded ribbon, moth-eaten but still whole. A gift tag attached to one lay open before him. Through the drunken haze, his mother's delicate handwriting resolved into view: *To our darling Alexander on his 19th birthday...*

Something round and hard stopped his throat. Over forty years had elapsed since he had first read those words, alone in his parent's home, in the minutes immediately following the End. But all that time seemed but a flicker, a blip in his memory, for right now he felt no wiser than he had then. Just as afraid, and clueless.

He stooped carefully and picked up the packages. Gathered in his arms like swaddled infants, the fire's flames glinted in the wrapping's golden filigree. For an insane moment a voice in his head urged him to throw them into the flames, watch them curl up in the grate. Instead he set them gently upon the mantelpiece, one on top of the other, and stepped back.

*If they could see me now, what would they think? Would they even be able to look at me?*

How could they possibly have been proud, if they knew all the hurt he had brought to the world, even if he had been trying to save it? As he stared at the beaten, sad packages, his father's voice echoed in his head: *Alex, some men have to put in the hours. They have to fight for everything they get. Men like me. But other men have something different, something else on their side. Some men have a destiny. And you got that, boy. You got that in spades.*

The same words Alexander himself had repeated to those whose destinies he had crafted. Little Norman, who had never wanted this life; and long before that, James…

Alexander gritted his teeth as his father's voice returned again and again: *Some men have a destiny.*

Where had it got him? To this place: knowing that he was responsible for both sides of the coin; the Alliance and their few twinkling hopes, and for the scourge that might bring it all to an abrupt, bloody end. He whirled from the grate and headed for his bedroom. It was time to throw some cold water on his face.

# IX

Charlie woke to the sound of screaming. At first he thought his dreams, fuzzy half-remembered images of his parents, had chased him into the waking world. But once their faces faded from his mind's eye and he was on his feet, gun at the ready, the screaming continued.

The campfire beside him still licked skywards. He couldn't have slept more than an hour or two. He blinked his aching eyes wide and stared into the dark, crouching painfully on his bad leg, perceiving the spread of fires across the treeless plain upon which the army had camped. By their glittering combined light he picked out silhouettes against the stars and the great swathe of the Milky Way.

The screaming came from his left. He ambled away from the fire. Darkness consumed him within a few paces, and he had to step carefully over the uneven ground. A misstep into a rabbit hole would mean a broken ankle. His leg was almost healed, but an injury now would put him out of action. He had no illusions: weakness would not be tolerated this late in the game.

He forced himself to slow despite the urgency of the

screams and inched his way by starlight.

*It's so peaceful,* he thought absently. *The wind in the grass, the silver trees under the moon.*

It took him a moment to realise that in transit, the screaming had become entirely academic. The horror he had felt in his heart on waking—the instinctive gut-yanking fear that came at the sound of genuine human anguish—had faded to a blank nothing.

*Christ, I don't feel anything.*

He was close now, only yards away. The screaming clawed at his ears and threatened to give him a headache. But his pulse was entirely steady. He realised he sought the screaming for curiosity's sake alone.

*No, that can't have happened. Not to me. She sounds like she* hurts *so much. I… I don't feel a thing.*

He paused in the darkness and gripped his head. Suddenly everything seemed so confused, the past few weeks a daze. How could it all have happened in so short a time?

Could it really have been only last month that he and Dad had been on their way to Kent with a cart full of preserved apples? Everything seemed so much brighter in his memory. They hadn't had anything in all the world but that stupid old cart and the clothes on their backs, but they had had each other.

New Canterbury had taken all that away from him. That grey old sack of shit, Lucian McKay, had been the one to put a bullet through Dad's chest.

It had been him upon whom all of Charlie's rage had

been fixed. James had promised revenge when he had found Charlie crawling through the forest. So Charlie had taken the grey bastard north with them, intent on keeping him alive just long enough to let him see the army in all its glory, to know that his friends would soon join him in oblivion.

But when the time had come to take his revenge, James had let McKay and his friends go free.

*He turned his back on me just like them. But I'm still here, marching right by his side, like it was nothing.*

What else could he do? He had seen enough second-guessers cut down over the past few hours to know that there was no slipping away, no backing out.

*Do I really want this?* Can *I do this?*

For a moment he wasn't sure. But then he remembered what the *good people* of New Canterbury had done to him when McKay had dragged Charlie screaming into their midst. Their trampling feet, saliva raining down on him, a turbulent writhing mass looking to carve off pieces of him. They were no different.

*We're all killers.*

His fingers twisted through his hair, and he bent over in the grass, clawing at his scalp.

Suddenly the screaming seemed real, actually there. Somebody was crying out to the darkness, a living breathing person. He ran the rest of the way, reaching a clearing in the grass. A fire just large enough to throw off a few slivers of light crackled to one side. Charlie stopped at the sight of Jason crouched over a tiny pale figure.

The girl couldn't have been more than fourteen. A dress

that looked as though it had been made from old floral sheets lay torn under her. She writhed under Jason as he held her to the grass, the long knife in his hand finishing its work and cutting away her underwear.

She yelped as the blade nicked her pelvis.

Jason tensed as Charlie took another step forwards and turned the blade towards him. His face creased into a wide, aggressive grin. "Charlie, boy," he hissed, snaking his tongue out into the night as though tasting it. His eyes glittered with starlight, but there was nothing in them to lend them any semblance of life. Black, snake eyes. "Want a piece of this one?" He grunted, wrapping his hand around the girl's throat until her scream faded to a dry wheeze. "You can have her when I'm done. If she quiets up." He shucked his pants down around his ankles, a bare lithe arse glowing in the moonlight. He leaned down upon her, and while his hand around her throat kept any sound from escaping her mouth, Charlie saw the scream perfectly captured in her round bulbous eyes.

She implored Charlie with her gaze, jerking with each of Jason's thrusts, tears trickling down her face into the grass.

Charlie stepped forwards, his hand held out towards Jason, but he paused.

*He'll tear me apart in seconds.*

Jason was James's lapdog for a reason. He had cut down more people than the rest of them put together. This one had never been recruited. There was no question in Charlie's mind that James had never had to convince Jason of anything. He only unleashed him.

Charlie's fingers wavered for a moment and then, shaking his head, mouth ajar, he let his hand fall back to his side. A strangled whimper escaped the girl's mouth as he stumbled away into the night.

# SECOND INTERLUDE

1

Beth tasted blood. To keep from crying out, she had bit down on her lip so hard that she had cut deep. She let loose the tiniest groan. It was all she could do to hold in the panic whorling in her chest.

Malverston loomed close by. She sensed him through the haze swirling around in her head.

When the blade first touched her skin, she had been sure she would pass out. It hadn't been the instrument itself, a scalpel fit to bore through leather hide without a mote of resistance, but the look in Malverston's eye.

*Why me?* she wanted to scream. *Why not one of the others?*

But she knew why. She had always been his favourite. There had been no shortage of passing temptresses over the years, born of the same vein as Malverston himself, happy to lie with him if it meant a life away from the wilds.

Yet he had never taken so much as a second glance. He had eyes only for Beth.

She knew it stemmed from her hatred of him. She would lie with him, but all the while she'd picture stabbing him through the heart, tearing his eyes out with her bare hands, peeling his manhood with a paring knife. Even if she could never do it, the thoughts were always there, and she was always ready, a single breath away from murder.

And he knew it. That was why it was her: she was something to conquer, something to whip and beat down and break—even if it meant slicing pieces off it with a scalpel.

The cuts burned, arcs of liquid fire traced in her skin. Her dress stuck to her skin where blood had run down her elbows, her shins, her shoulders. Nodding with satisfaction, Malverston stepped daintily around her and studied her with the precision of an artist and made nicks and incisions with passion and flair.

*God, he's killing me. Don't let it end like this.*

She had no idea how long she had been tied to the chair, but nothing had stirred nearby, not even a single distant footstep. They were truly alone, and she had a feeling he was just getting started.

She wouldn't give him the satisfaction of being beaten by a sack of lard, even if he took everything away from her.

"Curious, that I might have been wrong," Malverston whispered in her ear. "Beauty is more resilient than I thought." He giggled. "That's my girl."

He stepped away, the scalpel held up to the light, showing beads of scarlet blood upon the blade. His eyes roamed her body as he smacked his great flabby lips and nodded with approval.

The same look he'd given her since she had been no

older than Melanie. Twelve years old, taken into that den of sweat-stained sheets and stuffed with the fruits of the Moon's labour, candlelit and luxurious and suffocating, while her mother and sister starved at home. Not that her mother had ever lifted a finger. Being family of the mayor's favourite girl had its perks, after all; they had had food when the rest of the town starved, and they had got medicine when plague struck.

*Gotta keep my princess plump and delicious*, Malverston had whispered. *Can't have you slopping around with diseased ingrates. The things I do for you, my darling. The sacrifices I make...* The same words, every time she fought tooth and nail for those favours, gyrating over him, wishing she could choke the life from his wobbling form.

Presently, Malverston retreated farther towards the cart and set the scalpel down.

Everything inside Beth threatened to break in that moment. The pain amplified, the sheer horror of it all washing over her anew. She had worked so hard to blank it all out, to crawl into the furthest recesses of her mind and into her few memories with James in the peach fields— when, just once, she hadn't had to think of Melanie and her mother.

But the pain—she bled from dozens of cuts. How deep did they go? She could barely move, didn't dare turn her head lest those on her shoulders and neck widen further.

*No! I won't give in to him. I won't!*

She did the only thing she could think of: she bit down into the bloody groove in her lip, bringing back fresh pain.

There was no thought in the pain. The most horrible thing was that the pain was better; it was easier to hurt.

Malverston pursed his lips. "Now, now, don't look so glum. I thought we were having such fun!"

She glowered, biting down harder to bring out the fire in her eyes. She hoped he felt at least some of the hatred; all the brimstone and rivers of lava of the underworld gushed out from inside her head, beamed at his liquor-soaked beard and wicked, boyish face.

For a moment she thought that maybe his expression flickered, something akin to anger and frustration peeking out from behind his mask of superiority. Then he returned to the cart and picked up a mirror, turning it around to face her. "Maybe you'll change your mind when you see for yourself," he said, the flicker replaced by a victorious smirk.

Beth's reflection rotated into view, and she released her hold on her lip. Her breath whooshed out of her mouth as though he had sank his fist into her gut. The cuts weren't nearly as bad as she had thought, nor as bad as they felt, but they were everywhere: dozens of crescent moons cut into her face and neck, arms and shoulders, belly and thighs, even the delicate skin of her feet; brilliant dripping crimson against the marble pallor of her skin.

She knew they would scar. If she got out of this, she would be forever marked.

*I'll remember this every time I look down at myself. Every time I see my reflection in a pane of glass or pool of water. I'll remember being here, in this chair, with him.*

In that moment, Beth wished for death. It would be

better than living trapped in this place, replaying the here and now over and over until she grew feeble and the world had moved on.

She muttered, "If all you want is them, why are you doing this?"

There was no mirth in Malverston's eyes, nor mocking glee; just cold stones set in a rounded, immobile face. "Because nobody embarrasses me. You betrayed me, slut. You showed me up in front of that little shit—not for yourself or mummy or your little brat sister, but because you *wanted* him. That slick of nothing, that nobody—one wave of my hand and he'd be slime on the sole of my boot." He blinked. "You betrayed me."

She leaned into his face. "You're pathetic."

A plastic smile pulled his lips to one side. "We'll see, when I stop cutting and start carving."

Beth's pulse raced, for she saw no bluff in his eyes, but she squashed the panic with everything she had. If she was going to die, it would be on her terms. "You can't lie to me, George. I see you. You need something to hurt for you, something to play with, because if you stopped now all you'd have is fear."

His lips tightened and he returned to the tray. She steeled herself for fresh pain, taking note of her toes and fingers, her ears and nose, and wondered which of them she was about to lose. While his back was turned, she sobbed silently.

Then, footsteps. Malverston, a few paces away, froze midstride. They listened as the steps grew louder, echoing through the empty hall, rising the stairs.

Renner, chief slimeball—one Beth also planned to gut like a fish when the time came—appeared before them. His beetle-like eyes flitted from Beth, to Malverston, to the tray, and back to Beth. "We need to talk," he said, a sigh charged with thinly veiled delight.

*If it were him in Malverston's shoes, I'd be dead by now. He wouldn't have just cut. Not this one.*

"I'm not to be interrupted! What part of that didn't you understand?" Malverston bellowed.

Renner gave a sarcastic bow. A little while ago that bow would have been deferential, but now it was openly derisory, bordering on condescension. Before her, yellow-skinned and weasel-faced, with a greasy cap of black hair and fingernails that could have peeled potatoes, was a true tyrant in the making.

Malverston, underneath his gluttony and pride and callousness, was just a scared and jealous little boy who never grew up, turned rotten by too many sneers and jibes. He would never match the cruelty that poured from Renner's every pore. His lips pulled into a grin twice too large for his angular face. "The town is restless. Nobody went to the fields this morning. The women refuse to get water from the river. The mayoral stipend has vanished: most of the food, the tributes from the past month, the alcohol… most of the weapons."

Malverston turned slowly on his heel. "*What?*"

The smile remained unmoved on Renner's face. "As I said, mayor, you have a problem."

"We." Malverston strode towards him, towering a foot taller than Renner, outweighing him by at least a hundred and fifty pounds. "We have a problem."

A renewed twinkle bolstered Renner's implacable grin. "The town is gathering in the yard. They demand to see you."

"Tell those good-for-nothing slackers to get back to work, or I'll have their heads on spikes by the end of the day."

He was halfway turned back to Beth when Renner said, "We're having a bit of trouble getting them to leave. Some of them are armed."

Malverston stilled. "Shoot the ones who dare carry a weapon outside my home. Scatter the rest."

"I may have understated when I said they were adamant."

Malverston rounded on him, the mirror raised threateningly. In it, Beth saw his bulging—but unmistakably terrified—eyes twice over, real and reflected. "Spit it out, you blasted weasel!"

"It's McFadden. She's riled them into a mob. They sprang your bitch's mother and sister from the lock-up. They'll overrun us if you don't talk to them." That grin stretched yet again, almost reaching the bottom of Renner's ears. "The people demand it. My men and I will protect you, of course."

Malverston didn't move, his mouth working impotently. He let the mirror fall to the floor where it shattered and sent jagged shards skittering over the floorboards. "Fine," he said. "If my loving people are so desperate to lay eyes on their devoted mayor, then I shall deliver."

He whirled and strode to a cupboard beside the tray, pulling out something long and looping, his body blocking her view as he stuffed it into his jacket. When he turned around, he held a canvas bag and a cloak in his hands. "Come, dear, it's time to face the people."

Beth tried to spit blood in his face, but before she could purse her lips, the canvas bag had been thrust over her head. Her bindings fell away and she stumbled in darkness, half-dragged over the floorboards and down the stairs. As they walked, Malverston's heavy breathing in her ear, she became aware of another sound, rising from the ringing silence: the combined rumble of dozens, maybe a hundred, voices.

Fresh air filtered in through the cloak Malverston had wrapped around her, then she was positioned by beefy hands. She sensed they stood on the porch from which Malverston was wont to give his speeches. Even without the power of sight, she sensed something amiss. The noise of the crowd was unmistakable, threaded with anger and turbulence.

"My people!" Malverston boomed, summoning his usual tone of doting magnanimity.

In response, the crowd roared, a poisonous sound that washed over Beth and pressed her backwards.

"Friends, this is unnecessary. Please, go back to your homes and chores. If we do not keep up our precious work ethic, our great and fair town will grow weak, and if we grow weak, I cannot protect you."

The crowd gave another roar, no different to the first. Beth felt a surge of elation. Maybe they would rush the porch, cut him down where he stood.

Malverston's voice came again, stentorian and livid. "I have spoken, you great load of ingrates! Get back to work before I have you all put in stocks. I'd sooner use you all as fertiliser than have you question me. I have made this town great. Me, I, myself. Without me, you're nothing. You hear me? Without me, YOU'RE NOTHING!"

A lone, ancient voice cut through the crowd's racket. "We're not standing for your bile anymore, mayor. Too long have you starved us. We demand our daughter back."

Old Alice McKinley. Once upon a time, this town had been fair under her hand, before Malverston had moved onto the scene. For years she had lived in shame, cowering in her home. No longer, it seemed.

"My property is not of your concern," Malverston hissed.

"Your *property* is a young woman, one of us, our daughter and sister. Release her to us."

Hands seized Beth roughly by the arms. Gritting her teeth against the pain as Malverston thrust his nails into the cuts on her shoulders, she stumbled over the porch. She sensed the crowd's outrage close by; she could not have been more than a few feet away from them—from freedom. How she wanted to jerk free of his grip and dive. Would they get away in time before the shooting started?

*No.*

"You want your daughter, your precious sister? Here she is."

Darkness gave way to blinding light, and Beth cowered as the sun bored into her eyes. Newquay's Moon slowly resolved into view, a sprawling mass of cottages perched upon a hilltop by the sea, overlooking the peach fields. The bare-mud square before the hall heaved with farmhands, sons and daughters, smithies and tradesmen, milkmaids and cobblers. Their faces were etched with outrage, perched on the tips of their toes, ready to surge forth.

Malverston's few dozen armed guards lining the porch and stationed atop the roof held them at bay, wielding guns that could have cut down every single one of them.

*But they have guns too. Some of them are big. Maybe they can win this.*

No. The guns amongst the crowd were far too few. The crowd's mass was its strength; what would happen if they rushed the porch, Beth didn't dare guess.

Alice McKinley, bent almost double by arthritis, stood a mere four feet below Beth. Beth's sister Melanie stood beside her, marble-eyed and filthy, yelling along with the rest.

*McKinley sprang her from Malverston. That's all that matters. Even if he cuts off everything I have, at least Mel's safe.*

No sign of her mother. She would never have expected it—her mother had been a limp fish, silent and yielding, since the day Beth had been born. But still, not to see her now sent a tiny stake through her heart. Where had she gone? Probably retreated silently back home to bake bread and knit as she had always done with all the emotional and intellect of a goat.

"See your daughter, good people!" George boomed and whipped the cloak off Beth's shoulders, leaving her half-naked upon the porch, her wounds exposed to the open air.

Horrified gasps rippled through the square, and suddenly the great writhing mass seemed dimmer, weakened by the sight of her.

"George… what have you done?" McKinley gasped.

"This is what happens when people fail to appreciate all the things I do for them. Know that the very same awaits any of you if you carry on with this nonsense."

Beth cast a desperate look around, looking for some avenue of escape. The guards had their guns trained and ready, waiting for the word. Whether they still followed Malverston or not, they would be cut down along with him if the crowd surged. For now, they were bound to him; that meant he was still as dangerous as ever.

Renner stood close by, his expression stranded somewhere between puerile anger and intrigue. Out here in public, he was just another of Malverston's men. He couldn't make a move.

"Give her to us now!" McKinley cawed, banging her walking stick into the mud. "You give her to us now, or so help me God, we will tear the ragged lot of you limb from limb."

Malverston laughed, an exaggerated, jeering roar. He pushed Beth a step away from him and opened his coat, pulling out a leather handle, from which a trail of whipcord snaked down onto the porch. "You want this one so bad? Good, that means you'll understand what it means to defy me when you watch her get her just desserts."

"Don't you dare!" McKinley croaked. "I'll kill you myself, George. I swear it."

"Shut up, you stupid old bitch." He turned to Beth. "Turn around, darling. Unless you want to lose an eye."

Gritting her teeth, meeting Melanie's gaze, Beth turned to face away from him, leaning against one of the balustrade posts.

*Don't move,* she tried to say with her gaze. *Do not move. No matter what happens to me, don't risk yourself.*

Melanie wasn't like their mother. She was like Beth— maybe tougher. She hadn't shed a single tear in all her nine years. But right now, her eyes were red and bloodshot, her mouth ajar. Her slingshot was gripped tight in her hand.

*Whoom-psh!*

Beth was sure the first strike cut to her spine. The pain was that bad, dwarfing the fire of the scalpel's incisions. She managed not to scream, just.

The crowd gasped, straining against the porch. The line of guards tensed, their fingers trailing towards triggers.

The second strike was worse. This time Beth screamed. Then the third came, the fourth, the fifth. Each one seemed to carve entire chunks off her back, crossing over previous wounds. Each time she screamed. By the sixth, she fell to her hands and knees and wept. She cowered, but no more strikes came.

Malverston rounded on the square. "You think you can

take us? Well come on, then! Either come up and do your worst, or crawl back to your holes and rot."

For a moment it seemed the crowd really would charge, their bloodlust blinding them to their own imminent doom.

Then Beth was screaming. "NO! STAY BACK!" She shook her head. "He'll kill you all."

No movement, only bulging eyes. Just like that, she knew they were beaten. She had sealed her own fate.

*Better that than we all die. Because that's what would happen. Nobody would get out alive.*

The crowd fractured, and people backed away. Rage crashed over the town hall like a maelstrom against a sea wall. But they retreated.

"Go," Beth muttered to Melanie. "Stay out of this. Run."

Mel didn't seem to hear her, backing away, her hand shaking around her slingshot. She was lethal with that thing, could pick birds out of the sky from thirty feet. If she used it now, she could probably kill Malverston where he stood. But by then she would be shot to ribbons.

"I said run!" Beth screeched. "Get out of here."

Mel finally glanced at her, and a tear dropped from her eye. She turned and ran after the crowd.

"Be strong, darling," McKinley cried. "This isn't over."

"This is over," Malverston growled. Then the bag was back on Beth's head, and she was being dragged back inside.

# 2

Just north of Oxford, James burst into tears. Without warning a well of crushing sadness washed over him. He was resting the horse yet again, feeding a few of his pigeons in a fit of frustration. Presently he leaned on the saddle, breathing hard. A coldness had stolen into his chest since leaving Radden Moor, spreading from the secret place inside him that had driven him from home on feet that had moved of their own accord. The cold defied the summer air; a fizzing chill that didn't belong.

It whispered things. Black things.

Right now, it transmitted something he knew was real: a scream. The sound of rushing air and something being struck. With each echoing slap, fresh pain shot through him. His eyes swam with tears. James grunted against the chill, forcing it away. After a moment it grew quiet, and he breathed heavily. Time slipped through his fingers.

He grunted when a figure slid into view; quite simply popped into being from nothing. A few days ago he would have thought himself crazy, that he had cracked under the strain. Now he knew the world he saw was just the tip of something much larger and stranger.

The figure was dressed in a black coat, pale-faced and tall. The man from the tunnels, back in Radden: the man with dark marks under his eyes. "Please, stop. You must come back. Come back now," he said.

"You again." James wiped his eyes, sniffing furiously. "Go away."

Fol had abandoned the aloof and facetious air he'd flaunted when James had found him, deep underground in that strange place up north. Now he reached out to James, restless and maybe a little afraid. "I can't stay long. I'm breaking the rules just by being here. You have to listen to me: you can't do this."

"Beth's taken because of you! Stay away; go back to whatever faerie land you came from."

"You don't understand," Fol uttered. "More rides on this than you can imagine. You have to come with me. If you don't, all this is in danger. Everything that's left, and so much more."

James tightened his steed's saddle, scattering his pigeons into the sky. "I don't care. I'm not leaving her."

"You can't do this. You can't."

"Try to stop me. I know you can't."

He didn't know how he knew, but he knew. Just like he had known how to find Radden, and just like he knew he was special.

Whatever it was, he didn't want it. It had only taken him away from Beth.

"You have such power," Fol said as James swung into the saddle. Already he seemed a vague apparition, there and also not. "I can't just let you go. You can save this world and so much more. But you also have the power to end it. We can't risk it. You… you could bring it all crashing down if you don't follow the path."

James shook his head. He didn't have time for mystical nonsense, no matter what hung in the balance. Not if this was the consequence.

"I don't want to see you again," he said.

Fol looked crestfallen. "Please, James. Please. I can't do this again. If you go, we'll lose everything."

James paused for a moment, reins poised in his grip, and he met the eyes of the man… or whatever he was. "I'm sorry," he said.

Fol rushed forwards. He was barely there at all now, diaphanous as netted curtains. "You feel it, don't you? The Frost, inside you? James, if you let it, it'll work through you. It lives on pain. You have to turn back. You can't save her."

James jerked on the saddle. "Watch me, you son of a bitch."

He gave a roar and slapped the reins, starting the horse off across the meadow, leaving Fol to vanish from the land in his wake. All the while, his voice echoed down to nothing inside James's skull: "You'll kill them all."

He didn't stop. He kept riding. All the while, that strange cold grew in his chest, hardening and twisting.

# X

The cavern slammed down into place, replacing the darkness. Billy wobbled on her feet, disoriented from being bent through impossible angles yet again.

The others hit the floor, crumpling and wheeling as though they had spun in a circle for minutes on end. They tried to get up, then keeled sideways, breathing hard. The younger man called Richard was sick on the stone floor.

Billy looked at the Panda Man, who stood beside her, watching them all with patient detachment. He winked at her. "Amazing what you can get used to eventually, isn't it? Even this crap."

Billy said nothing and crouched beside Norm. Looking into his face, a green but still holding together, a little knife dug into her belly.

*He's like Daddy*, she thought. Daddy who had gotten so sick and gone away. Just like Ma and Grandpa left her all alone, to face the magic inside her.

"It goes away," she said quietly. "The sick feeling."

He gave her a weak smile. "You're a tough kid."

She tried to smile, but her face didn't want to. Maybe

people couldn't smile anymore after they had hurt too much.

She held out her hand, and he took it after his smile widened a fraction. She helped him up and they turned to the others, staggering to their feet in the cavern. The big man, Robert, picked Richard up off the floor like Gulliver plucking up the little people in Lilliput—Billy loved that book. Ma read it to her some nights, before she got sick. Before they had left home behind, so far away across the sea.

Both men still looked green, but their faces were determined. Billy liked Richard, the young one; he looked nice. Nice but weak. He shouldn't have been anywhere near this place.

*Like I should be here. I'm just a baby.*

*No,* another voice answered from the same place as the itch inside her. The Light inside that made her special. *Not anymore, you're not.*

It was a funny feeling, to stand at the waists of all the grown-ups and feel as though she was older than them all. Because none of them had seen what she had, knew what she knew. They had seen the dark place just now, but to them it had been just a nightmare. For her, it would never go away. Every time the coldness touched her, she brought a little of it along with her. She could still feel all those people even now, screaming, begging.

The little grey-haired man, the mean one, was baring his teeth like a snarling dog. "What are we doing back here?"

"The Conduits are set," the Panda Man said blithely. "We can't just move wherever we want, willy-nilly."

"You're such a freaking headcase," Richard sighed. "We just teleported to another dimension that I'm pretty sure was hell without the lava, and now you're telling us you can't just do whatever you want. Well it bloody looks like you have a trick or two!"

"You better not be lying about getting us home. All the card tricks and mystic shit in all the world won't save you," Lucian said.

Norm cleared his throat, and they grew grudgingly silent. "We've seen what we needed to see. What now?"

Fol nodded curtly. "Now I keep my word. We get you home."

The others sagged in relief.

"All right, that's more like it," Lucian said, looking around at the walls. "Beam us up."

Fol remained motionless. His eyes had fixed on Billy. "Well?" he said.

Billy took a step back. She felt as though he had reached out and slapped her. "What?"

"Where to, captain?"

She blinked, frowning. "I don't know."

"Sure you do." A small smile had appeared on his face, knowing and wolfish, just like the looks he'd given her way back in the cabin by the sea—when Daddy had still been alive. "The Light knows the way."

Lucian pointed at her, his eyes furious and fixed on Fol. "The kid? You're betting on her having something to pull out of her hat? You lying son of a bitch." He made to step forwards, reaching for his gun.

"Lucian." Norm was looking down at Billy. There was no expectation in that look, no demand, not even confusion. He just watched her, waiting. "Billy, do you know how to get us back?"

Billy wanted to shake her head. But the truth was she didn't know what she knew. She hadn't known that for a while. It wasn't a matter of knowing or thinking; that wasn't what had got her here or to any of the places on her long journey north.

"Maybe," she said.

She expected Norm to shake his head, maybe get mad like Lucian. All their friends were in trouble and now they needed her, and she said *Maybe*. But his face didn't change; he looked into her, and she let him. He had a piece of the Light too—just a flicker, but enough, she hoped.

He nodded slowly. "Okay," he said.

She looked to Fol. "What do I do?"

The Panda Man shrugged. "This is your show. I'm not allowed to meddle. Rules are rules."

"You've meddled plenty," Lucian growled.

Billy thought so too. All the times he had appeared to her since she had come to Enger Land flashed before her eyes. He was a meddler if there ever was one.

Fol seemed to know her thoughts exactly. A little smile hitched in the corner of his mouth. In her head he said: *All rules have a little bend in them. But this one's on you, Billy. It's all there. Just let it come.*

She stepped into the middle of them and looked around at the cavern walls. They were smoother than the tunnel's, worn and ancient. This place had seen many faces, known many feet upon its floors; every surface echoed with voices. In places there were deep gouges, as though a mad animal had clawed at the rock trying to escape. In others, complicated squiggles and pictures had been painted on or carved, not letters but something similar, and much older.

Nothing else. She sighed, sensing the others ready to deflate. But she also sensed Norm's gaze shooting out at them, keeping them silent. He believed in her. Like Daddy had believed in her.

She closed her eyes, took a deep breath, and looked at the cavern afresh. She let her eyes roam, landing where they may, and found that they had a will of their own, flitting rapidly back and forth as though searching for something. All she saw was black rock, etched or scratched or bare.

"Is she... okay?" Richard's voice suddenly sounded distant and fuzzy.

"Billy?" Norm, even from right beside her, sounded just as far away.

The itch in her feet: *walk forwards*.

She went, watching her body do what it wanted. It felt almost like being under the awning in the rowboat, when she, Daddy, and Grandpa had come across the sea. She had just watched then while they had rowed themselves to exhaustion. They hadn't known what waited for them ahead then, either.

There was something inside the walls. Lights sparkling out like rays of sun through a forest canopy.

She stepped forwards, her hands held out before her.

The others parted to let her pass, their faces fuzzy, as though they weren't quite there—or was it her that was no longer quite in the world?

"This is mental," Richard said slowly, throwing each word as though coughing up balls of phlegm.

"Shh!" Norm said.

The twinkling grew stronger, and she stepped up to the wall and placed her hands upon it. "Cold," she whispered. "Too cold."

"Sounds like a winner," said Norm. He was already walking over to her side. "Come on," he said to the others.

They crowded around, Fol included.

"What do we do?" Norm said, crouching beside her. She saw the way he looked at her in the corner of her eye: the trust still there. It made her feel strong.

"Touch me," she said.

A beat passed, then Norman laid a hand on her back. A long pause followed that seemed to last forever, because something was pulling her now, sucking her into the rock, and it took effort to stay in the cavern to wait for them.

Then she felt more hands on her: two big rough paws, a thinner fainter touch, then the cold dead feeling of the Panda Man's delicate digits.

"Well?" Lucian's gruff voice, mad and impatient.

"Don't look down," she said.

"Wha—" Lucian began, but he never got to finish, because suddenly the world had dropped away like stage scenery.

Billy gasped, looking around at empty space—yet not

the empty, crushing darkness of where the Vanished suffered. This place was different, infinitely larger and more complex and alive. Everywhere she looked hung great balls of shining orange, red, white, and blue. Some were far away and static, others close and hurtling past like speeding bullets; great tendrils of light spitting from them and splashing back down into their turbulent surfaces, so large that her mind gave up trying to appreciate their scale.

Before her lay a bridge. Translucent, faintly purple, with an almost imperceptible arch, it glittered and winked amid the blackness, cold underfoot.

*Frost,* she thought. *It's made of the Frost.*

"Stars," Richard hissed. "We're… in outer space."

"Uh huh," Lucian said. "Outer space have many bridges, Richard?"

"I… forget it."

"Where are we?" Norm said, beside her.

Billy shook her head, frowning. Everything had gone foggy in her head. This place wouldn't remain for long. It was here just for them. "Somewhere in between," she said quietly. "We have to be quick."

"Let's go then," Robert said. He didn't say much, but the big man didn't seem to care about all the crazy things. It seemed he just wanted to get home. Billy liked him too.

"We follow the path?" Norm said, still crouched down beside Billy.

She nodded.

He gave an unsteady smile and stood awkwardly as though he was terrified of falling over the edge. Billy had no idea what would happen if they fell.

*Nothing good*, said the Light inside her.

They set off in single file, Robert in the lead. Behind him Richard shook and cursed, his shoulders gripped by Lucian, who pushed him along from behind, snarling. Norman followed, his arms held out to the side like a ballerina. Billy and Fol brought up the rear.

For a stupid while that seemed to defy all sense, the group walked across the bridge in something akin to companionable silence, glad for a direction, and All Where moved overhead. Billy wondered how many people would have gone crazy at this sight.

*I'm probably crazy by now, myself. Maybe Daddy died and I'm still back in the cabin with him, gone cuckoo.*

Would that be so bad? At least then she would go away with him to be with Ma and Grandpa again.

*Sorry, Billy, but it's all here.* That same inner voice again. She kept walking, the Panda Man at her back.

Lucian called up from ahead: "What's with your head, Mystery Man? You look like a hard-boiled egg with its top broken off."

"Lucian," Norman said. "Really?"

"I'm about to lose my marbles, Norman. I need a distraction. Mr Mystery?"

Fol said nothing.

"It's where his hat used to be, before they broke it off," Billy said absently. She blinked, surprised she had spoken.

"What the bloody hell does that mean?" Lucian spat.

"His jester's cap," Norman said. He sounded spooked.

"Yes." Billy kept walking, certain that she would lose her balance and fall if she slowed. "Before they took it away."

Fol's shoulders tensed ahead of her, and she caught her tongue before she could say the rest: *Took it away because of what he did.*

"I'm sorry," she muttered. "I didn't mean to."

Still Fol didn't reply.

"You could have taken us here, couldn't you?" she muttered. "You can't come with us, but you could have showed us the way. Why did you make me?"

He looked over his shoulder at her, a twinkle in his eye. Since she had first laid eyes on him, one thing hadn't changed: she had never been sure if he was good or bad. Now, staring at him upon a bridge between worlds, with stars wheeling past and black infinity all around, she still didn't know. "I had to show you, and them, what your power really means. That you're not just some freak."

Norm was listening; he had dropped back. Their voices had been so quiet. How had he known?

*It's the Frost inside him,* she thought.

"Why the kid?" Norman said, turning around. "I know you put some... *thing,* inside me, because I'm supposed to fight. That's it, right? I'm supposed to stop this? Fine. But why can't we let her go home?"

*I can't go home.* The thought arrived fully formed and terrible in Billy's lap. She fought the urge to cry. There was nobody left. If she wasn't on her secret mission, she wasn't anything anymore.

Fol said, "She's more important than anyone. You can

fight, and you can win, but you can't stop what's coming without her."

Norman's face fell. "The End?"

"James and his army carry it with them like a sickness. They'll crush you, or they won't, but the very act of murder, of destruction, of trying to tear down what's left, will pull the trigger. And that'll be that." He laid a heavy, cold hand on Billy's shoulder. It should have been comforting. It wasn't. "Billy is the only one who can stop it. Another creature of destiny."

Norm stopped and turned despite the craziness around them. "She's just a little girl. Where we're going… People are going to die. A lot of people."

Fol just stared.

"I'm going," Billy said.

Norm sighed as though all the stars overhead rested on his shoulders. "Why, for God's sake?"

"Because I'm meant to."

"Norman? You and your voodoo pals better be keeping up, or I'm going to skin the lot of you," Lucian called from ahead. "If we get lost…"

They kept moving, now just her and Fol at the rear, following the others as they tiptoed behind the curtain of reality. "Why did you do it?" she said. "What you did?"

Fol didn't answer right away. She sensed he was mad; she could see into him, and he didn't like it.

"You did a bad thing, and you lost your hat… Banished."

"Yes, I did."

"Why?"

The darkened lessened ahead. Wherever they were going, it was getting close.

"Because if you live long enough, eventually you end up the bad guy," Fol said. He sounded old then, much older than Grandpa. "Now I'm one of the only ones left, and I have to put things right."

"You need me." It wasn't a question. "Like you need the others, out there." She gestured to the void.

"You feel them?"

She nodded. Other Lights, infinitely far away, fuzzy and indistinct, just on the edge of her sight. "They're waiting."

"Yes."

"We have to go to them."

"In time."

"Why not now?"

The light ahead grew, a brightness like sunlight at the end of a railway tunnel. The others became lost in its glare. She heard birds singing.

"Because if we don't stop the End this time, it won't matter," Fol said, his cold hand still on her shoulder; maybe friend, maybe foe. "Because... that is another story altogether."

# XI

Allison Rutherford watched the light bulb hanging overhead more intently than she would have thought possible. Something so insignificant, so commonplace as to be part of the world, another seamless element of the Old World's leavings. She had grown up without electricity, but the dormant technology had always been there, ready to be awakened.

*We're only going back to that,* she told herself. *It'll all still be here, waiting to get lit up again. As soon as we're back on our feet, it'll all return.*

So why did she feel as though she was losing a part of herself? That this was in some way a symbolic death, a sealing of their fate?

Before her eyes the bulb fizzed, spluttered, endured in momentary brilliance, then died to a glowing ember, fading fast to dull and lifeless tungsten.

All across New Canterbury, the same last gasp swept every home, street light and outbuilding.

Allie kept watching for a moment, hope lurking inside her that the bulb would pop back to life. When it remained so much inanimate metal and glass, she made her way out into the street, where Sarah and Heather were playing cards by a small fire on the cobbles.

"That's the last of it," said Mr Abernathy with a grimace, emerging from the generator shed.

Heather cursed. "I never thought we'd get this close to losing everything. Not really. I think, inside, I always expected some miracle to come and save us."

"Well, miracles can't replace gasoline," Abernathy said, wiping his hands on an old rag. "If Robert were here, maybe he could have squeezed a few more drops of power, but I don't think it would have made any difference." He shrugged. "Nobody works the fields, nobody tends the oil mills, no biodiesel, no power. People knew the stakes as soon as the wind farm got blown to hell."

"They're scared," Allie said. "We're all scared."

"That doesn't change anything," Abernathy said darkly.

"How would you like to work the fields, knowing that they might appear any moment, just come pouring out of the trees?" Allie was too close to his face, suddenly angry enough to reach for his collar. She took a breath and unclenched her hands. "Like I said, we're all scared," she muttered.

An awkward silence passed, then Heather shrugged. "Miracles might be just in my head, but we got something." She nudged Sarah with her foot.

Sarah threw her a look that was simultaneously dismissive and affectionate. "Don't do that."

"A little bit of adulation's in order, after all you've done."

"I did what I had to."

"That's just it: you *did* something, when nobody else would."

Sarah let her cards drop to the cobbles. "Don't put me on a pedestal." Her eyes flamed, but when she cast a glance around at the rest of them, her expression was sheepish.

"They're going to be having kittens in the cathedral," Abernathy muttered, arms akimbo. He chewed his lip, staring off into the middle distance. "And all those idiots sat on Cain's lawn. If they get wind of things going south, what if they get in a flap?"

"Don't let them," Sarah said, taking up her cards again.

Abernathy shrugged. "How? No power."

"Figure it out."

A note of alarm crept into the old man's gaze. "But… how? I'm sorry, miss, but what do you suggest?"

Allie noted the defensive contempt in his look and wondered what he saw before him: three young women, two in their twenties and one in her late thirties; and him, a self-professed handyman who had known the world before the End.

*Not our place to tell a man how to deal with a crisis*, she thought with an internal grunt. Some relics of the Old World she could live without.

"How about you pull your head out of your arse and start using it for something?" Allie said.

He rounded on her. "You got any bright ideas?"

"Candles. We've got stockpiles of them in the lock-up. Round up some of the kids and get them to run a batch out to every house. Send the rest to the cathedral."

He tongued his lip, eyeing her carefully. "What are candles going to do when *they* start showing up? We going to waft magnolia and coconut at them?"

"She's right. Give out the candles," Sarah said, setting down a straight flush by the fire.

"Bitch," Heather muttered.

"It'll give them hope. That's all we can offer."

The fight had gone out of Abernathy's gaze. His shoulders drooped. "You're right. I'm just…" He gave a tiny shrug and set off towards the cathedral. He sent a loose salute over his shoulder. "For what's it worth from an old billy goat, thanks."

Once he was out of sight, Allie turned to Heather and Sarah. Never before had she felt so close to anyone as she did to them right now.

*Even if it all comes to nothing, we did something,* she thought.

Allie climbed up onto the hood of what had once been some executive's shiny toy and poked her head over the barricade blocking Main Street. "They're really out there, aren't they?" she said. She stared out into the hills beyond the limits of the old city. The day was pleasant and balmy, a slight chill on the air countering the shining sun. A few butterflies winged in majestic dance between the shattered windshield panels of the Mercedes beside her.

She spoke to the wind but knew Sarah and Heather overheard. "It won't sink in." She recited: "People are coming to kill us. I thought we were trying to save those people. In the end, we almost killed everyone who was left." She shook her head. "We were stealing. Somehow it just didn't feel like it at the time."

"Don't think about it too much, you'll just tie yourself in knots," Heather said, pouring a few cups of dandelion tea from a pot off the fire.

Allie took in the sight of them for a moment, on sentinel duty with guns slung over their shoulders, slouched in the dirt playing cards, unwashed and hungry and exhausted. None of them had slept more than a few hours a day in the past week, and like a lot of others, they sent half their rations to the cathedral.

*What's become of us? How did we get here?*

She felt so different, so unlike herself. A little while ago, she had been so young and stupid. A dead weight with a big mouth. Now here she was, getting ready to stand against an army, waiting for Norman and the others to come back when she knew they were probably all dead…

Her heart lurched. *No, Norman isn't dead. He isn't. They're all coming back.*

She laughed. "Makes me feel like a damsel in distress," she said. "Waiting for the burly men to come home and save us."

Heather snorted around her steaming tea. "In our flaming tower, wringing our hands."

"I never got to have my honeymoon. As soon as Robert gets back, I'm going to make him *my* little princess," Sarah said.

"Filth," Heather said, shaking her head. "Absolute filth."

They laughed together, and for just a moment a bubble of warmth blossomed between them. They were themselves again, and it served only to highlight just how far they had come.

*We're all different. Living here, with all the lights and guards and crops... we forgot what it was to live in this world. Us and the kids, anybody young enough to forget the wilds... we were growing up green.*

That hadn't always been so for her. She had been tough before she had come here. She had had to be.

Before the famine, Allison thought she'd seen everything that could surprise a person. The End had ripped away most of humanity after all and left the rest of them crawling on their guts like flies with their wings pulled off. Her dad had brought her up to respect the Old World, but they had been alone, and Allie hadn't seen much worth in all the dusty books and dormant laptops and abandoned buildings—though she was careful never to admit that in front of him.

Theirs had been a quiet life, out on the east coast by the mouth of the Thames. She snared rabbits while her dad collected cockles from the rock pools. They had a little Old World cottage, and they kept themselves entertained at a little town a ways down the road, which made its way putting on stage shows.

They hadn't had much, but it was enough. The End had come, but the sun kept rising, the stars still wheeled overhead, and life went on.

"One day," her dad had said, clapping his hands as he worked on a bucket of cockles with his penknife, "all this will be yours, and you'll make it something better."

"Wow, thanks," she had replied, but she had never had the heart to say what she felt.

*I'll never make anything of it. What's the point? The world keeps on spinning anyway.*

Why risk rocking the boat? She wanted to be like everybody else: find a man and have a few kids. The simple life. She had had no intention of giving up what she had; her husband could find cockles when dad got too old, the kids could hunt rabbits with her, and they could all go to the performances in town in the evenings. Maybe she'd have made a few friends. That was the only thing missing: somebody to talk with. Her dad said she could *talk the tail off a donkey*, whatever that meant.

That was how Allie had seen her life, laid out before her like some comforting tapestry: simple and inevitable.

Then one night the little town had been torn down. The performance of the night had been Chekov's *The Cherry Orchard*, one of her favourites. She had been so caught up in the third act that she hadn't noticed anything wrong until her dad had clutched his throat, his eyes wide and blood gushing between his fingers.

The Snatchers ruled most of old Norfolk, a ragged clan of murderers with a penchant for casual arson. They seldom roamed outside their own territory, but that was what made their occasional raids so much worse. The coast had its troubles and thieves, but it was quieter than most places. None of them had even been armed.

The Snatchers had crept into the theatre's every corner

while the candles were dimmed. When they started cutting, there was nothing to stop them. The only thing that saved Allie had been her father's dying act: he had thrown himself onto the Snatcher reaching for her, and they had both gone toppling down the steps towards the stage. The town burned that night. Stage actors who might never be replaced, and a theatre that could well have been the last in all the British Isles burned on the horizon as she fled crying through the marshes.

Lucian had found her the next morning, on the verge of passing out on her hands and knees. By the time she came to, Heather had been hovering above her, and she had been in the New Canterbury infirmary. She had imagined she would stay a few days, recoup her strength, and chase down the bastards who had taken Dad away from her. She had been ready for it when she woke, had to be held down by Norman and Lucian. But then she had seen the city, seen its people, known what it was like to be one of them. There had been so many people to talk to, a community that she could be a part of; a real home.

She had retreated into this life, into gossip and chat. Here, in the city of the great Alexander Cain, seat of the Alliance of the South, people had fought all their lives to put thought before action. By then she had been all too eager to let them do the thinking for her. She knew the same was true for Sarah, who had breathed books, lived for books. Nowhere else in all the land—maybe all the world—could somebody spend the their days cataloguing and sorting masses of bound volumes brought in from the far reaches of the Old World by scavenging parties, tradesmen, and pilgrims come to see the city for themselves. Only here, a thin scrim of civilisation that had been nurtured and carefully tended, could *literature* ever be spoke of without snorts of derision.

Heather was no different. Her skills would have likely been limited to poultices and cutting off gangrenous limbs in the near-feudal communities beyond the Alliance's reach.

They had all been somebodies here, and in being somebodies, they had lost who they were underneath: survivors.

"They are coming," Sarah said, staring into the fire. "I don't know what to do."

"We've done all we can. Don't come apart on us now."

Sarah shook her head. "I just can't help but wonder how many people are about to die because of me."

Allie jumped down from the barricade. "What are you talking about?"

"If I hadn't started this, they wouldn't be playing hero." She blinked slowly. "We can't fight them off. We know we can't."

"So we'll die trying."

Sarah's face took on a haunted slant. "But they'll be out there because of me. It'll be on my head."

Allie leaned over and cupped her face, turning it up to face hers. "Shut up," she said. "We're all here because we want to be. You just gave us a kick in the knickers."

"Just promise me one thing," Heather said, her eyes darting between them. "Don't let them take me. No matter what, if it comes to it, you kill me before they… before they do things to me. They turn people, make them hurt. I don't want to end up marching with them, or worse."

"We'll do each other if it comes to it," Sarah said flatly.

They all nodded. The quiet that followed was punctuated by little more than the cooing of the pigeons, endlessly circling the city. Allie scarcely noticed them anymore, except in times like this, in the unnatural pauses when everything grew still, and the utter silence of the world after the End punctured the city's edge.

Then from afar, noise. Yelling voices.

The three of them were on their feet and stamping out the fire before Allie could utter what she had been working up to saying: "I'm glad for the two of you, here and now. But when this is over, I'm leaving. And I'm never looking back."

*

"There he is!"

"He's come for us."

Alexander held the doorknob tight for support, standing in the doorway of his home. They were everywhere, a carpet of beaming faces sprawled in a wide parabola. Blankets lay spread amongst meagre possessions and foodstuffs, the fragile remnants of so many lives torn apart—for many, the second time in their lives that they had lost everything.

*Because of me*, a cruel part of himself whispered.

He shook off the dissenting voice. He couldn't afford to

think like that if he was going to face them. For over an hour he'd been staring into the mirror at his own dishevelled face, waiting for the room to stop spinning and for the wine's grip on him to loosen. By the time he felt level-headed enough to walk unaided, his reflection had seemed entirely separate from him, as though he stared through the walls of some glass prison at a tortured creature he didn't recognise.

Aggie had been right: when the grips of dementia had been at their highest, he looked so very *old*.

He had stood before innumerable crowds through the decades and wielded them like clay upon a potter's table. Now, he felt himself shaking. He gripped the handle with such vehemence that he thought he might tear it from its fixings. Still they gabbled, scrabbling weakly to their feet.

*They come for me.* The *Alexander Cain*, he thought with a note of disgust. *The messiah.*

He licked his lips and cleared his throat. His voice had grown weak and broken—probably just from the wine, but it struck another note of fear in him nonetheless. "What do you want?"

A unified expression of confusion rippled through the crowd.

"We come for you," said the closest of the men. "We've come to stand by you."

"Why?" He sensed the harshness in his voice but failed to filter it out.

The confused expressions intensified.

Alexander wobbled on his feet as he released the

doorknob and stepped onto the front step, chagrined to realise the wine's fog remained. "You've come to hear me? Hear my plan?"

The confusion lessened some. A few expressions of unfettered hope blossomed like flowers amidst the carpet of vapid attentiveness.

"How far have you come?" Alexander didn't want to know the answer, couldn't bear to hear that they might have wandered any more than a mile or two.

*Please, let them be from the next town over.*

There was no such mercy.

Cries of *Lincolnshire, Nottingham, Oxford,* and *Southampton* filled the air. Some even claimed to hail from so far north as Leeds. He looked around at them helplessly and spread his arms. "Why?"

*People have been coming from as far and farther for years, before any of this was going on,* said that self-same sneering voice in his head. *Now that the shit's hitting the fan, how can you blame them?*

But he wouldn't be stopped. There was no solace in reason.

"You think that you can just pour from the forest like sheep and I'll take you into my arms and show you the light?"

They bunched together as though for communal safety. To see the bare, unflinching admission in the eyes of some that what he spoke of was *exactly* what they hoped for almost cut him to ribbons.

"Please, sir."

Alexander turned to a man in the second row, a broomstick of a figure, a nervous hunchback who angled his head to one side constantly as though afraid of being beaten for speaking out. The left side of his face was so bruised and swollen that Alexander wondered how he spoke at all.

"Please, Mr Cain. We… You must understand. We have nowhere else to go. They burned… everything."

Alexander hesitated a moment. "Anywhere is better than here, trust me." He raised his voice and spoke to the crowd once more. "I'm not what you think. I'm just another fool who forgot what was really important."

The man panicked, so much so that he took a step from the crowd; an act that seemed to terrify him, but he did so through apparent duty. "Please, don't!"

Alexander rounded on him. "Don't what?"

"Don't speak like that to them. Please don't. They need this. We all do."

"I can't help you. I really can't."

"I know," the man said, faltering then gathering himself as though afraid he would never speak again if he stopped now. "I don't reckon anything can stop what's coming. But we've lost everything. Most lost the last of their families on the way here."

"Then you should have stayed where you were."

The man's face paled. "You have no idea what you're saying," he muttered. "You haven't seen what we have."

"No, I haven't. That's why you shouldn't be here. I'm not going to save you."

The man gripped Alexander's sleeve. His brow twitched

as though electrified. "Please, just let us stay. We want nothing from you."

Alexander paused, looking down at the man's hand upon his sleeve. So long had it been since a stranger had touched him like that. Nobody had dared. He had been no mere mortal in the height of his power, after all. Now, the man's grip upon him had all the fierceness of one who had no intention of letting go.

"We're… we're the ones they didn't even bother to kill. If you send us away, we'll die out there."

Alexander looked over the homogeneous sheeplike gazes, tired and shocked into stupor, and knew them anew: the dregs left behind by James's army. These were those placid and infirmed or benign; exactly the people who always lost the most when egos grew too large, and the world's balance of power shifted.

*These are the ones I should have protected. Instead, they're the ones I took the most from. The worst part of it is that they're looking at me like I'm the good guy in all this, like I had their backs while the Bad Guys slaughtered their parents and children. The truth is… nobody would have had to die if I hadn't written them off like lines in a ledger.*

Something round lodged deep in his throat, so big and immovable he felt he might choke.

"Please, just let us stay," the man was saying, still clutching Alexander's sleeve.

Alexander wrenched himself free and stepped between the blankets and precious bundles of photographs, jewellery, and the myriad detritus of lives destroyed. The crowd parted like water around him, absorbing him into their bulk and reaching out to lay hands on him.

Fingers brushed his skin, flinching at the contact, as though he might invest some mystical charge if they let their flesh linger.

*They're dead no matter what they do,* he thought.

"Listen, listen to me," he said, turning on the spot, drawing in their gaze. "All of you, listen. We don't have space for you here. There is no food, there is no power. There is no shelter. The army that destroyed your homes is marching here as we speak, and there is nothing in between to stop them. If you stay here, you'll just have to watch it happen all over again. I'm sorry, I truly am, but our time is done. We had a dream, but it was only that; a dream." He stopped turning and pointed to the hills. "You have to go while you can."

A hundred blinking eyes, uncomprehending and deaf to his every word.

"Believe me, I'm telling you the truth. You will die if you stay."

Still, the maddening stare of the docile flock.

*They can't afford to think. They've had to turn it off. That's why they came here; they're all on autopilot.*

He gripped them one at a time, shaking each of them in turn. "You, you, and *you.* All of you. You have to go. Get out of here. Please, go!" He started pushing them, rushing through the crowd, staggering drunkenly between them, shoving shoulders and thrusting them in the direction of the fields and forests. "Get out of here, you fools! Save yourselves!"

By the time he came to a stop, panting and yelling wordlessly, they still stood, unmoved. The expectancy had gone out of their gazes—it was clear his words had extinguished their last flickers of hope—but he realised that was exactly the worst thing that could have happened.

Now they had nothing. Broken and beaten and lost, he saw a hundred faces birthing the beginnings of horror, of loss and fear. Any moment now, he knew, they would start screaming. And once the panic started spreading, there would be no wielding them. Somewhere in the crowd of hyperventilating, half-crazed glares, he caught sight of the bruised man who had stepped forth.

The blackened side of his face remained immobile and bloated, the unwounded part reddened and glittering with tears. Slowly, he shook his head. Alexander saw into him, as though the man had decanted memories of their long trek into his head like water from a bucket. He might have kept them together as the threads of refugees wandered south, from myriad places set ablaze by the scourge. While the screams died out and the fires burned low, this man and others had kept the rest moving.

Now they were here, and the messiah had thrown off his mask.

The weight of a hundred lives freshly crushed came down over him, and Alexander realised he had done the one thing he had never thought he would do: he had taken a crowd willing to lay down and die for him and shattered its resolve in under a minute. He watched helplessly as they began sinking to their knees, lowering their heads or crying out to the skies, clutching their belongings and one another. He could only watch, disbelieving. A moment ago they had been in awe only to touch him; now he seemed not to exist at all, and they transported back to the moments of destruction and death that had sent them here.

Then thunder. Everywhere, a calamitous roar that ripped the fug of woe and loss away and sent the entire flock jerking and screeching. Alexander crouched low on the balls of his feet by instinct and reached for a gun at his hip—a gun that wasn't there. Cursing, he waited for death, suddenly certain the army had crept up on them while he spoke.

*I never got to see the others, never got to make it right.*

After all this time, this was how it ended. He was on the verge of closing his eyes and accepting his fate when the roar stopped as suddenly as it had started. Blinking, he stood, alone amongst all the others who now cowered at his feet, arms over their heads.

Allison, Sarah, and Heather stood at the edge of his lawn, knee-deep in garden gnomes. Automatic rifles smoked in the late afternoon light.

"City's closed to outsiders," Sarah called. There was nothing of the mousy librarian who had once worked beside Alexander in the city vaults. Her eyes were dead, shark eyes, round holes in her head that seemed at once to see every one of the refugees, and also none of them.

"Sarah…" Alexander motioned helplessly. "What are you doing?"

Sarah, to his surprise, ignored him. "All of you are trespassing on the lands of New Canterbury. We're not taking refugees. All of you will take your things and leave now."

The crowd stood slowly, taking their hands from over their heads and staring wide-eyed. Some of them mouthed like fish out of water.

"All of you, get out of here!" Allison yelled. "There's nothing for you here."

As though to illustrate the point, Heather raised her rifle and fired a few more rounds into the air. The racket seemed to have trebled in volume since the first shots. The crowd burst into action, some sweeping up their things in a single scrabbling motion and others abandoning what they had altogether. They shuffled quickly away, looking fawningly over their shoulders all the way but going.

Alexander was left alone in the epicentre of what remained: a few blankets muddied by footprints, stampeded bags of bread and biscuits, a few water bottles. He watched, aghast, until the newcomers had fled from sight, jumping the wall and shuffling as a single ragged mass down the cobbled street, heading for the hills. Then silence.

"Thank you," he said at last. He had to say it again, for his voice had abandoned him, and all that emerged the first time was an airless gasp.

They nodded together and seemed to consider him.

Alexander realised he was still swaying, despite his efforts to hold a firm footing. "I'm sorry," he said, "I failed you all, again."

After an uncertain pause, they stepped forwards. The four of them met just beyond the semicircle of abandoned leavings.

"They'll live," Sarah said.

"Some of them, anyway. At least they have a chance, now," Allie said.

Alexander looked after the departed crowd, shaking his head. "I tried. I really thought I could convince them. The way they looked at me…" He turned to them. "How could you ever have followed a fool like me?"

Heather reached for him and looked carefully into his eyes. Her lip twitched disapprovingly. "You're drunk."

He blinked. "I sobered up."

A wry smile touched her lips. "It's hard to convince people to do anything if you've been on the booze."

"I'm fine. It wasn't that… I just… They didn't listen to me." He hung his head. "I couldn't even save them. If you hadn't…"

Heather's hand wrapped gently around the crook of his elbow. "They're lost. They came because going somewhere was all they had left, not because they wanted anything from you. Come on, you're in a state. You were out there a long time, wandering around the wilds. We need to get some food into you."

"I'm fine." He tried to turn for home, but her grip on him was vice-like.

"Don't even think about it. I might have hung the scrubs up for good, but I can still give doctor's orders." She and Allie began pulling him towards the street.

Sarah walked ahead of them, rifle swinging before her. "We need you strong," she said.

"You don't need me. All I've done is bring death on you all."

"Don't ever say that," she said, turning to face him. Her gaze shattered his miserable cascade, and left him staring blankly. "Not ever. We'd have nothing if it wasn't for you. The wars in the north would have spread. The Old World would be gone. We owe you everything."

Before he could retort, she had turned away and was walking again. He wanted to cry out to her, to scream: *But at what cost? So many died by our hands that we're no better than the lords of the North.*

But she kept her back resolutely to him, and he hadn't the strength left to fight.

"I don't deserve any of you," he said.

Allie laid a kiss on his cheek. "None of us deserve anything," she said, sounding so much older than he remembered. "All we can do is play the cards we're dealt."

Alexander went with them as the sun began to sink below the horizon, and the people of New Canterbury hunkered down to what he suspected was their last night of peace. When the sun rose tomorrow, there might be nobody left to watch it set. The voice in his head spoke again, but this time it was a shade less invidious—perhaps, just perhaps, it lent a sliver of new strength.

*She's right. If we're going to stand a chance, we can't afford to wallow. Now it's only about surviving what's coming.*

# XII

"Not this again!" Lucian barked.

Norman was on the verge of asking what when his body was stuffed through a slot the size of a letterbox once more. He gritted his teeth, abandoning all hope of making sense of any of it, and waited for it to be over. A cacophony of colour, icicles on his skin, a moment when he, the others and the Frost itself whirled into a melted Dalian monstrosity. Then suddenly, he stood quite still beside the others.

Light. Birds singing. Grass brushed his shins. It was late afternoon, the light already failing, casting orange and purple highlights over mossy rocks. A circle of rough cuboid-shaped rocks stood nearby, some standing and others laid horizontally atop the others; a ringed pattern that was eerily intentional.

*These are so much older than the Old World*, he thought.

"Stonehenge," Richard said. "We're on Salisbury Plain…" He mouthed wordlessly. "How is that possible? That's hundreds of miles from Radden…"

"You're really going to ask what's possible after the crap

we just saw?" Lucian said.

Richard kept shaking his head.

"I don't understand," Norman said, turning in a circle, then settling on Fol and Billy. "How could we…?"

"This is a special place, too," Billy said. "It showed me things. It helped me find you."

Fol shrugged. "What she said. It's as close as I can get you."

"That shaves five days off our travel time," Norman said. A weight seemed to have lifted off his chest. Maybe, just maybe, they really could get home first.

*And what then? Wait to die with the rest.*

*One step at a time*, he told himself. *We'll figure something out.*

"We're still a hundred miles from New Canterbury," Robert said.

"Maybe we can make London before sundown," Richard said uncertainly.

The look in Robert's eye shut him up. "We'll move through the night if we have to."

Norman ran a quick calculation in his head. "We're still two days' walk from the city."

"Then we better get going."

They made to move, but Fol remained before the largest stone pillar. "This is as far as I can go," he said.

"What?" Billy said.

"I can't go. It's against the rules."

"You can't leave us," Billy said. "You have to come." She stamped her foot.

"I'm sorry. But I can only show you the way. It's"—a moment of pain flickered amidst Fol's ever-shifting expression—"part of my punishment."

She glowered. "For what you did?"

"For what I did."

"What *did* you do?" Norman said.

Fol blinked solemnly. "Good luck. You're going to need it."

Robert stepped forwards, not saying a word until he was face-to-face with the Jester. "I don't know who you are, what you are… But, thank you."

Fol winked but didn't take Robert's hand. "Sure."

Billy still stood before Fol, her face red and downcast. "You really can't go with us?" she muttered.

He looked skywards and sighed. "I can't go with you any more than I could stop the End, or save your father. We're all bound to the laws of the Web, scuttling like bugs under the thumbs of powers so much bigger… All we can do is be brave."

"That's what you're doing, then? Dropping us off to go fight your battles for you?" Lucian said.

Fol ignored him. "You're going to have to be brave a little while longer."

Norman stepped forwards and placed his hands on Billy's shoulder. He almost jumped when her fingers rose to clasp his. "She can stop the End coming again?"

"Maybe."

"Doesn't sound like much of a shot," Richard said.

"It's all we've got." Already Fol seemed farther away, as

though he wasn't quite there with them on the plain, but only an echo of a dream. "I'm sorry I can't do more. I truly am."

"What do I do?" Billy cried, lurching from Norman's grasp.

Fol became translucent, and with one gust of the wind his body lost its form and faded away to nothing. Only his voice remained, a ringing tenor inside Norman's head: "The Web takes no sides."

Then they were alone with the ancient monolith, the great plains, and the whistling wind.

Robert was the first to recover. "Come on, we're wasting time. They're waiting." He set off at a striding pace. They turned their backs on the stones from the long-forgotten folds of prehistory and headed east.

"If we live through this, I'm going to need therapy," Richard said.

*

James Chadwick held an arm up high, and the army of the North grew still. Filling every square foot of the prairies and forests as far back as the distant hills, they watched as Jason and a few burly men worked on a set of gates set into the fenced compound in front of them. The military base lay sprawled over what had once been an airfield, now concealed under forty years of storm damage and infiltrating sapling groves. Between, rusted and faded by the elements but still intact, a sprawling mass of barracks and outbuildings thrust above the fledgling forest. They had taken this place months ago and secured it until the time was right.

Right here lay true Old World sorcery; what the Alliance stood no chance against.

Charlie watched from close at James's flank, chewing on his lip. Absently, he caressed his stomach; his guts ached constantly. Marching with this godforsaken army was turning him inside out, piece by piece. It wasn't just the poisonous hatred spewing off it like black exhaust; all around them the sky—the very air—seemed unnaturally darkened, as though they brought with them a cloud of shadow, blotting out the sun and casting shadow over the earth. Then when they grew still and bedded for the night, the cold would come. It was hardly noticeable most of the time, and so he guessed it was always there, made unnoticeable during the day by their progress south. But when darkness fell, something gnawed at him: a cold so deep that he expected to look down and see that he had become a block of ice.

*We carry that too. Whatever brings the darkness also brings the cold, and we're taking it with us wherever we go*, Charlie thought.

Every time he thought of New Canterbury and those who awaited them, his fists bunched with fresh anger. But in these brief interludes when all grew still and those around him ceased to be part of that great lumbering beast and became people once more, with faces turned black with dirt and lives turned blacker by grief and hatred, he couldn't quite believe any of it was happening. That people could be wrought to such mindless hate shocked him anew, and for a disorienting while he couldn't suppress a vague hissing voice deep inside him:

*What if you're on the wrong side?*

It didn't matter. He had made his choice. Even if he wanted to leave, he would be cut down—he felt eyes on him even now, as though some sensed his faltering allegiance.

While the army watched and waited, the burly men and Jason disappeared inside the base and returned a minute later carrying something black and heavy between them. They set it down with a metallic clang and stepped aside. Charlie took in the sight of a black length of tubing with a set of legs acting as a stable base, allowing the tubing to be pivoted on an axis. The word *mortar* filtered up from somewhere lost in childhood memory, and the knot in his guts tightened.

Charlie felt a wave of understanding rush by him, propagating through the crowd. Whether from intuition or stories told by elders or from books read long ago, the army came to understand what the black tube represented: devastation, fire, and death, far beyond the means of their bare hands.

"How many?" Charlie said.

James turned to him, and it was like looking into pits so deep that entire worlds could have lain hidden inside. "Many," he said.

Without a word spoken, the army started forwards through the gates.

# XIII

"It's up to four now." Latif shook his head in amazement, sitting back from the bench. "Only a few hours ago, it was three. Yesterday, two." His every nerve fired, willing him to run laps around the lab. With great effort he channelled that vitality through his hands, working fervently, making notes and pulling in as many people from the camp as he could—anybody with the vaguest hint of technical knowledge. If the walls fell and only a few survived, he was going to be damn sure that at least some of them knew about this.

By now he was pretty sure there was nothing special about this radio. It had simply been a matter of timing. This was the first one they had found in working order, and nobody had bothered fixing the Old World wrecks in so long that it was quite possible nobody in Canary Wharf had listened to the Blanket in over a year.

Lincoln had been by his side almost constantly. The old goat was no vegetable on any day, but now he seemed born anew—a man who had once advised governments and overseen the construction of nuclear submarines reduced to childish glee.

"The possibilities!" he cried repeatedly, striding about the workshop with his cane clacking over the floor and his hands in constant motion, gesticulating in wild sweeps and thrusts. "Think of what this means," he snarled into the faces of newcomers, his lazy eye wild and bulbous in its socket. "We stand here in this moment of metamorphosis."

"Stop bothering people, you old fool," Latif said at last when Lincoln crossed the workshop to double-check yet again, casting people aside with his cane. "It's not going to suddenly change."

"But a mistake could totally reverse—"

"Enough!" Latif laid his hands on Lincoln's shoulders, laughing despite his incredulity. "Look, we both sat here, didn't we? You and me, like when I was a nipper? We sat and took it all apart and put it back together, swept the whole band?"

"We did," Lincoln hissed, his wrinkled lips churning and working as he considered. "We did indeed. But it is so unbelievable…"

"That doesn't mean it isn't true. And it *is* true. Like I said, four open frequencies now." He swallowed, relishing the fact that he had the opportunity to add, "This one's clear."

Lincoln, on the verge of returning to his striding about the room, squawked like an exotic bird. "Clear?"

"Yes. We're getting no broadcast. Not the Blanket, not a voice, not music, just… white noise."

The few snoopers who remained in the workshop

seemed to sense Lincoln's burgeoning outburst from the way his crooked frame straightened over a period of several seconds. They shuffled out while Lincoln strode forwards, taut as steel cable, and laid a hand on the radio—so superstitious a gesture that Latif frowned. "What?"

Lincoln huffed quietly. "For so long I worked on these wretched things in the Early Years. It was different then; I still hoped things could go back to the way they were—half the time I was convinced it was all a dream. How many times I thought I was going insane, picking through each frequency, listening to that same wail... hoping there might be one sliver..." He broke off, his lip trembling.

Latif waited, said nothing, just watched Lincoln take his hand off the radio. "I'm sorry, my boy. I don't think I'll ever believe it, not quite. It's your time to do the real detective work."

"Fine," Latif said. He tried a smile but found there was too much adrenaline in his system; his face felt paralysed.

Evelyn appeared in the doorway, an imperious shadow draped in lengths of shawl, as much a part of the encampment as the walls themselves. "Progress?" she said.

"You have no idea," Latif said.

"Enlighten me." She stepped into the workroom and closed the door behind her, cutting off the noise from outside. In her doing so, Latif caught a guarded air about her, as though she were ready to voice disapproval.

A sliver of guilt stirred inside him. So focused had his attention on the radio been that he had scarcely given a thought to what was going on outside; while he had enjoyed an escape to a timeless world of exciting discovery, the others had remained out there, tending to those wounded in the siege, making ready what they could for the coming storm—twiddling their fingers and waiting for bullets to start flying.

His head threatened to crack in two, like a boiling engine head doused in cold water. To make this discovery now, when they might be snuffed out any moment. How could providence be so cruel?

"Mr Hadad?" Evelyn stood at his shoulder, her calculated stare trained upon the radio.

"We're picking up three transmissions, now. The Scottish distress signal—still on a loop; some kind of music that seems to be mixed on automatic, I think perhaps some old radio station server that somehow survived; and an emergency broadcast message, also on a loop. The latter two have opened up in just the past few hours."

"Opened up? You mean to say you discovered them? How could you have overlooked them all this time?"

Lincoln shook his head. "Mark my words: in my years I have scoured every part of the spectrum time and time again. These broadcasts were not there before."

"And these new ones weren't there yesterday," added Latif.

She glowered accusingly at the radio. "You're sure?"

"Trust me."

"I trust very little in this world, Mr Hadad. I need you to stop working on this curiosity this minute. Our scouts in the northern counties have returned to report an army marching on New Canterbury. I'm afraid we don't have long left before…" She cleared her throat. "We haven't long left. I need you to spend whatever time we have remaining on strengthening our defences."

Latif gaped. "There's nothing left to do. I promise you."

"Still, it would be time better spent, just in case something occurs to you."

Lincoln shook his head. "No, he will stay."

Evelyn rounded on him. "I know what this means to you, Oliver. I really do. But we can't afford this distraction, not now."

"This *distraction* might save us!" Latif cried.

She blinked and turned a cold eye on him. "Explain."

Latif blushed. Astonished at his own audacity, he reached out and grasped her shawl. "Madame, the Blanket really is breaking. If we wait, other frequencies will open up. I'm sure of it."

Lincoln cut across him, looking her in the eye, ignoring her troubled frown. "We have just discovered another. It is open."

"You mean…?" Evelyn's face had fallen slack.

"We may be able to transmit," Lincoln said. He too now clutched at Evelyn's shawl, and a youthful smile spread over his face. "Evvie, we may be able to call for help."

Silence reigned for a few moments, so potent that Latif could hear every footstep up on the catwalks outside. He watched Evelyn's face go through the same transformations that his own had: shock, rising hope, relief, then a troubled glitter that threatened to dash it all.

"Yes," he said, "it relies on somebody else out there listening."

Her lips had become firm and unyielding once more. "Nobody has bothered fixing radios in some time, Mr Hadad. You know this as well as I."

"Nobody *here*. That doesn't mean there aren't people out there who haven't given up. A few scholars, experimentalists, tinkerers."

"You underestimate how very fortunate you are to have the resources of the Alliance at your disposal," she said distantly. "Out there, it is about survival and little else… Nobody will have bothered for this long."

"They will! I know somebody will, somewhere."

"Mr Hadad, we don't have time for this."

He burst out, "Well we damn well better make time! We have a chance here. We can't let it slip through our fingers."

She shook her head. "Waste of time," she muttered.

Lincoln sighed. "Evvie, listen to me. Somebody put this radio down in that vault under the airport, shielded it somehow from the End. Somebody knew they would need it, perhaps because they knew that eventually the airwaves would be free again."

"We can never know what they knew," she hissed.

"No. We can never know. But the fact remains: somebody foresaw the Blanket fracturing. And that means perhaps others knew." He swallowed, his turkey neck throbbing.

Evelyn pulled herself free. "Very well. Stay in here, do your work." She blinked harshly. "I hope you're right, Mr

Hadad."

"So do I," he said with a meek grimace.

She left in a whirl of shawl, and the workshop door clanged shut behind her.

Lincoln sat beside Latif, and their combined gaze rested on the lump of wood and metal until all the world seemed to fade once more.

"Do you really think somebody might hear us?" Latif said.

Lincoln sketched busily, drawing out plans for a broadcast antenna. "I have never been a man of faith," he said quietly, then ever so briefly met Latif's eye, "but there comes a first time in one's life for everything."

*

As dusk fell, Alexander gathered up the refugees' leavings from his lawn, bundled them under a tarp, and loaded them onto a waggon. Slowly, savouring the labour, he set off down the street, hauling it from the city under the great flocks of wheeling pigeons. He was fully sober now, but the wave of embarrassment he'd expected hadn't come. What Allie had said had stuck: all he could do was play the hand he'd been dealt.

After they had cleaned him up and forced some soup into him, he had gathered his will and set out for the cathedral. It had taken every scrap of self-respect he had left to walk through those doors and face the people inside; his people, those he had lifted from their former lives and brought to this place, moulded to service his dream of a better world. Those who now stood to be torn to pieces because of what he had done.

In his mind's eye they had swarmed him, cut him down where he stood in the doorway, and paraded his body through the streets.

Instead, they had only stared as they had always stared, with the same acquiescent nods, even from the depths of their prisons of perpetual terror. Walking along the parapet had felt like a mile-long hike, but by the time he had reached Agatha standing by her podium, he felt something like his old self again.

"You're back," she said quietly.

"I've been back for a while."

"No. That wasn't you. Now you're back."

He had taken her into his arms, not caring if she fought him off in front of all those people—God knew he deserved it. "I've done such terrible things, Aggie," he muttered. "I've put us all here."

She pulled him to arm's length, and all the memories they shared throbbed between them. "You did what nobody else could," she said. "For better or worse. But don't think for a secon' it wasn't what we all wanted. You've got the gift of the gab, Alex, but you always forgot one thing: people aren't stupid. They ain't your flock, some rabble set up to follow you into darkness. We're all people, and we all believe. We all did this. An' we could never repay the debt we owe you, not in ten thousand years."

Alexander glanced to the majesty of the cathedral, its

high ceilings and ornate carvings, everything of the Old World they stood to lose. "We're about to lose everything. Look at them… They're so afraid."

All those pale faces, looking furtively at the two robed figures by the podium, peeking from hundreds of nests amongst the pews.

*So many faces…*

Her hand on his elbow had brought his eyes back to her, and her stony glare cut into him. "You think tha' matters? You think bein' afraid of the end means the journey wasn't worth it? If we were goin' to do it all over again, knowing we'd end up here, I'd do it all the same way. 'Cause even getting the chance to *live* that dream was worth everything. We did what I never thought we could: we stood up for what we believed in." She punched him on the arm. "We gave it a shot."

"I could have done it better."

"Stop that blabber. You look me in the eye and tell me you didn't do more than any other person could have done." She steered him to face the podium. "Now, one last time, be the one we need, tell us a story."

Alexander had turned to the cathedral then, to all those rising from the pews; the remnants of their order. He had let words come, any words. What emerged had indeed been a story, the first to come to mind: the first chapter of *Alice in Wonderland*.

Presently he hauled the wagon across the city limits and towards the hills. He mouthed the words of that story now, a story he had read to a little boy with emerald eyes, so long ago. He reached a clearing in the grass, and he began unloading the refugees' things, laying them out where he knew they would find them if they still lurked in the trees somewhere close by. As he worked, the warm glow the story had brought fizzled out.

The truth was he could have done so much better. None of them, not even Lucian, knew the truth of what he had done. Why James would never stop, not even when they were all dead; why he wouldn't halt until every last scrim of the Old World had been scoured from the Earth.

Alexander laid everything out neatly and returned to the city, dragging the empty waggon in his wake, already missing the burn in his shoulders. Pain felt good, felt right. He needed to pay at least some penance before the end.

*I'll settle for a sleepless night*, he thought as he returned home, and the sun set on his city for what he knew, quite simply knew, was the last time.

# XIV

Norman clutched his coat tighter around him, curled in a pile of hay. It was warm enough, but he couldn't shake the chill in his chest, ever-present as a shard of ice stuck through his heart. They had walked all day until their feet had been worn raw, across a landscape still smouldering with wreckage. They avoided London, skirting its edge for fear of remnant splinter groups of James's army or hostile refugees hiding out in the dense city sprawl; but they had been close, so very close, that the tower had been visible from across the Thames, lighting up all of Canary Wharf, one beacon ablaze in the dark.

Would it still shine when the sun fell tomorrow?

They had almost stopped too late, the sun having grown so low that they had barely discerned the barn by its silhouette. All the while, the cold had run rampant through him, and he wondered whether it would ever fade.

"Billy," he muttered.

Silence, a few snores from Richard's direction, somewhere out of sight.

Then tiny and soft and perfectly awake: "Yes?"

"Do you feel it too?"

Another pause. "Yes."

He nodded, couldn't think of anything to say.

*Only a thousand questions I could never ask*, he thought.

He was exhausted and every part of him ached in throbbing cycles, but sleep seemed so far away, the most abstract of ideas. Across from him he spied Robert lying on his back, the whites of his eyes glowing in the slivers of moonlight filtering down through the thatch. Norman thought he had never seen eyes so very vivid and wired, in perpetual glare as Robert's that evening; as though the cycle of day and night itself were an insult from destiny.

"Sleep now, Billy," he said. "You'll need your strength."

"For the fight?"

He smiled despite himself. "There won't be any fighting for you. You'll stay back, far away."

"But Fol said—"

"What that *thing* said is that you're special. There's no doubt about that. He didn't say anything about throwing a little girl into the middle of a war." He worded it carefully, aware he spoke as though to an adult instead of a child— something he couldn't help around her—but still spoke slowly, lest he mention the word *bloodbath*.

"I'm scared, Norm." That sweet soft voice cleaved Norman's flesh in the dark.

He turned over to look upon her in the darkness, knowing she probably couldn't see him but doing it anyway. "You'll be fine. I promise you. I'll take care of you." A helpless smile grew on his lips. "Me and Allie."

"Allie?"

"Allison. I can't wait for you to meet her. I know she'll love you." The smile died a slow death, petering out to nothing and leaving a hollow even deeper than before. Would Allie ever get to meet Billy?

Would any of them leave that city, even if they got there in time to warn them?

He couldn't afford to think about it. For now, they just had to get there.

Norman rested his hands behind his head and tried to get comfortable, staring up through the thatch to the heavens. Memories of walking over the bridge came of their own accord, too easily for comfort. Were those stars the same that had flown over his head, great elemental balls of flaming plasma so close he could have reached out and touched them? Or were they something else? It was all so absurd, dreamlike and ridiculous, and yet so fresh—he could still feel an afterglow of that strange sensation of being folded through impossible angles, a tingling in his skin too similar to that of insects crawling over him.

*Did any of that really happen? Could it have?*

Why not? The only rationalisation that brought him any peace of mind, had been his first: the End had been all the stranger, and there was no denying that had happened.

*But it's so crazy. Now I'm supposed to have some magic power inside me, and I'm pretty sure I'm the guardian of some Supergirl who's our only chance to stop the End from coming again.*

"Norm?" Billy again, even softer, almost lost in the

flutter of hay.

"Yeah?"

"What if we lose? All this goes away. Everyone." A strained pause followed, and Norman realised Richard had stopped snoring—he could feel the others listening, their attention pressing like a physical force. Billy hissed, "I don't want to go to that place."

"You won't. You won't go there, I promise you."

*Even if I have to put us out of our misery*, he thought. It was shocking, but irrevocable. If it came to it, he'd kill them both. Sweet nothing trumped eternal torture any day.

Fol's words echoed in his head: *The dead are safe from this place.*

"We'll win," he finished.

He could just about pick out her eyes in the pitch darkness. Even as the faintest of outlines, they cut deep into him like hot knives. Eyes that expected only hurt from a world that had taken everything from her. "How can you know?"

"Because," he whispered, sitting up.

She leaned closer, drawn by his voice.

He smiled grimly in the dark. "We're the good guys."

Those soft hurting eyes blinked slowly, and she lay back down.

Norman let himself savour his smile, even if he did so alone. He knew it might be his last.

"Up! All of you," Lucian growled from a little distance away.

Hay exploded in all directions as they surged to their

feet. Ignoring the icy throbbing in his toes, Norman scrabbled after Robert, who had launched himself up in a single motion and bounded out. Norman climbed through the glassless window onto the roof and perched beside Lucian, where he had been keeping watch.

"What is it?" he said.

Lucian said nothing, just pointed into the night.

Richard and Billy clambered out beside them, and together the five of them looked out over the land. The stars and the moon were bright enough to see by, a silver radiance that lent a calm serenity to a world otherwise fixing to be forever rid of the touch of man. But it wasn't the silvery washout that caught Norman's eye.

"There's destiny for you," Lucian grunted. Norman had never heard his voice sound so weak and hollow. "Ain't she a bitch?"

Norman followed his finger to the orange glow in the distance. A glow like a swarm of fireflies lay upon the horizon, crawling south-east. Hundreds, perhaps thousands, of torches.

His guts seemed to sink down through his feet, through the floor, down and down into the earth. Billy's tiny hand squeezed his in a death grip.

The lights were ahead of them, strung out across a mile. Heading for New Canterbury.

"We're too late," Norman whispered.

# THIRD INTERLUDE

1

The homestead looked exactly as James had left it. A part of him expected to find it a broken ruin, the roof cast off and the walls blown out. In his mind's eye, a great battle had waged before anybody would ever have let Beth be taken away. But it seemed that not a single shot had been fired. Even the gate at the end of the path lay untouched, bolted neatly shut.

Urging his utterly depleted mount along, he yelled wordlessly before he reached the cobbled square. The others were out on the doorstep before he had come to a stop.

"Back, filth! You swore we had a deal—" Oliver Farringdon's voice stopped in his throat, his eye pulling away from the barrel of his old hunting rifle, and dropped the weapon to his side. "James," he breathed.

Lucian was out the door and around Oliver before James could dismount, his hair flagging out behind him and his face a picture of panic. He half-pulled James from the horse and clutched him by the shoulders, his fingers digging in so hard that James winced as he looked him up and down.

"What are you—?" James began.

Lucian bared his teeth, shook his head, then pulled him into a fierce hug. "You son of a bitch," he muttered. "You go away for one week and everything goes down the toilet. How's that for proof of the Chosen One? I sent so many messages. Why did it take you so long?"

James pulled him off with some difficulty and held him at arm's length, watching him carefully. "Lucian," he said, "where is Beth?"

Lucian's face grew slack as the others spilled out into the square. "You didn't get my messages?" He looked around, frowning. "Wh-where's Alex?"

It was James's turn to grip Lucian, shaking him. "Lucian. Where is Beth?"

Lucian swallowed heavily. "They took her," he said. He blinked. "What happened out there? Did Alex…?"

"Tell us he's alive," cried Oliver.

"He's fine," James said. Agatha rushed forwards in a blur of maternal softness; despite himself, he allowed her to take him into her arms and realised how incredibly tired he was.

"Where is he?" Lucian said.

"Behind me." He extracted himself from Agatha's grip and made for the door, staggering a little as he went. "Tell me what happened."

"James, you can barely stand, child!"

"I'm fine!" He paused in their midst, surrounded by their concerned and ashamed eyes, and fought off a sudden overwhelming urge to break into tears. Helen and Hector Creek hovered in the doorway, only barely restraining a wriggling Norman.

James was home, finally back from the madness up north. An instinctual part of him knew it was safe to let his guard down here, begging for sleep, to drop to the floor and slumber for a week. But he couldn't. Not now. This was just the start.

"They took her, didn't they?" he said. "That's what your note said?"

"Didn't you… didn't you read it?" Lucian said.

"No. Alex… Alex didn't tell me."

"What? Why would he do such a thing?" Oliver cried.

James only stared. The others' eyes remained blank and shocked for a moment, then something seemed to register with each of them in turn, and they lowered their gazes.

*They know. We've all known, for a long time. He'd do anything for the mission, even if it meant the end of us all.*

There was fresh pity about them now, a heady stink that pressed in on James like a pillow pressed over his mouth. Through the pall of exhaustion wrapped tight around his head like a vice, he felt something give way—something that had kept him going all the way home, but could never stand up to their terrible, terrible sadness.

*Like they've already written her off.*

Tears pooled in his eyes and his shoulders grew slack. He took a few deep breaths, on the edge of hyperventilating, and it took everything he had to fight it off and maintain control. "Tell me what happened."

Oliver's lips parted, but he seemed unable to go any farther. He and Agatha's gazes drifted across the cobbles at his feet. Suddenly they both seemed so much older, wrought by shame.

Lucian grunted and stepped in front of them, a note of disgust on his face, whether for them or the very ridiculousness of the situation, James couldn't be sure. "They came in the night, two days after you left. A few riders, unarmed." He bade James stay quiet with a hasty wave of his hand. "We hadn't posted guards. We were too focused on keeping an eye on the men Malverston had already sent. When they came, we had no way of knowing who else they had out there. For all we knew, we were surrounded."

"What did they say?" James said through clenched teeth.

Little Norman had struggled free of his parents' grasp, scrabbling out into the square and standing just behind the others, his eyes wide and his mouth ajar. Never in his life had turmoil churned the group into such chaos. The last time something like this happened, James had himself been but a boy: the day Paul, the drunken zealot, had lost his mind and tried to kill him.

The day he turned on James like a rabid dog, it had been for one thing, and one thing only: his destiny. The destiny Alex had imbued him with.

It had been Oliver to save him with his rifle, but it had been Alex who had banished Paul: a death sentence.

*The signs were always there. Back then it might have seemed for the good of the family, but was it really? Hadn't it really been to save James—not for his well-being, but to make sure he could carry on the mission?*

Lucian had taken his arm as though to staunch a flood he knew was coming. "They wanted *her*, James. They said Malverston demanded his… his property back, and that we were to give her up, or the treaty would be nullified."

"Why?" The word escaped James's mouth as a bark. He had to close his mouth fast, lest the screams inside came spilling out.

"They didn't say, but I'm not betting on it being anything good."

"What about the ones already here?"

*For the classes*, he thought with disgust. They had been really about to divulge what they knew about the Old World to those slimeballs, knowing that they would use what they learned to push those beneath them even farther into the mud. Cruel men, bent on taking a world perched upon a precipice and giving it a solid push—the wrong way.

*And Alex was happy to let it happen if it gave us a shot at getting rid of Malverston and getting our hands on the south-west. That's all it was about for him; not the people, or the good we could do; it was all about the vision in his head. His legacy. I'm as much to blame for everything he's achieved as he is himself.*

That was the worst part, the gut-wrenching thing that he couldn't get away from. No matter how hard he tried to stop this ball rolling, it would always be him who had helped to get it started.

Lucian looked crippled by a medley of hatred and nausea. "It was like they smelled blood, James. They just up and went along with them. None of them said anything, they just went."

James stepped so close their noses almost touched, snarling: "Why didn't you stop them?"

Lucian's lips drew to a thin white line. He said nothing.

"What could we have done?" Oliver said. "I promise you, James, there was no way we could have known they didn't have people out there with guns to our heads. They had us right where they wanted us. And they knew you and Alex were gone. They must have had scouts watching us the whole time… so much for diplomacy."

James didn't wait for him to finish, darting off around the side of the house, heading for the row of coups lined up along the back edge. As he approached, a few of his pigeons fluttered down and alighted upon the hay laid out within. He skidded to a stop and peered inside. The birds welcomed him with a few docile coos, fluttering and buffeting in the darkened innards.

He crouched down and held out an arm. "Hey," he whispered, "it's me. I know you're tired, but I need you to help me out. You know what I'm talking about."

The birds had already started emerging, some hopping onto his proffered hand, some fluttering out onto his shoulders and head, others still rising into the air to circle him in tight loops. A fetid smell wafted into his face, bringing a wave of homely calm. Devoid of panic and fatigue in that brief interval, he saw just how precipitous the way ahead was. If he didn't get things right, he'd lose more than Beth.

"Always creeped me out, the way they do that." Lucian

spoke from a short distance away, eyeing the birds with guarded disquiet. "They always just… did what you wanted, always found you. Funny that we never guessed you were a freak. Now we've got proof: storming north and seeing fairies."

James shook his head. "That was a fool's errand, Lucian. If I hadn't gone to Radden…"

"If you hadn't gone, they still would have taken her. Oliver's right: we didn't know who else they had out there." Humiliation flashed over Lucian's countenance, reddening his cheeks. "I'm sorry," he said. "I tried."

James's anger fettered and died. "I know." He took a moment to offer a smile and thought his face might shatter like a pane of glass. He turned to the birds upon his arms. "I need you to send a message. McKinley, you hear? In the Moon, like last time." He reached into his pocket for a scrap of paper, but Lucian took a step forwards.

"James, I already did it."

He was holding a tiny scroll out before him. "The others don't know. They didn't want to do anything until we knew what had happened." He cleared his throat. "I sent a bird the morning after they left. She sent this back."

James reached out over what seemed an age and grasped the scroll. He unravelled the message, steeling himself, then sighed with relief at what he saw:

*Tell the little shit to hurry up and come get his princess. There's a toad that needs squashing. Hurry. - A.M.*

"When?" James said.

"Last night, just before sunset."

James nodded, taking deep breaths. Relief threatened to steel into his bones and flatten him. "She's still alive."

"I guess so."

James started forwards and threw his arms over Lucian. "Thank you."

"Uh huh. Get off me, you're smearing bird crap over me."

James released him and slapped him lightly on the cheek. "You're an arse."

"Yeah, yeah. Listen, there's one other scrap of good news."

"What?"

"We didn't let all of Malverston's goons loose."

*

The homestead farmhouse rang hollow as though the slime that had been let through its doors had forever besmirched its walls. James followed Lucian through the kitchen, which had been full of Malverston's wretched men the last time he had seen it; Renner, that yellow-skinned monster, and his competitors for the throne of Newquay's Moon.

In his mind's eye, James saw them even now, grabbing at Beth and pulling her into their laps, laughing and pinching at her, and all the while her immobile face, her jaw set and her eyes far away.

He shuddered with rage as they headed over the flagstones. Lucian stopped at the door to the cellar, and pulled it open. He smiled bitterly. "Stupid bastard drank himself half to the death the night they came. By the time the others realised what was going on and started off back to the Moon, he was dribbling under the kitchen table." He shucked and swept an arm, indicating for James to go down. "I bet he regrets that now. If he doesn't, he's about to."

James stepped into the doorway, listening to the hollow burble echoing up from the interior, and discerned a tiny noise mixed amongst the dripping of water and shift of soil: a tiny, human mewling. He stepped down into darkness, and in doing so, realised that he had his gun clutched tightly in his hands.

"No," Lucian said behind him. "All of you stay up here. We'll handle this."

"Lucian, don't be absurd…," Oliver started.

"I say we'll handle it," Lucian growled, and James was more glad for him than he could have thought possible. Oliver and Agatha were at least three decades their seniors—those who knew the Old World. But that was why they didn't understand, would never understand: what was at stake wasn't just another small town that had survived the End; it was the whole world Lucian and James had ever known.

He reached the bottom of the stairs and lit a match, touching it to a lantern hanging on a nail. Slowly, he turned towards the source of the mewling and found a man before him, gagged and bound with thick ropes to a palette set atop a pair of barrels. For a moment his eyes seemed murky, but then they settled on James's face and began to quiver in their sockets.

It was then that James realised just how far he was willing to go. If the man was afraid, then he was damn well going to use it. He nodded to Lucian up at the top of the stairs, and Lucian pulled the door closed behind him. James set the lantern by his side and crouched down to meet the man's gaze. "That's right," he whispered. "It's me."

## 2

Melanie Tarbuck shifted upon the threshold of Mrs McKinley's cottage and rattled on the door a second time, casting wild glances over her shoulder. Everywhere, voices rang out; shadows prepared to spring upon Malverston's men, who prowled the streets in watchful gangs. The door burst open, a black maw that framed a crooked marble-white figure.

"Come, child!" Alice McKinley lurched out and gripped her with astonishing speed. She had seemed on the brink of death since Mel had been alive, yet now she had grown as animated as a stuck pig. McKinley yanked her inside and slammed the door, then set to tottering over the cobbles, pacing back and forth. "Were you seen?"

"No, but they're close," Mel hissed, ducking down below the windowsill and waiting for a group of figures outside to pass. The mayor's men had patrolled the streets since the whipping. The way they held their guns told no lies: they would shoot to kill at the slightest provocation.

Mel skittered over Mrs McKinley's dusty kitchen as the old woman pushed open the window and thrust her arm out. Mel was about to hiss for her to withdraw it before she was seen, but by then McKinley was back inside and the window was closed. Upon her arm rested a bobbing pigeon, cocking its head and flapping its wings.

McKinley took the tiny scroll from its leg and unravelled the note. "Child, read it to me. My eyes."

Mel took the message, just as she had a few days before. This one was different, sent by the Pigeon Keeper himself.

*Coming NOW. Be ready. - James*

McKinley slapped her knee and nodded. "About time the snot got his backside in gear. Dunno what took him so long."

"He let Beth get taken in the first place," Mel spat. "If he never came here, none of this would have happened. She'd be at home. We both would."

McKinley laid a bony hand on her shoulder. "Home is where you should be, little lady. Your sister's wrapped up in this mess, but you don't have to be. You've been a brave little warrior, but things are going to get bad now. Go on, go be with your mum, there's a good girl."

Mel threw her off and glared. "I'll never go back there. Not with *her*." She had returned home after Beth's whipping. While Mel had railed at her, her mother had continued putting the house in order, torn to shreds when Malverston's men had taken them. Her face hadn't born a single crease of concern. She had shut down.

"I'm not going back!"

McKinley's face softened. "Okay, dear. But you're going to need more than that thing if you're going to be any good."

Mel took her slingshot from her belt and held it up to the scant light filtering into the cottage. "You want to bet?"

"Darling, they have guns."

*Don't talk to me like I'm a baby,* Mel thought. *You'll see what it can do soon enough.*

"Trust me."

The old woman's face creased into a wan, accommodating smile, and she sat heavily at the table. A moment of weakness followed, and she seemed to shrink; a brief flicker where her blue lips and rheumy eyes seemed to occupy her whole face. "The others?" she croaked.

Mel stayed by the window. She had scoured the whole town, sneaking past the patrols in shadow to knock on windows and back doors. So many had been afraid, their faces wet and ashamed, and had shut the door on her. "A few. Not many. They're getting ready now."

McKinley took in a deep breath and held it as though inflating a punctured old tyre. "Okay," she said. "Let's get on with it."

*

They moved fast in the dawn haze, bent low, following hedges and squeezing between fences. Around them dozens of others followed similar paths, brief flashes of bodies and winking metal between the fence posts and bushes, hurtling through Newquay's Moon towards the town hall. Most of the guards had retreated to change patrols; this was their only chance before the sun was fully risen and mayor's hold on the town was set for the day.

They took no chances. The few guards still heading back were overtaken before they knew what was going on and were set upon quietly, neatly: splinter threads broke off from the main group and circled in. Melanie paused to see the men seized from behind and held with their heads wrenched back, hands crushed over their mouths. Before they could struggle, pairs of shadows could rush forwards with knives ready. While their carotids spewed crimson pools across the dirt road, their twitching bodies were dropped to the ground, the shadows dashed back to cover, and the threads kept moving, converging on the hall.

Mel kept her hand clutched tightly over a ball bearing, ready to load her slingshot and fire.

This was it. The moment she had been waiting for since she could walk. All her life she had watched the mayor take Beth away whenever he wanted, and all the while Mel had had to watch Beth act like she wanted it. She knew it was just an act that kept Mel and her mother from being the mayor's playthings as well, but that didn't make it any easier; black gruel in her stomach condensed a little more each time. Today she was going to make things right.

"Stay close, child!" McKinley wheezed, staggering so much that Mel had half a mind on her, ready to catch her if she fell. But Mrs McKinley wouldn't be left behind. She led the first of the threads from the bushes to race out over the compacted-dirt square towards the town house.

*Catch them by surprise,* they had said. *Take no prisoners, don't give them time to regroup. We cut them all down and be done with it.*

But Mel had seen in their eyes that they knew the score. They had numbers and surprise, but that was all. If they hesitated, it would only take one guard to send a hail of gunfire that would send them all to the ground.

"Remember, don't stop!" McKinley cried. "Ready?"

The shadows emerged in full, several dozen strong, perched like cats with guns and anything sharp they could find in their grasp.

"Let's take our town back," McKinley hissed.

They rushed forwards, people who had for so long cowered, now made furious and alive by those years of drudgery. They covered the square in a few moments and raced along the porch to surround the door. Mel was left in their wake, a few steps behind, her little legs too short to cover the ground in time. McKinley tottered a few steps ahead. They both watched as the men and women gathered around the door and piled up around it.

*No, I need to be first. I have to be. The mayor is mine!* Mel thought.

So preoccupied was she with the thought that when the doors were thrust open and the gunfire started, she failed to quite absorb the sight before her. In a hail of flashing light and the cacophony of gunfire in an enclosed space, people fell like bags of wheat, lifeless and riddled with holes. The wrong people. Those by the door were torn asunder by a wall of shrapnel sent from within. Mel just had time to scream and throw herself into the dirt before the bodies in between her and the door were cut down. She pulled her hands over her head and kept on screaming, crawling into a ball. Terror erupted in her bowels, the likes of which she had never felt.

*I wanna go home, please let me go home! Please—!*

Suddenly, totally, the gunfire ceased. Silence rushed in to take its place, so loud that Mel thought it might make her go deaf. Shaking, she crawled for McKinley, who lay in a tangle of limbs.

A garble escaped the shaking old lady: "Don't… stay."

Mel stopped, was about to retort when the doorway filled with a dozen men and Malverston himself. They looked upon the carpet of dead without a mote of surprise on their faces. Over her shoulder, Mel heard the town stirring, people pouring from their houses. Some crept forwards, eyes peeking around walls. Others ran without a care for the guns aimed at them, screaming for loved ones who lay torn at Malverston's feet. In moments they were all around Mel, overtaking her, falling over the dead and hugging their ragged bodies.

"You think we're stupid?" The mayor roared triumphantly. "Behold the fools who think they can trick George Malverston!"

He laughed in great booming chortles. Behind him, Renner appeared with Beth held between his hands. Fresh cuts riddled her neck and ears, bleeding so freely that her shoulders had been stained red. She writhed in his grasp, and he stilled her with a sharp blow to her ribs.

"Beth!" Mel struggled to her feet, reaching for her

slingshot. She was on the verge of loading the ball bearing into the sling when she caught sight of Mrs McKinley rising before her.

McKinley held a hand to her stomach, her dress marked by spreading florets of red. She staggered forwards, and even those weeping grew quiet to watch her approach Malverston and the firing squad trained on her. She seethed like a boiling kettle, a kitchen carving knife in her hand.

"Old woman, I should have turned you into dog food a long time ago," Malverston said.

"You come and face me like a man for once in your life, you snivelling tub of lard," McKinley said. "Enough hiding behind your pet apes."

The guards tightened rank, preparing to fire, but Malverston waved them down. "No, no, allow me," he said. He addressed the crowd. "See what happens to those who challenge the natural order, folks. See it well."

"Mrs McKinley, don't!" Beth cried, struggling in Renner's grasp. "Please, don't."

"Be still, girl. I'll have you free in a trice."

"Is that so? You still mean to steal my property from me?" Malverston shook his head gravely. "You see, my fair people? Not a hero, but a common thief who has led you astray. Let justice be done. If it must be by your elected leader's hand, then so be it."

McKinley thrust a bony leg onto the bottom step, which shook from side to side. She paused for a moment and looked as though she might fall, clutching her stomach. But then she looked up at Malverston—even from behind, Mel knew what that look must have contained: distilled, cold hatred. McKinley gripped the banister and not looking down at the dead underfoot, launched herself up at the mayor and swung the knife with a banshee screech.

Malverston caught her hand almost lazily, her fist disappearing into his beefy paw. He smiled and took hold of her shoulder, turning her in mid-air, pulling her close to his chest and yanking the knife from her hand. She wriggled in his grip, but he held her fast around the throat. Already she had begun to grow blue.

"Don't do this!" Beth cried.

Mel started forwards through the crowd, scrabbling with all she was worth, plunging through the immobile stupefied bodies of the others. She was going to kill him, kill him if it was the last thing she did in this world!

She was frozen in place ten feet from the front of the crowd by a pair of stares: Mrs McKinley's and Beth's. Both wide-eyed, warning, as loud and terrible as if they had reached across the space in between and shoved her back. Gritting her teeth, tears filling her eyes, Mel let her slingshot fall to her side.

Malverston had been watching. He picked her out of the crowd and winked. "I sentence this woman to death for crimes against the town. We live in dangerous times. Alas, justice must be done."

He drew the knife sharply through the air, and Mrs McKinley's throat gaped wide. Her eyes rolled up into her head as Malverston dropped her like a bag of trash. She fell atop her kin and rolled down the steps in a series of bony crunches. Then silence.

Malverston's eyes grew hard, his face a tiny island in an ocean of flab. "Go home. All of you."

For a moment Mel was on the verge of calling out to them all: all it would take was one last push. Malverston's men wouldn't have enough bullets for all of them. But another stare lanced her way, this time only from Beth, taking up all of Mel's field of view. She gave the minutest shake of her head and mouthed, *Please.*

Mel shook all over as those around her shuffled away, heading back towards the town like zombies. The tears came fast and angry, and soon she stood alone in the square, before the bodies and the mayor's entourage. Malverston looked right at her and laughed; laughed down at her as though she was nothing.

The mayor looked around at his men as though expecting them to join in. They didn't, just stared. Mel saw the look they were giving him despite Beth's struggling as she was hauled back inside, and McKinley's body jerking at their feet. Through the tears swimming in her eyes, Mel saw: the guards weren't defending him anymore, only themselves.

No matter what, the mayor would die, die soon, and die badly. She wasn't going to let those men get him first, though. He was hers. Burning his supercilious grin into her memory, she turned on her heel and strode back to McKinley's cottage with her nerves crackling and fire in her veins.

# 3

"I know how this works," James said, standing over the quivering, gagged figure upon the palette. "And I know you do, as well." He crouched slowly, careful not to break his level gaze.

A week ago, he wouldn't have thought he could pull this off: the cold-blooded killer act. But right now, there wasn't a shred of doubt left in him: he would make this man believe he'd be cut into tiny pieces.

*Are you sure that isn't exactly what you* are *going to do to him, anyway?* muttered a voice deep inside.

"I don't want to hurt you," he whispered—

*Liar,* answered that secret voice, for he had strode across the room to pick up a pair of shears. Returning to the man's side, he bent anew, bringing the instrument into plain sight.

—"But I will, if I have to."

"I'd start talking really quick," Lucian said from the bottom of the stairs. "He might come off all peaceful and highbrow at first, but you don't know what he's done to people down here. It gets…" His face contorted into a ghastly mask so wholly unlike him that, at any other time, James would have laughed. "It gets pretty ugly," he finished with a whisper.

The man looked James up and down disbelievingly, yet his entire body shook upon the palette as James leaned closer.

"I'll start with your fingers," James said after some mock contemplation. "I don't think you value your face all that much, but a man without hands isn't much good to anyone."

The man thrashed, but he was stuck fast. James seized his hands, which were bound at the wrists, and drew them up so that the man could see them.

*Where am I going with this?*

He had no idea. He just knew he couldn't stop, or the illusion would be broken.

"I'm going to ask a few questions, and you're going to answer them. You tell me what I want to know, and you go free. It's that simple. Sound fair?"

*Jesus, I sound like…*

Like one of the Bad Guys.

All they had of the Old World was their art, the combined media of generations; a fantastical imprint of their lives, where good and bad were clearly separated. Light and dark. James's instincts rang like a gong to that sharp divide, but now he saw it was but a fantasy. In the cartoon world of heroes and villains, there was no doubt or anguish—none of the awful instability and morphing face that was morality in the real world.

He was on shaky ground.

The man grunted until James poked his fingers into his mouth and plucked the gag away. He made to speak, but James seized his face around his lips and squeezed hard.

"You're used to being the one in control. I bet you're feeling that you can't give in without putting up some kind of fight, throwing some insults at me, wasting my time. Let me tell you this: stalling is not part of the deal. I'll ask questions, and you'll answer them. Anything else, and pieces of you start going missing. We clear?"

His staring eyes bored into James, but when James released him slowly, he said nothing.

"Why did they take her?" James said.

The man was silent a moment longer, then threw his gaze over to the far wall. "The mayor's tired of the insolent bitch. I don't know why he kept her around so long. I'd have kicked her into the dirt a long time ago." His eyes filled with malice as he turned back to James. "It's you that turned the tables. The mayor could take her crap when only he had to stomach it, but she showed him up in front of you—and us. Now he knows he won't be top dog for long." His yellow, crooked teeth glinted in the lamplight. "Congratulations, boy, you've killed your sweetheart."

James gripped the shears so tight he thought his hands might break, but he kept his temper, just.

"He's waiting for us, isn't he?"

"We got him thinking you was going to cross him the first chance you got. As soon as he sent the girl, we knew all we had to do to set him off was make him think you wanted to steal her away from him."

"Malverston knew about us?"

"Him? The mayor's blinder than a mole. He don't see nothing but his own wants. But we saw what you really are." The man cackled. "What, you think you were so smart that you could hide it from us? Like it wasn't written all over your faces? We saw, boy. To get rid of him, all we had to do was let you two play your games and whisper what we saw into his ear. Once he got mad enough, the town would tear him down for us."

"Letting all this slip easy, aren't you?" Lucian said. "Why should we believe that?"

"Because there's nothing you can do about it," the man said. "Go ahead, go be heroes. He'll cut off her head while you walk into the ambush. Then the town will take him all the sooner. Or you can stay here and let her be her crazy bitch self until he kills her anyway." He shrugged. "Same result. We win."

"What then? I'm supposed to believe that you and the others are going to play nice and share the Moon good and fair?" James said.

The man cocked his head and shrugged. "Well, that's another story, ain't it? One step at a time."

James shared a look with Lucian. Half in shadow, Lucian's eyes were cold and hard. James rounded on his prisoner and ran a hand through his hair.

"How do we get her back?"

"I told you, she's dead one way or the other."

"We could bargain. We offered you knowledge, here: everything you need to rule."

"You ain't got nothing we want. All that song and dance about learning the *ways of the Old World* was just to get the ball rolling. Without us there to keep everything in line for him, it was only a matter of time before he blew his top."

"Then tell us how to beat the trap."

"How can I know the trap when I'm strapped down here?" He turned his head away to face the far wall. "I don't know shit."

James felt something snap inside him, deep down where muscle met bone. Before a single thought could register in his head, he reached down, drew one of the man's fingers up to full extension, brought the shears around the digit, and yanked both handles to a close.

The screaming cut at his ears like glass. Suddenly the man's entire body was thrusting and writhing, and blood spilled over James's hands in a hot gush. "You son of a bitch, you bastard!"

James blinked, taking a step back and looking down, shocked at his own bloody hands. A shuddering exhalation escaped his throat.

Lucian lurched from the shadows, blinking stupidly. "James…," he said.

"I…" James shook his head.

"You bastard, you shit, you promised!"

"Tell me what I need to know and you can keep the rest of them!" James roared.

"I ain't got nothing. I SWEAR!"

"Liar!" Some great beast welled in his chest and he surged forwards despite himself and seized the man's hand once more.

"NO!"

But it was too late. A moment later the man screamed anew, and another digit dropped to the floor.

"James!" Lucian's hand clutched his shoulder, vice-like. "What are you doing?"

"What I have to," James said and moved the shears

around the man's wrist.

The man wept. Nothing of the swagger and venom remained about him now. He merely wept as a child weeps, trying to crawl up into a ball, managing only a pathetic bending due to his restraints.

Lucian was pressed close to James's side, whispering in his ear. "James, stop. This isn't you."

James glowered down at the man, blood dripping from his fingers, a sickly and vivid scarlet in the lantern light.

"Let me go, Lucian."

"I'm with you until the end, but don't turn into him. If we do this, we're no better."

James turned to face him slowly. "If she dies, Lucian, it won't matter. None of it will matter."

With all his strength, he brought the shears together, and the man's mouth opened soundlessly, a terrible rasping emanating from his throat. A dull thud at James's boot signalled the severed hand hitting the dirt. His vision blurred. Everything seemed to happen at once. He fought nausea, swallowed bile rising in his throat, then Lucian's arm wrapped around James's neck, his other hand seizing the shears.

"Let go of me!" James writhed and kicked, but Lucian had a firm hold, and with a jerk of his arm, sent the shears clattering across the floor.

"I'm getting you out of here." Lucian hauled him towards the stairs, fighting him up the risers as the door banged open and the others spewed into the basement.

All of them started screaming at once, Agatha wailing

and Oliver roaring for a belt to tourniquet the wound. All the while, James bellowed at the man upon the palette, projecting hellfire down into the echoing abyss.

*

"He'll live," Agatha said in a tiny voice, emerging from the farmhouse. "I've put 'im out. Moonshine is all we got, but he took it gladly."

James sat in a pile on the floor, shaking his head weakly. His hands and face were still spotted with the man's blood. "I thought he'd talk."

"He can't tell you what he doesn't know," Lucian said. "You're not going back in there."

"I have to." James was dimly aware that he shook his head ceaselessly. "I won't leave her."

"Nobody's thinking about leaving anybody," Oliver said. "But we can't become that."

James blinked his way back to sense and realised they were all looking at him, gaunt-faced. They had never looked at him like that before, like he was dangerous.

Oliver cleared his throat. "We're in the same situation, flying blind."

"Our own bloody fault," Agatha spat. "I can't believe we were so stupid." She played with her hands. "Maybe she'll be fine, James. Like we always said, Malverston's a crook, but he ain't a monster. Maybe…"

James only looked at her.

She snorted. "Yeah, I don't buy it, either. I can't

understand what got into Alex. It's not like him. Why would he do this?"

"Why don't you ask him yourself?" James said, nodding to the path leading from the gate.

They all turned towards the bedraggled figure atop a limping steed, trundling a few yards from the square. Alex's face hung shrunken around eyes ringed with saggy bags. His horse looked as though it was fit to collapse to the ground and die that instant. The clopping of its hooves were the only sounds to be heard, for everything had grown painfully still. His eyes watery, Alex said nothing, only waited.

"Don't you dare presume to come back here," James said. "Don't you dare. This isn't your home, not after what you've done."

Alexander Cain—for that was who was before them now, Alexander and not Alex, the Messiah persona he presented to the masses, instead of their brother—was a master of disguise and manipulation, but James knew the mask too well. Beneath the placating, calm exterior, he saw his words cut deep.

"I did what I have always done," Alex said, dropping to the ground and approaching them guardedly. "I protected us."

"You protected your fantasy," James said.

"James, don't speak like that," Oliver said. "Nobody could have known—"

"We all knew!" Lucian rounded on him. "Like we all weren't just waiting for something like this to go down. We all smelled trouble the moment those bastards got here."

Lucian looked between Alex and James, a muscle in his jaw jumping. "I don't know who's stupider."

James blinked, stung despite himself. "What?"

"You, or him." Lucian's lips drew back from his teeth. "That idiot"—he pointed to Alex—"was always going to overstep his mark some time or another. Go pushing your way into other people's lives and sooner or later you're going to get beat down, no matter how smart you are." He turned to James and pushed out a sharp sigh. "But you… You let your balls get in the way of your brain."

James moved to strike him, but the fire in Lucian's eyes stilled him. He shook, jaw clenched, an inch from Lucian's face. "She's more than that. Her and the Moon. There are good people there, they don't deserve Malverston, his men, or us. Especially us."

"It's not about what they deserve," Alex said. "It never was and never will be. It's us or them. The world will fall on the side of light or dark. If we don't do everything we can to load the dice. It'll all be gone, and we'll never get it back."

"Don't. Just don't," James spat. "I've had enough of your bullshit."

"The game hasn't changed!" Alex strode forwards, a livid fire melting the neutral mask he had been hiding behind. "You think that one life could change the stakes?"

· "Not this, Alex. Not Beth!" James roared, raising both fists to his forehead.

"Anybody," Alex yelled. "Anybody it takes. If it comes to it, we all have to be ready to sacrifice, or we'll never get anywhere. That's the bare truth of it."

"She never did anything but protect her family, and now she's going to pay for what we've done."

"We don't know that."

"If it's not, why did the others go back as well? Why, if not to use this to take Malverston out when he'll be too focused on us to see them coming." He paused, sucking bull-like through his nostrils.

The cobbled square rang with fresh silence. A few pigeons cooed from the farmhouse rooftop.

Had it really been a week ago that they had ridden from this place, on some crazy mission to the far north? It seemed a million years ago. If only he could turn back the clock just that much, go back to that moment he and Beth had stood in the alley between the house and the stables, where she had begged him not to leave.

He'd never let her go.

*Oh God, please just let me go back.*

"We could use this," Lucian said.

James blinked. "What?"

"We can use it." He swept a glance around at them all. "If they've gone back to throw Malverston out, and Malverston's looking to use your girl to get to us, lure us into a trap or whatever, then a shitstorm is about to kick off in Newquay's Moon. We could use it."

"That's not our way," Alex said. "That's the whole point."

Oliver cleared his throat. "Alex, I think the time for politics is done."

Alex said nothing.

"It's too dangerous," Agatha said. "It'll only ge' us into more bother. We'll lose people."

James barely heard the others, looking deep into Lucian's eyes. An understanding had formed between them, something that only they could understand: no matter what happened, people were going to die today; and no matter what, James was going to be one of the ones doing the killing, whether the Alliance was behind him or not. He had to win Oliver and Agatha over now, or they would slip through his fingers. "We go, all of us, right now. If we get there in time, we can turn the tables in our favour."

Silence. He sensed Alex watching carefully from the corner of his eye, but he kept his gaze fixed on Oliver and Agatha.

"They'll be waiting for us," Oliver said. "That is the only thing of which we *can* be sure."

"Yes," James said, "they will. Say we don't go, Malverston's trap goes untripped, but those men take him while his back is turned anyway. They'll kill half the people in the Moon just to make a point. What do you think they'll do then, when they realise that we're still out there, a threat that knows all their secrets?"

For a heart-stopping handful of moments, nobody in the square moved. Then Lucian stepped around to James's side.

James's knees threatened to buckle with gratitude, but he kept his eyes trained on the others, heart racing, praying Alex wouldn't work his magic and tear it all down; he would take Alex's place one day, that was the whole point of his great destiny, but Alex possessed an unparalleled capacity for bullshit and manipulation.

James knew that if he wanted, Alex could turn them all around on a dime. They would go nowhere, and James would go it alone.

*I need him.* The thought arrived ready formed and incontrovertible in his mind. *They'll follow him anywhere. If we're going to save Beth, I need him.*

Hating himself, knowing it was going back on everything he had thought and felt over the long ride home, he said, "Please, Alex. If you ever cared about me at all, please."

Alex looked into him; not at him, but into him. They had worked for this their entire lives, building up to this moment. Not once had James thought in all that time that he would beg Alex not for reason, but mercy.

*He knows it: if he does this, he gets what he wants. I can see it in his eyes: the cheering masses in Newquay's Moon, shouting his name when we save them.*

"Okay," Alex said.

James managed to keep himself from sagging to the ground. He turned to Oliver and Agatha and the Creeks over what seemed like a thousand years. "I'm not going to force any of you to do anything," he said. "I'm not hiding anything. If you come, you're risking everything."

Their reticence endured for only a moment. They stepped up one by one, touching their heads to his.

"You kids always make such a frickin' mess," Agatha muttered.

"Thank you. Thank you…"

"We'll prepare immediately," Oliver said. He pointed sharply to James and Alex. "Get some rest, both of you. You are going to need everything you have."

Lucian squeezed James's arm. "We'll get her," he muttered so low the others wouldn't hear.

"An hour," Agatha said.

They disbanded, heading for the kitchen and the stables, leaving James with Alex and the Creeks. Shell-shocked, James turned to Norman, who still stood frozen before him, wide-eyed. "Sorry, Norman," he said weakly. Could a person ever feel so very defeated? "I really am."

Norman blinked, uncomprehending. "Go on back to your mum and dad. This isn't kid's stuff."

"I'm not a kid," Norman uttered. "I can help!"

James smiled weakly and nodded to the doorway, where Hector and Helen still loomed, mute and sheepish. "Go on, now. We'll be back soon."

Norman looked forlorn, his eyes darting between James and Alex.

Then a voice rose up, so unfamiliarly strong that James didn't quite recognise it. Hector emerged from the doorway, Helen clutched at his side. "We're coming," he said.

James and Alex shook their heads simultaneously.

"There's nothing you can do," Alex said.

They shrivelled, but with what seemed like every scrap of courage within them, they stood their ground, clutching Norman's head between them. "I know we're not like you.

We never were. But we're part of this Alliance, for better or worse. If you all go and something happens, we could never forget it," Hector said.

"We're coming with you," Helen muttered.

Norman seemed awed by his parents, his gaze fixed upon them. His big, round eyes drifted from them to James, then to Alex. "Please," he muttered.

James prepared to let them down gently, when Alex did the unexpected: "All right, you can come. But you keep your son safe. You stay back," he said.

Hector nodded firmly. Tight-lipped and victorious as though quite unable to believe what they had done, the trio retreated inside.

James caught the way Alex looked at Norman, something he had never been able to hide: like the kid was a bag of useless nothing; he wasn't interested in the mission, and so he was no good in the Messiah's eyes. Just dead weight.

*Is that why he's letting them come: hoping that they'll get a few scars and toughen up? Even now, he's looking for soldiers, for pawns.*

Everything that had been festering inside him the past few days returned with a vengeance, acid so vicious he felt it might burn through his stomach and bore a hole into the ground. The Creeks led their child inside to make their own preparations, and James was left alone with Alexander in the square. They shared a long, stony look, two men apart upon opposite sides of a fresh line in the earth, something neither of them would have ever dreamed of.

"We'll get her back, James. We can undo this."

James burned that moment into his retinas.

*Whatever happens, this is going to be the moment I look back on, because this is the last time we could have changed the course of everything.*

"If she dies…" James couldn't finish. He sighed, his heart ripped and warped by two inescapable truths: that Beth had been put into harm's way by the both of them; and that whether they saved her or not, there was no coming back from this. His great destiny had never seemed so fanciful and childish, so very far away.

He strode for his room, leaving Alex behind him, a single poisonous thought blossoming behind his eyes: *If she dies, I will take everything you've built apart, piece by piece. And I'll make you watch.*

# XV

Alexander woke to the song of larks outside his window and gripped his mattress as liquid fear seemed to seep into his body from the bed sheets. Immobilised, he could only stare about at his room, crushed by stark reality. To live a life of speeches and great journeys in the unknown, cast a romantic sheen over everything, turned fear into bravery and dimmed the sharpness of things to a rosy tint. But to be here, in the cold stillness of early morning, with everybody asleep and water dripping from a pipe nearby; an old man alone in his bed, everything was suddenly too sharp, too pedestrian and so very real.

Outside, the larks' song fought under a blanket of pigeon cooing. People rose for their breakfast, and somewhere out there in the wilds, people just like them were coming to tear them apart.

For a moment Alexander considered sending a prayer. What good would it do? He had never seen it save anybody. A lot of people had died praying in front of him.

Feeling so weak he wondered whether he might already be a walking corpse, he threw back the sheets. Splashing some water over his face from the basin, he looked at himself in the mirror and realised anew just how old he had become, how all the long years of struggle and work really had gone by, leaving him with a haggard ruin of a body. Clipping his beard, brushing his hair, he re-familiarised himself with his face's every wrinkle and divot, knowing each one had been hard earned—and had probably meant the end for somebody, somewhere.

He dressed slowly, intent to feel every moment, every slip of fabric against his skin, the carpet between his toes. This was what he had fought for, after all: to live in a home and enjoy running water and heated pipes, to have books on the shelves and linen on the bed. If this was to be the end of that way of life forever, he was going to savour it, one last time.

Descending the stairs took more effort than he could bear. His feet seemed encased in cement, and a childish cowardice inside him willed him to grip the picture and door frames as he passed. He made breakfast and ate in silence. Usually he read while he ate; in this manner he had slowly worked through the many thousands of volumes of his library. This morning he could only stare at them all, sat in his armchair and chewing bread made tasteless by cotton mouth.

Had he ever really appreciated the notion that it might all be for nothing—that he himself would certainly die before the Old World returned in magisterial splendour? In his daily speeches and plans he had stuck doggedly to a realist stoicism; but in his dreams, he saw the lights returning, lighting up the old cities, and planes taking to the skies once more.

*Did I ever really accept this life, or did I only hide away inside what was left of it?*

He wished it was a question he couldn't answer, but the truth was he could: that was exactly what he had done. That was why all this had fallen down around him, why—in the end—it would all come to nothing. He had forgotten the bare reality of his fellow men, chasing street lights that would never again be lit and telephones that would never again trill.

Alexander toured his home in the dead-quiet of early morning, touching things. He touched everything.

People had come here from across the country not long ago. Live-in scholars in the vein of Professor DeGray who boarded upstairs in the many rooms, poring over his library and the books from the city's vaults, excavating tidbits of know-how and nuggets of wisdom like archaeologists, rediscovering once great voices from across the sands of time. For that was what the Old World had truly become: already it was the stuff of legend, and to their children's children it was little more than a bedtime story, myth and whimsy to explain away the hulking metallic carcasses that littered their world of encroaching forests.

Now those scholars were gone, never to return. Where were they now, those who had been the sole conduits to the world's origin for many fledgling communities? Dead in ditches, burned upon pyres, or marching under the sigil of a pigeon?

By the time the first sounds of the city stirring began, Alexander had exhausted the many rooms and pokey crannies and retreated back to his study to stand by the fireside, wallowing in yet more nostalgic slime: all the times he sat here with Norman expounding a rhetoric that had never quite landed, raised a second heir—and what? Found him inadequate?

No. Norman had greatness in him, but he would never be what Alexander had before in James.

His mind turned to a memory he had cast from his mind for years: flames and screaming, the night everything had changed. He cast an eye at the mantelpiece, couldn't bear to look at what was placed there, and fled. Tearing open the front door, he strode from the home he had for so long fought to uphold and knew he would never return.

The sky had failed to grow lighter as the morning pressed on, a murky half light as hazy as a dream; pigeons whirled over the periphery of the city, an ominous black swarm that further blacked out the clouds hanging low in the sky. It had grown cold in the past day or so, not born of lack of warmth, a bone-chill he knew only too well but had felt only once: the day the world went away. As he walked the waking city's streets, the chill chewed on him, prickling his arms and yanking at the gristle of his core.

*Warn the others? No. There's no sense in that. They know only too well. Let them sleep.*

He passed by the cathedral, fighting off the urge to lay eyes on Agatha, Sarah, anyone. Perhaps with him far away, some of them stood a chance.

Beside him the Stour trickled, meandering parallel to the twisting paths and cramped lanes. Such history here, over a thousand years of condensed heritage. The seat of archbishops, site decrees, and games of politics and murders that had shaped the course of entire civilisations.

"I forgot how beautiful this place is," he said aloud. His voice died on the breeze, bleeding away into stark nothing. The world seemed set to eat up all that remained of man, including the voices of those who lingered.

Alexander didn't notice when he left New Canterbury behind, but at some point he looked down and saw that he trod over grass yet again, though gnarled and unkempt, touched by recent decay. The crop fields had been on the verge of recovering from the plague that had wrought the famine. They might have been all right. Now it didn't matter.

*The plague started all this*, his mind protested.

No. No, he had started this. Something would have brought this upon them, eventually. They should be thankful they had lasted as long as they did.

He headed for the hills under the shadow of a lacklustre sky full of flapping harbingers, spreading his hands to either side and brushing the wheat with his fingertips.

*

Allie shook Agatha gently. "It's morning. Time for the sermon," she whispered.

Agatha's face wrinkled so deeply that she didn't look

quite alive, more like a carving of wisdom incarnate in moss-ridden bark. Upon her lips, the slightest touch of blue had stolen into the whitish pallor. Her eyes flicked beneath her closed lids, but otherwise she didn't stir.

The cathedral hummed to the tune of a few hundred people's slow steady breathing. Most slumbered in their nests among the pews, covered in coats and blankets, gathered around candles that had died down in the night. A few sat awake, their eyes far away and fatigued by dread, hugging their knees and watching over children or elders. A few whispering appeals to the heavens rang in timorous echo under the high roof.

Allie shook Agatha again who lay in the hollows of the transept, but she didn't stir. She looked to Heather.

Heather smiled, a long-suffering and tired expression that cast her a decade older. "I'm done healing, Allie. I've left that behind."

"This is Agatha. We owe her."

Heather crouched by Agatha, touching her forehead and squeezing a finger over her wrist. Her wan smile stretched. "She's old, Allie. Old and tired."

"She's a fighter. She's done more for the city than anybody."

"Yes. That kind of strain has consequences."

"She was a vegetable for over a year before all this. Now she's finally come back to us—she's strong again."

"She's near the end, Allie. She's given everything she has to give."

They both looked down as Agatha groaned and her eyes

fluttered open. "Speak for yerself, Missy," she croaked.

Allie smiled. "It's time for the sermon."

Agatha's eyes flicked to her—which seemed to take a great amount of effort—and winked. "Time to shine, eh?"

"That's right."

Heather laid a hand on Agatha's arm. "I'm not sure that's such a good idea. Rest up this morning. Let somebody else take the sermon."

Others woke around them as though roused by Agatha's mere consciousness. Those who had been quietly praying crept forwards over the pews, waking yet more as they went.

"Are you volunteerin', m'dear?" Agatha said with a thin smile.

Heather said nothing.

Allie cleared her throat. "I could…"

Agatha shook her head, stroking her cheek. "My flock needs me. Now c'mon, get me up."

Heather made to protest, but Agatha cast a dismissive hand and looked out through the stained-glass windows.

"Bloody dark, this mornin'. Today ain't a good day, is it, kiddies?"

"No. It doesn't look too good," Allie said. She and Heather had spent the predawn hours with Sarah out at the roadblocks. At first light on the horizon, birds resting on rooftops and power lines had taken to the skies and begun their endless circling of the city.

"Something wicked this way comes," Agatha muttered.

Allie raised her brows. "Huh?"

Agatha flapped her hands and waved for them to get her

up. "We've stuff to do, souls to save, yada yada. C'mon, darlings, my legs aren't what they used to be."

Allie implored Heather silently, and after a moment she relented with a sigh. Together they pulled Agatha to her feet and guided her towards the podium. She took a steadying breath and whispered over her shoulder, "Best that you go join Ms Strong, girls. Somethin' tells me she's gonna need you."

Suddenly Allie saw the truth in her eyes through the misty veil over Agatha's countenance. Their job was done here.

"If you feel faint or tired, rest," Heather said. "Drink plenty—"

"Doc, you've been a saint, but you ain't got to worry about me no more. You said it yerself: you're done nursin'. Go on now, get outta here. Go be heroes."

Allie and Heather passed out through the side doors into the courtyard, and made their way towards the roadblock on Main Street where Sarah had gathered the militia's lieutenants for the morning briefing.

"I don't like this," Allie said, spying the birds milling overhead. "They're still up there. You'd think they'd get tired and just… fly away."

"I don't know. I don't know anything anymore," Heather said. A spot of pallor touched her cheeks. "I don't know if I can do this. I… I'm not a fighter."

"You'll be fine. We both will." Allie didn't feel nearly as confident as she managed to sound. They walked for a while, then Allie cleared her throat. "What do you think is coming?"

"I don't know. Maybe another siege like last time? One that won't end."

"I'm betting they'll starve us out. They can't have enough strength to rush us. All we need is for the militia to repel a first wave, and they'll keep their distance. But if they cut us off, all they have to do is wait." She swallowed. "I'm betting that's how it'll go."

"Great." Heather looked only paler, gripping her belt so hard her knuckles turned white.

Allie checked the pistol hanging from a holster at her hip, a practise she had taken to mostly out of obsession. None of them would ever have the time to become proficient with guns.

*We're idiots with sharp sticks, yahoos running around playing soldier*, she thought. *But we're all that's left.*

"We can't win," Heather said. She sounded half-strangled.

"No, but that doesn't change anything—"

They drew within earshot of Sarah and the others. Standing over them upon the hood of a beaten old cement truck, her proclamations slotted into the conversation so well that Allie let Sarah answer for her.

"We're not born for this," she called. "But we're going to give them all we've got. Our friends are still out there, looking for help, and we have to believe that they're going to come back. We *have to*. All we have to do is keep the city unbreached and hold out."

The congregation was silent. Every refutation had been

uttered, all doubts voiced. Now was the time for action.

"Go on," Sarah said. "Hold your stations and remember that we're not alone."

The group disbanded, heading out into the city's web of side streets. In mere moments Sarah was left with but a handful, and all around them the city had become as still and silent as the surrounding wilds. "All of you, hold this line. I'll be back soon," she said.

"Where are you goin'?" said Abernathy. He looked paler than ever this morning, but he stood fast.

"To the school. I'm late for my lesson."

The contingent turned to her as one, wide-eyed. A thought seemed to blaze between them as though it had been yelled aloud: *have you lost your mind?*

Sarah bore their incredulity with a calm stare. "I'm a teacher. The children have known nothing but fear and pain since all this started. If this really is the end, then they deserve to be kids again, one last time."

"But you can't just…," Tommy Doogan cried, a young lad who stuck to Abernathy's side like a limpet. The rifle in his hands looked comically large. "Don't leave us."

"I'll be back. I have to do this."

"Why, for the love of Christ?" Abernathy said.

"I'm going to read to them. If this is the end, that's what I'm going to take with me: knowing I made a difference."

"They should be in the cathedral where it's safe!"

Crushing sobriety smeared Sarah's irked expression. "It won't make any difference where they are. I've got a lesson to get to. Keep your eyes peeled." She stalked away over the cobbles, heading for the schoolhouse.

"Well that's just bloody brilliant," Abernathy said, deflated, turning his eyes upon the streets beyond the roadblock.

"Mental," Tommy Doogan muttered, climbing to a screened hide set into a pile of rubble. "Mental, mental…"

Sarah passed Allie and Heather and reached out a hand to touch Allie's arm. "Look after the boys. Not too much chocolate, make sure they're in bed by eight." She winked, and Allie returned a wan smile, but there was a tautness between them that could not be melted; in Sarah's eyes there was scarcely anything but glassy, churning fear—and Allie knew that if she looked into a mirror, she would see little else.

"Don't dally."

"One story. The kids deserve that." Then she was gone.

Allie and Heather took their positions at the roadblock and settled down to the watch. All around the city, Allie reckoned she could feel the others hunkering down, waiting for the first pieces of hot metal to come hurtling from the ether.

"I'm scared, Allie," Heather said quietly.

Allie took Heather's hand in her own and squeezed tight.

*

Alexander climbed the hills alone, freezing despite the stuffy air under the clouds. It felt as though ice ate at his chest, pushing in from all sides, setting his heart racing; an afterglow of those awful moments when the skies had turned purple and a deafening whine covered all the world.

*What the hell is going on?* he thought.

Maybe he had lost his mind. Maybe he'd died in his sleep and walked not through New Canterbury but along the road to the underworld to join all those who had vanished so long ago.

*Or not*, he thought as he looked at the pigeons over the city.

He reached the log where he sometimes came to think, an innocuous and gnarled old thing that wasn't at all sheltered from the elements but gave a good view of the city. Right here was where he had brought the first of James's signs to Lucian: the pigeon feathers he had left for them to find. The look Lucian had given him seemed to reach through time and wrap a tight fist around his throat.

He sat and reached into his robe, pulling out a green book so battered and torn that it was by now hanging together by threads: *Alice in Wonderland*. He stared at it in his hands for a while, but in time his thoughts turned to Lucian; Lucian who had stuck by him, even knowing what he knew.

*Stupid bastard was always too loyal for his own good. If he had any kind of sense, he'd have killed me…*

Alexander wondered if he would ever see him again. Was he even still alive out there with Norman and the others?

They were so scattered. Oliver in London, Norman and Lucian in the North, himself here with Agatha—who faded so fast she might as well be gone already. They had been so strong once, so bright that the entire world seemed malleable in their hands.

*How did I screw it all up this bad?*

He stroked the book gently, feeling the embossed golden filigree, remembering his parents. His father had been given the book by his own father, just as Alexander had given it to James. Of everything he had held on to, the copy of *Alice* held so much of who he was and where he had come from. What if he had never dug it from the detritus of his bedroom, the day he left his parent's home forever? Maybe the destiny of the world would have played out differently.

He dropped the book into the grass and turned to the city. How beautiful it was even now, its colours diminished as though washed out by rain, shifting with myriad shadows cast down from the flocks circling above. He closed his eyes and let thoughtlessness take him, going gladly to a place he had seldom allowed himself to travel: sweet blissful nothing, where there was only the air in his lungs and the wind against his skin.

When finally the cold in his chest seemed to encase his heart altogether, the masses of pigeons simultaneously ceased their orbiting and scattered, spreading out radially into the clouds. It was now mid-morning, yet the sky dimmed even further, throwing a lifeless pall over all the land, rendering the grass almost black and the city in a dead, flat grey. Footsteps behind him in the grass.

Alexander didn't move, just kept watch over his city, taking each breath deeply, savouring it. The distant treeline grew black, a lurking smudge stretching for a solid mile across the western flank of the abandoned parts of the city.

They were here.

The footsteps reached his side. In his peripheral vision, a figure sat beside him on the log and joined him in overlooking New Canterbury. Silence again, the wind. A few pigeons returned, circling down as they approached, landing in the surrounding grass. One landed upon the newcomer's shoulder.

James took a slow, ponderous breath. "Let me ask you something. When you found me—when you looked into that crib and saw me for the first time, did any part of you wonder? Did you ever have an inkling that one day that little creature you found inside would be sitting next to you about to end everything you ever cared for?"

Alexander, over what seemed like a millennium, turned from the city to face him. Despite himself, he blinked at the ruined face: the sunken flesh and the naked gums protruding through denuded cheeks, the missing masses of bone and patches of scar tissue. His immediate thought was that he really had died, gone to a place where undead things roamed. But those eyes were just as alive as the last time he'd seen them.

James glowered. "That's it. How does it feel to look at your work? There was a time when I would have done anything in your name. I would have killed for you, or given my own life. The destiny you gave me, like something wrapped up pretty in ribbon, made me special—made me better. I thought it was my duty to go out there and enlighten them all—poor defenceless cretins hugging to the edge of the world, waiting for us to come along and save them. We had the divine right to poke our collective heads into other people's business and do as we pleased… for the good of the mission."

He mused, a contemplative hum. "Say it like that enough times, and you see just how seductive it is. But keep on saying it, and you realise something else: just how much gall it takes to start you down that path. All it takes is one person to get the ball rolling, but that person… they need the kind of strength that comes once in a generation. A god among men. Or at least, that's what they have to think of themselves." James inched along the log. The pigeon upon his shoulder bobbed closer, fixing Alexander with eternal mocking stares. James finished, "Men like that can only ever be one thing inside: tyrants."

"Spare me," Alexander said. "To raise this scourge, to do the things you've done, that is the work of a tyrant. What I did was what nobody else dared. I tried."

"What you *did* is take the world into your hands and mould it as you saw fit, and never mind what anybody else ever wanted."

"That's what it takes to save the world."

"The world never needed saving, Alex! Except from you."

Alexander couldn't break his stare from that terrible, scarred face. "My whole life, people have second-guessed and condemned me for being what I am, and all the while they've lined up behind me and let me make the hard decisions. I'm not sorry for what I've done, and if I could do it over again, I'd do it the same way."

Those emerald eyes flickered. "That's it: the bare truth. You wouldn't change a thing. Even the things that make you a monster."

"I don't have to explain myself, least of all to you. If things had played out differently, you'd be exactly where I am now."

"But they didn't. You made sure of that." A pause; the fire in James's eyes tempered seemingly through force of will. "I have to thank you. You're exactly right: if you hadn't, I'd be right here with you. I'd have become the villain. What you did, Alex, was show me the light."

"That what you call this?" Alexander gestured to the treeline, where the space under the canopy had thickened to a treacle-like sludge, undulating and alive.

"That down there is the truth laid bare."

"That's a mob stoked to commit mass murder."

"Don't even try to turn this around. I've done nothing but bring them together. Alone, wronged, they were weak; together, they can find justice for themselves."

It was Alexander's turn to lean closer. "Are you going to tell me that you played saint and led the good people of the wilds to a new beginning? I saw the outpost in the forest. I saw the bodies, James. I've done some terrible things in my life, but I never killed anybody unless I had to."

James's eyes bored into his, and Alexander returned his own stare, and for a crackling moment the urge to leap upon James surged through his mind. A short scuffle, a single blow to the head with a rock, and it would be done. Decades of uncertainty and worry, of looking over his shoulder, would be over. Either that, or his own story would come to an end, but at least then he could rest.

*What would it change? He's telling the truth about one thing: he's not leading those people anymore. He's just uncaged them.*

Uncaged, after burning, kidnapping, twisting, torturing.

"Don't punish them for what I did. Nobody wants this."

"Nobody ever wanted this, Alex."

"What you're doing is… It's genocide. If you start this, it won't stop here. They'll keep going, and you know it. They won't stop until there's nothing left at all."

"I'm counting on it."

"But *why*? Just tell me why. What will it change?"

"It's not about changing what's done. It's about justice and the future. It's the only way we can ever begin to choose our own destiny. That's something you'll never understand: that the choice is what matters. Whether we succeed or fail, live or die—it doesn't matter; it's the choice to rise or fall that makes a life worth living."

Alexander licked his lips. "You're right. I'll never understand that."

"And that"—James leaned down into the grass and picked *Alice in Wonderland* from the dirt—"is how you corrupted everything you ever touched. After everything that happened between us, you haven't learned a thing."

"Don't pretend that this is for anybody but yourself. You're just another thug out for revenge."

"Everybody down there has had the same things taken from them. We're all the same." A sick, terrifying smile stretched over James's gaping lips. "We're your children just as much as the rest of the Alliance."

"I did what I had to."

James nodded. "For the mission."

"That's right."

They turned to face the city, side by side, just as they might have done if things hadn't gone so terribly wrong. A momentary peace blossomed when it was possible to forget the amorphous shadow hidden in the forest, even the pulsating ball of ice in Alexander's chest.

James flicked through *Alice* as the darkness spread from under the trees. Muttering lines and passages of the Mad Hatter and the Red Queen aloud, he ignored the emerging figures entirely. Alexander wasn't fooled: he sensed James's attention trained upon him, drinking in the horror spewing from that icy prison inside him. He knew they would come in these numbers, but to see it for himself, right here in front of him... There were no words.

Men and women, old and young, armed and not, poured from the forests bordering New Canterbury like ants bursting from a freshly-trampled mound. It seemed as though the Vanished themselves had returned to reclaim the Old World.

James inched so close that his scarred lips were but a few inches from Alexander's ear. "See your new world, oh creator," he whispered. "Tell me, do you see that it is good?"

The multitudes numbered in the thousands. Most bore

arms: from machetes to axes and pitchforks with those more emaciated wielding sharpened lengths of salvage. A smaller proportion—which still numbered over two thousand—carried guns. Most were pistols or single-shot rifles, things of antiquity or meant for buckshot, but more than a few had the unmistakable form of military-grade automatic rifles. The parade of human flesh kept coming until it flanked the city's entire western edge, stretching from the Stour to the beginnings of the foothills where Alexander sat. With the river blocking the way to the south, and the abandoned parts of the old city to the north and the east, there was no escape.

Not least because of their own roadblocks. They had bottled themselves in.

*We prepared for a siege, to be worn down over days. Not this… this is going to be over before it starts.*

"Don't do this," he whispered.

"It's done." James remained an inch from his face.

Alexander's thoughts turned to Agatha, Sarah, Allie, Heather… everybody down there following their lead. It was really going to happen. They would all just vanish. Was that how it would be told in times to come: the wicked who succumbed to the righteous deluge? Was that how they would be remembered?

"Do one thing for me. Kill me first," he muttered.

James laughed, a vicious sound that tore at him like a vulture stripping carrion. "Kill you? This was never about killing *you*, Alex."

"I can't watch this."

"Now *that* is what it's about. Killing you would serve no purpose, because men like you are like forces of nature. If we put you down, another would rise. But turn all that on its head and leave you the only man standing… now that's poetry. A shepherd without a flock, lamenting until a sad, lonely death that nobody will remember."

Alexander turned, aghast, to one who had once sat in his lap and asked about the magic of the Old World. "What happened to you?"

"You happened, Alexander." James touched his shoulder, tucked *Alice in Wonderland* under his arm, and stood from the log.

Alexander became aware of others converging on him. Not predatory, not murderous, just there, cementing his imprisonment. Hands landed on his shoulders.

James nodded to the cast-iron clouds. "So foul a sky clears not without a storm, messiah." He stalked away down the hill towards the city, followed by an entourage of a dozen men. Alexander's hands were bound behind his back. Cut off, adrift from home, he watched as those in the fields approached New Canterbury, and the first shots were fired.

*

*"Peter did not feel so very brave; indeed, he felt he was going to be sick. But that made no difference to what he had to do—"* Sarah blinked, her mouth ajar. The book in her hands tumbled from her grasp, its pages crumpling against the floor. The classroom full of beady-eyed kids started.

"What's wrong, Ms Fisher?" hissed Eddie Petrie, leaning forwards.

"She's Mrs Strong now," said Helen McKendrie earnestly, all pigtails and missing front teeth. "Mrs Strong, what is it?"

Sarah only swallowed, rocking on her feet. Something had passed through her, so visceral that she was sure somebody had crept up behind her and stabbed her in the heart with an icicle. Her hands folded over her bosom as she leaned against the desk for support.

*They're here*, she thought. She had never felt anything like it in all her life, but somehow she just knew.

Outside, the ghostly wails of hundreds of people across the city penetrated the schoolhouse. The others felt it too. For a paralysing moment the classroom rang with silence, and over thirty terrified pairs of eyes stared at her. Instinct clawed for her to gather them in the smallest crevice she could find, threatening to overwhelm her thinking mind.

*No! I will not be that.*

She took a powerful breath through her nose and strode for the door. "Children, up, everybody up now!" She clapped her hands so loud that they burst upwards out of surprise, clinging to her flanks as she passed. Without a break in her stride she flung the doors open and took them all at a jog into the hallway. "Careful, no pushing. Stick together!" She headed for the main door, took another steeling breath, and emerged into the street.

Had it really been so dark all morning? The light seemed so *thin*.

Screams rang out from every direction. Unseen in side streets and alleys, she could hear people running. She hoped they were heading home, or to the cathedral, and weren't trying to flee the city. If they managed to get over the roadblocks…

She couldn't afford to think about that now. There was only one task at hand: getting the kids to Agatha.

"All right, everybody, time to go see Auntie Aggie. She's waiting in the cathedral, come on." She made to set off but stopped herself to look down into their watery, staring eyes. "Don't stop. Not for anything. Promise me."

Thirty terrified nods answered.

Sarah sobbed then. Just once.

Then they were running. When the gunfire started in the distance, crackles and bursts that seemed to barrel up the street in haunting echo, the children screamed. Helen McKendrie wrapped herself around a lamp post, shuddering. Sarah swooped on her and peeled her away without stopping. The girl screamed in pain, but there was no time for soothing. There was only time to run. That time wound down fast as the shots grew in volume and frequency. Within moments, the return volleys had started as the militia sprang into action. Quite suddenly, Sarah and the children were in the middle of a war zone.

*

Norman burst from the trees and skidded to a halt. He dragged Billy in his wake, her head lolling as she muttered indecipherable words. A short while ago she had grown confused and simply stopped. Presently she didn't even look at the city. The others already lined the hillside, blocking most of the view, but Norman only needed a sliver of sky to see the smoke rising into the air.

*We really are too late.*

Lucian was on his knees in the grass, moving fast and talking even faster, checking their scant arsenal. "If we go in via the storm drains, we'll pop up close to the main hall. Go right under the bastards just like they did to us. We've got a few dozen rounds, maybe. I've divvied them up."

Robert snatched his share from Lucian's grasp and set off immediately down the hillside with enormous bounding strides. He didn't turn back when they called after him, just turned his head once so they could see his face. His expression said everything, as though he had yelled aloud.

"Just wait. We need a plan!" Norman said without much hope. Robert had already receded to a bobbing dark spot at the bottom of the hill.

Richard shook his head, his voice thin. The rattling pops and whip cracks echoing up from below, coupled with sharp yells of pain and panic, seemed to whittle him by the moment. "What's the point? We were coming back to warn them. We failed."

"Boy—" Lucian began.

"What's the point of going down there to die?"

Lucian lanced up into his face, teeth bared, and pressed a gun into his hands. "Stay here if you want. If it comes to watching my friends die or going down with them…"

He cast a look in Norman's direction, his lips tightened, and he said, "The girl."

Norman turned and knelt before Billy, holding her shoulders tight. Her eyes remained unfixed, wandering the skies as though seeing another world entirely. "Billy, I need you to stay here. We're going to go and do what we can, but I can't do that if I'm worried about you." He shook her hard, and her eyes shifted to him vaguely. For a moment he thought the fog in her eyes might have cleared. "Billy. Promise me that you won't move from this spot. If anybody comes, you hide."

"I thought we needed her to stop… I dunno, bad voodoo," Richard said.

"She's here, ain't she?" Lucian said.

"I don't think that's what the Jester meant."

Norman rounded on him. "You want to take her down there?"

Richard turned away, shaking his head.

Norman clutched her tighter. "Billy. Promise me."

The slightest hazy murmur: "Okay."

He remained a moment longer, her shirt bunched in his hands, then forced himself to say, "I'll be back soon."

Shrugging off a bloom of fear in his loins, he turned to Lucian. "We need a plan for once we get in there."

"Round up who we can and get them into the sewers," Lucian said immediately.

"What about the militia?"

Lucian gave him a stony look that said it all. There was no fighting back. He just didn't want to accept the obvious:

the city had been lost the moment the army showed up.

Lucian snapped his gun's chamber closed and addressed Richard with a tight sigh. "Look, kid. This isn't some book, this is balls-to-the-wall real. You go down there, you probably don't come back. But nobody's going to make you go. We got five seconds, so choose. If you're with us, you're with us. If not, mind the girl."

Richard's eyes lost their glaze, filling with hate as a bucket is filled with boiling tar. "Norman, do you still have my master's king?"

Norman smiled thinly and patted his pocket, where John DeGray's black chess piece still rested snugly to his side. "Right here."

"Keep hold of it until we're done." He turned a steely eye on Lucian and nodded, sweat beading on his brow.

Lucian grunted. "Maybe you're okay."

"You're still an arsehole."

The tiniest twitch bunched the side of Lucian's mouth, then they turned and ran down the hill. Norman remained with Billy a moment longer. "Be safe, Billy."

She nodded but still didn't see him, so very far away.

A momentary panic stabbed at his heart—*what if we need her; what if this really is going to bring the End if she isn't with us*—but he thrust it aside. There was nothing else to be said: he wasn't going to take a little girl down there. If it took that to save the world, then the world would have to end.

He ran a hand over her cheek, then tore himself away, chasing the others towards the crumbling bastion of New Canterbury.

*

Allie screeched, trembling uncontrollably. She could barely hold her gun straight, let alone settle on a target. Figures moved back and forth ceaselessly in her sights. They had lost precious moments when the army appeared at the far end of the High Street, pouring in from the fields in all directions and converging on the central parade.

She, Heather, Abernathy, and the others had just stopped. Not a single one of them had fired, dumbstruck by the sheer enormity of the crowd. It didn't seem possible. All the while, the army had approached, first at a cautious lope, then at a sprint. She and the others simply watched for what seemed like an age, frozen in place, as a thousand people had come screaming down the road towards them. Not until shrapnel started pinging off the cars around them had any of them squeezed a trigger.

Abernathy had been the first, taking the enormous 30-calibre in his hands and started spraying rounds down into the crowd. A dozen people hit the pavement, though most rounds went so wild they ended up embedded in masonry over fifteen feet up. It wasn't enough to scatter the approaching ranks. Instead they moved onto pavements, ducking behind lamp posts and postboxes, lunging from doorway to doorway, diving behind bushes and the rusted hulks of old trucks. The dark, unstoppable ooze gained on the militia with terrifying speed.

Allie could hear nothing over the sound of Abernathy's fire, the sheer volume of it thrumming in her chest. It seemed such a horrific thing of destruction, rending flesh and cleaving dozens of people by the second. But for every one Abernathy took down, ten more took their place. By the time Allie and the others had found their first targets, the front lines were a mere forty feet from the base of the roadblock. Returning fire began a moment later.

As soon as she and the others started shooting, she realised just how inadequate they were. Back on the ranges under Sarah's instruction, she had watched straw men cut in half and felt so powerful. Like they stood a chance.

Now any notion of their having become gunsmiths in the past few weeks melted away. She emptied her first clip with stunning speed. She thought she might have made a single hit, and she knew it hadn't killed. She cast a glance to her right to check on Heather and blinked in shock. Heather's gun lay against the hood of a Jeep. Heather herself lay behind its thick tyres, crawled into a ball, her hands over her ears, rocking back and forth.

"Heather!" Allie screamed.

Heather only kept rocking, shaking her head. "No, no!"

Allie shook all over. She hadn't thought a person could shake as much, a full-body trembling that threatened to pull her apart. She kept firing, missing almost every shot. The army grew close, resolving into individual faces wrought by terror and rage, some eyes wild and others streaming with tears, sweeping towards her like a wave.

Then silence consumed everything, and her heart almost stopped.

*I'm dead. I was hit, I died, I'm dead—*

She wasn't dead. Those in her sights still rushed forwards. But it wasn't silent; her ears still rang. She cast her gaze wildly to Abernathy and saw him bellowing soundlessly.

The gun had run through its reel of ammunition. Allie made to leap from cover to reload from the barrel beside him, when the side panel of the Nissan Micra beside her disintegrated in a hail of hot metal.

*They were waiting for us to run through the reel. They can afford to. There are that many.*

Allie gritted her teeth and started forwards, but another burst of shrapnel tore away the Micra's wing mirror, just inches from her chest, and she cowered back with a whimper. Abernathy scrabbled with the gun himself, hauling out a fresh reel. A thud reverberating through Allie's chest told her it was too late: the invaders had reached the bottom of the roadblock.

"We can't stay here!" she yelled.

"What do we do?" Abernathy wheeled away from a red-hot round that shattered a headlight by his side.

"Get to the cathedral. It's the only place we might be able to hold them!"

"Hold against this?" Abernathy's voice broke, so high was his scream. Before she could reply, he jerked. The tiniest sliver of red arced from his temple, and he rolled to the side, tumbling out of sight. It happened so fast that Allie didn't even have time to reach out to catch him.

She screamed a curse. Flinging herself after his lifeless body, she landed with a crack on the ground. Something in her back ripped, but she didn't pause, didn't give the pain time to blossom. She grabbed at Heather, slapping her across the face, pulling her hair. "Get up, get up, get up!" she screamed.

Heather shook her head quite calmly, staring at the ground.

"Don't do this, please don't do this. Please, Heather."

Thumping on the other side of the roadblock, now. They were climbing.

"Please!"

Heather's eyes cleared a tad. "Go, Allie," she said flatly.

"Get the bloody hell up, you stupid cow!"

That maddening calm voice. "It's okay. Just go."

"No, I—"

A high screech cut across her as a figure fell in her peripheral vision across the street. For a heart-stopping moment Allie thought they had come over the top, but then she picked out little Tommy Doogan spreadeagled in the rubble, the left side of his ribcage torn away.

Allie swayed, saw black, then gripped Heather's lapels. "Don't do this to me," she whimpered.

Heather looked dully into her eyes. "Go."

Allie ran. Glancing over her shoulder, she glimpsed what seemed like a tar oozing up over the head of the roadblock, a wave of human bodies thrust forwards by an unfathomable legion from behind. The first few crashed down into the street without grace, pushed by those behind. The next jumped, scrambling for cover, then fired along the street itself. Allie threw her arms over her head as rounds snapped and whizzed close by. She didn't dare look back again.

Elsewhere, the screams ringing out had changed from those of fear to those of pain. Already the returning volleys had died to a trickle. In place of the sound of gunfire was that of groaning metal and toppling cars. The city had been breached.

# XVI

Billy walked in shadow. Things amorphous and veiled in darkness shifted around her in constant motion. Cold rained down on her shoulders and slicked her skin, each moment seeping deeper into her, stopping her breath in her throat and weighing her down. She wanted to lie down and sleep in the grass. Right here would be fine. She just needed to rest for a while. On the verge of looking around for a comfy spot, she wondered how long she had been walking.

*Don't know.*

Where had she been before?

*Don't know…*

Who was she?

*Doesn't matter. Sleep now.*

She was about to start bending her legs when a sharp crack cut through the shadows, washing it all away like cobwebs parting in a gale.

Billy blinked. Light. Green hills, trees, an iron-grey sky. She turned on her heels and saw she was alone upon a hillside, three hundred feet above a city of wibbly-wobbly stone houses. A pall of loneliness fell heavy around her shoulders as she realised the others were gone—just gone.

*Poof,* she thought weakly.

She turned in a wide circle and found a pile of the others' things nearby in the grass. Darkness lay wrapped around the city's far side, made of thousands and thousands of people. Angry people, smirching everywhere nearby with darkness that slowly crept into the fields.

*I have to go down there.*

The itch in her feet that had carried her from the cottage with Daddy to the forests of Radden Moor awakened and bade her to advance. She started forwards, but an almighty burst of gunfire coming from the city's biggest road forced her back with almost physical force.

*I have to go, or we all go away.*

Already she could feel the Frost creeping about her heels, rising over her shins. Soon it would cover the whole city, if the Bad People kept rushing in, and then… once everybody was dead, it would spread.

Gripping the hem of her sleeves and biting her lip, she started forwards, heading down the hill. At first it was hard to take each step, and she jumped at every gunshot. But soon the itch took hold, and the Light lit up a path before her, guiding the way. The mindless haze crept back over her, and she went gladly to that place where there was no fear, where there was only her against the shadow.

*

"Down! Everybody down now!"

Sarah and the children flung themselves sprawling onto the cobbles as a blanket of hot metal spewed into the street. The town hall's cladding vanished in a puff of splinters. Inside, a few errant cries of pain rang out from the handful who had taken shelter there.

Sarah scrabbled up, grabbing at her belt for her pistol as a group of thin skeletal creatures appeared before her. Those at the front were armed, those behind holding knives and pickaxes. A beat passed in which she and the party stared at each other, then their eyes moved over the children. Their stances softened for a moment—the tiniest flicker of hesitation.

Sarah had been counting on it. She crouched down and took careful aim. It took everything she had to go through the motions and to not merely close her eyes and start spraying bullets, but surging adrenaline brought a strange outer-body deliberateness over her as time stretched, and she found her mark and fired. She missed.

*No!*

She aimed again, fighting back panic, and fired. The first figure dropped to the cobbles with a muffled *oof.* By the time the others blinked from their stupor, Sarah had found her second target, and a third. She shattered an elbow instead of hitting the chest she aimed for, and a round went wild and hit what would have been her fourth target. It didn't matter. She kept shooting. Five bodies hit the cobbles in lifeless heaps. None of them got a single round off.

Absurdly, she had time for a cogent thought to run

through her head, calm and ponderous as an armchair philosopher's: *so that's what it's like to take life.*

Then she was hauling children up by their hair, screaming, clawing, beating. They rose under her coaxing voice, shaking and weeping. Not fast enough. Even as she ripped them bodily into the air and placed them on their feet, a few lost their courage and sank back to the cobbles.

"Don't! Go, go all of you. Run!" she howled, scooping them up one by one.

Eddie Petrie wept and after a stutter in his stride, clipped her side and went hurtling off down the street. Sarah's heart stopped as she watched her pistol spin from her grasp and go wheeling through the air. She made to dive after it, but the children were all moving now, spurred into motion by Eddie's flight. As one, they rose, more terrified of being left behind than the remaining people loping forwards.

"Keep running. Don't stop for anything," Sarah called, waiting for them all to pass before turning in a horror-filled moment in search of the gun. She didn't have time to spot it. Arms seized her from behind, locking around her midriff and lifting her into the air. Sarah thrust her head back, made contact with flesh with a satisfying *crunch*, and a shriek rang out. A pot-bellied bald man stumbled back holding a nose pouring with blood, and she hit the pavement hard. Her cheek smarting, she rolled onto her haunches and searched for the gun. All she saw were feet sprinting closer, too close, all around her. Sarah watched a booted foot loom up towards her face with unstoppable rapidity, and then pain exploded in her jaw. Jerking back, her head made contact against the curb, and a moment of darkness threatened to swallow her.

With everything she had left, she screamed, "Run. Run, RUN!"

Then everywhere there were creatures laughing, fuzzy and bending over her. A few of them parted, and a figure holding a long curved knife appeared over her. A voice, high and predatory, washed over her as she blacked out: "Take her."

*

Allie reached the cathedral and felt she might have passed into another world. Inside, all was silent. For a horrible moment she thought everybody might have fled or been dragged away, but then she caught sight of figures gathered in the pews, their heads bowed, praying. She searched for Agatha, expecting to find her at her podium, but it was empty. Not a single person guarded the door.

Outside, the screams had died down enough to tell her all she needed to know. The roadblocks had been swept aside like dandelion heads in a breeze, and a scourge poured into the city, decanted from the sludgy ocean beyond, sloshing up the streets and cutting down anything that lay in its path.

She hadn't seen Heather since leaving Main Street. She couldn't afford to think about her right now.

"Everybody up!" she cried. Her voice returned in magnificent echo, the booming voice of the wizard of Oz addressing Dorothy. Eyes turned upon her in a wave that propagated from the rear pews forwards. Hundreds of eyes popped up into view, most wide-eyed and tearful, some blank, some angry. Children and the elderly lay in the centre of such clusters, surrounded by adults who stood slowly to face her. The entire cathedral stank with the expectation, the acceptance, of death.

Allison Rutherford never expected to stand before this city and be the one to whom it looked.

Harsh, taunting whispers from within: *The gossip. The dead weight. The nobody. That's who I am.*

She recoiled under the combined weight of their hopelessness, then caught sight of a slumped figure close to the transept. She was running before anything clicked in her mind, but by the time she leaped up onto the platform, she had started calling Agatha's name.

A groan answered, and the figure transfigured into Agatha's lolling body, her head drooping to her chest and her limbs splayed on either side. She sat teetering in a chair as though a diver preparing for a plunge. Allie crouched beside her and lifted her head and turned to those in the closest pews. "What happened?"

Nobody answered, just stared.

She scowled and cupped Agatha's cold cheeks in her hands. "Aggie, it's Allie. Come on, now. Look at me."

Agatha stirred and her milky eyes turned laboriously, but there was no trace of recognition in them.

*She's gone again.*

"Oh…," Allie said, deflating. Suddenly she felt weak, as

though gravity had grown stronger tenfold. Somehow, hearing her friends slaughtered outside paled in comparison to this: seeing one so wise and *above all this*, fade away before her very eyes.

No. She wasn't going to let this happen. Not like this.

Cursing herself, she shook the old woman hard. "Aggie! You hear me, you old bat. I know you do. You're not checking out that easy. You get your arse in gear, right this instant! You hear? Right this instant!"

Those milky eyes flickered with something, an oil-clogged engine sputtering and choking.

Allie gripped her hard, searching. "Come on, please. They all need you. I need you. One last time," she breathed.

"Ms Rutherford…" Suddenly those eyes were alive. A human being had dropped into place before her. The tiniest rueful whisper: "Let go o' me before I clock you one proper."

Allison laughed, a hysterical and delightful absurdity amongst the pain and woe in terrible oscillation about them. "Everybody's here now. We're all together."

Agatha looked for the source of the racket filtering in from outside. "It's started…"

"Yes. It'll be over soon." Instead of loosening her grip, Allie tightened it to get her point across.

Agatha's gaze filled with understanding, and she took a breath. "My flock?"

"All here. And more. We need to get out of here, right now."

Agatha smiled and rubbed her hand, bringing it to her

lips and kissing it. "So alive," she whispered. "I 'member bein' that way. Like you could do anythin'… Long time ago, that was. Like your heart is on fire." She winked. "Lemme tell you a secret: we don't ever get wiser, not a wink. But gettin' to be an old bat does give you some favours: you get to know when the time for some things has passed. We coulda got out of here before. But listen to that out there, child. There ain't no runnin' now. Now's the time to be together."

"No, no." Allie recoiled, pulling her hand away. She stood and turned to the crowd. "Come with me. There's still time to run. We can get to the forest if we go now. They won't get all of us, we—"

"Child." Agatha's hand gripped her harder than Allie thought possible, yet her voice remained soft as goose down, wafting high above the echoing carnage. "Anybody who wanted to run, ran already. The fighters fought. Us folk here, we got nothing if we don't have this place or each other. Here we'll stay."

Allie fought tears but didn't pull away. "Don't give up, please don't. I can't just leave you."

"You go do what you gotta. But right here, we're happy." Agatha winked once more, gave a smile so warm that Allie thought it might destroy her, and let go of her arm.

Allie turned slowly to the others as Agatha took once more to her podium and spread her arms. "Sons and daughters, brothers and sisters, I'm done with this bull-crap." She picked up the bible by her hand and tossed it aside. "It ain't gonna do us any good now. It's time to live all the time we got left with our heads in the here and now. We're all friends here, fam'ly. Whoever you got by your side, take their hand." She paused and turned to Allie. "Go on, now. You take care."

Allie bit her lip hard to keep the tears from flowing, backing away. "I'm sorry."

That smile again, so serene and everlasting, keeper of those who weren't for this world—those who before had been hopeless and tired of it all, but now seemed only ready. "Don't you dare be sorry. You take that pain and you use it."

Allie looked at them afresh as she reached the door. They had turned away from her now, their backs to the destruction, standing hand in hand. As one, they began to sing.

Allison turned and ran without looking back. As soon as she emerged, the sheer force of vibrating air stunned her. Everything was so very loud now, so very close. Her heart pounded painfully as she looked for somebody—something—she might be able to grab.

Sarah. Where was Sarah? If she had mounted a last stand then Allie wanted to be by her side. But there was no sign of anything she recognised. All around people were falling, shadows shifted, fires blazed. Bloody figures fought hand to hand, and bodies were being flung from upper storey windows into the roiling streets. A thin spattering of militia positions remained, but the approaching numbers were so vast that they were but islands in a foaming ocean.

A fresh wave of people breached the roadblocks with torches held aloft and scattered in all directions. They ignored anybody in their path, even those shooting at them, as though intent to penetrate as far behind enemy lines as possible, and lighted rags stuffed into bottles filled with liquid. As soon as these bottles were hurled through windows or through shattered doorways, great conflagrations belched to life, spewing flames into the streets and blowing out windows. New Canterbury began burning in earnest.

A gaggle of kids burst around a corner, sprinting for the cathedral. Allie watched them, frozen, but as soon as their terrified eyes turned on her, she sprang forwards with her arms spread wide. "Stop, stop! Where's Mrs Strong?"

"They got her!" the closest of the boys wailed.

Allie mouthed wordlessly, then shook herself and waved them away, to the east. "Time to go, everyone."

"What about my mummy and daddy?" the boy cried. The other kids began babbling at once, and Allie almost crumpled. Marshalling her strength, she clapped her hands, something she had seen Sarah do a thousand times but never thought she would do herself. Now, it might be all that could save them. "Enough! You do as I say. We're going to stick together, and we're going to run together and… and your parents are all going to be waiting for us."

The kids wheeled away from the cathedral once more.

*God, don't let that be the last thing to come out of my mouth*, she thought.

She made to run, but in the corner of her eye a tiny

figure tottered into view, tottering along the cobbles. A young red-headed girl wobbled drunkenly up the street, looking at and avoiding things that quite simply weren't there. One of the kids must have taken a hit to the head.

Allie cast a look after the main herd of kids disappearing up the street. If she left them, they might get lost and run right into the army. But she wasn't going to leave any more people behind, not one. Cursing under her breath, she ran for the tottering girl, who now seemed to be dancing.

Before she could reach her, the shelling started. The first explosion threw her sideways several paces. As the air unzipped overhead, a rumble fit to outstrip thunder tore its way down the street. Screaming, Allie caught a glimpse of flying shrapnel some fifty feet away, emanating from what had once been a rooftop, showering the street with razor-sharp detritus. Smoke and flame issued forth.

The air came alive with whistling. An instant of silence reigned, then ear-splitting pain thrummed in her head as cacophonous noise and blinding light lanced from all directions. The city seemed to disintegrate as streets overturned and spat cobbles at fighting men and women, houses vanished in puffs of dust, and the city she had known for the past five years suddenly belched death upon those within it.

Somehow Allie kept moving, heading for the girl. The explosions had banished her thinking mind entirely, and now she moved on autopilot, legs pumping and arms working. She swept the girl into her arms and yanked her to the side, collapsing against a wall and skidding to the ground.

"No," the girl slurred. She stared into the sky and shook her head. "I have to stop the Frost. The Frost is coming."

"What?" Allie yelled.

"I have to stop it."

"What are you—?" Allie threw her arms over the girl as a shell landed less than thirty feet away, and a power line twanged loose, slicing a brick wall clean in half.

The girl snapped her head around and looked over Allie's shoulder. Her face drained of colour. "What's happening?" she screamed.

*God help me.*

"Come on, we're getting out of here," Allie said.

The girl looked at her, blinking fast. "Where's Norm?"

Allie blinked. "N-N-Norman? Did you say Norman? *Where is he?*"

"Here. They're all here."

"Now?"

The girl nodded.

Allie cast a furious gaze around as though expecting Norman to emerge from the ether, but she saw only the same medley of destruction. Could they really be here, somewhere? A moment's indecision wracked her, for every fibre of her wanted to dash senselessly into the city in search of them. Even if just to see Norman one last time—

*No. The kids. Get the kids out.*

Allie choked, set the girl down beside her. "We have to get out of here, right now!"

"But I have to—"

"Right now!"

The girl flinched wildly as yet another shell rocked the ground but nodded.

Allie took her hand and tore away down the street. She had no idea where she was going, could make no sense of the streets, a whirling confusion of colours and flying debris. But she couldn't stop, not for one moment. She just ran.

*

Norman took Lucian's hand and hauled him up from the manhole, pushing him aside to join Richard. Robert already perched ahead of them, surveying the city, leaning forwards like a dog poised to spring from its master's leash.

All of them dripped with tepid sewer water, churned like rats in a spin cycle. The explosions had started just as they had passed under the feet of the invaders, using the same system of tunnels that Jason and his men had first used to get into the city. It seemed absurd that so short a time ago, they had believed the extent of the scourge's power to be a handful of terrorists sneaking into the city at night, to slaughter watchmen, send warnings, and tie Chosen Ones to chairs.

Norman propped the manhole cover aside, making sure they would be able to dive inside should they need a quick getaway. The others' faces grew slack and gaunt, looking over his shoulder. He joined them and wanted for all the world to squeeze his eyes shut and block out the terrible sight. It was burning, all of it.

"It's over already," Richard whispered.

"Oh no it ain't," Lucian said. "We've got a job to do, so

keep your crap out of your pants."

They crouched in the lee of a porch and watched a few figures dash across the end of the street. From here it was impossible to tell if they were friend or foe.

"Get in, take who we can, and get out," Lucian said.

"Sounds like a plan," Norman said.

"What about Alexander? The council?" Richard said.

Nobody answered him.

"Well?"

"Save who we can," Lucian said.

Norman saw the pain on his face, knew it was the same he felt himself. "We don't have time to search for anyone. We grab who we can. That's all."

"What about the vaults? My master's research materials? Years of work—decades. Irreplaceable stuff. We can't just let it—"

They all stared at him, and Richard's brow crumpled. "Yeah. Okay."

"Like I said, we don't search. We just grab."

"You do whatever you have to do. I have to find Sarah," Robert said.

"We'll find her. We'll find all of them."

Robert said nothing, just turned and started off along the street, keeping low, a hulking unstoppable machine animated by pure instinct.

Norman shared a grim look with Lucian and pushed Richard out before him. "Come on, let's make sure he doesn't get himself killed."

"And us," Lucian muttered, and they gave chase.

# XVII

Sarah flinched when the explosions started. All around her, her captors laughed and jeered. Those few with whom she was tied back to back wailed in horror. Before them, New Canterbury became a stack of smoking tinder. The gunfire had all but ceased, and by now the streets were dark with the invading army, systematically sweeping the streets, plunging into buildings and yanking any they found within out to be slaughtered. Slowly they converged on the cathedral—they could have taken it minutes ago; they were saving it for last.

Sarah worked at her bindings, yanking and sawing away with her fingernails. By now her wrists were raw and her nails bled, but she kept going, her teeth gritted together. Once she was free, she would kill as many as she could before they got her. That was all that occupied her mind now: getting as many as she could. The alternative was to die in whichever way they had planned, and by the looks of what was going on in front of her, it wasn't going to be anything pretty.

She had no idea how long she had been unconscious,

but she had woken in time to watch the fires start, and for the first tendrils of smoke to drift up into the clouds. She and a handful of other women had been hauled back behind the enemy lines, just past the main roadblock. Nearby bodies were scattered on the ground, full of holes. A few she recognised. Many more she knew she would have also been able to name had they not been so mutilated.

Explosions continued to pepper the city with firepower the likes of which she had never thought possible. So this was the power of the Old World, brought to bear. Ironic that it should be used to seal their fate.

Fibres gave way one by one. The fingernail of her index finger throbbed and burned. A few more stokes and the nail would tear free.

"How long?" A young man appeared before her, a soft-faced youth with a leg that dragged behind him.

The men who stood around Sarah jeered, pointing to the city.

*"It's done, already."*

*"Look at the bastards. They got nothing."*

*"This ain't a fight at all!"*

The young man cut across them. "Stop the shelling."

They turned to him.

*"Eh?"*

*"What the bloody 'ell for?"*

*"We've got them on the ropes."*

"It's unnecessary. As you say, the battle is won."

Sarah blinked, staring at him. There was something familiar about that face.

"We ain't gonna stop nothing until we get an order from—"

"*I'm* giving you an order. Stop it right now."

Those around her stiffened, and for a moment the young man glared at them. Something clicked in her mind at the sight of that brooding, confused expression, and she gasped aloud.

*That kid who Lucian hauled off the streets. What was his name? Charlie?*

He looked right at her then. She saw the recognition in his eyes, just as well as she saw the micro-expression give way to a mask of hatred. "What are you doing with these?"

A sickly grin from one of the men. "Orders."

"Well?"

Everybody stilled as a high voice rose up from behind her. The kid stiffened as a lithe figure stepped into view. Sarah shivered: the voice was the same she had heard just before she had passed out. The man was wolfish in appearance, holding the same long curved knife, which now dripped with blood, tendrils red and white clinging to its edge. "Keep shelling," he said. "Hurry up with the hay."

Charlie glanced back down at Sarah, and leaned close to the wolf man. "What are you doing?"

The wolf man followed Charlie's gaze and grinned down at her, waggling his eyebrows. "A little fun."

A geyser of fear erupted in Sarah's belly. The ropes that bound her suddenly seemed impossibly thick. She would never get free in time. More people arrived with baskets of hay, then long lengths of wood. Before her they started erecting long poles, to which they hammered crossbeams.

"Oh God," spat the woman tied to Sarah's back. "Oh God, no."

Sarah said nothing, just stared the wolf man in the eyes. She wasn't going to weep.

The wolf man's brow twitched, a touch of curiosity threading his malicious glare. He got down on his haunches, waving the bloody knife back and forth. "You scared, missy? I know you are. You can't hide it from me."

Sarah barely heard him. She fixed her gaze over his shoulder, and her heart lurched. It took a moment to realise what she was seeing: Heather's figure, wedged into a recess in the far side of the roadblock's remains, watching the procession with wide eyes, trembling.

"You can't hide anything from me. I see you," the wolf man was saying. He ran his tongue over his teeth and bit his lip. An old bandage wrapped around his face had suppurated and grown green/brown to the extent that infected flesh showed beneath. He didn't flinch a bit as he smiled and stretched the glistening skin—the perfect cap to his uncouth exterior. "Don't worry, not long now," he whispered as he stood.

As soon as his back was turned, Sarah mouthed *Run*.

Heather didn't move, hugging her knees.

*Run.*

Heather moved an inch, then flinched back.

Sarah leaned forwards, glaring with all the force she could bring to bear. *Run, now!*

Slowly, inch by inch, Heather began crawling out from

her hiding place.

*Yes!*

Charlie frowned in the corner of Sarah's eye, clocking her gaze. He was on the verge of turning when she yelled out, "Scared, of you?"

The wolf man, who had been ordering the wooden structures to be built faster, turned back to her quizzically, like a cat surprised to see a mouse bite at its paw.

"I know your kind: needing to see pain to feel like anything but a piece of dirt. Sick, pathetic men."

He sauntered around her, appraising her with a critical eye. His tongue darted to and fro in the corners of his mouth, like a snake tasting the air. "She speaks," he said, grinning. The bandage stretched to hideous proportions, such that she could see torn pus-ridden flesh underneath.

In the haze of Sarah's peripheral vision, Heather inched out into the street and slid along in the dirt.

*Just keep him distracted a little while longer,* Sarah thought desperately.

"You don't belong here," she said. "Most of these people are just angry for what we did. I get that. Maybe I can even forgive it. The others you would have killed if they didn't join you. It was them or us. I can forgive that too. But people like you... You're just monsters."

The knife appeared again in a blur, resting upon her throbbing jugular. "There it is," he sighed. "*Monster.* I lost count of how many people I've had where you are right now, and in the end, they all pick that same word. You can only hear that enough times before you start to believe it;

then you start to own it."

"Save it. Finish your work, coward," she spat. A horrified part of her cried out to take the words back. At least she would die fast, and Heather could get away.

"Jason," Charlie said. "You sure you want to do that?"

A flicker of anger behind the monster's eyes. "I do what I want, boy. When I want. I'd think you would know that by now."

Charlie paled but took a hesitant step forwards. "She's important to them."

Sarah and Jason turned to him.

Charlie hesitated. "I was here. When they had me, I saw her talking with Cain and the others. She's one of the top dogs."

*Try librarian, kid.*

If only they knew she led the militia. Her head would already be on a spit.

The wolf man, Jason, turned back to her with renewed intrigue in his eyes. He dropped the knife from her throat. "Is that so? Why didn't you tell us, darlin'? We had no idea we had such exalted company. We'll have to pull out all the stops for you."

The others laughed, belly laughs of wicked amusement. Suddenly work on the wooden erects redoubled.

Charlie's jaw tightened, his face a mask of fury and— maybe—regret.

*The kid wants out.*

Maybe she could use him. If she could get close, maybe she could slip away. If not, maybe at least she could get his gun and take a few with her.

"There are kids in there," she said, leaning towards Charlie. "Old folks, farmers. Nobody in there ever did anything to hurt you."

She felt hatred beamed at her from all directions.

"You people are the reason we're here," Charlie spat.

"Not *these* people. They didn't make the decisions. Most never leave this place."

Her words landed visibly. Charlie's face flickered once more.

"They're just as hungry, lost, just as scared. You don't have to do this."

Charlie's face darkened as he glanced at Jason's turned back. He leaned over, and she felt the others' attention on them. The boy felt it too; his eyes searched the corners of his sockets, and he spoke as a mere breath. "We all chose. It's too late."

"It's never too late," she hissed.

He glowered down at her, hovering a moment longer before drawing back. In his wake he left a whisper on the breeze: "Sorry."

Sarah gritted her teeth and rounded on Jason. She only had to keep going a few seconds longer, and Heather would be safe—by now she was under the awning of an outbuilding, moving towards an alley.

"Coward. You don't have the guts to do your own dirty work? Why hold a knife to somebody's throat if you're not prepared to use it?"

"Oh, don't worry. I have special plans for you."

He kept his back to her, yet his shoulders had tightened. But at what?

*Coward?*

She grinned. "Like every *coward* ever said. How does it feel to know that we all see you for the yellow dog you are?"

He whirled on his heels. His eyes livid and bloodshot, he snarled down at her: "I could gut the lot of you right now, flay your friends in front of you, piece by piece."

"Please, don't," wept the woman behind Sarah. "Stop it. I-I don't wanna die."

Sarah ignored her.

"Hope… she has hope," Jason hissed, his tongue searching the air once more. "That's the talk of somebody looking to get saved."

"My friends are out there. They'll tear your spine out when they get here."

"Is that so?" Jason spread his arms. "All I see is little piggies getting their homes blown down."

Sarah glared at him, if only to keep her eyes off Heather, who had stopped crawling and lay still, pressed against the wall, only a few yards away.

*Keep moving. Move!*

"They'll be here," she said.

Jason grinned and shook his head. "Darlin', do you have any idea how many times I've heard that, right before the blood started flowing?"

"Forget what I said before. When they come, I'm saving you for myself. I want to see the light go out of your eyes."

Jason sneered and inched closer. "A fighter. I like it. Tell you what, I've changed my mind. You get your wish: I'm going to take you for myself, after all." The knife once more snaked from his belt, and Sarah found herself inching her neck higher, waiting for the blade to start slicing.

Then screaming filled the air. For a strange moment Sarah thought it came from her own mouth. Then she saw Heather streaming from the shadows, wailing at the top of her voice with a fist-sized rock held over her head, heading straight for Jason.

The monster caught her in an almost graceful pivoting motion, taking her arm and spinning around with her held in his grasp, such that by the time their revolution was complete she writhed in his grasp, the rock dropping to the floor. "Vermin," Jason hissed. "Hiding behind every wall and under every stone, just waiting to be put out of your misery." He raised his knife, and before Sarah could scream, thrust it into Heather's back.

Heather's tear-strained, terrified face froze in a grimace. She and Sarah shared a look then, and Sarah felt a piece of herself vanish as Heather's gaze grew stony and distant and was gone. She went limp as Jason raised his arms in a grand *ta-da!* gesture, letting her body drop to the cobbles with a crunch.

Sarah bit down hard on both sides of her cheeks. She'd be damned if she was going to let him get any satisfaction. Inside, she felt as though the blade had torn through her own heart.

The monster sighed as though satisfied after a hearty meal. He squeezed her cheek and winked. "Don't worry, it's your turn next."

He jerked his head over his shoulder, indicating the uprights behind them, which now bore the unmistakable form she dreaded in her mind's eye.

Crosses.

*

James crossed the lawn towards the stately home sprawled before him. A well-maintained Victorian thing of three floors and enclosed gardens filled with flower beds and gnomes, its walls enclosed a space easily large enough for two dozen people. It stank of everything Alexander Cain. Reaching the heavy mahogany door, inset with a brass knocker the size of his fist, James stopped and waited for his entourage to catch up, buckets of sloshing liquid in their grasp. "The whole place," he said.

Without a word they kicked the door open and surged inside, vanishing from the atrium and scattering to the far corners of the house, leaving giggles of anarchic glee in their wake. James followed, taking his time, breathing the musty air and dust, enduring the sensation of stepping back in time—the very same smell had once pervaded the homestead: the smell of old things, mildew, leather and mothballs.

The smell of home. Once.

He walked along the long corridor and entered the study. He knew what he would find, yet still it stopped him in his tracks: the sheer embodiment of everything he had once desired, fought for. A wall made entirely of books, paintings everywhere, knick-knacks and instruments of every variety spread interspersed throughout the long room, arranged in concentric circles around leather armchairs by the fire.

He walked amongst the trestle tables, running his hands over globes, astrolabes, a brass sextant, a gleaming cello, intricate works of ancient pottery, working his way inward towards the fireplace. In the grate, the remains of last night's fire still smouldered. His mind went blank as he moved through endless layers of odour and colour and texture. This had been his destiny.

*Could have been.*

Reaching the fireside, he stopped and stood in ringing silence. Somehow the crash-bangs elsewhere in the house and the accompanying cackling, along with the distant whip crack and booming of the war outside, only served to deepen the silence of this place. He closed his eyes and laid his hands upon the headrest of Alexander's armchair.

The others came hurtling down the corridor and started knocking over tables as they sloshed the buckets every which way, splashing their contents upon bookshelves, Persian rugs, canvasses, everywhere. All the while, James stood unmoving until they had circled the entire room and moved back to the doorway.

"Go," he said.

They left without a word, marching out and vanishing across the gardens. James waited until he could no longer see them through the gaps between the curtains, then searched his pocket for a lighter. The flame sputtered to life, and he held it there before him, staring into the undulating flame. Within it, he glimpsed the echo of a town ablaze—a town by the sea.

James sent the lighter spinning through the air, into the recesses of the room, where it clattered onto the partner's desk. The oil caught immediately in a muted *whumf,* zipping in both directions, climbing the walls and cloaking the bookcase in flame. The heat puckered the skin on his arms and neck, but he remained there by the chair as the flames caught, watching every single canvas bubble, every book curl.

He patted the headrest of the armchair and headed for the door. He took one last keepsake: a glimpse of the mantelpiece, upon which a handful of brightly wrapped boxes lay nested atop one another, tied with intricate ribbon; all melting, ablaze.

# FOURTH INTERLUDE

1

The homestead made its preparations in heavy silence. The cries of the wounded man filtered up from the cellar on occasion as Agatha and Helen tended to his stump, but nobody spoke. They had drilled for emergencies countless times, and all knew what to do. Dried food was bundled with the water, handfuls that would serve for only a single meal. They needed the spare weight for ammunition.

James's skin crawled. Handfuls of ants crawled under his clothes. His mind tortured him with Beth's dead staring face, the Moon burned to cinders. The message from Mrs McKinley had been hours ago. Anything could have happened since then. His stomach churned at the thought of Malverston's grubby hands on her skin—his mind replayed the night of the feast, before they had left the Moon: Beth dressed in a revealing slip, held close to Malverston's chest. The mayor's eyes fixed on James as he ran his tongue slowly up her cheek, like a slug crawling over a leaf.

James's hands shook without pause.

Lucian appeared at his side. "Hey," he muttered.

James felt himself return from a great distance. "What?"

Lucian glanced over his shoulder to make sure they wouldn't be overheard. "Can you do this? I'm with you, but if you're going to get in the way, maybe you should stay back."

James only stared.

Lucian's grip on him slackened. "Promise me that you won't put the others in danger."

"We're all in danger, Lucian."

"You know what I mean. We're all ready to do what we can—I know we'd give everything if it came to that, but… I need to know that your family comes first, James."

James opened his mouth to answer but found that he couldn't.

Understanding filtered into Lucian's gaze. "Okay." He picked up a few clips, stuffed them into his bag, and turned to leave.

"Lucian."

He paused, head arched over his shoulder.

"She is family."

After a beat, Lucian went out, and James was alone. As soon as the door came to a close, his legs went out from under him. Collapsing against the bench, air rushed from his lungs and he clutched the wood so tight that his fingers throbbed. Groaning, his entire body shuddered in the gloom. He could have stayed there, never moved again, because he was sure that whatever happened from here on, it was moving towards somebody getting hurt.

*Get up off your backside, Chadwick. Move, now.* The voice rose around him like salt vapours, rousing him by degrees until the shaking faded. "I'm coming," he said. "Time to go." He threw himself for the door, taking up his satchel as he went.

Outside, the others were saddling up. Alexander had swapped out his white horse for a ruddy brown mare, looking decidedly less grand than usual. Oliver and Agatha shared a mature steady mare, and the Creeks were lined along the back of their largest dark stallion. Lucian waited with his own reins in his hands. All their eyes trained on James as he emerged.

"What about…" James cleared his throat.

"I put 'im out. Gave him a mandrake infusion. He took it gladly," Agatha said.

James pulled himself up into his saddle. "His wrist…?"

Agatha shrugged. "Either it'll get infected or it won't. Probably, he's a dead man. Ain't got the energy to care right now."

"Fighting talk, my dear. My, my, things must be dire," Oliver said behind her. "Shall we?" Without waiting, he turned their mare in a wide circle and proceeded at a trot towards the gate.

"Last chance to stay," James said to Hector. He clocked the Creeks' look of defiance and nodded. "Remember: stay far back."

"We'll do what we have to," Helen said, the most mousy whisper James ever heard, so diaphanous it hurt to hear it.

Little Norman's big eyes watched from Helen's lap, confused and alert and afraid. He kept his gaze on James even as the stallion set off after the mare, turning his head to watch, the eternal stare of a newborn, until Hector's body blocked his line of sight.

James watched them go. Then it was just him, Lucian, and Alex. The three brothers shared a look, side by side, yet apart for the first time in memory. James realised then that there really was no going back, even if they won today.

He pushed the thought aside. There would be time for that later. Or there wouldn't.

He kicked his steed's sides, and then they were moving. Once they had cleared the gate and headed down the Old World motorway, heading south-east, James looked skywards. His pigeons circled overhead in their dozens.

"They never followed you like that before," Oliver said.

"They know," James said.

"How? They're jus' birds," Agatha said.

James said nothing. They would never understand.

Lucian's voice rose up from the rear, sounding a touch gravelly and bitter. "This shit's going to make me go grey."

*

The ride was agony. They pushed the horses mercilessly—too hard. A two-day journey somehow vanished under their hooves, compressed into less than thirty hours. By the time they passed the open plains of Dartmoor, their mounts' heads drooped towards the ground and their legs shivered with lactic acid build-up. Yet they pushed on, not daring to stop, never once climbing down to flex their aching legs. Every one of them endured the pain without a word.

James's mind ran on an endless loop, replaying what he had done down in the cellar. In hindsight it seemed that he had been but a spectator, beyond control of his own body; a body that had lashed out and cleaved another human being like one idly snaps a fallen twig. That couldn't have been him.

But he knew he had meant every inch of those cuts. In the cold bleak daylight, there was no denying that down in the cellar with the lantern light shuddering and the man's rancid breath wafting over his face, James had wanted blood.

He shook himself free at last in the middle of a national reserve, wild and windswept like Radden Moor, the nightmare from which he had fled. Well, not quite: Dartmoor was like a sunnier, more verdant cousin of that bleak grey place, like the yin to that haunted yang. Yet it was enough to bring it all rushing back: the aberrant coldness, the feeling of undefinable *otherness* that warped reality and sent the skin crawling.

That man, Fol, with his talk of prophecy and *true destiny* and the End sweeping the land once and for all. Had all of that really happened? Had he really crawled down into a hole in the ground—literally tumbled down a man-sized rabbit hole—to reach that strange place where shadows not-quite-human had lurked, and the bracketed torches had refused to extinguish themselves?

He knew it should have felt unreal. Yet there was no denying it had happened. He might lose the only thing in this world he cared for because of that steaming pile of craziness.

*Why, oh why, is life so bloody insane?* he thought, over and over, a maddening taunt in step with the horses' limping pace. Soon it shifted to something ever more torturous, but at least gave him strength: *We're coming. Hold on. We're coming.*

The final change in the beat of their journey came insidiously, weaving its way into the atmosphere of the exhausted convoy such that James couldn't be sure when it had first arisen. By the time he noticed the blanket of dread laying heavy over them all—dread of inescapable pain and strife and danger—it had already cemented itself in place.

At last, Oliver spoke, clearing his throat with a croaky *harumph.* "Plan?"

"McKinley," James said. "She'll have done something."

"The old woman?" said Lucian. "She's our secret weapon?"

"Once we're in, what do we…" Agatha sniffed. "What do we actually do? Jus' remember, we ain't no gunslingers."

"Whatever we have to," James said.

Alex's voice rose up, low and muttering: "No. We need to take the Moon, without tearing it apart."

They all turned to him. James tensed, teeth digging into his lip to keep himself from roaring.

"Come off it!" Lucian barked.

Alex's voice, calm and implacable. "If we don't, all this

is for nothing."

Tension wound up from the ether until James couldn't keep his neck from wrenching around. "Stop talking, now."

Alex stared back at him blankly.

James kept his gaze level until he was sure nobody would speak again. He turned back to face ahead and said, "If we have to burn the whole place to the ground to get her back, I'll do it myself."


## 2


Melanie shivered in the underbrush, using her mother's old rug for a blanket. Damp and bone-cold, she didn't dare move. The shivers had hit bad the past few times she had shifted. Staying still was better; tricking her body into thinking it was comfy.

How long had she been here? She had no idea. Everything had blurred together. When she blinked, the horizon remained burned onto her retinas, a vibrant pink line amongst momentary flashes.

Mel had returned to Mrs McKinley's cottage, staring at the musty cramped kitchen, trying to absorb the fact that she would never return, never bustle about making dandelion tea or tell her and Beth stories of the Old World. She was gone, like somebody had come along and wiped her away and left nothing but cobwebs and cutlery behind.

Was that how it always was? One moment the person was there in front of you, and the next moment they were just... just memories?

She wouldn't let that happen to Beth.

Big sisters were annoying, but losing one wasn't in the cards. Mel refused to let the mayor take her away.

Without the others though, she was alone. Anybody who had been strong had been cut up in the square. The mayor's men hadn't bothered to clear up the bodies. A few families had taken their own to the little graveyard beyond the peach fields, but others who had no families or had left behind only children, remained where they fell.

When she realised it was up to her to carry on, she felt like the weight of the sky had fallen on her shoulders. She wandered the streets, not caring if they took her again, staring without seeing, hoping that somebody—anybody—would come to her side. Nobody did.

One thing she had been sure of was that there was no point going home to Mum: Grace Tarbuck, the wet blanket of Newquay's Moon, doing the town's laundry, folding and scrubbing, day after day, her gaze fixed upon nothing and nobody. Mel couldn't bear going home to see her now. Nothing had changed since the slaughter: she'd find her mother sweeping the floors, content as you like, even if the door was still off its hinges and the stink of the Mayor's guards still hung in the air. If Mel had to see that, she'd probably kill her.

Instead she started knocking on doors. Pounding, until somebody came out to face her. That was what it took: to have a little girl standing there staring them in the eye. She held her slingshot in her hand the whole time with the stone she had picked out for the Mayor held tight. After canvassing the remaining adults in the town, she had something resembling an underground resistance.

It wasn't much, a dozen at most. It had taken her a while to realise just how many more they needed. But there were no more. Stewing, her jaw aching from clenching, she shot peaches down from the trees in the orchards, to keep hateful tears at bay.

The boy. That stupid boy who Beth had gone soppy over. He was coming now. The last time she saw him, she really had been ready to put a rock through his head. No stupid *boy* was going to take her big sister away from her.

But if it came between no sister and a sister cross-eyed and loved up…

She had taken to the hills a little before dark the first night, taking nothing more than the rug, water, and a loaf of bread. And her slingshot, of course. She hadn't moved since.

When the horizon finally flickered with movement, she didn't see it. So deeply was it burned into her mind's eye that she was blind to the real world. Eventually, blinking in disbelief, gasping and shivering, she ran on shuddering legs towards the line of people approaching on horseback.

*

James hit the ground running. Melanie Tarbuck leaped into his arms and wept immediately, shivering and damp and *small*… So small!

"It's okay, we're here now."

"Why did you let them take her away?" she wailed, pounding his chest.

"I'm sorry. It's—"

*Complicated*, he almost said. *No, it's not. It's not complicated at all. I let this happen.*

"—It's my fault. But I'm here to fix it." He glared at Alex as he spoke, who stared off at Newquay's Moon, which slowly grew to twinkling iridescence as fires were lit, and the sun set.

Mel shook her head, spraying hair against his face. "You can't, it's too late."

"It's never too late." Momentary panic shot through him and he held her at arm's length. "He hasn't…"

"No. She's alive."

James almost sagged with relief. "What then?"

"Th-th…"—tears ran freely down her cheeks—"they're all dead. The others. We tried to get her back, and the mayor, he…" She wept as only a child who has seen too much can weep: with eyes fully open, face uncreased, eyes shedding twin salty rivers. "He killed them. Mrs McKinley, he…"

James clenched his eyes shut against the mental image. "Beth?"

Mel's face crumpled. She collapsed against him anew. "He cut her."

James hugged her to him, staring blankly off into the middle distance. He sensed the others milling about, talking, planning. He didn't hear a word, consumed by a sinking in the pit of his belly that turned to bile, then fire, slowly climbing up into his chest and throat, threading his limbs and pressing behind his eyes. By the time Mel pulled away from him, he shook from head to toe.

"What are you going to do?" she said.

"I'm going to kill him," James said.

Her searching eyes seemed to find what they were looking for. She stepped back from his embrace, her tears staunched, and addressed them all: "They're ready: the last ones who'll fight. They're waiting for me—for us."

"Where?" Lucian said.

"Come with me."

Lucian gripped her sleeve. "Kid, once this starts, there won't be time to get you clear. Just tell us where and stay back."

James gathered himself. "Leave her be."

Lucian turned an incredulous eye on him. "James, she's just a kid."

"She's a Tarbuck. She'd come anyway."

Mel wiped the tears from her face roughly and squared off against the others. They visibly wilted under the coldness of her stare.

"Okay, fine." Lucian cleared his throat.

"They'll fight?" James asked.

"All of them. It's our last chance, isn't it?" Mel said.

"Yes. Last chance."

She nodded, looking back over her shoulder at the Moon, now twinkling dully as the sky faded from purple down to midnight blue.

"No!" Helen said. "We're coming with you."

A short distance away, Oliver and Agatha were in close conversation with the Creeks, their gesticulations placating. "Just stay here. This is far enough to be safe. You'll be able to see," Oliver implored.

"Watch what?" Hector said, his arms tight around Helen, who in turn clutched at Norman as he strained to jump forwards.

"Whether it's safe, or if…"

Both Creeks snorted in derision.

"If it's all said and done, and we can sneak down like a pair of sheep, you mean," Hector said.

"Or watch you die, up here, where it's *safe*."

"We're coming!" Norman yelled, a little too loud.

Agatha sighed, pinching the bridge of her nose. "Oh, bloody 'ell."

"Let them come." Alex bore all their shocked stares with steadfast calm. "There's no time. If we're going to take the Moon, we'll need everybody."

Oliver and Agatha mouthed wordlessly, looking to James for help.

James hesitated. "Can you do this? If things go wrong, then Norman…"

Hector gripped Norman's shirt tight, raising his chin skywards. "If you all die, I'll never forgive myself, and I won't have my son watch me stand by. If that means we all go together, then so be it."

"We're coming!" Norman's voice dropped to a hoarse whisper. "Please."

James searched them in turn. "Okay."

Lucian tensed beside him, but James laid a calming hand on his arm. "We all go together," he said. "Mel, lead on. Let's end this."

Mel fled, moving with the nimble skitter of a young deer, bounding over the clover towards the Moon. They followed more laboriously, burdened by ammunition. Soon the town's lights splashed over their faces, and they got down on their stomachs.

"Just remember one thing," James whispered to Alex, drawing alongside him. "This isn't about the Moon. This is about her."

Alex's face said everything that needed to be said. In the half-light drifting through windows and under doorways, it sent a shiver up James's spine.

*He still thinks I'm his Chosen One. Even now, he thinks I'll come back. Without me, he has no mission; and what wouldn't Alexander Cain do for his mission?*

Squashing a tremble of unease, James crept forwards, and they made their way into the town as darkness fell in earnest.

# XVIII

Allie dove into an alley barely wide enough for her to squeeze into and yanked the little girl in behind her, gasping for breath. The girl clung to her side in the musty darkness, mute and wide-eyed. She peered out at the street, both ends of which had been blasted to pieces. Allie took a moment to steel herself and stifle the scream of unreasoning panic frothing at the back of her throat and gripped the girl's shoulder.

"Hey, it's okay, sweetie. We're okay. We're fine."

She gabbled for a few moments before she managed to stop herself and crouch down. She searched for something to say, anything that might displace the terror between them. "Tell me your name," she breathed, trying to hold the gaze of those wide, staring eyes, framed by flame-red hair.

"Billy." She spoke with an unfamiliar lilt—Allie had never heard an accent like that.

*She's from far away. God, what are you doing here, sweetie?*

"Billy, I'm Allie. I know this is scary, I know it is. I promise, I'll get you out and we'll both be all right."

Through her own panic, she saw that the girl looked shockingly unafraid. She clung to Allie, but there were no tears in her eyes, nor did she shake as Allie shook.

"Okay," she said.

"Okay," Allie said, taking a steadying breath. Somehow the girl gave her strength.

*That's the wrong way around…*

Billy said, "Where's Norm?"

"I don't know. Are you sure they're here?"

"They told me to stay in the hills but I…" She seemed to drift off a little, her eyes trailing the bottom of her sockets.

Allie gripped her tight as another explosion rocked the walls, which actually seemed to flex with the sheer force of the blast. Somewhere beyond in the street, grit and pebbles showered brickwork and shattered windows. A wave of heat rushed into the alley, and Allie knew they couldn't stay. "We have to get out. Get out, get out," she said, looking both ways along the alley as though hoping to see a glowing exit before her.

She took Billy by the hand again and, keeping low, took her back out into the street. The shelling had lessened, and the chorus of screaming had faded to occasional shrieks. Forty years of accumulated decay and dry wood in the uninhabited parts of the city provided the perfect tinder bed to set the entire skyline ablaze.

Inching towards the end of the street, skirting chunks of blasted cobblestone and pressing her back to garden walls, she peered into the junction. A parted roadblock lay ahead;

cars she recognised all too well. High Street. "No," she grated. She punched the wall, ignoring the pain. "No!"

How could she have got so turned around? She had led them right back to where she had started.

By the roadblock, people moved back and forth, cast into silhouette by the undulating fiery rooftops behind them. A group of hunched figures cowered at their feet. To one side, yet more silhouettes, those of three wooden crosses, twelve feet high and surrounded by hay.

"Oh, dear God," she whispered.

"What?" Billy said, wriggling by her side.

Allie held her back. "Nothing, honey. Nothing… Come on, we have to go. Let's get out of here."

She was on the verge of struggling to her feet and heading back the way they'd come when a single prone figure, not far away, resolved into focus. "Oh…" Her throat closed, and all the fight went out of her legs. Slowly she crumpled to the ground. "Oh…"

Heather lay in a pile on the ground, staring blankly upwards, her clothes blackened by blood.

Allie wept, shuddering all over, unable to break her gaze away from the sight. It wasn't until Billy gripped her sleeve and tugged that she broke out of it. She was about to push herself away when she was stalled a second time.

Sarah sat among the prisoners, her hands bound behind her back. Her face was set, scoured clean by a smouldering stare that could have etched glass. As Allie watched, Sarah was hauled up by an aquiline, predatory figure and hauled towards the nearest of the crosses.

Allie and Billy were close. Sarah would have to pass them to get to the cross. Allie felt her pulse then, a visceral electric thump in the meat of her chest; not racing, but strong; suddenly she felt all the fear melt away, cast aside and flattened by a rolling swell of rage. "Stay here," she said and peeled Billy's hand off her own. Billy said something, but she didn't hear. She had eyes only for the waddling duo in front of her, silhouettes morphing into struggling flesh and blood.

Sarah's captor became a man with a peaky, sick face, devoid of colour or trace of humanity. Where his eyes should have been there seemed to be only dark holes in his skull. Upon his cheek hung a bloody bandage that was almost certainly gangrenous.

Suddenly Billy struggled behind her with such force that even Allie's seething focus carved in two. "It's him!" Billy hissed. "It's the monster."

"Who?"

"The monster." Billy's lips pulled back from her teeth. "He took Grandpa away." A disturbing smile crept onto her face. "I cut him good."

Allie looked back at the man. The bandage didn't quite cover the great slash upon his cheek, which had probably sliced right through to the innards of his mouth. "You did that?"

Billy reached into her belt and brought out a small paring knife; small, but wickedly sharp. "Uh huh."

Allie gripped her hand afresh. "Billy, that's my friend. I have to get her. If I..." She swallowed heavily. "Run. You keep running until you get out."

"No!" Billy hissed, gripping her so hard that Allie flinched. "No, look."

They looked back into the depths of the old city. The clouds had vanished behind a veil of black smoke, sending the flaming skyline into brilliant contrast. The flames reached the Stour and arched over the still waters, great licking towers of conflagration leaning out into space, waving fiery digits at the opposite bank. All of Canterbury would be ablaze in a matter of minutes.

They had to get out now, before they were cut off. Already they were surrounded on two sides. Without knowing which streets were occupied by the invaders or had been shelled, their options waned by the moment.

*Time to go, Allie. Get the girl out. Find the other kids and get out.*

But she didn't move. Frozen upon the cobbles, something congealed in her gut. The figures ahead were suddenly maddening, inhuman things—the only object that seemed real was Sarah, wriggling against her restraints, a fire burning in her eyes to match that consuming the city.

"Billy, you heard what I said," Allie muttered. She took the girl's hand gently from her shoulder and rose onto her haunches. Before Billy could protest, she launched herself forwards, following the garden wall out into plain sight. The others' milling meant that she went unnoticed in her approach. Sarah saw her long before her captors.

When their eyes met, Sarah's gaze filled with defeat, as though she had just watched Allie gunned down or stabbed to death alongside Heather. So powerful and unfettered was that expression that Allie almost stopped, and only kept going through sheer momentum. Then she was on her knees and scrabbling at the bindings around Sarah's wrist, madly pulling at the knots.

"What are you doing here?" Sarah seethed.

"Saving your sorry backside. Keep still."

"Go. Get out, now."

The knots were tight, expert. Her ministrations had done nothing but tighten them. Cursing, glancing fretfully at the others' turned backs, she leaned over for a better look.

Sarah's air of resigned dignity had shattered, giving way to simmering fear. "Allie, if you don't go right now, they'll get you too, and trust me—trust me, you do not want to stick around here."

Allie kept pulling, cursing. She knew she had already lingered too long. Now every moment she went unnoticed was a gift.

A hoarse whisper in her ear: "Please help me. Help me!" The woman with whom Sarah was tied back to back leaned over, her mouth a smear of mucus and tears.

Allie didn't reply, working on the bindings. If she could work out the knot, she would free them all. Dad had been a dab hand at knots, always showing her all kinds of hitches and bends at the kitchen table when she had been small. What had they been called? Sheep Bend? Sailor's hitch? Which was which?

*Why didn't I ever pay attention to anything?*

"Please! You have to help us. They'll kill us all!" the

woman squeaked.

"Shut up. They'll hear you," Sarah muttered.

"You can't leave me. Hurry up and get us out of here!"

"I said shut up."

The woman's eyes bulged and flicked to the crosses. "I won't go. They won't take me. No, no, no!"

Suddenly the woman jerked, pulling her feet towards her and dragging her bottom over the cobbles. The bindings jerked in Allie's hands and tightened to impenetrable nubs. Sarah jerked backwards with a curse.

Allie looked to the woman with horror as her legs jerked desperately, and the three of them jerked sideways again.

"Stop it! Stop it now or you'll kill us all," Sarah hissed.

Allie picked at the knots with her fingernails, but they had become far too small. "Shit!"

"Allie, go," Sarah said.

"No."

Another jerk.

"Stop that!"

The woman wept wordlessly and jerked purposefully now, as though heading for the alley. Despite the commotion, they had moved but a spare few inches.

"I can't…" Horror seeped into Allie's chest, dripping ice-cold onto her stomach. "I can't…"

Sarah's gaze sought hers. "It's okay. Go."

"No. I'm staying—"

Allie felt the moment she was spotted as though an arrow had struck her. The pressure of a human gaze pinged in some primitive part of her mind; the very same sense that sings in the dark when one is not alone.

No cries of alarm came, nor the clatter of running footsteps. The main body of attention was still on the straw being piled around the crosses. Yet she had been spotted. There was only one thing for it: she didn't bother looking away, just kept working. She wouldn't leave, not now, not if there was the slightest chance. Her fingers found nothing but smooth rope, nor a single break where the twine had folded. Her vision blurring with tears, she devolved into a shuddering wreck. Sarah's head came down gently and rested on hers, and the both of them waited for whatever might come.

*Snick.*

Allie almost screamed as a blade shot into sight, expecting it would momentarily be embedded in her face. Then she noticed how short the blade was, though sharp, and the soft chubbiness of the hand gripping the handle. Billy crouched beside her, pushing her way roughly between Sarah and the sobbing woman, and began sawing at the bindings without a word. There was a dull thud, and then the bound women's arms fell slack, and Billy was yanking at loose twine, casting it aside.

Time snowballed in a heady whirl. They were free! But they had been spotted. Somebody, somewhere, was very close.

"Go, go, go!" Allie yelled, abandoning stealth and heaving at Sarah and the woman with everything her muscles had left. They made it to a half crouch when blinding pain exploded in her stomach, as something very solid sank into her midriff. She had time to glimpse a fist pull away from her body before she hit the ground, and all around her everything was in motion. She crawled into a ball and watched the figures whirling above her.

The man with the sick face cast Sarah's fellow prisoner and Billy to one side with careless flicks of his fist. He had eyes only for Sarah.

Sarah had adopted a boxer's stance. She seemed ready to take on an army all on her own, but there was no denying the obvious: though small, the man had at least fifty pounds on her, and he moved with the easy assurance of one who had fought all his life.

Sarah lashed out with a wild fist, and he stepped back so that her fist went whistling by harmlessly. He gripped her free hand, span her around, and licked her neck from shoulder to the bottom of her ear. "Silly girl," he uttered, a high-pitched sigh, eerily clear despite the commotion, shelling and city-consuming blaze.

Allie found herself standing before she knew what was happening, somehow uncurling her body and diving forwards with a yell born of adrenaline and wild abandon. She hit them off balance, and three of them toppled in a spinning pile of clawing limbs, skittering over the cobbles. As they span and a hand gouged at her cheek, narrowly missing her eye, she caught sight of others, dark shapes running towards them from the crosses.

Allie fought madly, punching, scratching, wheeling her arms every which way in a desperate bid to separate herself. Beside her, Sarah's own clawed hands worked away at the stinking thing under them.

*"Over there!"*

*"Get 'em!"*

The cries reached down into Allie and wrenched at her insides. For a moment it looked as though between them, they might beat the man into submission, pummelling his chest and arms and neck like crazed apes. Then Allie's head exploded with stars and she toppled sideways, her ear singing and gorge rising in her throat. The world span, and amidst the medley of confusion she picked out fire and slanted running shadows. Then rank breath snorted into her face, and a livid pair of murderous eyes bored into her own. Hands closed around her throat and tightened.

*This is it.*

Allie realised in a heart-stopping moment that there was no getting away from this. This was no fairy tale. The life was about to be choked from her and nobody was going to come riding in to save her.

The world seemed a remote and inconsequential place from which she was rapidly receding. Pain throbbing in her cheek dropped away, and she realised she was dying; the very fact that she didn't mind was the most horrific thing of all, reduced to an academic curiosity. Shadows drew in from all sides—whether by her narrowing tunnel of vision or the approaching figures from the crosses, she couldn't tell.

*This is what it's like to die*, she thought peacefully.

A roar of rage reached her from a great distance, and the pressure around her throat was gone. Allie coughed explosively, surging up as fresh air hit her lungs, and gagged.

The darkness flew back as though a curtain had been torn away, and before her the man writhed on the ground. Upon his back, riding him like a horse, was Billy, her flushed rounded face drawn into a terrifyingly adult snarl.

As the man struggled to his feet, waving his hands over his head, Billy stabbed down with her paring knife, jabbing at his fingers, his shoulders, and his scalp.

"You bitch, you bitch, I knew it was you!" he roared, twirling on the spot. His hands flailed until he caught hold of Billy's heel, and then with a single merciless yank, he ripped her from his back and sent her sailing through the air. She hit the cobbles hard, rolling end over end in a boneless heap, and he was upon her within the moment, eyes bulging.

Allie stumbled, fell, saw yet more stars. The woman to whom Sarah had been tied had run screaming—right into the figures approaching from the crosses. They took her to the ground with a single jab from a rifle butt and kept coming. Any moment now and none of this would matter, for they would be surrounded. She had to get him off Billy and go, just go—somewhere. She got up again, managed a few steps, fell again. She spat vomit onto the cobbles and touched her head. Blood came away with a few strands of hair. The world revolved, a graceful, terrible dance. Allie could only watch as the man beat down with his fists, consuming the tiny girl's figure with his gritty, bloodied bulk. With unmistakable joy, he pinned Billy down and reached for the curved blade at his belt.

Sarah collided with him with the force of a freight train,

and they went end over end on the cobbles, not scrabbling at one another this time, but both rendered utterly senseless by the force of the impact.

Allie crawled over the cobbles to reach Billy, shaking her until her eyes rolled back to focus. "Come on, come on!"

The man was already on top of Sarah, his knife already unsheathed and put to work. "Run!" Sarah screamed. "Run, run!" As she wailed, the knife cut down in rapid slashes at her face and forearms. Criss-crossing, merciless slashes.

Allie cried aloud as Sarah's skin split in a thousand places. Closing her eyes, she tore Billy up from the ground and ran. The world turned, still, upending every other moment, but somehow she kept her feet.

"Run!" Sarah bawled in her wake. "Run, run, run, RUUUUN!"

*

Sarah shivered on the ground. Pain, everywhere. Her face was numb, a mass of crackling nerves. She had no idea how long the cutting had gone on. All the while, Jason's livid, bloodshot eyes had glared down into hers, hungry and glittering. Now, curled in a ball, she waited on her side while those around her talked.

"They're gone!"

"I want that little brat found. She's mine!"

"I tell you, they're just gone. Ran towards the fire, didn't they?"

A pause.

"Towards the fire?"

"Yeah."

A half-amused huff. "Stupid bitch."

Jason's face popped into view, blocking out the featureless sky, and grinned. His face was already swelling from the pounding he'd taken, but it only added to his menace; just another accoutrement to the seeping wound upon his cheek.

*Not human*, Sarah thought. *He's not human.*

His fist closed around her shirt and lifted her up as though she was but a feather. "Time to face justice," he sighed, a sickly delight radiating from him into the others, who grinned in turn.

Head lolling, Sarah caught sight of the woman she'd been tied to, lifted lifelessly up onto the bed of hay surrounding the nearest cross. She realised then that she glided over the ground, moving towards the central cross. Her heart gave a great lurch as some primal fear locked into place, something her hazy mind couldn't quite process.

She was being dragged, her feet bouncing over the cobbles and her armpits painfully hitched up by two pairs of hands. Expressionless men hauled her towards the hay bales as she bled from countless places, leaving a trail of scarlet droplets in her wake.

*I thought I'd die at home, in bed, an old, old lady.*

There wasn't time for more thoughts. By the time even that single coherent musing had coalesced, she was being lifted onto the hay, and Jason hopped up behind the post, and yanked her against it, pulling her hands behind her back. At her flanks, upon the other two crosses, her fellow captives screamed shrilly.

People gathered around below as though they didn't hear a thing, frank curiosity and bated excitement hanging about them like a stink.

She fought to the last, but in moments she was stuck fast to the central upright. Jason stepped around the hay and observed her with something resembling lust. His hand rose up to her cheek and trailed the bleeding slashes, his lip caught between his teeth. "How does it feel to know there's nobody coming?" he said, almost as though to himself. His gaze was upon her, yet not; he stared only at the flesh. "That you're all alone in the world, and there's nothing you can do to stop the darkness?"

Sarah stared back at him, squeezing the last of her energies into bringing the world into sharp focus. "I'm not alone."

*Robert is out there.*

In all her struggles, she had almost forgotten him. Thinking of him now almost broke her in half, a straight fracture from top to tail.

Something behind Jason's face twitched. She knew he saw it in her eye: he hadn't broken her. She would never break, not so long as she drew breath and Robert waited out there for her. She would never stop fighting her way back to him.

Jason stepped down from the bales and backed up, addressing the small crowd. The distant shelling shifted: a momentary respite rang loud in the ash-strewn air, and then fresh explosions rang out, altogether louder and, somehow, more solid. It took Sarah a moment to realise all the shells now landed upon the cathedral. The centuries-old stonework burst into florets of stony fragments, showering the air with the craftsmanship of masters long dead. The shells landed in their dozens, and in a matter of seconds the spires were reduced to rubble, and the beauteous stained-glass windows succumbed to shrapnel.

For an errant moment, she thought she might have heard hundreds of screams emanating from within.

Jason took a flaming torch, just one of many being lighted in the crowd, and held his arms up high. "Witness, all, justice done to those who would have us all dead and buried. Justice. Justice!" He turned to face her, a wicked glint in his eye: he didn't believe a word of it.

The crowd, however, was sent into hysterics, roaring, "Justice! Justice!" Fingers pointing, faces livid and searing. The encircling crowd stepped closer and lowered their torches into the hay.

"Please, don't do this. We're innocent," cried the woman to Sarah's left.

The woman to her right kicked and thrashed, weeping. "I want to go home. I wanna go home, I wanna go home. *Please!*"

Sarah said nothing, just watched the torches descend into the bales at her feet, which caught the instant the flames touched them. The heat bloomed under her, and smoke rose up in choking plumes. After that she focused on Jason, keeping his gaze, boring down into him as though she could punch through the back of his head.

One way or another, he was going to remember her.

By the time the pain started, the smoke was too thick to see the crowd anymore. Falling away into darkness, starved of air by searing smoke, she shifted her gaze to the horizon, searching for her husband. Her gaze was met by a bare horizon, except the crumbling spires of the distant cathedral.

# XIX

Billy screamed in the firestorm. Flames reared up in all directions, arcing between dried-up houses flanking either side of the street. Behind her, one house collapsed with a calamitous groan, pouring flaming debris across her last route of escape.

One moment Allison had been pulling in a rollicking dash that threatened to send them both rolling into the dirt with the Bad Men at their backs. The next, the fire had been everywhere, the Bad Men had been gone, and Allison had stopped. By the time Billy struggled from her grasp, Allie was mumbling to herself, her eyes rolling in her head and her legs bowing. Billy had managed to grab hold of her just as Allie sank to the floor. The grown-up was far too heavy; she barely managed to keep Allie's head from cracking against the cobbles.

Presently she crouched beside Allie's prone form, shaking her shoulders. The flames were monstrous, like beasts made of hellfire, cutting off all escape as they pressed in closer. There was nowhere to go. They were trapped.

"Allie! Allie, wake up!"

It was so hot and the air so dry that she could hear her hair crackling. Each breath burned her lungs as though the glowing embers were airborne and creeping down her throat. The flames licked closer, swirling and dancing with terrible choreographed grace.

Allie groaned, her eyes rolling. The blood on the side of her head had congealed into a dark clot.

"We have to go. Get up, *get up!*"

Allie gave a soft sigh, and she moved no more.

Smoky fumes fingered their way into Billy's chest and took the world cartwheeling away.

*I promised Daddy I would keep going. Daddy.*

His face appeared in her mind's eye, and new strength leaped up inside her. She pushed *out* with her mind, and the Light inside her sparked to life. Reaching through the flames as though they were but puffs of cotton, she searched the city—though for what she had no idea.

*Pull. Pull.*

Pull what?

She didn't know, but she flexed her mental muscle nonetheless, and she felt something—no, everything—draw in towards her. Something intangible yet irrefutably *there* sucked into a sphere about her head, swirling and twinkling and cold.

Smoke clogged her throat, and her eyes streamed with acrid tears. It was getting harder and harder to keep her head raised. She flexed once more, and another surge of cold gathered in around her. The cloud of otherworldly death the army had cast over the city like a veil, yielded to her command. Head thrumming and crackling, only distantly aware of blood trickling from her nose, Billy held back the flames. The heat receded, just, held at bay by the most tenebrous barrier.

*No such thing as magic, Daddy? I hope you can see this now.*

That barrier began fading as soon as she pulled it into being. Each breath came with a crackling wheeze in her chest. The flames sapped her strength as fiery tongues lashed out.

Then something. A pique somewhere on an internal compass, on the edge of deep eternal nothing. Dark figures racing towards her. As Billy's head touched Allie's chest and she blinked blearily, she picked out a horse at full gallop ahead, then another. In moments they went from undulating fire demons to solid, yelling men, and then they were reaching down, lifting her into the air. A face swam from the ether, a face she knew well.

*Norm.*

Somewhere, perhaps very close, perhaps far away, more horses were racing past, surging down the street and leaping over the burning rubble. Allison was lifted beside another rider.

A distant, warped voice: "We're surrounded! Where do we go?"

Taking a deep breath, Billy dredged one last flex from the base of her being, casting the bubble of Frost down the road. A gale whistled forth, and the fire along the street whittled down to chest height.

That same warped voice: "There! Go now!"

Then they were moving, the air grew clearer, and they left the fire in their wake. Yet the explosions, the terrible rending of stone and earth, never faded, not even when they left the city behind.

*

Norman rode hard into the hills, cresting the foothills to the south-east. All around scrabbled the few who had managed to escape the city: some of the militia, a gaggle of wailing kids, and some families who had removed their homes' barricades and fled before the fires had started. So few, perhaps eighty. There had been eight hundred people in New Canterbury.

Ahead, Lucian climbed down from his horse with Allie cradled in his arms and laid her down gently in the grass.

"Is she all right?" Norman yelled.

*I promised I would come back to her. I promised.*

She stirred feebly.

"She's fine, Norman," Lucian said, his lips white as marble.

Allie's eyes fluttered open, and she sat up slowly in the grass.

Norman let loose a puff of breath and sagged on the saddle. He could only sit there for a moment, trembling and coughing on ash and a gob of panic stuck in his throat. Steeling himself, he dropped to the ground and pulled Billy after him. Sooty and limp, she slid down into the grass but found her feet.

"Wha-whassapanin?" she mumbled, rubbing her eyes with her knuckles.

Norman crouched and took her into his arms. "Are you okay?"

"Mmm…"

"Billy, what did you do?"

His heart was pounding like a rabbit's; not only because he had been afraid he could have let the kid die, but because now he knew what she really was. They had been springing the city's horses from the stables when a horn had blared in his head; a whistling fit to deafen him. His chest shrank to a prune, and he felt the Frost cut at his bones. He had known it was her as if she had screamed in his ears. She had wielded it like dough. He had followed the gale right to her.

The Jester hadn't lied. If she had that kind of power, maybe she was the one to save them. If she had died, there would have been nothing to stop the Frost from consuming the city and everyone in it.

"Billy… talk to me."

"Norm?"

"Yeah, it's me, kid."

"It's too late…" Her bleary eyes turned to the city. "It's too big. Too much. So much… cold."

Norman turned to the burning city and knew he was seeing the same thing as her: a crushing chill, overbearing, a thousand-fold greater than any he had felt before.

*How could that be so? How can we be looking at a city on fire and feel nothing but cold?*

He didn't know. But he did know that his entire body

felt as though he were encased inside an iceberg.

Did the others see it? Feel it?

He didn't think so, not in the same way. But they felt something; he could see it in their faces. Not only those upon the hillside, but those of the enemy, which now spilled from the ruin of New Canterbury on the far side, out into the crop fields.

The shelling had stopped. Without the accompanying yells of battle, gunfire, falling rubble or explosions, the fire sounded eerily peaceful. Blank expressions trained upon the city and the sky, searching for something just out of sight: the source of an unsettling shiver. Shadow had fallen over everything, cast by nothing and never quite touching the ground, merely hanging like smog, slowly spreading, feeding off the fear and destruction and pain and death.

"This is bad," Norman said. "They've started something…"

"It's the End," Billy said, sounding far away still. "Soon. It spreads from here."

"To where? London?"

She ignored him, her glassy eyes on the city. "I can't stop it now. He's too strong."

*James. It's him who started all this.*

Norman gripped her hard, and her gaze crept slowly over to him. "He's not won yet—"

An earth-shattering *crack* rang through the air, and every pair of eyes—upon the hillside and in the fields—turned to face the cathedral. The spires had long ago succumbed to the bombardment and lay now as only so much rubble in the surrounding grounds. What remained was a smoking windowless husk, scorched stone made shapeless, pockmarked and trembling. A great well of dust billowed from the northern edge, obscuring the burning city behind.

Those on the hillside cried out and gathered on the crest, none daring to stray any closer. Hands were held to chests, arms wrapped around anybody who would have them, and a single unified breath held painfully.

*No. This can't happen*, Norman thought.

He was sure of it: so grand a masterpiece of Old World engineering could bear anything. All his life it had been a symbol of the unchanging tapestry of the world, immune to their comings and goings.

The terrible sound came again, a whip crack that shot over the landscape and blanketed all else. A black fissure unzipped the entire superstructure across its centre, and the emanating dust built to an unending billow. The two halves of the cathedral, ever so gradually, separated.

Norman could only watch, his mouth ajar, as the roof split into countless sections, a spiderweb of fractures lancing through the masonry. Then with dreamlike slowness, the slabs fell inwards, dropping down into the pulpits and transepts, the magnificent delicate carvings, and all those who prayed at the pews. The walls followed in short order, toppling inwards, and the entire cathedral vanished in a monstrous cloud of ash and dust.

Those on the hillside fell silent and dropped to their knees in the grass.

"How many people were in there?" Norman said.

Allie answered weakly from nearby, a whisper on the wind. "Hundreds."

*

Alexander had gone numb. Motes of chalky dust accrued on the crop-heads by his side, upon his clothes, his lips. Dust that had moments ago been the cathedral, and his friends.

*Agatha…*

He felt so weak, as though he could just fade away from the world. Judging by the gnawing cold in his chest, underneath the stabbing well of heartache, he suspected that wasn't far from the truth. The dark smudge hanging over the city grew still, weaving its fingers over the last of the burning rooftops, encompassing the city proper and spreading out into the fields and forests, bridging the river as though it wasn't even there.

"It's over." Charlie stared after the city with a gaunt expression.

Alexander would have felt sadness at the first sight of him here, amongst all this, if he had any feelings left to feel. The doe-eyed young man they had brought into their clinic so short a time ago—just a kid—who they could have saved, if they had had the mind. It hadn't had to be this way. None of it had. He had failed even this stranger.

"Not yet," James said, thigh deep in the crop heads.

Alexander yelled at the top of his voice, struggling forwards against the guards, but all that emerged around his gag was a muffled warble.

The wicked leering creature who James kept for a pet loped from the city, away from High Street, where a blaze of hay bales had been ignited. "I see runners," he hissed hungrily. "Give me a hundred men. We'll finish this." He started off to flank those on the distant hilltops, but James raised a hand.

"No. Leave them."

"They're chickenshit cowards. Let me finish them!" The creature's eyes were livid and bulging.

"No. We go." James didn't once look away from the burning skyline. "Their debt is paid."

*I hope somebody's over there. Somebody*, Alexander thought.

But what could anybody do now? London alone remained, they were outnumbered five to one, and outgunned.

"Isn't it done?" the young man said. "Can't we stop this, now? Cain's mission is done."

James said nothing.

The young man stumbled through the grass. "I've stuck with you. I did everything you asked because I believed that we stood for something."

"We stand for balance. Everybody standing here has been wronged."

Charlie crept closer, hesitated, then hissed, "Everybody stands here because you would have killed them if they ran."

Again, silence.

Alexander watched the creature unsheathe his knife

behind Charlie's back, an ugly and disgusted glower about him. He began to inch closer until James waved him to be still—he complied, just, a feral bare-toothed sneer taking over his face.

James took a long breath. "We're going to stop this ever happening again. As long as there remain those who remember the old ways, this world is in danger."

*Liar,* Alexander thought. *I feel what's coming, what you've brought to this place. So does the kid. It's not justice, and it's not revenge. It's darkness and pain, and—and nothingness. You bring the End with you. And you know it.*

James laid a hand on Charlie's shoulder. He turned his back to the city and whispered—though loud enough for Alexander to hear: "Question me again, and you'll join them."

He replaced his balaclava and trudged away through the grass. Passing by, he fixed Alexander with a dead, shark-eyed stare—glittering with the reflected blaze of New Canterbury—then was consumed by the ranks of his army.

Charlie took a shuddering breath and tightened before facing the others. A momentary flicker of disquiet cracked his outwards calm when he saw Jason only paces away, his gore-streaked knife still in hand and his feral leer very much in place. With visible effort he composed himself and called out to the ranks in the fields. Slowly, inexorably, the great bestial machine tore its gaze from the city and turned its back, heading back into the forest, heading east.

Alexander's guards turned him away from his home and pushed him through the fields, his white tunic splashed across its front with a figure painted in red ochre: the sigil of a pigeon.

"Walk, *messiah*," the creature hissed in his ear.

Tears fell into the grass as Alexander marched into the east, followed by creeping tendrils of cold and darkness.

*

Norman waited until the army had vanished before breaking his gaze from the fields. His mind raced with wild thoughts of escape routes, of how he could rally the refugees into the forest. He quickly realised it was fruitless. If the army came for them, there would be no running.

Those who had escaped lay crumpled in the grass like broken birds. As one stunned being, they watched the fires consume everything and slowly burn themselves out, all they had built and come to know and love, turned to so much ash. A great streak of darkness spread across the fields like treacle, a snail's trail left by the departed army. The flocks of pigeons pursued close behind.

Norman knew they all felt it now: the cold. Everywhere people shivered despite the heat.

"Any sign of Alex?" Norman said.

Lucian paused beside him, gaunt faced. "Nobody saw him all day."

"Maybe he ran."

"He wouldn't have done that." Lucian's throat worked. "James has him." He didn't wait for a reply, just headed away to watch the city, alone.

Once the last of James's forces disappeared into the trees, Norman couldn't look at the fires any more. Staggering through the grass, he knelt beside Allie, shame filling him to the brim. He couldn't bear the look she gave him as he approached, that steady non-accusing smile.

*She should hate me. How can she even look at me?*

"I said I'd come home."

"You did."

"Too late."

Still weak, she cupped his face. "You're here now. Tell me it was worth it. Tell me it wasn't for nothing."

Norman swallowed. "I don't know. I still don't know."

She looked pained. "The radio message… the Scots…"

Norman shook his head.

"Nothing?"

Norman looked over his shoulder at Billy, who still stared into space, muttering to herself. "I'm not sure."

Allie followed his gaze. "Who is she?"

"She might be our only chance."

"I don't understand."

Norman suppressed a grimace. "I gave up on that a long time ago."

Lucian stepped into view. He seemed in a trance. "Robert," he said quietly.

Norman drew a long sigh of relief. They had become separated in the firestorm; Robert had been like a man possessed. If he had survived, perhaps they were not lost yet.

The glimmer of hope winked out as Allie's eyes filled with tears, looking down the hill over Norman's shoulder.

"Norman…," she muttered, and the tears spilled over down her cheeks.

Norman turned to look down the hill, everything seemed to stop.

Robert Strong walked slowly up the hill towards them, his face utterly expressionless. In his arms, a figure hung limp, arms and legs swinging to the beat of his stride. One side of the body had been charred to uniform blackness, even the fire-red locks of hair. One remaining eye stared sightlessly, forever blind to the grey skies.

Robert laid Sarah in the grass, placing her down as though nestling an infant into a cradle, and sat back on his haunches. He reached out to touch her, but his fingers froze an inch from her blackened shirt. Instead they hovered, tracing the contours of her stomach, and gradually his lips parted. He took one breath, then another, deeper, and another. After that the heaving started, great breathless gasps that ripped away the sheer enormity of his frame and left in its place a small child.

"Norman," Allie wept quietly. "You…"

"I know," Norman said, rising. It took everything he had not to look at Sarah, walking through the grass to Robert's side. He crouched down and tried to ignore the horrific stench of cooked flesh—

*Like bacon*, an insidious part of his mind chimed.

"Robert… Robert, I'm sorry."

Robert didn't react, just sucked in gasp after gasp.

"I'm so sorry. You did everything you could. And she saved so many. All these people are here because of her."

Norman steeled himself for what had to come next—for he had to win Robert back now, before grief consumed him. "I need your help. There's no time. They're moving."

Robert stood slowly, giving no indication of being aware of Norman's presence. His entire body had turned milky pale under his coffee-coloured skin. He stood over Sarah with fists bunched, taking those same long, gasping breaths.

"Robert—"

Robert ran. Before Norman could react he launched away, skirting the crest of the hillside, charging around the edge of the city in pursuit of the departed army.

"Norman!" Allie cried.

Norman was on his feet before he had fully appreciated what was happening. People still dead-eyed and distant tumbled aside as he made after Robert, who bulldozed his way through the crowd and was gone, gaining ground by the second.

*He's so fast! I'll never catch him.*

Robert stood two heads taller than Norman and was animated by pure rage. By the time Norman cleared the crowd, Robert had vanished into the forest. It was a lonely thirty-second race to the gloomy forest, with only his own panting and the crunch of his footfalls to fill the silence.

*The city is so quiet, now*, he thought. *As soon as the fires go out, you'd never know it had been there at all.*

He plunged into the forest, slapping branches from his path. "Robert, stop! You have to come back."

Crashing up ahead, receding ever farther away.

"Robert, please. We need you!" Twigs tore at his cheeks,

gouging for his eyes, and gnarled roots threatened to trip him up and sever a tendon.

He skidded to a halt as the trees ended. Robert stood not far from where the canopy's shadow ended. Peering over his shoulder, Norman caught sight of two dozen horses grazing in a small clearing; those they had freed from the stables. Forest lay on all sides, a small glade in the hills where neither smoke nor shadow had yet reached. The sight of such pristine, peaceful scenery stabbed at Norman like a hot blade.

"She's… she's gone, Norman," Robert said, a broken whisper that couldn't have been further from his usual deep tenor.

Norman made to comfort him, beg him, to do something, but he couldn't find a single word worth uttering. He could only watch the horses, spooked but feeding, watching him closely.

Robert sank to his knees and bunched his hands into claws. His breath came in seething gasps once more, building in intensity until he threw back his head and roared, an unending bellow that seemed to tear open the skies and shake the entire forest. Birds exploded from the canopy, and for a brilliant moment the sky was alive with them in their teeming thousands, whirling and scattering away into the grey nothing. By the time it finally ended, Robert seemed a wisp of his former self, stunted and bent double on the ground.

Norman found strength enough to step forwards. The horses, having spooked and regrouped on the other side of the glade, stood ready to take flight, no longer grazing.

"Nothing any of us say or do can change what happened. But we have the choice to keep going. This isn't over."

Robert shook his head, tears beading on the tip of his nose. "I can't, Norman. I'm done."

"They're on the move, right now. In hours they'll be in London, and then… then it really will be over."

"There's nothing to do," Robert spat venomously. "We're *done*."

Norman gripped his shoulder, suddenly seething. "No. No, I refuse to believe that. I haven't been put through this crap all my life just to be told that there's nothing to be done, when the time finally comes. I *won't* believe it. Even if all that waits for me is a quick, stupid death somewhere out there, I'm going to it anyway, because that's all I've got."

"I had everything," Robert said.

Norman dug his fingers into Robert's shoulder.

*He's not listening.*

"Robert, I can't do this alone. I need you next to me."

"What's the point? Maybe they're right. Maybe we are evil."

Norman endured a bolt of impulse and grabbed hold of it. Without a moment of consideration, he punched Robert in the face. The blow landed like a fly glancing off a windshield, hardly making a dent in Robert's skin. For a moment he thought Robert would peel the skin off his bones. Instead, Robert blinked. Something stirred, a flicker of presence.

Norman seized it. "Listen to me, *listen*. This was never

about getting back at us. It's all about the End. That Jester wasn't lying. It's coming, now. I feel it."

"Don't. Just… don't."

"It's going to spread if we don't stop them. This is our last chance. It's going to take all of us—it's *meant* to be all of us."

Robert was silent for a long time. "We can never go back, can we?"

Norman shook his head.

Robert blinked, looking at his shaking hands. "I'll go with you, but I'm not part of this. I'm going for her."

"Fine. But we have to go now."

Norman clocked the horses on the far side of the glade and nodded to them. "We'll use them. If we leave now, we'll make it in time."

Robert turned without a word and headed into the trees, back towards the hillside.

*

"Fol," Billy whispered to the skies. "Panda Man." She willed him to appear and tell her what to do.

He said she was the only one who could stop it. But she hadn't stopped anything.

"Where are you?" she hissed. "Stop hiding!"

Nothing, not a glimmer of otherworldly elsewhere, nor glimpse of those mischievous dark-streaked eyes.

"Please!"

*I can't do it all on my own.*

The Jester did not appear. He had said he could go no farther, but she hadn't really believed it until now.

She was on her own, without a clue of how to fight the darkness. It was so strong here, filling her up and eating away at her insides. How could she win when she had no idea how to use the Light?

Allie took her into her lap like Ma used to. She didn't smell the same—Ma always smelled of lemons—but the way she stroked her hair made Billy relax. Watching the darkness moving slowly up the hill, she sighed. "I don't understand," she said.

"Me neither," Allie said.

"I'm supposed to save it. But I don't know how."

Allie gave her a queer look, but she looked too sad to ask more. Tears stained her face. Even grown-ups hurt and cried when they lost friends.

Billy realised she had been betting on being a hero, saving everyone. She hadn't remembered that she would still be *her*, that she would still be clueless, that it would all be so very strange.

"None of us ever understand," Allie whispered in her ear.

The sky was growing darker still. Grey had given way to black, bulbous clouds that sagged under their own weight. The air cooled, charged with static, creating the phantom sensation of cooling sweat upon Billy's skin.

"Storm's coming," she said.

Allie wiped her eyes as she watched the last of her home burn up. "Looks like it'll be a big one." She tittered, a little madly. "It would come after the fire."

Billy didn't answer, just sat in her lap and stared. Eventually, Norm and Robert reappeared. Watching them approach, Billy muttered, "We're on our own, aren't we?"

Allie held her tight. "Yes, dear. In the end, we're on our own."

*

"What is it?" Allie said.

"I don't know, but it's going to be everywhere if we don't stop it," said Norman. He had gathered those who would listen, anybody not totally lost to shock or injury, and explained the shadow over the city as best he could. It was a rambling, stuttering affair, but nobody questioned him. They all felt the Frost around their ankles, working its fingers into their bones. "It's spreading," he said. "I don't know how it works, but it has something to do with the mission. Maybe it's us holding on to the Old World that's keeping the End from coming again. Once they get rid of us, there'll be nothing to stop it. We can't let that happen."

"How? How can we stop so many?" Allie said.

He looked to Billy for help. Allie leaned over to look into the girl's face.

"It's you believing that keeps it away. The little lights inside everyone. Now they're all going out, and it's creeping in," Billy said. "We have to make the monsters go away."

Lucian broke in. "They're not monsters. For all they are, we've learned that much."

330

Billy looked him in the eye. "Some are. They have to go away. Only Light can make it better," she said, a tiny voice, no more than a sigh.

"I thought it was you with the magic Light," Richard said.

"Everybody has some. I can't do it by myself."

"How? How do we do it? There are thousands of them," Richard said.

"I-I don't know."

Richard put up his arms and turned away, running his hands through his hair. "We can't do this, Norman. We don't have time for all this mumbo jumbo. This is real. Real people, real lives. We have to talk strategy."

"Shut it," Lucian said.

"I've had enough of you telling me what to do! I'm telling all of you now to wake up. We have one world, one chance to fix this before it's all lost forever. Everything we worked for, all the years we spent teaching, learning, saving those books and machines and…" He gestured down to the smouldering city.

Lucian said nothing, only glowered at him.

It was Robert, standing over Sarah's covered body nearby, who broke the silence. "We've all seen enough to know there's more going on. I know what I feel, and I know what I've seen."

"I don't know what's real anymore," Richard said.

"This is real," Robert muttered, looking down at the white sheet covering Sarah.

Richard's gaze softened. He lowered his head.

"Tell us what we have to do," Robert said.

Billy looked startled. "I-I really don't know."

Norman tried to keep the crestfallen expression from his face. "Nothing? The Jester didn't give you any clues? Think hard, Billy."

"I never know. It just sort of… happens. Then I know. But now…" She shrugged.

Norman swallowed.

Allie hugged Billy close to her chest. "We can't take a little girl into a war zone, Norman."

Norman looked around at them all, a mix of incredulous and downcast faces. It was too much. Like it or not, the macabre nonsense had no place here. If he was going to get any of them moving, they had to talk sense. "I know. We can't risk bringing you, Billy."

"But—"

"We'll have to go, do what we can. If we turn the tide, we'll bring you in. Then whatever happens, happens."

Billy made to protest, but Norman cut his hand through the air to silence her. "I won't risk you again." He addressed the others. "I'm not ordering anything. It was never my place—or anybody else's—to order anything in this world. But if you're with me, find what you can and say your goodbyes."

A quiet moment passed between them, and then they were in motion. Lucian took a group off towards the city to find weapons, and Richard went with them for medical supplies, food, water—anything they could give to those who would remain behind. Robert never moved from

Sarah's side.

Norman sat in the grass with Allie and Billy and held his head in his hands. "I can't do this. What if I…" He trailed off, looked into Allie's eyes, and stopped himself. All his life he had moaned; that he wasn't meant for the destiny thrust upon him, that he wasn't strong enough. Things had changed now. Looking at her now reminded him just how much things had changed.

*It was never my destiny to save the world. I was never chosen. But I'll be damned if I'm going to let this happen.*

"You have to take me," Billy said quietly. "You have to."

"We will. When it's over."

"No. There won't be time later. It's—"

"Billy." Norman shook his head. "I made my decision. Stay with the others, help who you can. Be brave. I promise I'll come back for you."

Billy lifted Allie's arms off her and backed away from them. "You won't come back."

"Billy…"

She turned and ran.

Norman made to chase her, but Allie gripped his arm. "Let her go."

"But she's—"

"She's safer angry, Norman," she said. "At least she'll stay."

"What if she's right? What if we never come back because we didn't take her?"

"It's still the right choice."

"Even if it means the End?"

"Even that," she said. "Because I'm not taking a little girl to die, even if it means saving everything. That's not who I want to be."

Norman drew her close, not holding or caressing, but holding on for dear life. "You've changed," he said.

"So have you. Funny, isn't it: becoming who you always wanted to be, right at the end?"

They held one another until the two dozen horses had been retrieved from the glade, and Lucian and Richard had returned. By the time they were ready to go, time seemed to have congealed, running through Norman's fingers like water. They saddled up fast, not leaving time to think. Norman took his place at the head. There would be no hiding behind Robert this time—even if he had wanted to. Robert wasn't leading anybody now.

*So this is it*, Norman thought as he climbed up onto his saddle. *This is the last goodbye.*

"Oh, great Chosen One," Richard said, appearing at his side. "You lost something." Between his fingers he held something small; half-black, half-white. John DeGray's king chess piece, charred but unmistakable. "You dropped it down there."

"You stopped to pick up that thing?"

"It's all I have left to remind me of who I am," Richard said. "But it still doesn't belong to me." He held it out to Norman. "Look after it, until it's time."

"If it's not time now, it might not ever be."

Richard shook his head and pressed it into his hands. "Give it back when it's over."

Norman forced himself not to say any of the thousand things racing through his head. He placed the charred king in his pocket. "When it's over."

Richard made to leave, then hesitated. "I don't believe in what I can't measure or quantify, and I never will. This End thing, the Frost, I don't care. But I believe in you."

"You have any idea how corny that sounds?"

Richard smiled glibly. "Take it or leave it, Chosen One."

Norman looked over his shoulder at them mounting up around him. He felt he should say something rousing, proclaim assured victory, give some great inspirational speech.

A beat passed.

"Well, let's go then," he said.

They rode down the hillside in pursuit of the army and the thickening storm clouds as the first peels of thunder rolled across the land.

# FIFTH INTERLUDE

1

*S* nick. *Snick.*

Blood pattered onto creaking floorboards in the candlelit gloom.

"I'm not an unlikeable man, you know. I'm a good man. A fair man. It's these people."

*Snick. Snick.*

"They're evil. Greedy and spoiled. When I think about it, it's my own fault. Things have been good for so long under my hand that they forget what it means to live in this world. Managerial oversight, you might say."

*Snick.* A pause. Then a longer, measured *snick.*

Beth flinched as the blade cut deeper. The pain was everywhere now, a burning ache all over her body, threading every square inch of exposed skin. It was only these longer, deeper cuts she felt individually. The world revolved as she sagged against her restraints, forever turning and undulating, as though the walls and floor were but painted upon a canvas flapping in the wind. Cogent thoughts formed fleetingly as she coasted on the edge of consciousness, undulating back and forth along a long dark tunnel. The deep cuts brought glimpses of a dark room and a pair of piggy eyes, and fear dribbled through the unfeeling veil.

In those moments she wanted nothing more than to cry, not beg or scream or spite, just weep. There wasn't enough of her left for anything else.

*Just let me lie down on the cold ground and be, let me fade away, let me rest.*

She never let one mote of the overbearing urge show on her face. That was all she had left to hold on to: not letting him win. Through a head full of throbbing cotton wool, she refused to respond to his cutting.

Malverston resumed his steady pacing around her, his expression as academic and detached as a gallery patron observing an oil canvas. Slowly he bent forwards and made the tiniest incision below her right earlobe, leaned back on the ball of his foot, and nodded. "Don't worry, there's time to fix this. A few more hours and we'll be rid of those meddlers, and then we can get back to establishing order. A fairer, newer world, where people know their place and show their betters proper respect."

Another dainty cut, longer this time, crosswise over her breastbone. *Snick.*

Darkness drew in frighteningly fast, receding just as quickly when Malverston's hand came whistling up to strike her chin, snapping her head sideways.

"Now, my dear," he whispered, "you mustn't drift off like that. It's rude." He cupped her cheek, stroking the shredded skin.

Beth tried to spit in his eyes but managed only a pathetic whistle between her lips.

"Such fire," he muttered and pinched her face between his mitt, scrunching a hundred lacerations and spilling fresh tears over his fingers.

The pain cleared some of the fog. Beth coughed, shook her head with as much vigour as she could muster, and glared at him anew. "If you're going to kill me, do it. You're running out of time, George."

He shook his head solemnly. Without the fog to cloud her vision, she saw just how changed he had become. His eyes had sunken and his lips had turned down and grown pale, his cheeks blotchy and loose, hanging in pendulous jowls. He wilted like a flower in a cold snap, stuck in here with nothing but her and his knife. Somewhere under her pain and misery, Beth felt her own slither of pleasure. "You're afraid," she said.

He blinked and straightened with a jerk. "Afraid? Of what? Those peasants? They're beaten. You saw that old bitch bled like a stuck pig yourself."

Beth pushed away the memory of McKinley's throat splitting open. "You'll never be sure, not ever again. There's blood in the water." She took a breath, ignoring the whistle in her throat, and slurred at length, "It could come from anywhere. From out there, from in here; from those *peasants*, or from your own men. How does it feel to know that every heart that beats wants you dead?"

What little colour remained in his face drained away,

leaving a puerile, green countenance of childish fear. He raised the knife to her nose, eyes bulging, held it trembling against her for a moment, then let out a scowl and whirled away. Staggering across the room, he collapsed against the trolley of wicked instruments and growled like a caged dog. "They do not. They love me. They love their mayor!"

"They'll have your head on a spit before sunrise," she sang softly.

"No!" Malverston cringed. "I could leave. Precautionary, of course, but perhaps I should seek shelter until—" His head jerked, and in an altogether more savage voice he cried, "No! I'll stay until every last fucking peasant who'd say *boo* to a goose is dead and buried."

Beth was watching him jerk back and forth when something close to the stairs drew her gaze: a huddle of shadows creeping forth so slowly as to seem utterly still. For a moment an unreasoning part of her thought McKinley had survived. The old woman had come for her!

No. It wasn't McKinley.

It was Renner, and two of the other men Malverston had sent to James's homestead. Abreast one another, crouched with eerily still, predatory expressions, they emerged into the light.

Excitement sizzled over her entire body like the electric shocks travelling magicians used to give her when they came through the Moon. Even her hair seemed to crackle.

Malverston kept jerking on the balls of his feet, oblivious. Close by, Renner's yellow livid eyes seemed to pop an inch from his face as he licked his lips.

The bastard was finally going to get what he deserved. He wouldn't even see it coming.

Finally Beth could get out of this place. Where was Mel now? Mum? She would beat that stupid little girl for trying to save her when she got out of here—beat her then kiss her and never let her go.

When they let her go…

She shuddered as her excitement came to a stuttering halt.

*Once they're done with Malverston… You really think they're going to let you go? Untie you and shoo you out the door: see ya later?*

Not with the way Renner had looked at her. She didn't doubt that his own fun with her would begin—she was willing to bet it would be all the worse than Malverston's.

Renner and his companions were feet away now, hungry and quickening.

*I can't save him. I won't save him!*

But she had to. If she wanted to live.

Closer. A single creaking floorboard. Malverston stirred but didn't turn. Renner's knife rose to his shoulder.

Clenching her eyes shut, Beth screamed, "Look out!"

Malverston leaped back just as Renner's knife came sailing down, slicing through his sleeve and opening his forearm. Howling, he wheeled away as one of the others jabbed down.

Malverston sidestepped with the deftness of a man half his size and caught the man around the midriff, crushing his arms against his sides. Before a beat could pass,

Malverston smashed his forehead into the man's nose with a sickly crunch. A moment later he dropped the man to the ground like a sack of rocks and punched Renner's elbow hard enough to send his knife spinning to the ground.

He snarled as the third man slashed low along his thigh. But the man had left himself open from above, and Malverston's elbow came whistling down to hit him between the shoulder blades, sending him to the floorboards with a muted *oof!*

The rest was a blur of scrabbling from all parties: three men racing to their feet, and one hulk of a mayor reaching into his belt.

Renner and his companions only made it to their knees by the time Malverston retrieved his gun. Three short bursts of light accompanied by as many reverberating cracks that sent Beth's head spinning anew.

By the time the attic settled, Malverston stood on the nearest man's coat, one foot resting on a gaping chest wound. "Where are the others?"

"Please," the man gasped.

The mayor's weight pressed down on his chest, and blood spurted from ragged holes in his flesh as he squealed. "Away!"

Malverston lessened the pressure. "Beg pardon?"

"They ran."

"Why would they do that?"

"Cain… Cain's lot. They're here."

Malverston nodded pensively. "I see. Thank you for bringing me this information, Johnson." Without a moment's pause, he stamped down upon the man's chest.

A muffled crunch filled the room. Then a long, slow sigh escaped Johnson, and his eyes faded to lifeless buttons.

Malverston turned to Renner's other fellow, found him already still and sightless, and shrugged. He then approached Renner himself, who was attempting, without success, to crawl back towards the stairs.

"The fool uses a knife to stage his coup? How romantic." Malverston looked down upon Renner, shaking his head. "Don't get me wrong, friend. I have a proclivity for knife-play myself." He winked in Beth's direction. "But a man needs to know how to use a gun when the time calls for it. Like now."

He trained the gun point blank at Renner's chest and pulled the trigger. And again, and again.

Renner jerked with each round, his jacket showering into confetti and his face twisting into a grotesque grimace that remained forever fixed on his yellow cheeks.

Silence reigned as Malverston assessed each man in turn, nudging them with the tip of his boot. His lip curled as he turned them over, taking their knives and throwing them onto the trolley. "Surrounded by fools," he muttered. "Whole world's gone crazy… Crazy."

He paused as a scream rang out into the distance, not a woman's or a child's, but a man's. His eyes grew wide, searching the rafters as though expecting attackers to pounce.

"They're here," Beth said. Her heart was in sudden fervour, stirring limbs and digits gnarled by numbness and blood loss. The pain suddenly increased tenfold as the last of the fog receded and she strained against her bindings—

*God, every part of me is going to split open if I move an inch!*

—but she didn't let it show, powering through the tears. She laughed as loud as she could, laughed right into his face. "They're here for you, and there's nothing you can do to stop them! Because you just put down the only dogs you had left."

Malverston's eyes swivelled down to the bodies at his feet, then back to her. He seemed to be two people in that moment: a blubbering confused baby, horrified to find itself alone in a strange and hostile place; and a fat, mean little man who has just realised his end is upon him.

"No. No, I'm only safer. Safer! A few less vermin to exterminate."

"But who will protect you now? The other guards? They're hired hands, or their families are held to ransom just like the rest of us." She played at a momentary musing. "Oh! That means you're… alone. You're alone. You've got nothing."

He rounded on her. "On the contrary, my dear," he hissed, tearing the back from the chair with his bare hands and lifting her into the air, "I still have you. You'll be my guardian angel. My darling."

Beth struggled, but each time she wriggled he pressed a hand against the deeper cuts in her side, and she howled. By the minute's end she stood before him at the back of the attic, facing the stairs, waiting.

Somewhere out in the Moon, gunfire warbled, for what Beth knew was the last time. They were coming.

*Hurry, James.*

# 2

The Moon had grown quiet. Families had retreated to their hearths or beds for the night, mourning those they had lost. Crickets sang where usually there was chatter and laughter of smiths and cobblers in the tavern.

Among the side streets, silver shadows flickered. James watched a dozen men and women hurtle down alleys and through azalea bushes, converging on the guards out on patrol. Waiting was torture—he was so close to Beth, to tearing the mayor's heart out through his nose.

He stayed put beside Mel and Lucian with great effort, watching as the first guard was yanked back by shadows, his yelp of surprise cut short. He didn't rise again. A few moments passed before the next man was taken down, more roughly this time. The third was rougher still, resulting in a scuffle that resulted in a baker taking a bullet to the belly. The noise alerted the remaining guards more each time, until by the fourth, the game was up.

"That's it, it's time to move," James whispered. "You ready?"

Lucian's eyes twinkled in the twilight. "Let's get your girl."

Mel's tiny hand squeezed his arm fretfully. "What if she—?"

"We'll get her, I promise."

"You can't promise." Her eyes were enormous and sorrowful in the gloom.

"I won't let it happen. Stay close."

They left their hiding place behind the forge and ran for the square, bent double. Around them the sound of struggle was building. With their element of surprise gone, the attack's success rate diminished fast. Seconds before things could have passed for peaceful. Now everywhere people died in the dark, screaming and tearing at one another. The three of them were out in the open; if anybody so much as shined a light on them, there would be nothing to do.

*Keep your eyes on the carrot*, James thought, willing the armed men on the town-hall roof to remain distracted long enough. A few seconds, that was all he needed.

From the other side of the square, a second party approached, led by Alex, with the Creeks bringing up the rear. If one group was gunned down, at least some of them would make it.

"We're going to get there ahead," Lucian uttered. "We ought to wait up."

"No!" James hissed as they skirted a rickety fence. "If they see us…"

"But inside—"

"I know."

They skittered across the square and James fought the urge to close his eyes, feeling utterly naked. It was so dark now that he couldn't even make out the outlines of the guards on the roof. They would have no idea whether they had been spotted until the bullets started flying.

Elsewhere in the Moon, the screaming had intensified tenfold. It seemed everybody in the town had emerged to join the fight.

"They're hurting," Mel moaned. "We have to help them."

"Shh!"

James leaped up onto the porch and landed upon his haunches, rolling with his momentum to dispel the thump of his boots. Reaching down, he pulled Mel up behind him. Lucian landed beside them with the stealth of a ghost. They were under the porch now, safe. Pressing themselves against the wall, they turned to watch the others as they approached.

Alex stepped foot onto the square, paused, and waved for the others to follow. Then horribly, sickeningly, the crack of a snapping twig rang out. It seemed louder than any gunshot in the strained silence. James just had time to close his eyes and utter a curse.

The gunfire began explosively. Ribbons of white-hot metal sprayed into the night from overhead, sending Alex and the others diving to the ground for cover.

"Alex!" Lucian barked, starting forwards.

James threw himself over him, smothering him against the ground. The two of them scuffled in the dark, but James held fast; Lucian wouldn't hesitate to throw himself out there, and there was no sense in losing more people. The three of them were safe, and they needed everyone they could get.

"Get off me!" Lucian snarled.

"Shh! Stay down."

The others had scattered into the murk, and James couldn't make out a single figure.

*That's good. If I can't see, that means the shooters can't either.*

Yet the guards had a solution: spraying spare bursts of fire methodically into each quadrant of the square.

*Battleships. They're playing Battleships with my friends' lives.*

"We have to stop them. There's no cover out there," Lucian said.

"We can't. They have to go back."

"You really think they're going to go back?"

A whimper emerged from the dark, the mewling of a terrified animal. After a moment, James realised it was Norman.

Before the next burst of gunfire, a howl joined the mewling. "Norman... Norman, no!"

"Helen," James muttered, closing his eyes against dread. "Shut up, Helen. Shut up. They'll find you!"

"James, we have to do something," Lucian said as he strained under him.

"We..."

"James!"

A sprightly presence appeared beside him in the dark, and Mel's voice floated into his ear: "Get my sister." Then she was gone, a light patter of feet along the porch. In a glimmer of starlight, he caught a glimpse of tiny limbs scrabbling up the balustrade, feet kicking in mid-air.

"Mel, no!" James seethed, but his voice fell on dead air, for she had gone up onto the roof.

The bursts of fire came twice more, lighting up innocent patches of soil before the young Tarbuck got to work. A nearly-silent fizz of air was followed by a sickening crack that could only have been breaking bone, for the next moment an unfettered scream tore the night open. One of the sources of gunfire vanished.

"That kid has balls," Lucian said.

A storm of feet thundered over the tiles on the roof, accompanied by fresh gunfire sprayed into the square.

*Now, it has to be now.*

"Lucian, we have to get inside while they're distracted."

"I'm not leaving them."

"We can't help them. We have to get inside now."

Lucian broke from James's grasp and wriggled off the porch. "I'm not leaving them." He stood such that their heads were the same height once again. "I'm sorry, James."

"Lucian—"

Lucian vanished back into the square, windmilling his arms as he zigzagged along, illuminated sporadically by the remaining streams of bullets.

Alone, James felt a sinking in his gut. It could all go wrong right here, right now. If Mel took a hit, if the firing squad found their targets in the square, if the guards out in the Moon got the upper hand—if any one thing tipped the wrong way, it would all be over.

James scrabbled to his feet and approached the door. He

brought his pistol to shoulder height, reached for the handle, and hesitated. If there was anybody on the other side of the door, the cover of darkness wouldn't save him. But it was the only way in. He moved now, or they really had lost.

Cursing, he inched closer to the handle and gripped the brass. He took a long breath, knowing it might be his last.

He almost jerked out of his own skin when a hand landed on his shoulder. Whirling, he brought his pistol around, but another hand seized the barrel, and in a moment of blind panic he prepared to die.

"James. It's me!"

The slightest outline in the dark, slightly taller than himself, unmistakable as that calm, quiet voice.

James slackened. "Alex?"

"Come on, let's go." Alex released James's gun and pattered over to the other side of the door. He hissed off a three count, reaching for the handle while James covered him.

*It would be you to make it here while the others are still out there. Did you leave them, Alex?*

The door burst open, a gaping gullet leading into blackness. They dove inside, skidding on their shins over the dusty floorboards. A pungent waft of countless feasts and drunken celebrations sloughed off the floorboards, a sharp contrast with the crisp night air, so heady that it brought Malverston's grinning face rushing into his mind's eye. Hatred filled him as he came to a stop against one of the long tables, ducked down behind one of the legs, and roared into the night: "Malverston!"

*

"Norman! Norman!" Helen lay flat over her son's prone body, unresponsive to Hector's incessant tugging at her arm.

Lucian fought the urge to rail at them, surrounded by streams of bullets thudding into the dirt just feet away, and crouched down before them. "What happened?"

"They shot him, they shot him! His head, there's blood everywhere. He…" Helen broke off into senseless wailing.

"I can't move her. She won't come," Hector croaked.

Lucian made to put the boy on his back. If he had to, he'd drag the kid's body clear himself. As he groped in the shadows and laid hands on the young boy's neck, a tiny groan floated up from him. He was still alive.

"Come on, Lucian!" Oliver's voice rang out from the porch.

"Get your bloody arse over 'ere, right now!" Aggie screamed.

"Norman!" Helen said. "Speak to me, honey!"

Norman groaned a second time.

Lucian thrust both Helen and Hector aside and pulled the boy onto his back. A voice in his head told him it was dangerous to move him, that doing so could kill him as surely as a bullet. But if they stayed out here, they would definitely die. If they moved, they had a chance. Laden with the boy's weight, he dashed for cover, Hector carried Helen in his wake.

*If I die because of this, I'm going to kick God's arse*, he thought.

The stretch of ground between them and the porch seemed like miles, but could have been thirty feet at most. By the time they passed under it, the scuffle on the roof had died down. A terrible silence rang out, and Lucian grimaced.

Stupid! How could they have let the Tarbuck girl go up there alone?

He laid Norman's body on the porch. Groping around the boy's head, his fingers met a wet slick above the collarbone that didn't stop until the hairline. Lucian lightly probed the edge of a wide gash upon Norman's forehead. A sick twist hit his gut. If Norman had been brained, maybe the moaning had just been reflex, for now he was utterly still and silent.

"He's dead, isn't he?" Helen wept. "He's dead, they killed him!"

"No," Lucian said. "It's a ricochet. Bounced off the ground and hit his head."

"Will he be okay?" Hector said, cuddling his son's face. "Norman, wake up, boy! Come on now, talk to Pop!"

*How should I bloody know?*

"He'll be fine. We just have to keep—"

A bloom of orange bathed the whole porch in soft light, streaming through the hall's window. Norman was illuminated in horrible detail, a pale vampire with half his head coated in what looked like tar. His forehead had split in a jagged hole along his hairline. It was a miracle the ricocheted bullet hadn't demolished his skull.

"Fire," Oliver cried. "It's on fire!"

"What's going on in there?" Agatha said.

"I don't know. We have to get in there."

"We can't!"

"I'm not leaving either of them," Lucian cried.

Agatha's face twitched with fear, then she threw her arms over her head and ducked inside. Oliver followed a moment later.

"Well this is just bloody brilliant, ain't it?" Lucian yelled at the Creeks. "How about you, you want to go in too?"

"You're not... you can't," Hector said.

"I have two brothers in there."

*This crap...*

"Take care of your boy," he said. Before they could respond, he too dashed into the flaming building, where all was heat, chaos, and groaning wood preparing to buckle.

*

Melanie jerked awake with a silent scream. She took a stertorous breath and bent double from a vice-like tightness in her leg.

Stars twinkled above. The rooftop was silent, and the only sounds now came from under her—muffled shouts, scuffling feet, and something else—a spreading crackle.

Shaking and taking shallow breaths, Mel uncurled herself by degrees and searched one-handed for her slingshot. She had gotten three men, she knew. At least three, right in the head. They had dropped to the tiles like bags of peaches. It had been so easy that she had actually grinned as she turned in search of the last man. Her hand had been quick with the smooth, aerodynamic pebbles she had fished from the brook down by the fields, socking each one into the leather seat at the end of the string.

Mel Tarbuck, the deadly cat. So long had she shot birds and cats and rabbits, wishing they were the mayor's men or the mayor himself.

*That's right, you stupid sister robbers!* she thought with spite as she had spun for the last.

She found him just like the others, put the stone in its place, and pulled back the sling. It all felt so right, so justified, that in that instant she had been sure she would be in Beth's arms by the minute's end. She had laughed aloud when the stone whistled through the air and hit the man full in the nose, and he dropped just like the others.

Then something very hot and sharp had punched her in the thigh, and the world had gone dark from the pain.

*Shot*, she thought with wild panic. *I got shot, I got shot, I'm going to die!*

Presently she steeled herself. Big girls didn't cry. Gingerly, she checked her leg, whimpering when she neared a ragged tear in her jeans. She inched her way around the wound until she was sure the bleeding had almost stopped. It hurt far too much to stand on, but she could still move.

She had to. Beth was still in there.

She crawled towards the roof's slanted peak. If the other man was still alive, he would find her and finish her easily. But what else could she do?

As she crawled, a strange warmth spread in the tiles

under her elbows and thighs, so slow at first that she scarcely noticed, then faster. It clicked in her mind as she neared the peak: the crackling, the heat. The hall was on fire.

She groaned and lay flat on the bulge of the roof's peak, holding on to her sling with the last of her strength.

Big sisters were such a pain. But she only had one.

*

James's voice returned in a cascade of retreating echoes, reaching into the hall's many chambers and crannies: *Malverston, Malverston, Maalverstooon!*

The longest, strained silence followed. Then a voice drifted down the stairs: "Master Chadwick, welcome. You've caught my faithful mistress and me at something of an awkward time. Could you call later? She's ravenous for me, you see. *Ravenous.*"

"Sack of shit," Alex muttered in the dark.

"Let her go, and it's over," James said.

"I imagine it would be. Quite over."

Was that the tiniest tremble in the mayor's voice?

*Under all that bravado, he's scared out of his mind. Good.*

"Stop this now, and we'll let you walk," Alex called.

James stiffened. *Let him go, be damned!*

"You don't really think me that stupid, do you?" Malverston called. "I'm the mayor of Newquay's Moon, gentlemen, wisest man in the land."

James let the words roll over him, squinting into the dark, expecting the goons to make their appearance any moment.

Would they sneak down and hunt him and Alex out? Were they already seeded about the room, lying in wait?

To his shock, a rotund figure appeared at the top of the stairs, illuminated by a faint orange glow. Malverston held a lantern aloft with one hand, and Beth held tight against his chest with the other.

James felt that he could have lifted the world and torn it in two in that moment. Somehow, he kept still.

"Ah, my friends." Malverston cast the hand holding the lantern from Alex to James with a magnanimous sweep.

"George, it's over. You know it is," Alex said.

"Ah, I beg to differ."

Beth writhed until her mouth was free and cried out. "James, don't—" The mayor clamped his hand back over her mouth.

"Get your hands off her…" James paused, squinting. There was something odd about Beth's skin. She seemed almost striped in the strange flickering light. And her eyes… She looked to be on the point of fainting. "What have you done to her?" he breathed.

Malverston continued as though James hadn't spoken, smacking his lips. "You see, I find myself surrounded by those unworthy to be my subjects. I'm on something of a cleanse." He smiled, turning his eyes on James. They were wrong, those eyes, broken and wild.

James fought against a leaden anvil of panic, which threatened to tear him down through the floor. "Please let her go."

Again, Malverston pretended he hadn't heard. "I should thank you. If you hadn't come, I'd still be surrounded by those greedy, conniving scoundrels who sought nothing but my chair, after I had done so much to nurture and love them."

For a beat, James thought he was talking about McKinley and the others who had died earlier. Then he looked around in earnest, and was at once certain that Malverston was alone.

*His bodyguards have left him... or he took them down himself. Either way, all he has left is Beth.*

A cocktail of excitement and terror filled him. Nowhere to run, and out of men. That meant his grip would be all the tighter on his last bargaining chip.

The mayor's grin twitched. "Unworthy, all of you. All out to get poor old George, who did so much for you." Spittle flew as his mouth twitched into a childish grimace and he bawled, "Unworthy!"

James swallowed, clutching the table leg. Neither he nor Alex said anything.

Malverston nodded, pursing his lips. "You think *I'm* unworthy. I see now." He tutted and looked at Beth as though to share a derisory scoff. Then he rounded on them and held out the lantern. "Let's see who's worthier," he spat with a paroxysm of cackling—of a man totally unhinged— and sent the lantern tumbling down the stairs. Oil cascaded down in a carpet of igniting red and amber flames, splashing crazy shadows across the walls.

James made to jump forwards but flinched back when a

round fizzed past his head. Cursing, he could only watch as the rich draperies, curtains, throws and tables burst into flame. Light flooded the hall, and he just had time to glimpse a flash of paunch vanishing up the last step. The fire spread fast, zipping over the ground, following tassels of rugs that made for perfect kindling. Before he could move, a river of flames had shot by, dividing him and Alex between opposite sides of the hall. James alone stood on the same side as the staircase.

They shared a long, tense look. "Go," Alex said. "Go get him!"

James was momentarily stilled by the cacophony: the screams from the Moon, Mel's struggle on the roof, the gunfire in the square and the Creeks' wailing, coupled with that single solitary look from Alex that said so much.

*I can't do this without him.*

"Come on, jump!" James cried.

"I can't."

"You have to!" He searched his brother behind the mask of Alexander, imploring. "Please."

Alex's lips stiffened. Gritting his teeth, he turned one shoulder towards the fire and dashed forwards, hurtling over the tabletop and crashing against the far wall. James was on him in moments, slapping out the flames that had caught on his sleeves, pulling him to his feet.

"Thank you," he said.

"Come on, let's go."

Together, they rushed for the stairs.

# PART 6

# THE BATTLE OF CANARY WHARF

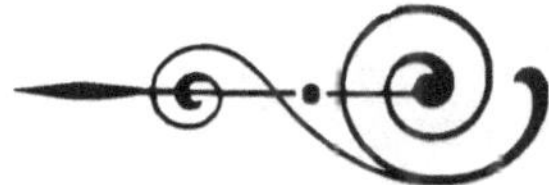

When the sun has set, no candle can replace it.
— **George R.R. Martin**

I

～✦～

Latif's voice drifted through the workshop door, strained and haunted. "Is it done?"

Lincoln waved Evelyn and Marek inside, following close behind. They had brought in halogen lights to make work easier, but the lights seemed only to highlight how dishevelled Latif had become. His eyes were cupped by purple crescent moons, and his skin had grown so sallow he looked sicker than the wounded in the tower. "Is it done?"

"It is," Lincoln said, stepping over the cables snaking away through the door.

Latif nodded solemnly, hunched over the radio with a comforter gathered about his shoulders. "Good, that's good."

Lincoln squinted, noting Latif's slouch, the distant glint in his eye.

*What's wrong with the boy? So fatigued... No, it's more than that. He looks ill.*

He put it aside as they gathered around the radio. There were bigger things at stake. It had taken all of two days to prepare and install an antenna close to the roof of the tower's pyramidal cap, diverting manpower from vital preparations for their defence.

"Mr Hadad, tell me we didn't just waste our last chance to ready ourselves," Evelyn said, skirting the worktop with a distrustful glare aimed at the radio.

Latif took a long, rousing sigh, blinking heavily. Even his eyelids were pale. "Only one way to find out."

"We can't afford maybes. Can we send a signal or not?"

Latif shrugged. "I never promised anything. We might just get static. Nobody's done this in forty years… so far as I know."

Evelyn stiffened.

"If you want certainty, go to another universe, where people don't vanish into thin air like puffs of confetti," Latif mumbled, fiddling with the tuning dial.

"Watch your mouth," Marek warned. "You may be hot shit with your new toy, but you're still addressing the High Councillor."

Latif didn't seem to have heard. He flipped the power switch and the Blanket's screech filled the workshop. Their faces scrunched up against the pain.

Lincoln felt the urge to join him at the controls. They had drawn up the antenna blueprints together. The airwaves had cleared so much that they had been in a frenzy of excitement, mapping a dozen channels, with more emerging all the time. A few channels were occupied by looping messages, though who had set them up eluded them. A few were empty, just white noise—perfect for broadcasting their own message.

*With more time we could have rigged up an antenna grid for ultra-low frequency broadcasting, as well. Even with our power supply, it would bounce off the ionosphere—all over the world! We could talk with anyone.*

He forced himself to drop it. There was a very good chance there would be no more time for anyone.

"I still don't get why we bothered," Marek yelled over the screech, his arms folded tight over his chest. He had donned the same tight-fitting Kevlar bodysuit as the guards on the catwalks and hadn't taken it off in days. "We could run out of time any moment, and we're fiddling around with a bucket of wires."

"If we send a message and somebody picks it up, they can send help," Latif said, his fingers moving with dainty finesse, tuning the dial to the empty frequency. The Blanket fizzled and petered out, replaced by a jumping crackle that was blissful in comparison. Latif smiled, his pale lips stretching. "There. Isn't it beautiful?"

Marek huffed. "Uh huh. So we send a little message, and a magic army of heroes comes to save us?"

"Somebody might hear it."

"*And?* If there was anybody out there strong enough to help us, we'd know about them already."

Lincoln bristled. "We knew nothing of the Scots before. And the party gone north may yet bring them back. This serves as a redundancy. We can't afford to delude ourselves one moment longer: if we fight without seeking help, we don't stand a chance."

"We can hold them!" Marek said, rounding on him. He

blinked and checked himself. "Councillor," he added.

Lincoln let it pass. "No, we cannot."

"My men and I have protected this encampment for years. Nobody, not a soul, has ever passed through our gates without my say so. I'm not about to let that change for a bunch of mangy scroungers with sharp sticks."

"You lost your head, mate?" Latif cried, rolling his eyes. "The siege ended two weeks ago, and you've already forgotten how they had us pinned down under their bloody thumb!"

"We held them," Marek glowered.

"Oh yeah? Were you out there, like me and the old goat were? Did you see just how they moved, how they positioned us just how they wanted us? Hunting us, like their little playthings?" Latif's brow twitched.

"Nobody is questioning you commitment, Mr Johnson."

Marek stabbed a finger at Latif's chest. "So why retreat? I'll tell you: because they're cowards with no real strength. They need mind games and tricks to make us cower in here. They'll never take this place. Our walls can stand against anything."

Lincoln strode forwards to stare Marek in the eye, their noses but a few inches apart. "Mr Johnson, are you not in charge of our scouting parties?"

The fire in Marek's gaze fizzled. "I am."

"Then you know as well as the rest of us what they saw marching towards New Canterbury yesterday. Thousands, you hear? Thousands of people. A force unlike any other, one we stand no hope of repelling alone. We are going to do everything we can to the last moment, to reach whomever may be out there. Even if only to warn them."

Marek fumed but stepped back. "It's a waste," he said. "It's a damn waste."

Evelyn seemed torn. She straightened and turned back to the radio. "We must do all we can, while we can. There are too many counting on us to fall victim to pride."

Marek scowled behind her.

"Mr Johnson, please prepare our defences for incoming hostiles. I expect we shall soon have company."

Marek remained staring at them all for a moment, a touch of forlorn hesitance about him. Then he bowed. "Yes, ma'am." He left without another word of retort.

Latif and Lincoln turned to Evelyn, who now stood with her arms wrapped about herself, observing the radio with the same potent glare.

"Why?" she muttered. "Why now?"

Latif's eyes glimmered, and Lincoln saw in them something that made his heart lurch.

*He knows something.*

"I don't know," Latif said.

Lincoln felt her gaze on him. He cleared his throat. "Just another mystery."

"To gain something so powerful as radio, just as we face our end."

"Life's a bitch," Latif said.

Evelyn didn't respond. She seemed consumed by the little box. "That so much could ride on so little." She swayed on her feet. "What do you think our chances are?"

Lincoln took his hat from his head. "Not good."

She nodded. "Do what you can, Mr Hadad."

Latif pulled a plastic, toothy grin. Upon his pale face, it looked grotesque. "Have I ever let you down?"

She didn't answer, just glanced back at the radio, then turned on her heel and left. Before the door closed, she threw one last comment over her shoulder: "If only it had come sooner."

Then she was gone. Lincoln wasted no time, striding forwards to take a handful of the boy's hair in his hand. He pulled hard.

Latif squawked, eyes bulging. "Steady on! What are you playing at?"

Lincoln held up a forefinger to silence him. "You tell me what you know right now. This is no time to play at games and secrets."

Latif grunted as he yanked harder, yet Lincoln saw what he wanted to see: a glimmer of resistance.

*Yes, definitely hiding something.*

He yanked still harder, and Latif seethed.

"Let go of me! What are you doing?"

Lincoln kept the pressure, slapping the boy's ineffectual hands away.

"All right, all right!"

Lincoln let go.

Latif seethed, rubbing his scalp. "Mean old bastard, you are. I was going to tell you."

"When? Once the gates came crashing down and our

throats were cut?"

"No." Latif blinked. "When I knew for sure."

"What?"

Latif hesitated.

"Must I scalp you, boy?"

Clearing his throat and addressing the radio, Latif said, "It speaks to me."

Ringing silence. Marek's voice audible in the distance, ordering a doubling of the guard on the wall.

Lincoln fought a sinking in his chest. "You haven't slept. I shouldn't have left you alone so long." He made to reach out for Latif's arm, but the boy withdrew.

"You think I'm crazy."

*Damn right*, Lincoln thought, taking fresh note of Latif's slouched, pale form upon the stool, swaddled in his dirty blanket with those dark bands of exhaustion around his eyes. "No, but we must have you in fighting form."

Latif held up his hands in protest. "Don't play dumb, old man. You know there's more going on here. You heard that music just as clear as I did."

Lincoln hesitated.

*The music. I had been hoping that had just been a dream.*

He knew it hadn't been. His heart wouldn't be racing like it was if he thought it was so.

Yesterday, they had been scouting the ninth open frequency, but this time it hadn't been a looping transmission, nor quiet bubbling static, but something he had never expected to hear again in his lifetime: Led Zeppelin.

Latif had frowned at the electric-guitar chords as Jimmy Page worked his magic, and Robert Plant's voice blasted out the lyrics to "Custard Pie". The lad had never heard music like that before outside vinyl records, not in a world where only classical instruments remained. They had sat in the dark, staring at one another with mouths ajar as the track had played all the way through, come to its resounding close, and been replaced by static. They had waited for an hour on the same channel, but nothing more had come.

Lincoln thought perhaps, somewhere out there, some insane Old World enthusiast was playing DJ.

Why bother, when next to nobody in the world knew about it—when most of Britain was sliding back to feudal barbarism?

They had been spooked, but let it rest. The world was a strange place, and they understood so little about how the Blanket worked. There was no time to dwell.

Then it had happened again, this time a half-garbled AC/DC single. A little after that, they had come across the tail end of something Lincoln was pretty sure had been Van Halen's "Runnin' with the Devil".

It was as though the Old World echoed over the electromagnetic spectrum. Somehow, the Blanket had preserved decades-old broadcasts. Apparently, the universe had a thing for classic rock.

*Yes, I heard it. And something strange is going on. But talking about the airwaves themselves speaking to you is going over the edge.*

He laid a hand on Latif's arm. "We have a few hours,

yet. Come, rest."

Latif slapped him away. "Don't." There was nothing facetious or tired about him now, just a simmering stare. "I mean what I said."

"That the static talks to you?" Lincoln said.

"No, it's… Something talks to me *through* it. It started before I found the second frequency. I felt cold inside my arm, like it was coming through the dials into my fingers. I knew something had to be tipping me off about where to find the channels—nobody's luck is that good—but it was so mental that I couldn't believe it. I'm not into mystical crap, never was. Numbers, cold numbers, that's all there is." He cleared his throat. "But I kept finding them. Over and over, like I knew exactly where they were. That cold was like ice eating my insides, telling me where to go, guiding me."

Lincoln listened with mounting dismay. The boy had cracked. He should have stayed with him. To put so much pressure on one so young; he should have known better.

Latif seemed to spot something in his gaze and stiffened. "I'm telling you, I'm not crazy. That's what crazy people always say, but I don't have time for semantics. I'm just telling you what I know. The Blanket fractured because something broke it."

Lincoln scrutinised his apprentice with all the rigour he could bring to bear. The boy was jittery, weak and so very tired. But his poise, his speech, his gaze, they were perfectly lucid.

*He really believes it.*

Chiding himself for entertaining Latif's ravings, he drew

up a stool. "Something?"

"It's just feelings, but not hunches or tingles; I mean… knowing. Suddenly, absolutely, knowing. Like something reached inside you and injected truth into your head. It sounds stupid, I know. But I can't say it any other way." Latif touched the dial. "Something out there is fighting for us. It knew we needed help and bent the rules just this once, to give us a chance."

*The rules?* Lincoln thought. *Good God, this has turned into Mystic Meg hour.*

"Rules about what?"

Latif frowned. "Dunno. I get the feeling it's something much bigger than us. Some war of the titans that goes back and beyond. Every war's got rules, I suppose." A thin smile spread on Latif's face, as ephemeral as the glint of dark humour in his eyes. "Whatever's going on, I don't think anybody's playing fair."

Lincoln's mind turned back to what Evelyn had said just before she left: "Why now?"

Latif paled still further, a chalky whiteness under his copper skin. "I get the feeling that night is coming, worse than that army. It's what the army's got with it."

"How could you know that?"

Latif looked at the radio, and for a moment Lincoln saw him anew: a frightened kid with an entire city's last hopes resting on his shoulders. "I don't know," he said. Suddenly he was trembling, and tears spread into the hollows of his eyes.

Lincoln reached out to touch him, and Latif jerked.

"What is it, lad?"

Latif swallowed hard. "Earlier today, I found another channel. I didn't say anything about it."

"More music?"

"No."

"What?"

Latif's haunted face searched the room as his lips twitched. "Screaming. More voices than I could tell apart, so much pain, and they were all… working. Working and screaming. Just for a moment, I felt so cold, like I could never be warm again."

Lincoln shook his head and sat back. He was too old to start working his fingers into some spooky world of *other powers* and magic signals.

*Stick with what you know, old man. Get out there and do some good. Leave the boy to do his work.*

"Latif," he whispered. "If we send this broadcast, will anybody hear it?"

Latif shrugged. "I don't know. I got nothing but hope, same as you."

Lincoln stared at him a long time, then nodded. "Send it. We need every man and woman."

*

"Accept one thing right now: a lot of people are going to die today." Marek stood before the ranks gathered before him at the foot of Canary Wharf tower, shouting loud enough for all to hear. "Our last scouting party returned five minutes ago." He stopped pacing and turned to them. "An army of ten thousand marched into Alliance territory from the North. New Canterbury is gone."

Muttering rippled through the crowd, not conversation but a unified spat of cursing. A moment later, even deeper silence took hold.

Above, the sky grew dark, the clouds an angry black. The temperature had dropped precipitously in the past half hour, and even sunlight seemed to wilt. It was as though a blanket slowly draped over the land, the vanguard of something malicious amongst the vast twisted mangroves of town houses, skyscrapers, office buildings and tube stations.

Marek continued. "The scouts barely kept their lead. That army is here, in London. They're circling from the south to cross the Thames, so they'll bypass every land mine we've laid, every outpost, all our outer defences. Last sighting had them heading for Westminster Bridge. They'll be here before the hour's out."

No muttering this time, just a carpet of unbroken silence. The entire camp had frozen mid-action: people cleaning bandages for the wounded, cooks, mechanics, smiths, refugees, guards. He even felt eyes upon him through the tower's windows. They had waited for so long that fear had grown thin and turned to anger; anger they were ready to use.

Marek saw Evelyn emerge from the tower's lobby in the corner of his eye but didn't acknowledge her until she was right in front of him. Her cold stare seemed to focus the light around her into a scalding beam, aimed squarely at his head.

"What are you doing?" she said.

"Mounting our defence, m'lady."

"We have been doing just that for days." She drew close and lowered her voice. "Everybody is on edge enough without this spectacle."

Before she could continue he spoke again, loud enough for all to hear. "If I'm going to die, I'm not going to do it cowering in a hole. This place is all I have, and everybody I ever cared about is inside these walls. I'm not letting them get anywhere near this place. I'd never order any of you, but I'm going to meet them head on. Who's with me?"

In his mind's eye, he heard crickets, saw a crowd of blank staring faces—himself apart, one solitary shadow wandering into the city.

Evelyn gripped his arm. "Marek, have you lost your mind? We can't—"

The clatter of soles upon compacted mud interrupted her, five hundred strong. Every able body in the courtyard had stepped forwards.

Marek turned to Evelyn at last. "I couldn't tell you."

"You didn't ask the council's permission."

"I've served the council for a long time," Marek said—

They both knew what he meant to say: *I have served you for a long time.*

—"and that will never change. But this needs doing, and none of you would have signed off on it."

"Because it's crazy!"

"That's why it'll work. They won't expect us."

Evelyn seemed to struggle with articulating her rage, and

Marek couldn't keep himself from smiling.

"You dare laugh at me?" Evelyn glared.

Marek shook his head and laid a hand on her wrist. He wasn't a man of words. He was a fighter. He would never be able to explain why they had to go, not to her, not if he had a week. But in the decade he had stood by her side, he had never laid a hand on her.

That one touch did what his mind could not. Evelyn's gaze softened, the inferno diminishing. Then all front vanished, leaving the woman who cared so much who he knew had been just under the surface. "You'll die, Marek," she said. "You'll all die."

Marek let his touch linger a moment, then drew back. "The whizz kid and the old man have it covered. Somebody will come."

"If it doesn't work—"

"It'll work. Those two are batty as anything, but they know their stuff."

"We need you here. If they reach us…"

"If they reach us, you'll give them their medicine. They'll never get through these walls. What we need is time, and I'm going to make sure we have it." He nodded to the five hundred before him.

Evelyn swept around to look at them all. He had never seen her look so agitated, like a lioness losing her cubs. "How can you know it'll work? Tell me you know, Marek. If I let you go now and nobody hears us, I'll never forgive myself. I don't want to die knowing you went out there to be slaughtered for nothing."

Marek pointed to the gate. The klaxon sounded and the iron gates clunked, lumbering open. The volunteers dispersed to gather their things. Every scrap of weaponry, armour, and ammunition had been distributed days ago. Together, they comprised the most formidable armed force the country had seen in memory. So few, but a deadly few.

In moments they were reforming at the gates. With last looks back at the tower, they filed out through the gate and into the city beyond. Marek and Evelyn watched until most had passed through, then he turned to her anew. Before decorum could stop him, he reached out and touched her wrinkled face. "I'll tell you how I know it'll work. Times change, people come and go, but you can never quite kill hope. Not totally. We don't know anything about this world, not a single bloody thing. But, like my Grandma used to say, where science ends, you fill in the blanks with a bit of faith." He smiled. "Goodbye, my lady."

Before she could say a word, he crossed the square and passed through the gates. "Seal this thing tight behind us. Make sure you boys see hell before you let those bastards in here," he called to the guards on the catwalk.

He stood before the five hundred, and a moment of stillness passed. As one they looked over the wall, at the tower that had been the beacon of the Alliance. Lightning flashed somewhere in the city, and a few moments later thunder rolled between the great skyscrapers of old.

"Nice day for it," he called. "Let's go."

The gates of Canary Wharf rumbled shut as Marek held his rifle aloft and headed west. High above, an electric sizzle cut the sky in two, and thunder sounded again, directly overhead this time. Great waterfalls of dust rained down from the rooftops. As they moved out onto a dual carriageway, one cohesive amoeba engulfed by miles of nothing, the first drops of rain darkened the asphalt.

By the time the walls had fallen out of sight, the heavens had opened in earnest, and the rainstorm crashed down over them and the once great city.

Billy shivered, curled into a ball. The canvas sack in which she hid was soaked, jostling violently with the horse's gait under her. The nausea was intense.

Only the cold eating away inside her kept her from vomiting. Every nerve thrummed, every finger and toe screamed. The Frost was everywhere now, woven into the fibres of her clothes, hanging in every molecule of air. She felt she would drown in the swathe of treacle-thick death left in the Bad Men's wake.

Holding on meant being strong, like Daddy had told her. She had had to sneak into the sack on the back of Norm's horse, which hadn't been easy, especially with so many people looking to him. But she had wriggled, and crawled, and she had made it. Now she wished she hadn't.

It seemed that the world wouldn't stop spinning if she lay still for a hundred years. Since leaving the burning city they ridden without stopping, hours of stifling headaches that abated only when she poked her head into fresh air— she had only dared a handful of times, lest they saw her. She knew they couldn't send her back, but maybe they would leave her.

She wouldn't be left again. She still had no idea what she was supposed to do, but she knew she had to be there. Even if Norm and his friends won, the Frost would come.

A little while ago they had sped up to a canter, driving the horses through unending meadows. Billy risked a peek through the opening in the sack's neck and caught sight of dark shapes racing parallel to Norm's horse. Not far away Allie bounced up and down, her clothes hanging slick and heavy with rain and her hair flagging out behind her. Ahead was Robert, who looked like he would tear the world apart with his stare.

Rain splashed her face, freezing and stinging. The clouds overhead were monstrous, black things hanging low over the plains. Not far away a ghostly outline of great spires filled the horizon, made hazy by the downpour.

Billy gasped at the sheer size of the city—so much larger than those she had seen on her travels in Enger Land. How could men build so much?

Awe gave way to dread as she noted the clouds over the city's centre, where the buildings thrust up into the storm and out of sight. The clouds there had whipped into a whorling vortex, reaching black tendrils down towards the ground.

It was starting.

Trafalgar Square looked much the same as the rest of London: frozen in time, scattered with red double-decker buses and cars, cleared of the clothes and goods of the Vanished by scavengers long ago. The air still seemed to hold some memory of its bustling history, where flocks of tourists and city workers had passed between the fountains and statues over the centuries.

The bronze lions stood untouched by forty years of solitude, the fountain beds were filled with leaf litter and dust, and the great central column atop which Nelson surveyed the slumbering metropolis.

Marek crouched low in one of the divots lining the square's eastern edge. They had dug these foxholes years ago, long before the compound walls had gone up, miniature trenches set behind the weathered window frames of chain stores and souvenir shops. Along his flanks, he sensed the others join him in a unified gaze trained upon the storm.

The far side was barely visible through the slashing rain and a heavy mist that had come with the storm. Coupled with the ever-decreasing light, it had cut their visibility down to less than a hundred feet.

He knew they would come through here. He felt it. But they wouldn't know the army had arrived until they were right on top of them. That gave them the element of surprise, but it also meant they had to be ready. They wouldn't get another chance.

A patter of feet behind him signalled the return of a scout, a man named Ian with a jittery avian likeness. "Well?"

Ian panted, shaking his head. "Mist is too thick. There's no way we could have seen our hands in front of our faces out there."

"The bridge—did they cross the bridge?"

"There's no way to know. You can't even see the Thames."

Marek turned away with a scowl. Why did the weather have to turn now?

Every part of him sang with tension, every sinew screwed tight. He thought of checking on the others, but stopped himself. In the forty minutes they had been holed up here, he had tuned their positioning and attention to the optimal. They were as ready as their motley crew of civilians, mercenary guards, ambassadorial security and traders could be made.

Ian settled down beside him, and the roar of the slashing rain overtook them. Thunder shook the city, and lightning glanced off myriad panes of glass, casting the city aglitter in flashes of twinkling white. Hunkered against the wind, with their breath frosting the air, five hundred heads bobbed just in sight.

"This stinks," Ian said.

"Quiet."

Ian grumbled. "I don't like it. They should be here by now."

"I said quiet!"

A moment of silence passed, then Ian muttered, "They could have gone right past us and we'd never know. What if they're at the walls right now?"

Several faces turned towards them, visibly concerned.

Marek couldn't allow the slightest break in concentration. He rounded on Ian. "Look, I know they'll come through here. The road behind us leads right to the gate, and they'll know the gate is the wall's weakest point."

"You can't know that—"

Thunder thrummed the air directly overhead like a titanic gong, accompanied by a flash of lightning that sent everybody flinching. For a horrible instant Marek thought he'd been shot. He reached out to steady Ian's rifle barrel as it bucked in his hands, and waited for the rumble to dissipate. They looked at one another, and Marek allowed himself a smile.

Ian returned it, laughed unsteadily. "Phew, I thought we were—"

A black figure hurtled into view from above, crunching against the pavement. A tangle of broken limbs were visible for a moment before a rain slicker fluttered down to cover the body: one of their lookouts, his face frozen in open-mouthed surprise, a neat red bullet hole punched through his chest.

"Ready!" Marek roared. He hunkered down behind the door frame of what had once been a Starbucks while his vision narrowed to a funnel, the sounds of the storm grew faint, and his finger hovered over the trigger.

When they appeared, they did so without warning. From the riotous obscurity of the storm, suddenly and totally, they were there: thousands of figures lurched from the mist. Their battle cry reached Marek a moment later, the wild screams of those made feral and mad by hunger, desperation, and hate. With astonishing speed they covered the square, pouring over the statues and fountains and vehicles as though such obstacles were but leaves upon a forest floor.

Marek didn't have to give the signal. The first wave brought the air alive with cracks and whizzing ricochets, sending half the encroaching front line toppling back. Falling like sacks of wheat, they were trampled by their comrades, who rushed ever onwards, a single subconscious behemoth.

Return fire crashed down from surrounding buildings, and those in the square scrambled back for cover. Marek jumped behind the door frame and yelled, "They're using their unarmed as fodder, laying down covering fire until the ground troops get close enough to use what they got. Get your bayonet ready, Ian, we—Ian?"

He turned, saw the bloody pulp of flesh that had been Ian, spilled over the counter beside him. Marek leaped out and fired once more, taking out two more before he was forced back.

*Too many. Far too many.*

He had been hoping they would attack in waves. But that wasn't the way of this beast. They had sent in everything they had.

*We can't hold ten thousand for long, not if they don't care how many they lose. How could I not have seen this coming?*

Metal sprayed the Starbucks and reduced the panelling to pulp. Marek curled into a ball until there was a let-up, then threw himself out into the street and dived through the adjacent window, skittering into an old souvenir stall. Five wide pairs of eyes stared from sheltered nooks, trapped and shaking.

"Keep fighting," Marek said. "We have to hold them."

"We can never stand up to that!"

Marek pulled them out one by one. "We're going to. We have to."

They fired, were hit, kept firing. Despite the Alliance's relentless barrage, thousands of ragged bodies had crossed the square and were upon them. In moments the sky became blotted out by their writhing shadow, and puddles of rainwater ran red with blood.

*

Alex tripped clumsily up a flight of stairs, pushed by an overzealous guard at his back. Any thought of resistance was kept in check by the will to see this through. Beaten or not, he wouldn't cower. Ahead of him, James and the boy, Charlie, ascended to the top and vanished from sight.

As he too stepped from the stairwell, the guards manhandled him into an office much like the countless others in the skyscraper, around twenty storeys off the ground. From here they had a clear view across the Isle of Dogs and Canary Wharf. The wall-height windows were blacked, weathered to opaqueness by the howling winds and driving rain. A shorter intermediate building cut off any wayward onlookers from street level. The air was heavy about this place, the panic-inducing atmosphere of a predator's den.

"This is where you watched us, during the siege."

James said nothing, heading towards a small slit excised in the glass to look out. In his reflection Alexander saw a blazing, mad certainty—an unstoppable drive to finish a job half-completed. If Alexander could have looked him in the face just then, he was sure he would have seen fire in his eyes.

"Yes," Charlie said beside him, gripping his arm and leading him towards the centre of the room, which had been cleared of stationery and desks, leaving only their ghostly impressions in the dust.

Alexander grunted as he was forced down onto his knees, and his bindings were cut. Massaging his wrists, he addressed Charlie from the corner of his mouth: "You could let me go, Charlie. I know you don't want this."

A stinging slap arced across his face. Charlie hissed, "Shut up!"

Alexander cupped his cheek and rose up slowly, lowering his voice still further so not even the other guards could hear. "You're not like them. There's still time to stop this."

Charlie crouched behind him and made a show of fixing Alexander's kneeling position, yanking the threads of his bindings off his arms. "There was, once upon a time. You remember, don't you? When your friends trampled me half to death, and then you left your mutt to put a bullet in my head."

"Lucian was never going to kill you."

"Don't lie to me. You might be lauded as some great sage by peasants from here to Penzance, but I don't give a crap. I see you: you're nothing. So don't even bother. I've picked my side—and I picked right!"

"Then why are your hands shaking, Charlie?"

Charlie froze, then rose sharply. "Make sure he doesn't move!" he barked and made his way towards James.

Alexander watched him adjust his limping stance from hesitance to a sheen of familiarity, but it was surface level.

*He may be my only chance*, Alexander thought. *He's not yet too far gone. I may not fool him, but he doesn't fool me, either: he's chosen the wrong side, and he knows it. He's trapped.*

Charlie drew level with James and said, "What now?"

"We watch." Alexander realised that James hadn't really been looking out into the city at all, but rather into the office's reflection: right at Alexander and Charlie.

*He knows. Of course he knows. How could he not?*

But if that was so, why keep a chief lieutenant so close when they could stab you in the back at any moment?

The answer clicked in Alexander's mind. Even after all this time, he could read James's mind like a book—a mind he had formed with his own hands.

*The boy is why I'm here. I've already seen one city burn; another won't add anything. The boy's the final demonstration. That's how he's going to finish me: a battle of wills.*

"We should kill him now," Charlie said.

"No. We watch."

"This fight is done. They don't stand a chance. We don't even have to stay; nothing's going to stop them now."

"That doesn't mean we're not going to watch our plans come to fruition, to see the job done," James said.

Charlie looked over his shoulder, but this time Alexander didn't see anger or hate in his gaze, but barely veiled fear. "We should kill him."

James returned his attention to the tower. "We have messengers returning. I want their report."

Charlie hovered on his mangy leg, sweeping an uncertain look about the room as though some angel would leap forth and save him, then staggered from the room and descended the stairs.

Alexander, James, and the complement of guards watched the storm rage over Canary Wharf in strained silence. Contrasted with their long walk through the reverberating streets, everything seemed hauntingly quiet.

"When all this is done, what are you going to do with the people marching under your sigil?" Alexander said.

James replied after a beat. "I never did anything with anybody. I let them choose."

"Is that what you call burning towns and kidnapping an entire country? Burn or convert? That's a choice?"

James didn't rise to it, his voice measured. "People have to live with the consequences of their actions."

"What did any of them ever do to you? It was me who wronged you."

"It's not what they did that matters, but what they didn't. This island let itself get swept up in your sweet narrative and turned its back on the truth."

"The Alliance spreads nowhere near across the country!"

"For once, you undersell yourself. Your name is known in every hamlet and hole in the mud across all the land, and the sickness you bring as though bearing gifts has eaten into the very fabric of this world. If we don't cure it now, we will never know freedom."

"All I ever tried to do was help—"

"No, Alex. Enough. All you ever did was what you wanted. I can't let that decide our fate."

Alexander couldn't contain himself any longer, his voice rising to stentorian roar. "So your answer is to cull us like cattle? Because of something I did—I, alone? They deserve to die because of me?"

James whirled from the window and crossed the floor in a few bounding strides, his balaclava falling away and his head descending to Alexander's height. "You deserve to die. You, and only you. But that wouldn't solve anything, and it won't change the past."

Alexander muttered, "Neither will genocide."

James's gaze flickered with something sick and, perhaps,

not quite of this world. "The genocide of the innocent is part of what this world is now. I've seen it. The End changed things, forever. A new peace. But you and your meddling, everything I helped you do and everything you've done since, threatens that new balance—something we have to put right before it's too late."

He stepped around to Alexander's side and crouched beside him, sweeping his arm skywards, above the towers, to the vortex of blackness hanging over London, arcing down as the maw of some great beast descends upon its prey. "See balance restored before your eyes."

The cold in Alexander's limbs throbbed, pulled to the forefront of his awareness. He realised James cared nothing for beliefs, ways of being or justice—not even about the wrongs he had done or those who had succumbed to the mission's fervour.

This was about the End.

*He was always different, always had power. Something's got ahold of him, working through him… something bad.*

"What are you doing, James?" he hissed.

James gripped his shoulder. "I'm putting things as they should have been from the start, Alex. There's only one scratch of truth to be had: we were never supposed to survive the End. We're nothing but shadows in a world that doesn't belong to us."

Alexander couldn't break his gaze from the black storm clouds. "What is it?"

James whispered into his ear, "What you always taught me to reach for: our destiny."

*

Marek dived from the souvenir store just as it was overcome by a flood of men and women bearing sharpened farming implements and kitchen knives. Tucking and rolling, he discarded his rifle with a curse and managed to curtail a headlong tumble with his elbow.

He glimpsed a bloody raw patch upon his forearm but didn't feel a thing, already pushing to his feet and pulling his hunting knife from its sheath. Before he could lament how small it looked compared to the blades crushing limbs and hacking flesh all around him, he swept forwards.

He slashed across the hand of a middle-aged woman bearing down with a woodsman's axe, and she screamed, jerking back, shocked from her murderous reverie. For a moment, a person stood before him, her mask of fear pulled back. Then she was gone again as she snarled and swung wildly.

Marek knew he had won. The axe handle was as long as her torso, and she had nowhere near enough mass to counteract the head's momentum. Like the rest of her comrades, her skin hung in loose folds from her bones. He was surprised she had strength enough to stand.

Marek was small, and his weapon was but a thimble to hers, but he had speed on his side. Untrained and top-heavy, the woman toppled forwards, and he sidestepped with ease, not letting himself move until it was just right, and cut deep across her knuckles.

She shrieked and the axe clattered to the floor. The

horror written into her face almost stopped Marek, but he had been waiting for it—for the humanity, for the fear, for the begging—and before she could utter more than a screeching plea, he put the knife down behind her collarbone.

The woman dropped without ceremony, and behind her the square was revealed in full, turned into a riotous mass of warring, screaming bodies. Now that their guns were useless, they had fought their way from cover through sheer force of will.

If they had stayed put, those firing from above would have picked them off one by one. Being in the open wouldn't save them—they were outnumbered twenty to one—but they would take more with them. Their numbers wilted by the moment, yet despite everything being thrown at them, they were holding their ground.

Marek ran, never stopping, forever darting back and forth on the balls of his feet between struggling dog piles. Desperate enemies, swinging oversized makeshift weapons, never stood a chance; all he had to do was wait until their own weight committed them to a strike doomed to miss, and then he would go in from the side, make a quick vital plunge with the knife, and move on. In this manner he weaved away from the front lines and into the meat of the army. It was here he knew he could do the most damage, where those behind the front lines were concentrating on pushing forwards, not expecting to find one of their targets alone. Slashing, plunging, jabbing, Marek made dozens of small wounds almost unnoticed; wounds that would have his targets bleed out in a minute or two.

His luck finally ran out when he neared the square's centre. Voices rang out, arms pointing in his wake, lifting his veil of anonymity. He did the only thing there was to do: kept moving. If he stopped for an instant they would be on him, and once his avenue of escape was cut off he would be just another corpse.

*I need a bigger weapon*, he thought, and at once began scouring the ground for something with greater reach. He couldn't run forever, and once he stopped, the knife wouldn't do.

His trained eye picked out glints of blade, broken rifle butts, all half-buried under bloody bodies or crumpled into uselessness.

The enemy ranks milled like starlings to cut off his escape. His run was done. From everywhere came bloodcurdling cries: "Get him!"

Scrabbling from the hot stinking masses, Marek leaped into the rusted carcass of a London bus, kicking back in his wake until his boot met somebody's jaw with a sharp crack. Then he was in slippery darkness amidst mulched leaf litter and rotted upholstery, writhing for the stairs. He stepped over a bleached skeleton and seized at a glinting, long blade. Pulling it up in his wake, he bounded up the stairs and emerged onto the open-topped roof.

Backing away from the stairs, he looked at the blade he had retrieved and his heart sank: a three-foot-long antique sabre with a ruby inset in the hilt.

*A bloody sword?* He thought incredulously. *Seriously?*

Before his dismay could manifest, shadow fell over the stairs, and he swung down, cleaving flesh as a scream was cut short.

Around him the battle raged, all colour drained by the black sky and the driving rain. He knew he couldn't keep this up much longer, for his arms already burned and every move he made was less coordinated. After all his long years of training to keep the upper hand, he was limited by the very same thing that made these people such weak fodder: hunger.

They were weak, emaciated by the ravages of the long winter. This was less a war than a vague scramble; leagues of walking skeletons, barely standing, eyes huge and faces gaunt. This would be over soon, one way or another.

Marek swung again and met another body. Again, again, again, each time a harsh hacking motion without thought or finesse. If he could get enough, he could block the stairs. He just hoped the snipers weren't still watching.

His arms were so weak that lifting the sabre became an almost elastic motion, his arm trembling. There was no fighting it, but he had almost blocked the stairwell.

*Come on. One more, one more.*

Then from the heavens, a low whistling rose above the storm. For an instant everything froze as heads turned upwards and the whistling became a high shrieking whine.

Marek just had time to perceive the bus erupting under him, unzipping across its long axis like tissue paper. Then he was cartwheeling through the air and intense heat seared his back. Half-blinded, deafened by a percussive rush of air, all sense of orientation vanished, bar the vague sensation of spinning and falling.

He hit the ground rolling end over end, skittering in a scree of decay. Stones cut at his face, and a barked shin wailed as he cartwheeled to a stop. The world turned over ceaselessly and were it not for the solid ground under him, he would have been sure he was still flying.

The ringing dissipated just enough for a single thought to run through his mind: *move*.

Willing his senses to clear, he rolled up onto his knees. He overshot and tumbled onto his other side but sent himself back to his knees before he could settle, holding his head in his hands and smacking at his temples. Fighting dizziness and tasting blood, he groped until he found the sabre and slogged to his feet.

All was in slow motion. He still heard nothing but the same unbroken ringing, an eerie contrast to the destruction being wrought. In every direction flowers of fire and flying rock blossomed between the ranks of friend and foe, lifting people by the dozen from their feet, tearing their bodies and sending the remains spinning into the mist.

Marek blinked, something that seemed to take forever. His mind coughed, chugged, and finally clicked.

*They're using artillery on us. On their own.*

The fog in his head cleared, cast aside by instinct. Pain came in progressive waves, giving him just enough time to grit his teeth in preparation for its full force—he started running before the throbbing in his leg paralysed him.

He passed people who had moments before been bent

on cutting him down. Now, like dodos before the cooking pot, they merely looked into the stormy skies as death rained down upon them. They stared until the peppering of shells became continuous, and Marek felt the spell of shock stretch, strain, and snap. Then panic erupted and the square was alive with churning bodies—not fighting, but fleeing.

Marek ran, limping with the sabre clutched to his side. Close by the fountains belched detritus into the air, and the magisterial lions vanished in puffs of vaporised bronze. He crossed No Man's Land—a band of cratered stone patched with bodies and rubble—in a few moments that could have been years, his heart hammering as grit and pebbles sprayed his face, praying his luck didn't run out.

By the time he reached the eastern side of the square, the shelling had petered out. He risked pausing to look back, and saw the army gathered on the far side. Despite the terror of moments ago, hunger filled their unified gaze anew.

He gripped surviving Alliance fighters and threw them ahead of him. "Go! Get to the gate."

"What about our position?" somebody protested. "We have to hold them."

"Get behind the wall!"

He turned and shuffled east on legs screaming for mercy, leaving Trafalgar Square with now Nelson alone atop his column, surveying the swirling shadows over the capital.

# FIRST INTERLUDE

1

James took the stairs two at a time. Ignoring the flames at his heels, he rolled over the attic threshold and called, "Beth?"

His voice receded into the gloom. Alex rattled up beside him, and together they stood in the doorway, sweeping back and forth over the shadows. It would be so easy for Malverston to shoot them both right now. No cover lay in sight. All he needed was a gun and a clear line of sight, and they would be dead before they knew where the bullet came from. But nothing happened. In the aftermath of the headlong race, inaction yanked at James's insides with physical force.

"Beth?"

From the darkness, a scuffle of feet upon floorboards.

"There's no way out of here, George. Let's talk. We're not here to collect heads," Alex said, sweeping his rifle in the opposite direction to James, inch by inch.

From the darkness, somewhere to their left, Malverston hummed. "And what is it you're here for, I wonder?"

"We just want to stop this, before you destroy everything you're holding on to." Alex spoke carefully, each word smooth and calming.

"Don't talk down to me, you arrogant little maggot!"

James and Alex zeroed in on the noise's source, thirty degrees to their left. Excitement flooded through James as he stepped forwards into the dark. "Found you," he snarled.

Below he could hear the others' voices. It sounded like they had all made it. Too late to help Beth now.

Another scuffle, a satisfying stiffening akin to a deer wheeling in fright. Then slow, echoing footsteps. Malverston inched into the amber firelight filtering up the stairs. Before him he held Beth tight to his chest, a knife flush against her larynx. Before James could move or say a word, Malverston whispered, "Not a flinch. She'll be dead before you can squeeze that trigger."

James froze, fixating on Beth: her square jaw, hard features, and short-cropped hair, all consumed by a maze of tiny surgical cuts. In a fraction of a second the ache inside him turned to bile.

"James, Alex?" Oliver called from below.

"Up here," Alex replied. He turned back to Malverston. "It's over, George. The others are downstairs. Your men are dead. It's done."

Malverston's leer wilted, and James saw that he knew it was so.

Alex muttered in James's ear, "Wait for the others and we'll move in together—"

"No, he's mine!" James surged forwards, using every

scrap of his hatred, flying forwards with such suddenness that Malverston's only movement was to widen his eyes.

He heard Alex from a great distance yelling, "James, no!"

Then James was yelling, lowering his head and colliding with Malverston's shoulder. The mayor was twice his size, but with Beth in tow he was poorly balanced. Malverston's arm fell away from Beth's throat, and the three of them went spinning into the dark in a ball of scratching and yelling.

James clawed meaty jowls, pawing for the mayor's eyes, fighting enormous flabby arms. The mayor howled, then James touched something much slimmer, fairer—Beth. Abandoning his attack, he seized her around the waist and threw her through the air. Her hand clasped his briefly—so very briefly—then she flew from him and the mayor, landing several feet away.

*He had done it! She was away, she was free!—*

Blinding pain exploded inside his skull, radiating through his nose as a meaty fist pummelled him with the force of a hammer. Seeing flashes, James threw a wild punch that met nothing but air, then a leg swept out of nowhere and took his feet out from under him. James slammed to his knees with a crack that made him cry out, and then his arms were pinned to his side. He blinked his vision clear and writhed in the mayor's grasp, but before he could do any more than spit blood he faced Alex on his knees, and Malverston crouched behind him with a triumphant laugh. James felt something cold and sharp press at his neck.

"Well, this is tiresome," the mayor said. "Looks like

we've swapped one brat for another." Pleasure trickled into his voice. "This one I know you couldn't bear to lose. Am I right, messiah?"

Alex's eyes were huge in his head, his hands shaking so much that the rifle waved back and forth. "Let him go."

"I'll be glad to release your beloved Pigeon Keeper, as soon as I'm given safe passage." Malverston exaggerated a sniff. "Better hurry now, it's getting warm in here. We'll all be roast chicken in a minute."

James surged against Malverston, but the mayor started cutting the delicate skin of his neck immediately, slicing into the tendon. He yelled, gasped, and grew still. "Don't do it, Alex. Shoot him."

Alex shook, his mouth retracted into a pencil-thin white line.

"Now, Alex!"

Beth groaned somewhere in the dark, and upon the stairs a rattle rang out as the others scrambled over the flaming risers.

"Stop them now, Alexander," the mayor snarled.

"Stop!" Alex yelled over his shoulder.

The patter stilled. "*What?*" Oliver said.

"Stay back. He has James."

A pause, then a spate of curses from all parties.

"Wha-what do we do?" Agatha cried.

"Get out. Get out now."

"This whole place is burnin'. You gotta get out now."

"We'll be right behind you, just hurry!"

James swallowed and searched for Beth. The floorboards

were hot underfoot now, and the whole building groaned as the wooden supports gave way. Already his vision was blurring from the acrid build-up, and smoke was drifting up into the attic in bulbous clots, pooling at the ceiling.

"Beth, get up," James hissed. "Get up and go."

She stirred in the shadows. "James!" She moved forwards, but Malverston tightened the knife against James's throat.

They all became still, an immobile triangle standing in the growing orange glow of the spreading fire.

"Let him go or we all die," Alex said.

"I think not. I think I'll have you do something for me," Malverston said.

Alex made to retort, but the mayor cut him off. "If you want your precious saviour back, you'll do this one thing for me."

Alex's eyes twitched. "What?"

Malverston pointed to Beth. "Shoot her."

*

Melanie gagged, smoke filling her lungs as it seeped between the tiles. The roof was hot enough to burn, but she kept moving, gritting her teeth, moving towards the lee in the nested roof. Her gaze was fixed utterly on a ragged hole in the boards, just big enough to fire a well-aimed stone through. Inside she heard Beth and James and the mayor. They and the others were all screaming at one another. She willed flashes of gore from her mind's eye and kept inching upwards, gasping as her leg wound dragged on the tiles' sharp edges.

She screamed as the entire building shuddered, sinking an inch on the left side. Clutching the tiles, she waited for the roof to cave in, for her body to drop into the waiting flames.

It held. Swallowing the bile slicking her tongue, she inched for a stronger patch of tiles, and finally reached the tiny crack in the beams. She fingered her waistband and found her slingshot. Flame-lit floorboards met her gaze, a pool of light at the edges of which stood a frozen trio of silhouettes. Mel took a moment to recognise Beth—Beth free!

The mayor hunched over a slim young figure with long boyish hair. James.

She took a breath. Now that Beth was safe, she could focus. With practised familiarity her fingers found the rock in the pouch on her belt and brought it up to the sling. All the while she stared, judging dimensions in the murky, ever-shifting half-light. They were all shouting, the fire roared like a great beast under her, and the building juddered and groaned each moment.

She would only have one chance. She had to make it count. Mel drew back the band and aimed.


2


"We have to get out!" Oliver said.

Agatha reeled from the stairs as a flaming drapery twirled

down in a shower of embers. Oliver lifted her clear with an inch to spare.

"We can't just leave them," she yelled.

Their eyes streamed with smoke and ash. The fire climbed the walls, working into every crevice. The crackling and burbling blanketed out any sounds coming from upstairs. Oliver and Agatha stared at each other for a long moment, then with a tortured whine the beam above their heads buckled inwards, spraying embers into their hair.

A scream rose above the racket. Whatever was going on above, it wasn't good.

Every fibre of Oliver wanted to tear up the stairs. But they couldn't. They had no way of knowing what the consequences might be.

*When this is over, I'm done with people. I'll play with my clocks and gadgets. At least they never try to kill me. I'm done with this life, this name: Oliver Farringdon, and all the tosh that goes with it. I'll get a workshop, start over; I'll go by what the boys at the shipyards used to call me:* Lincoln.

A hand gripped Oliver's arm.

"Both of you go. I'm staying," Lucian said.

"We all come out of here together, or none of us will," Oliver said.

Lucian took Agatha's arm in his other hand. "You have to get out."

"We can't go out without them," Agatha said. "They're the lifeblood of the mission! Without them it'll all fall apart."

A cross-brace toppled onto the dining table and set the

chairs ablaze. They crouched instinctively, dropping to their haunches as the smoke grew thicker. The air was breathable close to the ground, but it still seared Oliver's lungs.

Lucian mouthed like a goldfish, then gripped them both harder. "If we all die here today, it'll be because of that mayor. We can't let the bastard have that. We can't let him win."

An ache shot through Oliver's chest. Lucian was right. But to leave now when they were but feet away…

"They're my brothers," Lucian grated. "I'm not going."

A crash shook the front of the building, and they turned to see Hector and Helen out on the porch, crouched over Norman. Oblivious to the flames, they stroked his cheeks, their expressions filmy and distant. Hector held a compress to Norman's forehead, which had soaked through with blood.

Oliver's chest sank. He turned to Agatha, who stared up the staircase with a pleading gaze as though she could will Alex and James to appear. There was the same knowing forlornness about her. They had to get out.

He nodded to Lucian, and the boy released them. Oliver touched Agatha's face, turning her gently to him. "Come, my dear," he coughed. "It's too late."

She shook her head, pale-faced and red-eyed from the ash. "I won't leave my boys, Oliver."

"Aggie, we have to—"

"No, Oliver! No! I haven't raised this lot of little toerags so they can jus' go and die on me. I won't ever leave 'em, not now and not ever—"

The front facade of the hall squealed like a stabbed pig. Wood tore with a wrenching, pistol-shot crack. The three of them just had time to turn and watch the lintel splinter along its centre.

Oliver saw what was about to happen in his mind's eye. A brief flash of his engineering from yesteryear projected stresses, shear forces, where the rubble would fall.

His mouth was only half-open to call out to the Creeks when the wall became an avalanche of flaming beams and cladding and tumbled onto the porch.

The Creeks saw. Screaming as one. Helen and Hector bent over Norman as the deluge of fire and splinters consumed them.

"Lord, no," Agatha muttered. She shared a look with Oliver, and they made an unspoken decision.

He turned to Lucian. "Get out before it comes down." He hesitated, then added, "Please." Then he was running after Agatha, leaving Lucian at the foot of the flaming stairs.

Coughing and gagging as smoke scratched at their lungs, Oliver and Agatha danced over the charred wood chips and cross-beams, calling out. They received no answer but that of the evening breeze, shockingly cold in contrast to the oven from whence they had come.

"Helen, Hector. Call out," he cried.

Nothing.

They kicked at the rubble, clearing swathes with their booted feet. The pile had formed a ventilated network of twigs and splinters; the perfect kindling. Already it was almost too hot to stand over.

He knew they must be dead but kept digging beside Agatha, unable to stop, to do nothing.

At last they uncovered a delicate hand. Oliver braced himself, dug down with the point of his toe until he had the proper leverage, then took away a tangle of splinters, revealing Helen Creek. Just beneath her he could make out Hector's shirt, torn and bloodied. Both their bodies were crushed, misshapen and contorted.

Oliver felt all the fight drain out of him.

*No. No, not the boy. He was so young.*

There was no sign of Norman.

Agatha was screaming at the heavens, cursing God and all his temerity. Oliver seized her. "Aggie. The boy. Where's the boy?"

She blinked, looked down, then scrabbled madly around their excavated hole.

Oliver did the same. Ignoring their burning hands and shins, their eyes streaming and their lungs crackling, they sent splinters and scraps of wood flying, until eventually they crouched beside one another and Agatha shook upon his shoulder, slamming her fist down on his arm.

"He's not here," Oliver muttered numbly. "He's…"

They grew still, defeated. Only then did the tiny moan reach Oliver's ears, barely audible above the fire.

They wheeled from Helen and Hector's bodies and peered over the porch's edge. In the moonlight, Oliver made out Norman's spread-eagled figure nestled in a halo of shrapnel.

*They must have pushed him off the porch, just before it hit them.*

A scrap of Norman's trousers had caught light.

Oliver leaped down and slapped the fire out. Norman twitched. Giddiness swept through him as Agatha landed beside him. "He's alive."

Agatha kissed Norman, croaking, "We have to get him away from here."

Oliver glanced back at Lucian standing in the midst of the inferno.

*The boy will let the flames take him before he moves an inch.*

Still no sign of Alex or James.

*Can we really just run away?*

Another look at Norman told him the answer: here was one they could save.

Oliver swept Norman into his arms while Agatha held on to his head. They dashed into the night, crossing the square until the heat of the flames left their skin, where they laid him on the ground.

"Will he be okay?" Agatha said.

Oliver shook his head.

They turned back to the town hall, crackling and whistling as it succumbed to the hungry flames.

"Come on, come on, come on," Agatha whined, jumping on the spot.

The Moon had grown silent and peaceful. It seemed the town had won its fight. Somewhere out there were people who had just taken freedom for their own.

Rain spattered down, first in tiny droplets, then in a steady downpour. Too late to save the building. The fire's damage was done. As they watched, it teetered on its foundations, flames spurting through gaps in the cladding.

*

"I said *shoot her*," Malverston said.

James thrashed in Malverston's grasp, but the knife cut once more at the tendon of his neck. He cried out, drawing Alex's gaze through sheer will. "Alex, don't listen to him."

"I haven't got all day," Malverston warned.

"He's not going to let me go. Take Beth and go."

"I am a man of my word, little cur. A man of my word."

Beth started forwards. "Don't hurt him. Don't! Just… take me back. Take me instead."

A combined roar came from James, Malverston, and Alex simultaneously.

"No, Beth!"

"Back, bitch."

"Stay where you are."

Beth stalled mid-step, her jaw clamped hard together. "You won't do this."

Malverston laughed, a rancorous booming. The smoke was thickening fast: in moments it would be too thick to see anything. The fire had breached the attic, climbing through the wall spaces and blossoming through cracks in the boards. James felt the noxious gases working at his mind, marbling rational thought.

*If we stay, we'll be dead by the minute's end*, he thought.

"Beth," he gasped. "Go. Go now. Get to the others." He

silently pleaded with her, mouthing over and over: *please*.

Her lip trembled. "I can't."

Mustering his strength, James forced himself to smile. "I'll be okay. I promise. You have to go now."

Her throat worked, and she backed up a step. His heart leaped. So long as she got out, whatever happened next didn't matter.

*Just let her be safe. Go, Beth. Faster, faster. Go.*

She took another step, breaking the triangle, moving towards the stairs.

James was on the verge of sagging in relief when Alex said, "Stop."

His last moorings of sense came loose. "Alex?"

Malverston interrupted. "What would you do without your Pigeon Keeper? Your line would come to an end... all you worked for, come to nothing."

"Don't listen to him, Alex!"

"Shh," Malverston whispered into James's ear. "Come, boy. See the way of man." Uttering each word with savoured ecstasy: "*See... what... we... are.*"

James stared disbelievingly as Alex mouthed unspoken words, his eyes throbbing in their sockets. In his twitching gaze there was only desire and obsession and coldness: the call of the mission.

"Alex...," he whispered.

Alex's mouth drew into a pale, flat line, and something faded behind his blue eyes. "I'm sorry, James."

In that last moment, Beth looked not at the gun Alex trained upon her, but at James. He had time: time to know life wasn't like in tales. In Beth's look there was no fear, nor anger or even love; just the empty stare of one totally alone, as a reverberating gunshot filled the air.

*

Mel's world vanished. Frozen holding her slingshot trembling at full extension, she watched Beth fall backwards, stretched out on the floorboards, her body striated with a thousand bleeding cuts and the centre of her forehead marked by a clean red hole.

Screaming, screaming everywhere. As ground became sky and everything inside Mel's chest came crawling up through her throat. Time seemed to stop, and a film reel played behind her eyes: the parody of life. For what could this be but some silly fantasy? How could real life be so cruel?

Then time snapped back, and she realised it wasn't her screaming. It was James.

A drum beat sounded deep inside: Mel decided to feel everything. Marshalling every mote of strength from the hard callous she had nursed against the harsh Tarbuck life, she took all that pain and formed it into a tight ball in her core.

*The mayor.*

Her arms stopped trembling. Mel blinked tears from her eyes and found Malverston's face. He had fixed James with the same leering, wide-eyed stare that Mel had seen countless times, when he had come calling at their house as

Beth had walked dutifully out into his clutches—to protect her.

Beth, who now lay in reach of the fire. Beth, who would never wake.

Mel's vision clouded for an instant before she could blink it clear. Malverston's pudgy, sweating face took up all of her gaze, seemed to fill the world with all its jeering malevolence. She took a slow, steady breath and released the band. The stone whipped through the gap in the boards, and the mayor's eye burst like a pus-filled tomato.

*

Malverston squealed, and suddenly James was free of his embrace. The knife's pressure on his neck went slack.

A new fire ignited in James, one to dwarf that which raged about them. With a howl he seized the knife from Malverston's hand, took it up in a wide arc as he stood, and plunged it into the flabby folds of neck fat. Screaming a scream that would never end, he gripped Malverston's lapel and stabbed again, and again, and again. The remaining eye bulged as the mayor wilted, his lips open and trembling, bubbling with blood as tiny gurgling sounds escaped his throat.

All the while, James bellowed—one that became an open, wretched gape as Malverston twitched his last twitch, fell to the ground with a thump, and lay still. James dropped the knife, turning on legs that seemed to belong to another person, and went to Beth. Crouching, he put his hands out to her, but some invisible force made him flinch.

If he touched her, it was real. And that just couldn't be.

Everything went quiet as he took in Beth's blank, ruined face. The world melted away, pushing back into the far distance. Only the two of them existed in eternal night, floating together.

"Beth," he said. "Beth, it's okay. He's gone. You're safe now." His voice broke as his fingers finally touched her skin, brushing a stray piece of hair from her forehead. "Beth," he choked.

"James, come on. We have to go."

James didn't recognise the voice. It seemed so far away, so warped beyond human tones. He looked up at a blond-bearded man standing ten feet away, a rifle in his hands. All around him, fire raged. A fire that he couldn't hear, nor feel. It was an abstraction, that blaze: it could have been happening on the other side of the world. He could only stare at the thing that had once been his brother.

"Get out of here, Alex," he croaked.

"No. Come. We can't do anything for her now."

"I'm staying. I'm not leaving her again." James took her hand in his and held it to his cheek.

Alex rushed forwards and seized his collar. "This whole place is coming down, we have to go."

Somewhere even farther away, he heard Lucian bawling: "The stairs are going. Get out, both of you!"

Alex was hauling him away from Beth. They both choked on acrid smoke, barely able to see a foot in front of their faces. The floor seemed made of putty now, bending underfoot. Alex dropped his rifle to grab James with both hands.

Snarling, James threw Alex away towards the stairs. "Go. I never want to see you again."

"The whole building is burning. You'll die!"

James said nothing.

"James, I-I did it for you."

James wanted in that moment nothing more than to tear at him, claw his eyes—reach for the knife and plunge it into his head. He returned to Beth, brushing her face. "Go."

The roof cracked with a high whine, and the east section caved in behind them.

"Alex! James!" Lucian bellowed.

Alex ran. In his peripheral vision, James saw him dash away down the stairs, leaving him alone with Beth and the mayor. Coughing and wheezing, James cradled her in his arms and brought her forehead to his as the roof above him groaned a final time, and then all around him was roaring inferno.

*

Lucian almost fainted when Alex came crashing down the stairs. "Take your bloody time, eh? You want to give me a heart attack?" He gripped Alex's arms and pulled as Alex jumped over the flaming steps—not a moment too soon, for the staircase buckled and wilted into the pyre behind.

Lucian threw Alex clear and looked up into the attic. "Where's James?"

He glanced at Alex and back to the ragged opening of the attic. "We have to get something for them to slide down. Get the table!" He ran for the burning edge of the dining table, unbuttoning his shirt and tearing it off. Slapping out the flames, he dashed for the end of the table and nodded to the opposite end. "Quick. This place is coming down."

He glanced to Alex and dropped the table. The look in his eyes said everything. "No," he muttered. "No."

He ran to where the stairs had been and bellowed up into the attic. "James, I'm coming. I'm coming!" He dashed forwards but wheeled back immediately as a spurt of flames leaped into the air.

Alex seized him from behind and dragged him away.

"No, no we're not leaving."

"He's gone, Lucian."

"No!"

"We have to go."

"James. James, answer me," Lucian roared. "You answer me right now, you stupid bastard. James!"

He kept calling as Alex hauled him thrashing and kicking from the building and down off the porch. He didn't stop until the roof's spine buckled as though sucked inwards, and the entire building toppled in on itself. A fireball burst from the conflagration and rose fifty feet into the air.

Lucian sank to the ground. Even when rain began to extinguish the dying flames, and the others wept and crooned over Norman's prostrate body, all Lucian could do was stare.

James couldn't be gone. He couldn't. It wasn't in the cards. He was the Chosen One with the funny powers—the one with the destiny.

Wasn't he?

Lucian realised he wasn't alone. A figure stood in the square, a black profile against the dying fire. A slingshot hung loose in her grip.

Over what seemed an eternity he went to her. They said nothing, just stood together until the rain had done its work, the hall was a black smoking ruin, and the square had turned to thick mud. All the while the same look remained on her face: that of a much older person, one who had been beaten down all their life, and expects nothing but strife from the world.

Mel turned and walked away towards the Moon.

"Wait. Where are you going?"

She blinked, a slow, lost expression on her face. "Home. Mum needs me."

"Come with us. We can take care of you."

She shook her head, her gaze on Alexander. Lucian expected to see fury there, but instead he saw only sadness, something irrevocably broken. "I have to be the big girl now." She didn't look back again, vanishing into the night.

Lucian watched her go, then headed back to the others.

"It's dangerous here," Oliver was saying.

"We can't... I..." Agatha's face had become a haggard wreck.

Alex spoke over them, a hard-edged baritone. "We're going home. It's finished here."

"We can't leave them. We have to bury them," Lucian said.

Alex laid a hand on his shoulder, and for a terrible moment Lucian recoiled. "Norman's bleeding. We have to get him back, or we'll lose him too."

Lucian looked at Norman unconscious in the grass, his head tightly wrapped in gauze and his body swaddled in a makeshift stretcher.

*Just a kid… and now he's got to live without his parents because of one stupid mistake. Will he ever forgive us?*

It didn't matter, because Lucian knew he would never forgive himself. One thing they could do was get him home and get him well.

"Okay," he said, fixated on the ruin behind them, and the glistening skyline of the newly liberated Newquay's Moon. "Let's go."

# IV

L atif sat back from the radio and sighed. It was done.

Fighting exhaustion, barely balancing on the stool, he stared at the worktop and gathered his strength. He had sent the distress call on every channel the Blanket had relinquished, over and over, for two hours. Cycling back and forth between the channels, finding them with the same guiding force working through his fingers, homing in on blissful breaks in the unearthly squeal, he had sent his voice into the world.

All his life he had dreamed of talking with those elsewhere, anywhere, bringing back what the Old World had taken for granted.

Now it rang hollow inside him. To find all this, when the barbarians were quite literally at their gate. It would all be for nothing, and when the smoke cleared and this generation had passed on and the world had been consumed, nobody would ever know what they had done here.

*They won't know anything because they won't be at all*, a voice said in his head. *If we don't win, there won't be anything left.*

He shuddered, shaking it off. He didn't believe in that crap.

But nothing could rid him of the certainty that had set like cement in his gut. He simply knew it was true. Just as he knew that his voice would be heard.

He had hit the nail on the head when he had said it to the old man: there was something out there fighting for them. It might have left them to struggle and die all this time, watching and waiting, but now—just this once—it had stepped out of line to guide him. Out there, just maybe, it had told others to listen.

He shucked and stood, shedding his blanket from his shoulders and flexing. His work here was done. It was time to go do what he could outside.

Latif paused at the workshop door and looked back. "This better work."

He headed out into the courtyard, flexing legs that had grown unused to walking of late, approaching the wall and scaling the catwalk stairs. Ignoring the rain, he checked the wall for signs of weakness, not through concern but by force of habit.

The last of the nursing volunteers were moving their antiseptic baths into the tower, and a few burly men hauled the last of the food stores inside. It seemed they felt it just as keenly as he did: the unyielding sense that a ticking clock somewhere had come to a stop.

Latif drew parallel with Evelyn. "May I?"

She didn't respond for a moment, standing drenched in

her shawl, which stuck unceremoniously to her body, her hair lank around her face. She stared for so long he thought she might banish him, but instead she reached out and cupped the back of his head. "You're just like him, you know," she said.

"The old man?" Latif scoffed. "Never in a million years, not that old goat…" He cleared his throat. "I'll never be as wise as that."

He caught a wry look from her in the corner of his eye.

"Do you think we'll be heard?" she said.

He could only shrug. It was so cold now, so very cold—a thousand tiny insects nipped at his bones. The clouds were lower every time he looked up, as though the sky itself were falling.

*Maybe it is*, he thought.

A gush of fear ran through him as he realised all this was really happening. While he had dallied with the radio and everybody had moved around him, he had lost himself in the work. Only now did the realisation truly hit home.

Something squeezed his fingers, and he looked down to see Evelyn's hand around his.

The ice in her gaze thawed, and she squeezed tighter. "You scared?"

Latif nodded as the wind rustled his hair and the rain slashed down without end. At the far end of the dual carriageway stretching away from the gate, a dark mass had appeared at the edge of sight, made fuzzy by the storm. A hard sphere formed high in his throat. "I'm scared," he croaked.

She blinked as a reverberating rush faded into audibility: the roar of thousands of voices. "'Atta boy," she said.

*

"You son of a bitch!" Charlie barked.

Jason vanished in a blur before Charlie's knuckles could come within ten inches of him. A moment later Charlie's cheek was a mass of pain, and the world hazed over. Then he hit the floor, his gammy leg splayed awkwardly to one side. "How could you? They were our people!"

He whirled onto his back and looked up at the wolfish thing standing over him. He was on the verge of throwing another insult when Jason's long curved blade swept down to touch his chin.

"Stay still, pup," Jason said. "Very still." He cocked his head, observing Charlie with the curiosity of a child watching insects scurry under a magnifying glass.

Charlie looked at the bleeding, torn people around them. Grit and pebbles lay embedded in faces, razor-sharp metal sticking out from bellies and shoulders. They had lost over a thousand people back in the square, half of them cut to pieces by their own artillery.

Jason had given the order. Before Charlie had been able to fight his way to the front line to countermand the order, the damage was done, and the fight in the square had been over.

"How could you?" he spat. "Our own!"

"No, not ours. We are not brothers. They're just things."

He waved to those bleeding out not ten feet from him. "*Things.*"

Charlie looked to them, gaping.

*Why don't they kill him? There are a hundred people in earshot. They could cut him down in a moment.*

But could they? Looking at Jason afresh, all hope drained out of him. Their sheeplike, languid forms watched, just watched. They visibly wilted as Jason turned to survey them, holding out an arm as though in welcome.

"Anybody have anything to say?" he called. He grinned, a horrific thing that sent Charlie's nerves crackling. "No? Then what are you still doing here?"

The silence that followed could have stopped hearts. Ever so gradually, those still able to walk headed east, towards the Alliance compound. Jason's mad stare persisted until the trickle had become a steady flow. Those whose blood oozed over the ground watched from the pavement with long, laboured breaths, babbling in horror as they were passed without a second glance.

"You can't do this," Charlie said.

"I am doing this." Jason danced the tip of his knife over Charlie's cheek. "Are you going to stop me, little boy?"

Charlie remained frozen in place, watching the blade sweep down under his chin and up over the other cheek. He winced as it rested against his temple and pressed inwards sharply, slicing his hairline.

"I asked you a question, pup."

Charlie shook his head fractionally.

"I don't hear you."

"No."

The blade carved fire along his cheek and Charlie grated his teeth until it was level with his ear. Then the knife dropped, and blood beaded on his chin.

"I'll take it from here—oh, and I'll be back for you after. Run if you like. I'll find you." Jason winked. "Have fun."

Then he was gone after the others.

Charlie lay dripping blood as mortar pipes pushed past him, moving east, while the main body of the army passed in earnest.

Suddenly he felt hollow. Not horrified, but empty. He was nobody.

Thousands passed, staggering on legs barely working, dead-set eyes trained forwards, following the ragged mass that had consumed them. They vanished into the storm, and Charlie was left with the fallen.

His father's voice spoke inside his head: "Time to wake up, boy. Time to get out of this."

*No! I won't let them get away with it.*

He couldn't give up. It was all he had left.

Ambling to his feet, he steeled himself against the long searching gazes of those dying beside him and limped away in the wake of the army—Jason's army.

*

The storm gathered about the compound, smothering the Isle of Dogs in milky tendrils. Evelyn shivered constantly but no longer felt the cold, nor even her feet under her; all bodily senses had abandoned her.

Distant rumblings and cracks reached them; the sounds of stone and metal being torn and people dying. The world seemed to be losing depth and focus, a fading so gradual as to be almost imperceptible. It was as though reality itself was fizzling.

"Ma'am, you should go inside," said Marek's deputy, a wall of muscle towering over her.

She turned her stare on him, and he stalled. She enjoyed a glimmer of satisfaction. She might be old and frail, but she wasn't done yet. "I am going nowhere."

"It's time to seal the tower."

"Then do so. I am not going to cower in my keep."

"We can't protect you out here." He gestured between her and Latif. "Neither of you."

She waved a sharp hand at him. "If I am to die, I will do it standing!"

From the corner of her mouth, she said to Latif, "You get inside while you can."

He jerked. "Run? Now? Get lost... Ma'am."

"Oliver is preparing whoever can put up a fight. If the walls fall, we're going to need everyone. He'll need your help."

"I can't help them!"

"You're no good here. Go, darling. Please."

Latif looked forlorn, blushing. The noise ahead was building, the ghostly sighing of some titanic being on approach.

"I'll be back. As soon as we're secure."

She pulled his hand from her arm. "Go on."

He whirled and pattered down the stairs. She watched him cross the empty courtyard and vanish into the tower lobby. The doors slammed shut behind him, and she caught a few winks of activity through the revolving doors as hasty barricades were thrown together on the marble floor.

The catwalk's length was lined with dozens of their best fighters. They were few, but she stood among the closest things to soldiers this world had to offer.

*Let them come*, she thought.

Lightning arced overhead. As one, they stared into the mist. Then from the monotonous rumble of pattering rain, noise from ahead, and the skies. The medley boggled her momentarily, and she searched for the source.

The strange double rumble took on form simultaneously, resolving into the roar of voices ahead, and a strange whine from the sky. The darkened streets morphed into a rushing mass of people, more people than she had seen together since the End, sprinting for the compound. Above, the whine became ear-splitting as somebody bellowed, "Get down!"

The next instant, a section of the wall to her left spattered into a thousand pieces as fire burst upwards. Evelyn blinked, dumbstruck.

"No," she breathed. "No, they can't have—"

Another section of the wall detonated. Evelyn saw the deputy running for her, shouting inaudibly. He came to within five feet of her when the air became a solid wall, and a giant hand thrust her clear from the catwalk. She tried to scream as fiery teeth chomped at her legs, but it was too late.

Darkness.

*

Marek ran. His leg throbbed, threatening to buckle, but he kept going. Everywhere, other survivors from Trafalgar Square were shot in the back as they fled.

*Christ, we're being mown down.*

There was nothing else for it. If they stopped for cover, they would be swarmed in seconds. If they crouched, their gain would diminish, and they would only be easier targets. All they could do is run.

"Keep going! Don't—"

A ginger-haired woman he had been reaching for dropped out of sight, red mist spraying Marek's cheek.

Canary Wharf loomed from the mist that had entombed it, amorphous shapes emerging from the milky blanket. Relief flooded him as he picked out the antlike figures on the catwalk. They were so close.

Another minute and they would reach the gate. It would be a huge risk to open and close it in time, but they had to take it: there were still two-hundred people out here, two hundred they couldn't afford to lose.

Marek got ready to give the order. They would have to time it perfectly. In his mind he was already scaling the catwalk stairs to take control, picturing the battlefield in his mind, where he would concentrate fire—

A whine he recognised all too well built suddenly

overhead, plummeting down with ferocious speed.

"Get down!" Marek yelled with everything he had, tearing something in his throat.

The ground shook as the wall vanished in a hail of rubble. Hammering down from above, no less than a dozen shells landed together and obliterated the wall along a twenty-foot stretch.

Marek could only gape, running still as the dust cloud swept down over him.

*The wall was all we had. And our firepower just went along with it.*

Breathing vaporised concrete, he reached where the gate had been. Before him lay a buckled twist of iron, gaping wide. On either side the wall was pockmarked with ragged holes, denuded to a few feet in height.

Already the whine was building again.

"Get under any cover you can find. Be ready!"

Marek passed through the gate and got behind the wall's remaining cover. With the creeping dread of taking a bullet to the back stalled momentarily, he searched the rubble in a mad frenzy, checking smoking bodies for anything useful.

Maybe they could lay down enough fire to cover the bottleneck at the gate.

Every body he checked bore a face scorched and inhuman. Any weapons were twisted, useless. Cursing, he yelled, "Here they come."

While the others took cover, Marek kept searching, yelling in pain as his leg cracked ominously. He stopped when he unearthed something that punched all the air from his lungs: a single scrap of shawl.

Marek stared dumbly while the world span, until the moment the gate darkened and the first of the emaciated figures came rushing through. In the same moment, the next wave of shells hit, peppering the courtyard.

Marek ran for them, swinging the sabre, slashing with wild abandon, knowing he had only a few moments left. The sheer ferocity of his swings sent the first wave sprawling back, but there was no fooling hard numbers: the sheer mass of their ranks continued pouring through the gate and gaps in the walls like a scourge of locusts. A bulbous beachhead formed in moments.

Hot metal flew down from the tower, spraying the wall and the asphalt, eliciting screams and grunts that were half-drowned by the intermittent explosions gouging the ground.

From the mass of skeletal bodies, Marek spotted a figure moving with such grace that, for a moment, he thought he was dead already, and he watched the pirouetting of an angel. Then the figure resolved into a snarling man with a face like a wild dog, cutting through people as though they were inanimate slabs of meat.

Marek rolled hard to the left, bringing them to face one another. The man halted for a moment, and they looked each other up and down. Marek lunged, sabre in hand. Only then, seeing the man feint to the side with the fluidity of water, did Marek realise how weak he had become. All he could do next was watch the sabre carry him uselessly forwards, while the dog man crouched with easy grace and brought the knife up under him.

Pain shot through him and set a thousand bells ringing. For an instant the man was by his side, breathing hot stinking breath over his face. Then the knife was pulled back, and Marek watched the floor rush up to strike him in the face.

The world receded as fast as the pain, spinning down a long black corridor. As Marek died, the orchestra of destruction wound down and warped into a deep, gloopy hum; and for just a moment, that sound became the laughter of something beyond the world, a mad staring evil that closed its fist over the dying earth.

# V

Norman kicked at his horse's sides and rounded the corner of what had once been the NatWest skyscraper, followed by two dozen riders. The explosions had reached them minutes ago, and the sound of battle had begun soon after. He knew they were already too late, but it took all his resolve not to haul the reins.

*The city, the storm,* he thought as the dream that had plagued him for so long flashed before his eyes. *The day all this started. We've come full circle.*

Canary Wharf lay in turmoil. Hordes surged in through the broken gate, smoke rose from a hundred craters gouged into the street, the wall had been shattered to so much rubble, and about it all, a swirling leviathan descended upon the tower from the black clouds.

The shelling of the walls ended, and a moment of comparative deathly silence followed. Then with a tinkling that sounded like a thousand ringing bells, myriad panes of glass blew out on the tower's western flank. Moments later a second volley tore the guts from a floor close to the tower's peak, sending shredded office furniture spinning out into

"

space. Constant shelling resumed, peppering the great spire of chrome and glass with holes.

Norman cursed into the rain. How many kids and injured refugees were in there? Hundreds, or thousands?

The Frost inside him thrummed to effervescent life, threatening to burst out of him like a moth emerging from a chrysalis.

*It's here. It's from here the End will spread, once and for all. This is no rainstorm, and those are no clouds.*

One way or another, this fight was going to be over fast.

He kicked harder, urging the horse onwards. If he stopped now, the others would halt, and if that happened they would be fodder in the open. They raced down the street towards what had once been the wall.

Norman brought his rifle up to head height. Jouncing along, it swayed wildly in his grasp. He let go of the reins, squeezing the horse with his knees. Beside him, Robert rested his own rifle on a forearm, taking aim.

Norman fired, and a moment later a dozen other blasts sounded over his shoulder. Several figures dropped to the ground—a handful from a crowd that seemed infinite, stretching into the mist as an unbroken carpet of bloody faces and bony bodies.

"Hit them head-on!" Norman said.

Their only chance was to penetrate as far in as they could. Most of the army had passed in through the walls, blind to their approach. But if they got caught outside the wall, they wouldn't last a minute. They had to get into the courtyard and make for the tower.

He gritted his teeth. The ragged figures ahead heard them too late: they turned just in time for the horses' bodies to collide with them, screaming as they fell under dozens of hooves. As one they plummeted headlong into the crowd, passing through the gate and parting the crowd as a boat ploughs the waves, leaving a bow wave of flying bodies in their wake.

He cast a hasty look about, stealing the lay of the land. The lobby had lost all its glass panes, and the battle raged for the most part inside or immediately outside it. Other pockets of resistance held near the stables, Lincoln's workshop, and near the catwalks.

He stabbed down with the butt of his rifle, beating unsuspecting heads as he passed, praying an errant shell didn't hit ground and bring an abrupt end. Behind him he could hear the others sticking close as he steered towards the lobby. Seventy feet, then sixty, fifty.

*We're going to make it!*

A lone figure leaped from the crowd, one he would have recognised anywhere, even now amidst the surging chaos. Jason leered in Norman's path, standing perched with his dripping knife held out to one side.

Norman bent low on the saddle and brought his rifle butt up high. For a giddy instant he thought he had won: either Jason would be trampled, or he would dive aside to be clobbered. Then in a show of litheness that defied all logic, Jason passed to the side and down in exiguous pirouette, bringing his knife over the horse's knees.

The world revolved. The horse's rear came up as the

forelimbs crumpled, and then Norman was flying, wheeling his arms as his forwards momentum carried him through the air. He landed upon a pile of bodies two deep and rolled.

He scrambled, willing pain not to come, certain that he would be dead in a moment. He grabbed blindly as the others rocketed by, surging ahead towards the tower, and found his feet. He searched the writhing madness for his own mount. If he could get to it, his rifle still might be close by. The horse had cartwheeled in a spectacular slide, crushing at least four people under it.

Beside it, a canvas bag had come loose from the saddle and slid twenty feet in the mud. It twitched, alive. The neck of the sack opened and fell away, revealing a tiny, tearful figure. Norman's heart stopped.

Billy.

"No," he breathed.

A blur in his peripheral vision drew his gaze: Jason hurtled for him with his tongue lolling and eyes bulging; an inhuman archetype of carnivorous malice.

Norman ran for the saddle. "Run, Billy!"

The girl stood staring, her lips pale, surrounded on all sides by people being stabbed, hacked, and beaten. She cringed and fell to her haunches, locking her hands over her head.

"No, Billy, go!" Norman yelled, waving his hands over his head. "The tower. Get inside!"

She only stared, still crouched, shaking.

Norman leaped upon the saddle, grabbing wildly in the dirt and torn leather for any sign of a gun barrel, stock, trigger—anything. For an agonising handful of seconds all he could do was feel blindly, watching Jason sprint towards him. There was no time! No time!

A whoosh of air was accompanied by a one-ton shadow surging past. Allie rode headlong for Jason, slapping the reins viciously.

"No, Allie!"

Jason snarled as he rolled away. Already he was coming up behind her as Norman's pulse surged behind his eyes and he found his gun's barrel, and he yanked at it.

Allie yelled, thrown bodily from her saddle as her own horse's legs were cut to shreds.

Norman almost abandoned the rifle—he wasn't about to watch Allie torn apart—but Jason had whirled back towards him. Norman tore at the rifle with renewed desperation. It was caught on something, budging just a little more each time, but wouldn't come free.

*Please. Oh God, please just this once!*

"I've waited a long time for this," Jason grinned. Then he was a blur of motion hurtling forwards.

Norman ran his hands along the barrel, found a snag of netting looped over the sight, and yanked it free. Threading it out, he brought the barrel up as the last few feet between them closed. His finger had just begun to depress the trigger when Jason's knife swept in from the side and knocked the gun whirling from his hands.

*No.*

Jason sneered. The knife was already coming over his back.

Norman closed his eyes and waited to die.

Then Jason was yelling, and when Norman opened his eyes he saw Billy's paring knife sticking from Jason's arm, just above the bicep. Convulsing with his teeth bared, Jason batted the knife free and whirled towards her.

His eyes narrowed in something beyond wildness: a visceral, rending hatred, spraying spittle from his lips. "*YOU!*"

Billy screamed and ran.

Before Norman could move, Jason was gone in her wake as she scrambled for the tower. His hands grabbed at the ground for something, anything, and found a sticky handle. Then he was being dragged up to his feet, and Allie was before him.

"What is she doing here?" she screamed.

Norman couldn't answer, just looked at what he held in his hand: an antique French sabre.

*A sword?* he thought distantly.

"We can't let him get her." He grabbed Allie's arm and gave chase. They fought through the crowd, pivoting and diving, cutting through legs and behind backs, until they burst into the scant space between the courtyard and the tower.

Ahead, Billy vanished inside, dwarfed by everything around her: the sheer scale of madness and sound, and the debris cascading down as the shells continued to pummel the tower's peak.

"We have to get her, Norman. We have to get her!"

They passed through the buckled revolving door, which

snagged Norman's shirt as he passed and left a gouge along his left flank, and then they were inside the echoing marble cave. The noise was rancorous, every collision and scream amplified a hundredfold; coupled with the echoing rumble of the explosions high above, it sounded as though the gods themselves fought within these walls.

Norman had a queer moment of clarity, watching the tower's defences crumble, the barricades being overrun, people rolling upon the floor in desperate struggles. In the chaos he had forgotten the cold; cold he now clearly felt.

The Frost was right here, inside this building. The one person who could stop it was sprinting from a creature hell-bent on cutting her in half.

He and Allie leaped fallen bodies and shredded barricades in pursuit, watching helplessly as Jason closed on Billy.

"Run, Billy!" Norman bellowed.

Ahead, Billy and Jason vanished from sight, cat and mouse, moving up into the tower's bowels.

*

Charlie took the stairs two at a time, breathless and groaning, dragging his bad leg behind him. "We have a problem!"

James watched him approach without moving an inch. "Yes?"

Charlie glanced between Alexander and James. "It's Jason. He's firing on our own."

"Did they push through?"

"Yes, but he fired the mortars behind our own lines."

"Where are they now?"

Charlie blinked, wordless. "They… they're behind the walls. It's done."

James's cold, measured voice: "How long?"

Charlie paused, heart throbbing in his throat. His breath echoed loud and hollow in the empty office, with so many blank uncaring faces staring back at him.

"Minutes. They lost their front line in the first wave. But Jason won't stop. He's just throwing them in like meat into a grinder."

James's eyes fixed so sharply on him that Charlie could barely move, X-rayed down to the last molecule.

*What if he sees what I am underneath? He's different, he knows things; maybe he sees.*

Who was he kidding? Charlie had known that all along. He had sided with the devil to get a chance to right the Alliance's wrongs. Yet, when the time had come, and McKay had been in his clutches, James had let him go.

*He used me just like he used everyone else. Lies all the way down.*

He should have been dead. He had seen the way they all looked at him, as though they were just waiting to leave him by the roadside, no matter how hard he tried to hide it.

He had been kept alive for something.

Looking at James now, he realised that that purpose had come to the fore. A beat passed in which he sensed Cain glance between them, and the guards shifted on the balls of their feet.

"Why am I here?" he said.

James took a step forwards, such that Charlie could see the edges of the twisted scar tissue peeking around the side of his balaclava. "I've killed hundreds like you."

"I know," Charlie said, intent to keep his gaze level no matter how far his guts twisted.

"You're here to show him"—he pointed to Cain—"why we do what we do. I could burn that tower to ash, hunt down every last person who knows his name, and do you know what would happen?"

Charlie said nothing. The guards' guns seemed to glare at him from the corner of his eye.

"Nothing," James said. "Nothing would happen. He'd just start all over again. And again, and again, no matter what it took and no matter how many people ended up dead. Because that's what he is. No amount of killing is ever going to change that."

"So why are we doing this?"

"Because it's what must be done to put things right for good. There will be no starting over." He nodded to the black clouds outside. "The world was supposed to end, truly. A final peace. We're correcting that. Once this storm clears, all will be as it should."

"You can't really believe that," Cain muttered.

James ignored him. "Before that happens, I need him to see in front of his eyes the moment somebody chooses to do terrible things, because to do nothing would be so much worse."

Charlie fingered his belt, resisting the urge to reach for his knife. The guards would gun him down before he could reach it, but in that moment he sensed an aura of madness—of something *cold* and *wrong*—and found himself wanting nothing more than to stab James and run.

*I've helped end the world.*

He stammered, "Why me?"

"You can decide to do what must be done—what you know is right. So many have died for their obsession. If we burn them now, they'll spawn again like cockroaches, an eternal cycle trapping us all in misery and ruin."

*I thought the storm following us was just me going crazy. But it's not that. It's him. He's the harbinger.*

Fingers of strange cold reached around Charlie's ankles, probing him, penetrating him. In time, he knew they would consume him.

"I can't."

"You can. We have in us the chance to be more than what we are. But we have to choose to make it so. So choose, Charlie."

Charlie thought he would remain frozen forever. But then he laughed, a tiny bitter huff. "You're a liar. This was never about choice, or justice. You used us all. It was always about you. You're just another murderer."

James gripped his collar. Charlie closed his eyes and prepared for the end.

*Just a moment of pain and it'll all be over.*

No end came. He peeked through one eye and found James staring as though he were some curious specimen. "I thought you would be different. Of all people, you would understand."

Charlie thought of his father, the sweet man who had once put chestnuts in his cheeks and capered about by the campfire, when they had been robbed of their inventory and lay destitute on the roadside. They had had nothing but each other, and starvation had been close. In times like that, Dad had always done the thing nobody else did: he smiled and stared death in the face with the biggest goofy grin he could muster.

That was what mattered, when they had all passed on and they were but dust in the air: what they chose to do when things looked their worst.

What would Dad think if he was here, now? What would he do?

His father's voice spoke from the ether: *I'm through telling you what to do, boy. I'm dead. Go with your gut.*

Charlie looked to Cain and back to James. "I know what it's like," he said. "Like the world's going to tear open if you don't do everything you can to get back at them. But I won't be this."

"I'm giving you a choice, Charlie. All things will end here today, one way or another. The only thing that matters is who's right and who's wrong. You have the chance to light up the darkness."

Charlie forced himself to smile. "I am. Go to hell."

James's eyes twitched, darting between him and Cain. A flash of uncertainty, maybe fear. Then it was gone and the deadened gaze fell back into place. "Fine." He launched

Charlie across the room. "Go and die." With a harsh wave of his arm, he bade his escort follow. "Both of you as well. We're done here."

Charlie swallowed, backing away. The escort filed out warily, pattering away down into the street. Charlie neared the doorway, his gaze drawn to Cain. Cain, the source of his pain. The look on his face said everything there was to be said.

*There's still time to stop it.*

Charlie reached the threshold and took one last look at them both, two leaders of men lurking in the shadows. Then he was ambling down the stairs, dragging his lame leg after him.

*

Billy tripped on the last flight of stairs. She managed to keep her feet as she reached the next floor in a lurching half run, then a sack of grain caught her foot and she went sprawling. Dusty tiles slammed her cheek and she skidded painfully. All the while her heart pounded *thum thum thum!* in her chest.

The monster would get her. She felt him just behind her like a needle pressing into her head.

She span onto her back, expecting to see him standing over her with his bloody knife. But he was still on the stairs, sprinting up as though on a cushion of air. He moved so fast!

Billy scrambled to her feet and ran down a long corridor.

The building touched the clouds—so big that she would never find her way out again if she got lost. What if the monster chased her where nobody could follow, and it was just the two of them lost in the metal maze forever?

There wasn't time to think. No time for anything. Just running, breathing, and pumping her legs even though they wanted to fall into useless lumps under her.

Half her mind struggled with the darkness raining down from the sky. It was going to gobble them all up if she didn't fight it. The cold was already more than she could bear, eating away at her. The Light inside shone bright, thrumming through her and out and away, but she felt like she was holding up a tent which had no poles; as soon as she stopped fighting, that darkness would come crashing in and it would all be over. It was so hard to keep the Light shining. And if the monster caught her…

They had to stop the darkness for good. There was only one way: everyone had to stop being afraid.

*How?* she thought. *How can you make people not afraid when there's so much to be afraid of?*

Behind her the monster reached the top of the stairs. His shoes squeaked over the floor after her. The same monster who had taken Grandpa away, who had tried to kill Allie, who had burned Norm's home to the ground.

Daddy had said that there were no such thing as monsters, that they were just imaginations from fairy tales.

*You lied, Daddy. You lied about the monsters.*

Ahead, light. She passed through a pair of doors and the corridor expanded into a much larger space. A throng of grim-faced men and women held sharpened table and chair legs like spears, crouched tight beside one another to form a wall of sharp points.

Billy skidded to a stop, trapped between them and the monster at her back.

*No, no, no, he'll get me!*

The monster was right behind—just seconds.

"Please!" she screamed.

The wall of spears dropped, revealing not soldiers but loose-skinned old folks and people whose arms and legs were bound by days-old bandages.

"Get the girl back!" somebody yelled.

A gap appeared in the wall of spears and Billy's head filled with squeaking footsteps rushing up behind her like thunder. Drawing her shoulders together, expecting a knife to dig into her back, she pushed between the spears, pushing through sweating unwashed bodies, the smell of fear and sickness filling her nose.

She found more people behind, and more going all the way back. As she went, each layer looked weaker, holding yet more pathetic sticks, slouching ever closer to the ground.

*Grown-ups get scared, Billy,* Daddy had said once when the merchants came by the farm and their faces had been creased up and scary. *They look mean and talk mean, but they all get scared. They're still little boys and girls inside.*

Billy hadn't been able to believe that until now. These people looked just like she felt. Then the squeaking came through the doors and they too saw the monster, and the yelling started.

Billy screamed when an old man grabbed her roughly by the shoulder and lifted her from the crowd. He had big tufts of hair along the side of his face, and a long hat on top of his bald head. "Child, what are you doing here?" he shouted.

Billy screamed. "Let me go, the monster's after me, let me go!"

"What are you—?"

"Lincoln!" cried a skinny young man, pointing over her shoulder.

Billy twisted in his grasp to see the spear-holders go shrieking to the ground as the monster slashed down at them. That moment slowed to a crawl as the monster turned, his face dripping with slicks of red broken in half by a grin so wide his lips seemed to touch his ears.

The old man dropped her. "Run, child."

Billy ran past the last of the sick people and on into older, dustier parts of the building. Fresh screams spurred her on. The rush of more feet coming up from below chased her as she plunged into the dusty building, a great silent maze. All the while her insides turned to icicles, until she was sure that she would shatter if she stopped for even one second. By the time she found more stairs and dashed up and up, her breath puffed in front of her face, and she felt the Light inside her sputter and fade.

There was no itch now, no knowing. There was just her running feet and the monster's prowling footsteps, coming closer.

*

Lucian ripped a last cartridge from his rifle and cursed. He had managed to keep on horseback for almost a minute before being brought down by mob force, spilled like the others into the teeming masses. It had been a matter of fighting his way to one of the rapidly-fading Alliance strongholds, letting instinct guide him.

Emerging from the rabble was like sinking under the ocean surface during a tempest. Not far away, Robert's hulking form swerved in vicious swings of his arms, beating people with blades, splintered wood, his bare fists—anything. With each strike he bellowed with a ferocity Lucian wouldn't have known had been in him—before Sarah.

The last survivors headed for the tower. There was seldom any resistance left; the fight now took place inside the buckled spire—a silver thread being trashed from below, blasted from the side and consumed by darkness from above.

He was on the verge of running for the lobby when a skinny figure stepped through the crumbled wall. Charlie dragged his leg behind him, and Lucian saw in his mind's eye a flash of New Canterbury. Not too long ago, Lucian had sent him limping away into the hills at gunpoint with nothing but his clothes and grief—grief for the father Lucian had cut down.

Something inside Lucian snapped.

He had been so angry, so afraid. All he had wanted was

to keep his family together. Norman, Alex, Agatha… he couldn't lose it all again. It had blinded him to his own cruelty.

Lucian realised he was walking towards Charlie, no longer fighting, not even dodging. He was just walking, and for a time the whole terrible mess seemed to fade away. Charlie had spotted him and froze as Lucian stepped over the bodies of his friends and those he had himself slain until the two of them stood but a few feet from one another.

*He's broken now, just like the rest of us.*

Lucian dropped his rifle. "Hello, Charlie."

Charlie's mouth tightened. "I only helped them because they promised me I could kill you," he said. "I want you to know that. All this, everything I did."

Lucian could have sank three feet into the mud. All those people… because of him.

"I'm sorry for what I did," Lucian said.

"That doesn't change anything."

"I know." He nodded, raised his arms out to the side. "I know."

Charlie raised a pistol to Lucian's chest, hand shaking, eyes budding with angry tears. "I have to."

Lucian nodded. "It's okay."

Charlie's eyes twitched, tears welling up in great clots and spilling over down his cheeks.

"Do it."

Lucian took a breath and looked off towards the tower. "Do it!"

Lucian blinked, for in the next moment Charlie dropped

the pistol and reached for him. Lucian struggled and they rolled over the ground, yelling into one another's faces as they came to rest under the stable awning. Lucian pounded Charlie's side and dragged himself up on top of him, reaching up to pound his face.

"Wait!"

Lucian paused.

Charlie spluttered between his teeth: "I need your help." He arched his head towards the swirling black clouds that had now engulfed the tip of the tower. "We have to stop it."

Breathless, Lucian tightened his grip and pulled Charlie up to face him. "What?"

"The cold, the dark, we have to stop it."

Lucian looked once more and realised just how monstrous those clouds were, how ominous, as though the gods themselves were reaching down to wipe them all away like ants.

"How?" he said.

"The others, we have to stop them. That's how it'll end. We brought the storm, and the storm will take us all."

"How can you know that?" But as Lucian spoke, watching the tower slowly vanishing into the bowels of the tar-slick sky, he knew it was true.

Lucian's gaze flicked back and forth between Charlie and the tower. How could he throw in his lot with a kid who had tried to kill him for countless weeks—kidnapped him, tortured him?

*What choice is there?*

Lucian scowled and yelled, "Robert, I need your help—"

Robert was gone.

*Christ, they even took him.*

Steeling himself against a spate of cursing, he turned to Charlie. "Can you do this?"

Charlie blinked and hesitated, and in that moment Lucian saw him as he really was.

*He's still just a bloody kid. A stupid kid.*

He reached out and took Charlie's shoulders. "Pull yourself together. We can do it."

Charlie stammered, "How? There are so many…" He gestured to the lobby, writhing with people squeezing inside through the ragged bottleneck of broken glass.

"We'll do it by doing it."

They ran for the tower as the last of the warmth left the air, and from the ether built a distant, low buzzing.

Lucian's gut twisted into a tight knot at the noise. He didn't recognise it at first, but some primal part of him knew it well. By the time they reached the lobby and began waving their arms, calling for attention, he realised how he knew that sound: he had heard it once before, only once, on a day when he had been but eight years old.

The day the world went away.

"It's coming," he yelled to Charlie. "Hurry!"

# VI

The woman was young with bright grey eyes. A pretty round face, the kind that sweeps away the cobwebs of the day's comings and goings. Latif had seen her before, he realised. In the mad jumble of memories that was his life, shuffling back and forth between the workshop and his bunk, he had caught flashes of her bright smile, glimpses of her face. A face now in his arms, pale and frozen in a last gasp for air that would never come. The girl's shuddering stilled and he slid to the ground with her, touching the knife sticking from her back.

Blinking stupidly at his hands, slicked with crimson, he groaned.

Everywhere, screaming. Those whom he had worked with, dished out meals with, washed clothes with, played games with: all caught in howling frenzy; dignity scraped clean away as they scratched, chocked, and pounded. The spears had gone now, snapped and thrown to the floor as the first wave of invaders had been impaled upon them, pushed ever forwards by the next wave at their backs.

Latif had actually thought they might have had a chance

at stalling them, right until the lines broke and people poured into the tower. Outside they had seemed many; inside they became countless, a single unbroken wave come to sweep them away. When the wave broke over them, the snarling beasts became people, just as afraid as him.

The horror was nauseating: there were no good guys, no bad guys; no justice to be had; no victory to be taken.

For every person that fell, the room grew colder, and the air thicker, as though the atmosphere froze to the lining of his lungs, working away at him from the inside out.

He still stared at his bloody hands.

*Move, Latif. Get your arse going or you're dead.*

Still he stared, until a gnarled, white-haired fist closed over his arm. Lincoln's grizzled face had grown pale and was twisted by a grimace so deep that Latif suspected his wrinkles would never flatten. He had somehow kept hold of a length of table leg. "No time to stop, boy!" he yelled, throwing Latif ahead.

"What do we do? We're cut off."

"Hold them!" Lincoln boomed above the sound of another explosion rocking the tower. The shelling moved progressively downwards, bombarding lower and lower floors. Soon destruction would be wrought upon them directly.

*That's if the fires don't burn or suffocate us first,* he thought.

He never thought he would die this way: trapped between raging lunatics from below and flames and smoke from above.

"There are too many!"

Lincoln seized the post of a bed in which an unconscious man lay. Around a hundred such beds lay before them, their occupants barely conscious. With their last stand rapidly crumbling, nothing lay between them and the army's ranks. "We have to get them back. Hold them as long as we can."

"Why? What's…"

*What's the point?* Latif thought, a sour taste in his mouth.

To his astonishment, Lincoln smiled and pointed out through the windows behind them.

Latif whirled to face the window and gaped. The city was almost invisible through the barrier of clouds, but still he could see the ant trails moving towards the tower from all directions. Trails not part of the army's ranks, neither blackened nor marching under the sigil of the pigeon. Hundreds of people hurried along the roads in a vast uniform trickle, as though the tower were a beacon calling them forth from the wild's enormity.

*But that means…*

Then he was laughing with such force that his insides seemed to be crawling out through his nostrils, great hacking peels that doubled him up. "They heard us. They heard us!"

The radio transmission had worked. He had hoped that somebody, somewhere, might have heard it. But not this, never this.

The first of the newcomers reached the crumbled wreckage of the concrete wall and sprinted into the courtyard.

Lincoln thumped Latif's side. "Let's get these people out of here."

"Right." Latif turned from the window. They took an end of the bed each and shuffled back into the building, moving through old office doors until they reached the cavernous council chambers. Others close by took up the initiative, shuffling more beds behind them. Soon a trail started up, and the last survivors retreated into the chambers that had once reigned supreme over the land.

"All we have to do is hold out until they get here," Lincoln said.

Laughter turned to bile in Latif's gut, for as they passed through the mahogany doors he squinted at strange striations all around. Frost grew on the walls like growths of mould, blossoming icicles and spreading spindly arms to floor and ceiling. Before his eyes the arms joined together, icicles spread onto seats, entombed light fittings and tables and guard rails. Inside him, Latif felt it slowly freezing his blood in his veins.

Not just chill anymore, but arctic cold with intent to kill.

They ran back for more beds, and Latif prayed the others would hurry.

# VII

Allie groaned aloud when she and Norman found themselves back at the stairs.

*A circle*, Norman thought wildly. *We've gone around in a big circle.*

They hadn't had a glimpse of Billy or Jason since the lobby. Each time they ascended to another floor, there was only one thing for it: scour every room, calling her name, pushing through anybody fighting on the upper floors. If Billy had gone up even a dozen storeys, they would never find her. Not in time, anyway.

*We will find her. We have to.*

"What do we do?" Allie cried. She turned in a wide circle with her hands over her head as the echoes of battle floated up the stairs in haunting echo. "We can't keep this up, we have to find her now… Norman?"

"Look." Norman stared at the wall beside the stairs: a wave of whiteness swept down from above, blanketing cracks and dust. "It's here."

Allie moaned. "Norman, what if she's—"

"She's not."

The certainty came from the shard of ice in his chest that had plagued him for so long. Feeling all that pain and confusion, seeing the Echoes; all of it had been building towards this. Something had known that eventually he would need to find Billy. He felt her, as though the cold bound him to her.

*She's so bright. If she hadn't fought it, the darkness would already have taken the tower. Maybe London, maybe everything.*

A new voice spoke from the cold itself, close to his midriff. *She can't win. She can only hold it back. It'll take all of you to stop it.*

*How?* he thought.

No answer.

He cursed while the Frost spread past them and down the stairs. Watching it go by, Norman caught sight of something that made him curse aloud. Their head start was up. Thirty people came wheeling up the stairs and fresh struggle broke out. Norman pulled Allie back and they ran for a desk, crouching behind it. Hiding like this would have crushed him any other time, but they needed their strength if they were going to get Billy back.

They watched carefully, waiting for a break to appear close to the stairs.

"We haven't got long," Norman said, pulling his hand from the desktop as ice oozed across it.

He was on the verge of making a dash for the stairs when Jason skidded around a corner. His shoulders were hunched in the unmistakable pose of a stalking predator, head darting up and down the corridor.

"There!" Allie said.

*Billy must be close,* Norman thought.

Norman grunted as Allie sprinted off ahead of him and gave chase. He bawled for her to stop—all Allie had left was a blunted hatchet. Besides the sabre Norman found outside, they didn't have anything to fight with. If they were going to bring Jason down, they would need a lot more.

His words fell on deaf ears. Allie yelled wordlessly as she charged and headbutted Jason's chest, sending them both toppling end over end. Norman put on a spurt, but Jason was already spinning around on his back.

Jason gripped Allie by the ankle and slid her over the smooth marble to face him. She writhed as he climbed snarling atop her and gripped her throat. "You bitches don't give up!—"

Jason barked as something soared in from the side and caught his flank, spilling him over the ground. The blur tumbled aside and landed beside Allie, resolving into Richard. Wide-eyed and armed only with what looked like a curtain rail, he wheeled back from Jason's growling form.

Norman yanked them up from the ground.

"No, I'm going to gut him!" Allie roared, pulling against him.

Jason was already on his feet, shaking his head back and forth like a disoriented mutt.

A tiny figure in Norman's peripheral vision sent him spinning to see a flagging length of flame-red hair, squeezing onto the stairs.

"Billy!" he yelled.

The others whirled in turn as the briefest glimpse of red hair appeared once more, vanishing upstairs. A moment of agonising stillness pursued in which Norman willed his legs to move, but his body seemed stuck in quicksand. He was thrust aside as Jason came hurtling past, loping with the gait of a gazelle. Norman's mind offered a replay of the instant Jason had passed by: his face contorted into a bloody sneer, inhuman and wrought with fury.

Time snapped back into place and the three of them were in pursuit. Richard took the lead and ran bawling for a trio of men blocking the stairs. He breasted the curtain pole in his grasp and caught all three men across their chests. "Get the girl!" he cried, his heels slipping as the men pushed back with strangled cries.

"What are you doing?" Norman yelled.

Richard gave him a queer look. "Earning my stripes."

The three pinned men gave a united yell, and he returned his own. Their feet skidded on carpet as Norman and Allie eased past and reached the staircase. As Allie raced up out of sight, Norman paused and looked back just in time to see Richard press the men against the railing, his teeth bared and his young academic face transformed into a warrior's grimace. With a grunt he gave one last shove, and the men toppled together over the rail.

Richard let fly a whoop of victory as one of the men's hands took his sleeve in a death grip. Richard slammed against the railing, his shocked gaze trained on Norman, then he was gone over the rails.

Norman blinked. Tearing his gaze away from the banister was like tearing apart two halves of Velcro.

Then he and Allie were running again, driven by the distant wails of a little girl being chased by a monster.

*

Charlie waved his arms and bellowed, and beside him Lucian did the same. Both of them stood upon the lobby reception desk, their voices eaten by the echoing roar.

"It's not working," Charlie said.

"Keep at it."

"I can't stop them. I never could."

Lucian seized him. "You can. We just have to get their attention."

"How?"

Lucian's mouth worked, but no sound escaped. He was in the process of cursing when his eyes bulged and his face slackened. Charlie followed his gaze, and all the air punched out of him.

The courtyard outside darkened with fresh masses of people coming in through the walls. As they passed inside, with shocking suddenness, the rumble of shells impacting the tower died.

*Who? How?* Charlie thought, stunned.

"You said there were no more!" Lucian hissed. "We can't handle more."

Charlie shook his head. "They're not ours."

Lucian stiffened, then a gravelly laugh erupted from his chest.

The lobby became surrounded by the newcomers gathering at the shattered revolving doors. Unwounded, unfatigued by battle, they looked almost Olympian compared to the rest, most of who could barely stand. One person at a time, a wave of realisation swept through the lobby. At last ringing silence permeated the space.

*There's enough of them to actually make a stand. Maybe… maybe they can win.*

But no. There were many, and they were strong, but they were nowhere near enough. All that could result was a stalemate. If they fought to the last man, there would be nobody left.

Already Charlie could feel tension building, straining the armistice brought about by shock. A few were already stepping forwards.

Lucian's voice filled the lobby, rising even above the hammering rain. "Stop! All of you, stop now. I am Lucian McKay of the Alliance of the South, aide-de-camp to Alexander of New Canterbury. You will listen to me!"

Charlie frowned.

Lucian muttered from the corner of his mouth, "Never thought I'd say that kind of crap."

*But it's done the trick*, Charlie thought. Everybody in the lobby span as though mounted on turntables.

Lucian said, "This ends now. None of you want this. If we keep down this path, there won't be anybody left to talk about it. I know you feel what's coming. That's no storm out there, it's something worse." He pointed to Charlie. "Those of you who marched on this city know this man.

You know his station." Lucian paused. "I killed this man's father. I stole from him, beat him, did all the wrongs to him that the Alliance has done to you all." Lucian looked to Charlie. "He'll speak to you now."

Charlie could only stare back at him as though from a great distance.

*I hope you saw that, wherever you are, Dad,* Charlie thought.

Then he was looking over those he had helped bring here, numbed by their combined stares. "I…" He cleared his throat. "Some of you are like me: you got so scared you started to hate, and that hate brought you here. A lot of you never wanted this… We just took you. We took a lot of you. But none of us have to be scared anymore. We can stop this."

Blank stares speared him, and his stomach sank.

*They won't listen. They don't see me.*

"You don't have to be afraid." His voice echoed back from afar—a nasal kid's voice.

Somebody spoke from close by. "You know what we're scared of. He still breathes."

*Jason. How many did he kill on the march south because they wanted to stop?*

"Are you all going to die today because of a madman?"

Blanket silence. The storm crackled outside. The cold deepened.

Lucian gestured to the newcomers. "We leave them be." He pointed into the storm. "We still have a lot of people out there. Draw anybody upstairs into the courtyard. Bring everybody into one place. We need to spread the word and cut down anybody who won't stop, no matter what side they're on. There isn't much time." When nobody moved, he slammed his hands together. "*Move!*"

Then, astonishingly, they were in motion. Those who had been in death duels moments before looked to one another distrustfully, fawningly, but started heading towards the stairs. Charlie watched hundreds pass by with his heart pulsing in his mouth.

"It's a start," Lucian growled.

Charlie nodded numbly. A nagging truth ate at him, still: this wouldn't be over until Jason was taken down. They might have won the lobby, but the army would never stop until the mad general was dead.

# VIII

"It's done," James said, staring out at the storm. "Finally, things are being put right."

The vortex of darkness now sheathed the entire length of the tower, pooling upon the ground and spreading towards the compound's shattered walls. The surrounding skyscrapers were beginning to ice over, despite the endless sheets of rain pouring down from above.

*No ordinary ice. It's the End. It's here*, Alexander thought.

"It's you, isn't it? You're doing this," he muttered.

"We are all doing this," James said.

"But you started it. You're…"

"A catalyst. No more. Make no mistake: when the End comes, it will come from within. I was told that a long time ago."

"By who?" Alexander said.

*By what?* he thought.

James said nothing.

They had watched people arrive from all over the city in stunned silence. Alexander had no idea where they came from, or why they came. Their messengers couldn't have reached that many in so short a time. Yet they had come, hurrying onto the Isle of Dogs and passing through the walls.

They had caught glimpses of people emerging from the tower, drawn outside by the new arrivals, before the darkness had engulfed the compound. Now there was no knowing what went on inside. What they could see were bright red flashes bursting across Canary Wharf, colliding with other buildings. The mortar positions had been overrun, but the fire still came, undirected and random, as though trying to take out the reinforcements.

Alexander couldn't take his eyes from the ice spreading radially outwards from the undulating blackness hiding the tower.

*If the End really is coming again, it's going to start there. It looks like the fight is nearly done.*

James spoke from the window. "It was latent in all of us: the power to end things for good. The biggest irony is that if you hadn't caused so much pain, we might never had managed it."

Alexander shook his head. "I'm done fighting you, James. I can't take any of it back. Why are we still here?"

James left the window and stood a few paces in front of Alexander. "Because I need you to see it, Alex. I need you to know, before it all goes away."

"Why?" Alexander said. "Why end it all? These people have lives."

"They had lives! Before you and the Alliance, they had a chance at making a new beginning. Now their minds are poisoned, and their families are gone. Better we all go to our fate, as we should have done in the beginning."

"If we were all supposed to die in the End, why did we survive?"

James said nothing.

"You don't know any more than the rest of us. You might be different—I don't pretend to understand it, and I don't care. But I know you can't really think you're doing what's right by destroying what's left of the world. I know you better than that."

James tittered. "You don't know anything about me. You never did. All you know is what you wanted me to be. If the world kept spinning, you'd do it all over again, wouldn't you? You'd find some other poor sap to take Norman's place, look into their eyes and tell them they're special—that they have a great destiny. You'd fill them with hope and false dreams, and squash anybody who got in your way. You'd dig any memory of him and me out of your head and begin all over, wouldn't you? Wouldn't you?"

Alexander said nothing.

James's lip curled. "Even now, you can't see that it was all for nothing."

Alexander sank lower to the ground. All he wanted to do was sleep. "Just do it."

"No. You're going to watch. You're going to see this through." James pulled him to his feet, marching him to the window, pressing his face against the glass. "Watch the whole world end because you couldn't let go."

Alexander gasped, struggling for breath. "You can stop this. We can. Together."

James turned him around with a wordless yell. His eyes were wild, and in that moment Alexander saw a little boy that he had once known. "Together?" he roared, his balaclava falling away, revealing the scars, the bare cheekbone.

"It wasn't…"

James pulled them face-to-face. "What?"

Alexander forced himself to look him in the eye. "It wasn't for nothing—"

A high whine built from nothing, and in the last moment Alex saw a shadow fall over them, staring over James's shoulder through the window. The shell detonated twenty feet from the building, and for a silent instant a concussive blast rushed out towards them, forging an empty bubble in the sheets of falling rain. Then the roar was upon them, and the window blew out, and they were both yelling, tumbling end over end.

Alexander's ears sang. For what seemed an age he stared at the ceiling, breathing shallowly as the wailing ebbed, replaced by a thousand sources of tinkling glass, and the rumble of the unfettered storm. Then James's face was hovering over him, and hands wrapped around his chest, lifting him up to a sitting position.

"No," James hissed.

Alexander struggled for breath, sharp pain stabbing his lower back. It felt very warm down there, too warm.

James's hand probed his back. Alexander cried out when the hand pulled away, holding a six-inch shard of bloodied glass.

Alexander tried to move, but the pain only intensified. He coughed, tracing his hand over the ground and catching on the ragged shards until he found James's arm. "James," he slurred. He receded back now, falling away from his body, retreating under the surface of some inky ocean. "James…"

"No." James's stretched, scarred face contorted. His voice grew strangled, watery. "No!"

Alexander pulled him close as he fell under the ocean's surface and whispered, "It wasn't for nothing."

# SECOND INTERLUDE

1

By the time they reached London, the rain had become a relentless cascade. Their horses were exhausted; and being driven straight back home had proved too much. Alex had tried cutting through the capital to get back faster, but once they had entered the paved streets proper, the horses had simply stopped in united rebellion.

They piled to the ground and stood looking around at the empty city, huddled together for warmth.

Alex's mind turned dully about in circles, caught in an endless cycle.

*I lost him. He's gone. James is gone.*

Those same thoughts, replaying over and over, a maddening mantra recited without end.

He knew he should have felt guilt, anger, loss. He should have felt a lot of things. But the truth was he felt nothing. He had done what he needed to do, and it would have worked—if James hadn't done what he did. They had been so close.

*He chose to stay.*

In his mind's eye he saw a little boy, no more than eight years old, sat upon his bed begging to be read a story. Alex had read *Alice in Wonderland* for the thousandth time, but only after changing the boy's life forever.

They could have been great. Together, they could have saved it all. Now the dream lay smouldering at his feet.

He knew the mourning would come later, in the light of day when he was confronted with decades' worth of collections back home, all gathered with James by his side.

Everything he had invested, every scrap of effort over the past twenty years, all gone to nothing. The fate of the mission hung in the balance. What were they working for now, if there was nobody left behind to take up the mantle?

Lucian and Oliver took an end of Norman's stretcher each and brought him down to the ground. The boy had scarcely stirred since they left Newquay's Moon. They removed the tarp that had been erected as a rain-shield, revealing his head turning from side to side, splashed with fat droplets of rain. The others gathered around in silence, weary and cold.

The child's eyelids flickered. As he stirred, the others gasped and bent close. Alex stood very still as something somewhere deep in his mind sputtered and chugged to life. The boy…

A stinging blow came from nowhere, and Alex wheeled away into the rain, turning to find Lucian before him, fists bunched, his face a picture of agony.

"I know what you did!" he roared.

"Lucian, what are you doin'?" Agatha cried.

Lucian ignored her, taking a threatening step forwards. "I know it."

Alex held up his hands. "Lucian, James—"

"I heard the shots. I heard him screaming. You would never have come down if they had come from Malverston." His eyes bulged from their sockets. "It was you. You killed him."

"No, I didn't."

Lucian's eyes searched the air, flitting back and forth as his lips worked. Alex could see the cogs turning in his head.

"The girl." Lucian fell slack, just staring now, all the anger gone out of him. "You..."

Alex said nothing. Agatha and Oliver had remained by Norman's side, just out of earshot, but their gaze on him felt just as potent, burned just as deeply. He made to lay a hand on Lucian's arm, but Lucian recoiled as though he were a leper.

"Don't. Don't."

"I had to. To save him."

"But you didn't save him."

"I tried. You have to believe me."

Lucian swallowed hard. He seemed to have aged in the past few hours; some spark of youth had winked out, replaced by haggard callousness. "All my life I've believed you. We all have. But James..."

"I did everything I could." Alex took a step forwards.

Again, Lucian backed away. "You used him, like you used all of us." He shook his head. "Damn you. Damn you."

Alex rushed forwards and pulled Lucian's head to his chest, and Lucian came limply, beating feebly at his arms.

"Damn you!"

"I'm sorry."

They remained like that until Lucian's fists stopping windmilling and he stood with his head lowered in Alex's grasp. Alex let him go and took him by the shoulders. "We can't stop now."

"How? He was the one, wasn't he?" Lucian muttered. "The one with the destiny."

Alex looked to the boy twitching between Agatha and Lincoln and swallowed hard as an idea solidified in his mind.

*Am I really going to do this?*

Yes. There was no other choice.

"Maybe not," he said.

He approached Norman as the rain slicked off his brow and into his eyes. Norman blinked, squinting up at the world and whimpering. He tried to grab at his head, but Agatha took his hand gently down again, crooning and hushing.

Alex stepped between them, gesturing for them to give him space. Crouching down beside Norman, he thought of the boy's parents, the lackadaisical sheep who had inhabited their homestead for so many years—feckless lumps to his eyes, for all the vision they had ever had.

They had never once shown a sign of desire for the Old World, nor interest in the artefacts they horded from the wilds. Never had they been *awake*. The boy was on the road to being the same. James had pressed Alex to teach Norman, but Alex could never bring himself to entertain the notion. Every time he looked into his eyes, all he saw was the place where light should have been, but none shone; a sad and lonely sight, like that of an extinct hearth.

*No choice. It has to be one of us, one who knows our ways. He's young enough. Maybe I can change him.*

All the while in his mind's eye, that twinkling brilliance of the boy with the emerald eyes.

"Norman, can you hear me?" he said. "I know you're afraid. I know it hurts. But I need you to listen to me."

"W-what's going on?" the boy moaned. "Who are you?"

Alex looked to Oliver, then Agatha, saw the sunken dismay on their faces, and sighed.

"Friends," Lucian said over Alex's shoulder. His voice broke as he croaked, "We're friends." His brow was twisted into a twitching frown. He pursed his lips and nodded. "Go on."

Alex could only stare at him for a moment, then turned back to Norman. "What do you remember?"

The boy only blinked, his eyes searching the city above their heads, breathing fast. "I-I…"

Alex hushed him, laying a firm hand on his shoulder. "It's okay. I'm going to take care of you."

Norman's eyes rolled around to focus dimly on him. A fine boy, a nice boy—but that spark… that spark was just not there. How could Alex overcome that basic element so vital to it all?

*I'll do it by doing it. The mission demands it.*

He crouched low over Norman Creek, begging forgiveness from the heavens as he whispered into his ear: "Let me tell you a secret: some people have a destiny…"

2

James tried to scream and found he couldn't move. Lightning bolts of pain throbbed upon his face.

In his head echoed the tumultuous crash of wood, the roar of fire, the flash of live embers rushing down and mashing under his eyelids. It was burning him! He was being burned alive, he was—

Light swam above him, cool yellow shafts of morning glory. Somewhere, a bird twittered a snippet of morning chorus. He lay on a soft bed. His body was whole, still very much alive; he knew as much because pain threaded every inch of him, as though it were a resonating piece of glass on the brink of shattering. And his face—his face!

*God, let me die. Let me die, now. I can't take it, I can't!—*

"Don't move," said a voice beside him.

He inched his head to the side and caught sight of a small, blurry outline. He blinked his eyes into focus, and his heart burst open.

*Beth. She's alive!*

He made to surge forwards, but his entire head rang like a bell and he sank back with an agonised cry. With the pain came the realisation that the person sitting next to him wasn't Beth, but Melanie. He sobbed quietly as liquid fire crawled over his skin, and he concentrated on breathing, nerves tortured as though dug from his flesh and rubbed with sandpaper.

"Lie still," Mel said, standing over him and gripping his hand.

He squeezed back with everything he had. He heard her grunt, but he couldn't loosen his grip. "Wha-what?" He coughed and moaned at fresh pain running from his tongue down and into the meat of his chest.

*Crackling. I can hear my lungs crackling.*

Why had they pulled him here? If he was this close to death, better they had shot him like a lame horse.

He searched her eyes as his own streamed silent tears, begging for death.

"You'll live," Mel said, squeezing his hand in return. "You have a chance if we keep the bandages clean. The doctor said—"

James managed to mouth around his aching face—every minuscule twitch felt like pressing his head into a pool of molten lead. *Doctor?*

Melanie nodded. "I found one in the next town. He dressed the burns, used ointments to cover your... your face. He kept you asleep for a long time, to let it heal. He said you should be dead—that anybody else would have died." Her eyes glittered with something that might have been fear. "But you didn't die. He was here so long I ran out of things to trade, and Mum"—her brow darkened—"Mum is Mum. But I have medicine."

James turned from her, shaking his head despite the pain.

*Just go, leave me to fade away.*

She leaned over farther. "I'm the big girl now. I'm taking care of you."

James swallowed, bracing himself for the exertion, and wheezed, "Beth?"

The modicum of light left Mel's eyes. She turned from him and busied herself with something behind her. Glass tinkled, metal clattered. When she turned around, she had a straw dropped into a tumbler filled to the brim with light amber liquid. The acid smell hit his nose.

It seemed moonshine qualified for medicine now.

Even shaking his head or pressing his lips together was too much. The pain increased by the moment, creeping towards unbearable. In moments he would begin screaming, whether doing so would split his face wide open or not.

When the straw came within reach, he lunged and sucked desperately. His throat clamped shut on contact with hard liquor.

*It'll either dull the pain or make me go blind*, he thought.

It seared his blistered lips, gums, and throat, but he sucked greedily until it sent him into a coughing fit. The convulsions sent fresh ripples of pain through him and Mel had to use both hands to keep him still, but already he could feel the alcohol at work, marbling his mind.

When the coughing stopped, the world warped, turning of its own accord as though somebody rotated the ceiling about his head. The pain remained, but the urge to scream had passed. He risked talking and heard his rasping voice as though from a great distance. "Beth…"

"We buried her." Mel's eyes were dry, but the same emptiness stole into her gaze.

James gave her a lingering stare. With the alcohol inside him, an agony all the greater came crashing in; something no drug or poultice could treat. "Take me," he said. "Let me see her."

Mel shook her head. "The doctor said we can't move you. He left for Penzance yesterday. If you fall, I don't have anything left to trade. If the burns get infected, you'll die. You have to—"

James reached out to grip her sleeve, pulling her close. He saw fear—or was it revulsion?—in her eyes at being so close to his face.

"Take me," he said. "Please."

She swallowed hard with an expression so much older than he would have thought possible for her tiny round face and nodded. It took a long time for her to reposition him, incrementally lifting his torso and stuffing pillows under his back to prop him up. Then came the business of swinging his legs out, swollen yellowish-purple lumps. He had to stop several times to groan and cry, the salty tears stinging his face—a fine garnish of misery from the powers that be.

Melanie straw-fed him more liquor, until the world undulated without pause, before she risked trying to get him into the wheelchair. Even then he screamed, a high-pitched wail trapped mostly inside his own head, for his jaw remained immobile, held shut by an entrapment of bandages. Eventually he was trussed up in the seat, and she pushed him out into the street.

Outside people hauled baskets of peaches in for packing on trade waggons. It was harvest time, and all hands had been brought to bear. The fields had yielded their bounty and filled the dusty ramshackle streets with round bags of vibrant colour. The atmosphere was one of quiet contentment. There was no sign of a single guard.

*So it all really happened. We did it…*

No. Mel and the other Mooners were the ones who had fought and died. They had freed themselves.

James almost jerked onto the floor when he caught sight of the dishevelled lump of cinders that had once been the town hall. It stood alone, the square quiet and abandoned—as though nothing of any consequence had ever passed there at all.

Mel wheeled him away from the topsy-turvy streets and up to a slight rise. James realised that this was where he had been with Beth most often, overlooking the peach fields with the wind in their faces, when every movement had been heart-stopping, every word a separate passion.

Upon the crest of the rise, a tiny white cross had been erected in the grass. There was no epitaph, no date, no name.

"I think she would have wanted it that way," Mel said.

James stood over many minutes, ignoring the pain, no longer feeling but accepting it. It took him a long time to take the three steps to the cross and kneel before it in the grass, tearing up handfuls of grass.

*She's really gone.*

"I tried, I…"

He couldn't finish. Speaking made him realise just how *wrong* his face felt, as though he had no mouth at all, instead just a gaping hole. He knew he would never look the same, never be anything but a freak. And without Beth, what was there to live for?

A chill swept over him, a queer shiver that swept through his burned skin and penetrated to his core. It was the same feeling that had driven him north and parted him from Beth in the first place, so long ago it seemed like another lifetime. When a voice emerged from somewhere inside him, it wasn't the same as the dark-eyed man in the caves of Radden, but something else entirely.

*It's time, James. They tried to keep me out, keep us apart, but now you've seen what they are. At last, we can be together.*

The voice bore a silken, lilting tone that could have been benign, almost beautiful, were it not for an undertone of flatness. It was as though something were missing, some key component lost in translation; the near-perfect but yet emotionless emulation of a cold, calculating machine.

*You were lied to. All your life, they all lied. Time to realise the truth.*

James saw: deep down under his grief and fury, a door opened, one that had always been there but had been held closed. Through it truth shone like moonbeams. Their whole existence, the world after the End, the mission— everything had been a lie. They were never supposed to survive.

But there was hope. He could fix it. It might take years,

but he could bring them all back to righteousness… and when he did, they would all be together again.

*Your beloved awaits. But first, you have work to do.*

Far away, he heard young Melanie Tarbuck speaking over him, her ten-year-old voice hard as diamonds. "Somebody has to pay for this."

The pain came afresh, steeling into him, becoming one with his flesh and forever entombing him. He welcomed it with open arms, for amongst the agony he glimpsed their real destiny. James wept upon the ground as that pain turned to bile, and in turn became boiling, unending rage.

# 3

Alexander stood alone, robe wrapped tight around him in the bleak afternoon light. A high wind had blown down from the north, washing the colour out of the world. Lucian strolled out from the farmhouse to stand by his side. They remained together for a long while, not speaking, just looking out.

"I forgot how good the view is out here," Alex said. "That's why we chose this place. The land's so flat. It's like you could hold it all in your hand… Makes what we're doing seem that little bit easier, doesn't it?"

Lucian said nothing.

Alex held his robe tighter to him. The cold had more bite than usual, but perhaps that was just psychosomatic. He had felt constantly exposed of late. He cleared his throat. "We can't stay here anymore."

"Why?" Lucian's face seemed permanently contorted into a half frown, his voice gruffer. It was as though all the bounce had been dug out of him with a penknife, leaving a bitter old man in a teenager's body.

Grief did strange things to people.

"There's nowhere to expand. We got word from Southampton and London: they agreed to a coalition. Permanent trade routes. We did it. We're finally building something. If we're going to do that, we need beacons that will attract people."

"This is our home, Alex. We built it with our own hands."

"It was our home. Before."

The empty rooms were like rotted teeth staring them in the face—as galling as the empty spaces at the dining table.

"Where do we go?"

Alex breathed cool, crisp air. "My parents took me to Canterbury once. We took a tour of the cathedral. I remember thinking it was impossible for men to have built something so big and beautiful all that time ago." He muttered into the wind, "It's perfect."

"You looking to start a religion?"

Alex smiled wanly. If only that weren't so very close to the truth.

"The others are worried. You haven't been inside all day."

"I just needed to clear my head. There's a lot to think about."

"If you had to get away from the kid, you could have

just asked one of us to pitch in."

Alex shook his head. "He's a good kid."

Norman had forgotten everything; amnesia from the impact trauma of the ricochet wound to his head. There were no doctors within the homestead's area. All they had were books that said his memory might return, and might not.

There had only been one thing for it. Patiently, Alex had closed down every part of his mind eager to get back out into the world. If they were going to keep the mission alive, they had to begin with a fresh slate, no matter how long it took. He could have been bitter, could have given up, but there was only one way to look at it. Tabula rasa: a new Chosen One.

It turned out Norman wasn't a dull boy. Quite the opposite. His reading was exceptional, his wits sharp. He lacked the spark he would need, but one thing made it bearable: he looked to Alex with undying devotion.

He never called him Alex. He always called him Alexander.

Alex liked that. *Alexander.*

He would need that guise if this was going to work. Their order might turn to Norman one day, but until then Alex would be alone. If that was so, he had to become more than just a man. He needed a throne.

"Yes," he said. "Canterbury." He turned his gaze on the wilderness, intent not to look back at the homestead.

Lucian gripped his arm. "What's wrong?"

"Nothing. Just thinking."

"You can't lie to me, Alex. I'm your brother."

Alex's gaze dropped to the ground like a bird sprayed with shot.

*Brothers. Three brothers against the world. Brothers who stuck together, no matter what—*

"Alex?"

Alex pointed back to the homestead. He wished he hadn't seen it, for it could never be unseen in his mind's eye. He knew the moment he turned to look at it anew with Lucian that it would be with him always.

"No," Lucian muttered. "No…"

It wouldn't be the fire that Alex remembered, nor the tyrannical mayor, not even emerald eyes. It was the sight of the pigeon coups before them, lined against the garden wall, their doors bent open, empty save for a carpet of downy feathers.

Their master had called them.

# IX

James watched Alexander Cain's face slacken. Eyes that had been so full of wakeful intent faded to a flat, glassy sheen. James didn't close his eyelids, nor lay him down on the floor, just remained entwined with Alexander's body, cradling the blond head that moved no more.

Numbness had taken him, so deep that not a single errant thought entered his mind. He went to unfeeling bliss gladly, adrift on a peaceful ocean amidst an inky void. Time passed. Somewhere on the very edge of his perception, titanic forces battled for supremacy.

When he finally emerged from his torpor, James's eyes moved to the floor before him. His gaze focused on a pair of booted feet, leading to muddy torn trousers. James followed those trousers to a hulking torso, chocolate-coloured skin over enormous arms, and a boulder-shaped head. James at last met the man's gaze and the two of them shared a look that could have lasted an aeon, for James knew the pain that rested behind the man's eyes.

A pistol rose from the man's waist and pointed at James's chest. James didn't break his gaze, and for the briefest moment he felt a caress upon his neck: the ghostly touch of a girl who had once grown peaches.

The sound of the shot was lost in the pain: an iron fist punching him in the chest. His body grew weak under him, sliding downwards, and he flopped upon a bed of glass. At once the shattered window became a thousand autumnal leaves, soft against his skin. Beside him lay Alexander: for an instant his eyes were beady and blank, set in a pale lifeless face; then he was young and smiling, pointing up into the sky. Grass surrounded them upon a hillside close to the homestead.

Happiness filled James as he followed Alexander's finger skywards, learning the clouds Alexander named: *cirrus, stratocumulus, cumulonimbus…*

He smiled as he uttered those names over and over, and the warmth of the sun tickled his skin. It was important he remembered. One day he would need this knowledge, when people looked to him. It was meant to be, after all.

He had a destiny.

X

A wave of rainwater crested ahead of Norman as he rounded a final corner, and the bottom fell out of his stomach. Panting, soaked from their mad dash through the bowels of the tower's eighth storey, he and Allie came to a halt before a ragged hole in the tower's side. A waterfall ran off the jagged edge of the carpet where the exterior wall had been gouged away by mortar fire, ending in a snarl of girders and reinforced concrete. Below, a new battle raged in the courtyard; a chimera of writing struggle, and a scattered separatist movement. The fighting was coming to an end.

Not fast enough. In moments, the darkness would blank out everything.

*Then we all go to that other place*, Norman thought.

Beyond the compound, the storm raged with unfettered vigour, but London had vanished, not behind clouds or smoke, but an impenetrable curtain of blackness.

Before them, Jason made a slow, sauntering approach towards a red-haired figure upon the floor.

Billy wheeled back on her palms, sliding in the rainwater, hair lank over her face, which had paled to the

480

colour of chalk. Her mouth hung wide in a grimace of terror.

"Together," Norman said. "No matter what."

Allie said nothing, just started down the hall. Norman followed, heart thudding in his chest.

The fighting below seemed far away. Even the raging storm became deadened as they splashed through the water side by side, and Jason's shoulders tensed, sensing their presence. He turned to face them.

Billy scrambled back, skittering to the far wall. Her expression was glazed, her face contorted as she fixated on the darkness outside, as though every part of her mind was concentrated on it. Then she vanished from Norman's attention, for Jason began throwing his knife from hand to hand.

"How's the chest, Norman?" he called over the storm. "Still breathing through a straw?"

Norman said nothing, just kept walking.

*Let him think I'm still a cripple. Like he'd ever believe that I got healed by magic Frost.*

Maybe, just maybe it would give them a moment's advantage. They would need every piece of luck if they were going to stand a chance. In his mind's eye he saw countless faceless people Jason had cut down as though they were but cattle.

He and Allie fanned out to either side. Norman knew neither of them knew what they were doing, but he kept moving. Allie too walked with steadfast intent, her face pulled into an emotionless grimace.

Norman felt every bump and groove in the sabre's handle, hypersensitive nerves firing; sensing the balance of the blade, the form of its curve. And something else: the ice in his chest—which had somehow melted the pain of broken ribs and brought him to Billy, and all the weirdness that had come since then—filled him, binding to his deepest tissues. Something reached out from an impossible place and acted through him.

*So that's why I'm here: to protect Billy and slay a monster. There's a legend to be going on with.*

Or, just maybe, a destiny.

"How does it feel to look out there and know it all falls on your head?" Jason said.

They were feet from one another now, storm run-off pouring around their ankles and over the ledge. A bolt of lightning struck a nearby skyscraper and for a moment the darkness became diaphanous, sending London's skyline into harsh relief, complete with thousands of writhing figures in the courtyard far below. In the blinding flash that whited out everything, the three of them leapt.

Norman put all his weight into swinging the sabre. His wrists yanked back almost immediately as the blade was thrust back over his shoulder by Jason's parry. He tumbled as Allie moved forwards in the corner of his eye and unleashed a vicious punch. Her blow landed square upon Jason's jaw and sent him wheeling back with a look of shock. Allie unleashed more blows in rapid succession, making contact with his bandaged face again and again, splitting his wounded cheek like a second mouth.

Norman regained his balance and risked a glance at Billy: her gaze remained hazy, struggling in an unseen battle of her own.

It seemed to take an age to rise to the balls of his feet and thrust himself forwards once more; an eternity in which all he could do was watch Allie face James's hound, somehow maintaining the offensive. By the time he splashed towards them, her luck ran out.

Allie screamed as Jason's bandage fell from his face, revealing a horrific yellow-green mass of freshly-torn, infected flesh. Eyes streaming and blood red, he launched himself backwards, drawing her on. Allie tensed, hesitating an instant—

*Wait for me!* Norman thought. *Just wait and we'll take him together!*

—then she charged with a banshee wail, running straight for the knife in Jason's hand.

Norman expected to watch her die; readied himself to watch and keep fighting.

But Jason didn't impale her as he had done in Norman's mind's eye. Instead, he danced to the side—

*Even now he's playing with us*, Norman thought.

—and gripped her by the hair, yanking her in a wide arc onto his other fist, landing a brutal punch to her solar plexus.

A guttural *uurgh!* escaped her as she doubled upon Jason's arm, and he delivered a sharp crack to the back of her head with the knife handle. She fell slack and almost carelessly, he sent her sliding on her stomach across the floor.

Norman yelled aloud, thinking she might slide into space, but Allie flipped onto her back and dug her heels in, coming to a stop six feet from the edge. Before he could call out to her, Jason was on him, teeth bared in a crazed leer, and the knife was a blur, coming from above and below in a blinding flurry.

*

Lights fizzed overhead, a roiling blur. The firmament itself shook with the force of Billy's transit through the *sideways* impossibility, infinitely faster than the last time she had travelled. She wasn't flying this time but being torn across space with such violence that she felt the fabric of this strange place stretching and tearing with her passage. All around, things screamed, multitudinous and agonised, and somewhere in the frenzy of pain and fear, she too screamed. The Frost had taken her body, converted her to so much ice—any moment she would strike a sliver of matter and shatter into fine dust.

Then with a suddenness that should have knocked her eyes from her head, she jerked to a dead stop. Below lay the dark place, alive with the enslaved, writhing Vanished.

She wasn't alone. Things hung just out of sight, so big her head gave up on appreciating their size.

*Can't help them, can't help them*, she thought.

"No. You can't. No more than you can help yourself, meddler," sighed a voice.

Billy jerked as a figure emerged from the darkness,

winged and haloed by a cone of white light. An immaculate face fringed by ash-blond hair and a slight body wrapped in flowing silk. The eyes set between those chiselled cheekbones were enormous, staring, and filled with rage. Almost hidden from sight—but not quite—where the hands should have been, were instead black, footlong talons. A voice washed over Billy, sighing and insidious. "You are too late."

Before Billy could react, liquid blackness the consistency of tar gushed forth from the figure, itself alive and snarling. She reacted instinctively, putting up her hands to shield herself. From her fingertips lanced a white jet, connecting with the blackness. The two bolts struggled, sending the Vanished glittering with scattered light. Billy stared, disbelieving, as the Light reached out from inside her, running down through her arms and out. She felt herself being drained, her very being whittled by standing against such a creature.

She knew that had the Light not protected her she would have disintegrated in an instant, dashed like a leaf in a hurricane. But now, with all the anger and fear inside her— from Ma, Grandpa, Daddy, and all the people dying and afraid —she took the Light and *used* it. Just as she had taken up her dagger and cut the monster's face back in Radden, she took up the Light and struck out.

Screeching as though feeling pain for the first time, the creature shrieked. "*You dare?*"

"Go away," Billy said. "Go back to the dark place. Leave us alone."

A harsh laugh from behind the arcing jets of light and dark. "This is my world. Mine!"

"No!"

"You are all at an end. There is no stopping it. You finished what I started—brought about your own end. Now, stand aside."

*It's now. It's now.*

Billy felt the full force of all the world push down on her. She closed her eyes and opened herself to the Light, let everything go and dropped away into the Frost. With a gushing roar the Light grew tenfold, pouring from her in a torrent. The jet of darkness trembled and fell back.

That voice again, high and outraged: "Stand aside."

"No."

"I have worked too long. I will not be stopped. Give me what I am owed. *Give me this world!*"

"NO!" Billy screamed, an unending cry that wound down into infinity, pushing the darkness back in a rush of light to strike the marble-faced thing.

With a snarling wail, the figure snapped back into the inky void, uttering the guttural rumble of a beast robbed of prey. For the briefest sliver of time, Billy hung suspended in space, as though floating upon her back in a brook, spent and defeated. Before her lay All Where: the magnificent scale of what lay beyond Enger Land and all the world. Standing above it all, eight titanic furry legs led to a black abdomen the size of the Earth, and a head inset with beady eyes in which whole galaxies swirled. From a pair of working pincers, a stentorian, benevolent voice: "Well done, Peyton child."

Despite the horrific sight, she saw true: it was this thing that had worked through her, guided her.

*You fought for us*, she thought.

A tug pulled her back through the endless tunnel from whence she had come, just as urgent and reckless, but this time a peaceable whisper followed from the eight-eyed behemoth. "I did nothing. Now go. Slay one last demon."

*

Norman ran for Jason. In the corner of his eye, Allie's prone form twitched and groaned; and beyond, Billy held her hair bunched in her hands and wailed—her whole body aglow. From a seemingly infinite distance, he heard her voice: *It's now. It's now.*

*I have to hold him until she's done. This better work, Billy.*

He could do nothing to stall his forwards momentum. Jason had bent down in a defensive stance, knife held at the ready.

There was no time to think or plan. Norman swung, trusting to instinct, but knew chance alone couldn't deflect all Jason's blows. Then they came together, and all was in motion. His arm thrummed as the sabre met the knife, then followed Jason's every move, as though drawn by magnetic attraction. With every dexterous spin and pivot Jason made, Norman's arm followed, blocking a barrage that came with such speed that Norman saw nothing but silver. He could only watch, shocked and spellbound, as his body moved of its own accord.

Ice-cold snakes slithered from his chest, into his arms, and down into his legs, guiding him. He didn't dare fight it. There was only one thing to do: use it.

Jason's face creased into a snarl of surprise. Norman drove forwards, baiting Jason with a wide attack that sent him diving to the side, bringing the sabre around in a sweeping undercut, following Jason's retreat. Jason yelled as lightning flashed, bringing the knife between them just in time. The blades clanged with a resonance that threatened to break Norman's arm.

Jason's putrid stench filled his nose, the pungent carrion odour of a carnivore.

*One more and I'll have him. One more!*

Something exploded on top of his head and he fell backwards into the running water, stunned. Pain radiated down through his skull, threatening to blow his teeth from out of their sockets. He scarcely felt the impact with the ground—what he did feel was his fingers releasing the sabre, which went spinning away out of sight. Blurred by the rain splashing into his eyes, Jason descended on him.

Straddling him with a satisfied sigh, Jason took his time, as though the darkness wasn't now threading into the tower itself. He flipped the knife over in his hand, grinning with unveiled glee. "I want you to know something, Norman: I'll skin the little one last."

Norman struggled in vain, trapped like a bug upon a pin. He gargled as Jason wrapped a hand around his throat and lifted the knife with the other. In the corner of his eye, Allie struggled to her haunches, her shoulders shaking, groaning. So close, yet infinitely far away.

*This is it*, he thought as the knife came down. *All I needed was one more chance.*

Jason roared in outrage, and the pressure around Norman's neck was gone. A tiny pair of hands reached around from the back of Jason's head, digging into his eye sockets. He wheeled back, waving his arms over his back, howling.

Billy dangled from his back. There was nothing distant about her now. Methodically, avoiding Jason's clawing hands, she withdrew her fingertips from his eyes and dug her nails deep into his face, drawing back across his skull, catching the suppurating wound as she went.

Her fingers sank deep. Pus spurted, infected tissue split like wet toilet paper, and a childish scream erupted from Jason's throat. The knife clattered to the floor as Jason span in an aimless circle, his arms flapping.

Norman forced himself up to his knees. A haggard shadow stirred not far away, and Norman looked over to see Allie struggling to her feet. As he dragged himself up, he took Jason's knife with him.

Jason was roaring over and over, and Billy hung on with the tenacity of a limpet, her hands embedded his face, having carved ten long gouges leading back across his entire head.

Norman braced himself to strike.

*It's me. It was always going to be me. That's why I had the power—*

He blinked as the knife was ripped from his grasp. Allie

moved forwards and thrust the blade into Jason's belly.

Jason grunted. His arms stopped milling. Bending slightly, his eyes grew wide and his mouth fell ajar.

Allie pulled Billy from his back, hurrying aside as though he were a rabid dog. Instead of running, she put Billy down, then bent so that she and Jason were at eye level. "That's for all of them," she said.

Jason wrapped his hands around the blade handle sticking from his abdomen and pulled it out. Gurgling, he dropped it to the floor and straightened with a low growl. He remained still for a beat, then swayed. He bared his teeth, ignoring the flowers of blood spreading over his clothes and dripping globs of red in the water at his feet.

"Bitch," he muttered. His gaze wandered to Norman, then finally to Billy. "*Bitch*."

He reached out to strangle her. Norman was already sweeping her into his arms when something changed: Jason counterbalanced backwards, then he fell slack at the shoulders and staggered back.

Norman dropped Billy, moving before he realised what he was doing, following Jason towards the precipice.

"Norman, no!" Allie screeched.

Norman reached out as Jason's torso moved into empty space. Then his hand closed around Jason's jacket, and they both came to a skidding stop upon the very edge. Jason dangled hundreds of feet above Canary Wharf, his heels barely touching the ledge. They wobbled together, Norman's grip teetering.

Allie and Billy splashed over to stand at his side.

Together, they stood before the choking monster.

"Let him fall," Allie breathed.

Norman stared hard into Jason's face; the last thing so many people had seen in this world. It should have been so easy, he shouldn't even have had to think about it.

*I wanted to see his eyes*, Norman thought. *I wanted him to know we beat him.*

Billy's high voice was utterly flat, without mercy. "They won't stop fighting until the monster goes away."

Jason gripped Norman's hand. Through a feral snarl, he pulled a bloody grin. "You can't kill me, Norman. You're nothing. Nobody. You're the *good guy*."

Norman stared into those mad twinkling eyes. Then he opened his palm, and Jason fell into space. He went silently, spinning back and down. Another crack of lightning illuminated his toppling form as it plummeted to the courtyard below.

The three of them watched his tiny figure hit ground, scattering people fighting below. Allie gripped Norman's hand, and he drew Billy close.

In the courtyard, those beside Jason's body paused mid-action. Their struggle forgotten, they looked from the fallen creature to the trio standing upon the ledge.

"You beat the monster," Billy said.

Norman shook his head and looked at Allie. "I thought I was meant to. But I didn't."

Allie didn't look away from the body down in the courtyard. "Nobody is meant to do anything," she said.

A distant echo of something he once told her rose to his

lips. "There's no such thing as destiny."

More heads turned up towards them, a wave of stillness spreading from Jason's spread-eagled remains. First a few dozen, then hundreds. The wave passed through the remains of the wall and out into the city, until eventually every person in sight stared at the tower.

A gale kicked up from nowhere, and at once the darkness began fading, just as morning mist evaporates under the rising sun. The vortex that had consumed the tower widened, losing form and spinning off in myriad spiracles, away into the city, and was gone.

Somewhere, Norman heard a malevolent force scream with rage as the chill in his chest peaked, thrumming, then winked out, leaving him swaying on his feet. For a sickening moment he thought he would fall, but Allie's arms were around him. Then it was only her face, her rosy rounded cheeks. He pressed her forehead to his.

Streaks of gold erupted through the clouds as sunbeams thrust brilliant fingers into the city. Suddenly everything seemed more real, more *there* as though balls of wool had been pulled from his mind. The last of the rain dribbled around them, and the clouds passed on, leaving behind wisps of baby blue.

# XI

Norman passed through silent crowds, stepping around body after body. Alliance survivors stood beside the ranks of James's army, every weapon on the floor. Allie walked beside him, Billy in her arms. Everybody they passed watched them go by. They left the crumbled wall and headed to the foot of a nearby skyscraper. Muttering floated through the crowd; Norman picked out the odd word: *Alexander, Chadwick, Creek.*

He hurried inside and upstairs, Allie close behind. He was so exhausted, utterly spent. But he couldn't stop, moving as though in a dream. He knew what he would find, but that did nothing to deaden the blow. He entered a blasted office and found Lucian crouched over two forms upon the floor.

Alexander Cain and James Chadwick lay side by side amidst a carpet of shattered glass, gazes trained upon one another.

Allie released Norman's hand. He crunched over glass. The edge of room was lined with people—army and Alliance—all staring, all muttering.

Lucian crouched between his fallen brothers. Norman knelt beside him.

"All this, because of these idiots," Lucian mumbled, his brow furrowed to hide his watery eyes.

"It's done," Norman said.

Alexander's robe was spotted a neat streak of red. Bar that, he was uninjured, a pasty-faced mannequin of the man who had wielded a nation. Beside him, James's scarred face was peppered with glass; yet in his eyes was the ghost of peaceful twinkle.

Charlie stood close by. He and the other invaders held their heads low, their palms visible; waiting for judgment.

Lucian gave a simian grunt, the smallest nod. It was all they needed. Charlie swallowed heavily, and his chin fell to his chest.

"Last kings of men," Lucian said, staring at the dried blood on his hands. "What do we do now?"

"Finish what they started," Norman said.

"Norman. After all this, we've proven—"

"That we can only ever save anything together."

There was no fear now, no doubt. Norman knew what he had to do.

"Norman," Allie said. "Outside."

The floor-length window had been blown out. A few storeys below, people once more stared up at him. Norman could feel the pressure of their combined gazes, joined by those around the edge of the room. He drew himself up, looking down into the courtyard. Thousands of faces watched and waited; from adolescent to octogenarian, every shade and shape; all covered in dust and mud, and the blood of those they loved. Nothing moved except spots of light cast down by the breaking storm clouds.

They all gathered at the foot of the building. Norman expected his throat to seal in the face of their expectation, but he felt only the sure knowledge of what came next: they would go on. He beckoned Allie and Billy to his side. They shared a look, their hair caught in the wind, framed by a halo of sunlight before the people of North and South.

*There's no such thing as destiny, but maybe some things are meant to be*, he thought.

# XII

Norman traced circles in the grass. "It's today," he said. "The negotiations are over."

Before him the graves of Alexander Cain and James Chadwick lay side by side, slabs of granite from the tower's lobby. Around them lay hundreds more, lined along the edge of Greenwich Park. Nearby lay the remains of Twingo, the mercantile township that had fallen to the army.

*We'll rebuild it just like we'll rebuild the Wharf. We need all types in this world*, he thought.

Amongst the tombstones others walked, their footfalls deadened by birdsong and the whispering wind. Norman took a moment to take in the sight, bracing for the day to come. It would be a long one.

He laid a hand on each of the stones and made his way back to the tower, charred and pockmarked, but still as majestic as ever in the early morning sun—perhaps more so.

Negotiations had lasted for days after the Battle of Canary Wharf. Standing before delegates from as far as their scouts could reach over land and sea, he had argued as he would never have dreamed. No more running, no more hiding. They would rebuild what they had lost, through their own labour. It would be a long road; it would mean sacrifice, it would mean work for all of them, but that was the way. The Old World had wonders and horrors to offer. It was up to them to take the best parts from those who had come this way before and would never come again.

But not all of them. Many left London after the battle. Bandaged up with water on their backs, they had returned to whatever homes awaited them; not to retreat or flee, but merely to rest. There had been enough bloodshed for a lifetime. There would never be any great society for them: the quiet isolation of the lone survivor would be their solace.

Presently, Norman made his way to a fledgling encampment beside the old wall, entering one of the infirmary tents. Volunteers from as far away as Leeds and even Radden tended to the wounded, cleaning bodies and changing bandages.

Charlie passed by, carrying a pot of soup, and their eyes met. Neither said a word, just nodded to one another. Charlie sat upon a wooden palette before a young woman, solemn as a monk, and set about ladling into a bowl.

Norman moved on and felt a pang in his gut as he realised was looking for Heather. He stopped before a bed at the far end of the tent. Richard lay breathing steadily under the sheet, his face swollen and purple-green with bruises. His right side was bound in plaster.

Norman watched him sleep as the camp went about its business, and the past few days revolved in his mind. So many burials, endless talks, speculations on what freakery had almost ended the world a second time. They had gained more ground than in the previous forty years combined. Through it all, Norman had wanted Richard by his side.

It was for this that the professor had schooled his disciple. It was with Richard's kind that their future lay.

They had a long way to go. New Canterbury was cinders, thousands of innocents lay dead in the wilds, having taken countless memories and skills and titbits of knowledge with them. Leaders of a calibre that came about but once in a generation had been exterminated. All their faces swirled in his mind as he watched Richard's eyes flicker under their bloated lids.

Alexander, James, Agatha, Evelyn, DeGray, Heather, Marek—even Robert, whom nobody had seen since the battle's end. Norman didn't expect to see him again, even if he had survived. If he had learned anything, it was that some things, once broken, could never be whole again.

Norman reached into his pocket, found the charred king piece that had belonged to Professor DeGray, and set it upon the bedside stand. "You earned it," he said.

He remained until Allie appeared by his side. They watched Richard sleep until she said, "It's time for the ceremony."

Norman nodded. "I wonder if they felt like we do now, before the lies started: are we as blind as they were?" He turned to her. "How do we know we're doing the right thing, Allie?"

She drew close and laid her hands on his chest. "We never will. All we can do is what we can."

He nodded. "And if I fail?"

She smiled, tracing his cheek with a fingertip before slapping it gently. "I'll be there to put you on your arse."

They left the tent and headed for the foot of the tower. A crowd had gathered at its base, filling the courtyard. The ground had been cleared of bodies, but otherwise remained untouched.

They would not hide what had happened, lest they forget, not until they saw who they stood to become.

Norman made his way to the front of the gathering, numbering some two thousand in total, and took note of a few faces. The surviving councillors of the Old Alliance: Robert Oppenheimer, David Rush, Emma Thompson; those who had once sat upon high as gods to their flocks were now lost among their peers as the everyman.

Southerners stood beside Northerners, survivors of the fiefdoms of the feudal lords and free peoples of the Old Alliance alike. A handful were Scots, emissaries from the reaches of the highlands.

All had been drawn by the voice of Latif Hadad. The radio Blanket had fractured in full, leaving a spectrum utterly clear. The white noise had lasted but a few days before voices had emerged from the static. Not all spoke as they did. Some spoke languages only a handful of survivors had heard. There was a world out there, and it remembered. Perhaps, across the world, millions awaited.

Latif and Lincoln were nowhere to be seen, and Norman smiled, knowing they were both locked away in the workshop, toiling over their next broadcast. There was much work to be done.

*Whoever's out there, we'll find them*, he thought.

"It's time," Allie said.

"Where's Billy?"

Allie pushed him forwards gently. "She'll be watching."

Norman searched himself and found no trace of the chill that had bound him to Billy and the strange other world. He stepped from the crowd to meet Lucian, whose silver hair blended with the white robe he had donned: the robe of the elders of the Old Alliance. Though he wore it with visible reluctance, he wore it well.

Norman said, "I've been remembering a lot lately. From before this"—he gestured to the scar upon his head—"and before…" Flames in his mind's eye, flashes of a much younger James, whole and brave and scared, racing into the heart of a faraway place called Newquay's Moon. "I know it was never supposed to be me."

Lucian's eyes creased to slits. "Don't go talking about things *meant to be*. Those are his words. Be yourself: that's what we need." Lucian held out a woodsman's axe. "Do your brothers proud."

Norman lifted the axe and approached a sheet covering the wall above the lobby. A rope held by a peg in the floor bound it in place. He stepped to one side and took a long look around at everyone. "There is no future set in stone. We are who we choose to be."

He swung the axe into the soil, cutting the rope. The sheet fell away and revealed the crest of the New Alliance: a white-robed figure with an arm outstretched, upon which a pigeon alighted.

# EPILOGUE

Billy sat cross-legged on a vent grating, high above London's streets. Up here the wind was cold and mussed her hair, fresh and clear. Far below, Norm and the others disappeared into the tower.

"We did it, Daddy," she said, kicking her heels. "We beat the Bad Men."

She reached out inside, searching for a glimmer of Daddy's voice, his face, hoping the Light might bring him back to her just this once. But not this time. She had only her memories.

"We did it," she muttered.

A piece of her hadn't wanted the quest to stop. Since arriving in Enger Land she had been hurt and scared, seen things that swept away pieces of her like dandelion petals in the wind—but she had had a purpose, and she hadn't been so alone.

Without Daddy and Ma and Grandpa, she had nobody.

*No*, she reminded herself as Allie and Norm's faces floated in front of her. Things had changed.

"It's okay, Daddy. You don't have to worry about me."

The wind swept her hair under her chin, tickling her neck, and she smiled. She imagined Daddy by her now, and the wind became his hand on her skin, his lips kissing her cheek.

Stranger things had happened in Enger Land.

"It's over," she said, watching the sun climb higher in the sky. She let herself drift off, just staring, wondering whether maybe, just maybe, the world had grown a little brighter.

She wasn't sure when she first sensed a presence close by, but when she returned from drifting in the clouds, cold crept up the vent under her legs, and somebody sat beside her. She didn't look over, didn't need to, just kept watch over the city twinkling in the sun.

"I did it," she said.

"Yes. You did," said Fol. He drew a long sigh.

"It's not over, is it?"

"No."

She looked at him. His pale face bore his signature half-friendly expression. His thin body was covered by the same dark overcoat. But something was different about him. The cragged cap to his head that looked like hair—but she knew had been the seat of his Jester's hat—rustled in the wind. His clothing crumpled as he moved.

He seemed more *there*…

Billy reached out and prodded his arm. Her finger bent on contact with his overcoat. Cold, touched with Frost, but there.

"You're…"

"Things are different now. We're playing a whole new game. You saved this world for now, but the Vanished still labour, and All Where is still in danger. The gloves are off, girl. It's time to take the fight to them."

Billy swallowed. She knew she could say no, if she wanted. She could stay here with Allie and Norm and the others, and she might be happy.

But the Light would never fade, and one day soon, it would all go away for good—not just this place, but all places.

"We have to find the others," she said.

"You feel them?"

Billy searched herself. "They're so far away."

Fol stood from the grate, dusting his coat. "Better get started then. Are you ready, Billy?"

She stole one last look at the city, held it in her mind like a glowing ember, and hopped down from the grate. "Where now?"

Fol walked to the roof-access door, gesturing with theatrical flair. "Our chariot awaits," he said.

"You're mad."

"No," he said, his face consumed by a leer lost between humour and insanity, revealing his pointed teeth. "Just a little foolish." Then just as quickly, the grin fell into a solemn stare. "Comes with the job."

He pulled the door open, revealing a perfect oblong of darkness; leading not down into the building, but elsewhere.

"Where?" she said.

"Now that would be telling."

*The start of a long, long road,* she thought.

Fol held out the crook of his elbow, bowing slightly. "Shall we?"

Billy threaded her hand through his arm, hesitated, then led them through the door and into darkness. For a moment she thought everything had come to an end. Then came new light and beyond.

*No. Not the end. The End was just the beginning.*

# GET THE PREQUEL: FROST

Phew, what a ride! The *Ruin Saga* has been a thrill to write, and I hope it was just as fun to read. It's sad to be closing off this story, but there's good news: things don't end here.

*Frost*, a prequel novella, explores the secrets behind the series. What is the blanket? Who knew about the End? Who are the mysterious vanguards of All Where?

**Find out at:**
**www.harrymanners.net/signup/buyfrostbook**

# LEAVE A REVIEW

If you have a spare moment, I'd really appreciate a review from you. It's a huge help in bringing new readers to the series. Thanks!

Review by visiting:
www.harrymanners.net/signup/reviewfray

# JOIN THE MAILING LIST

Join my list to get free stories, hear when I have a new book out, and get the latest news on discounts and deals.

http://eepurl.com/bv9Njv

# ACKNOWLEDGEMENTS


My sincere thanks go out to everyone who helped me put this book together. My family and friends I'll mention first; their support gives me the strength to keep sitting down to write each day. My editor Claire Rushbrook has once again helped me craft a better book, and it wouldn't have been the same without her. Several readers who followed the series as it was written also contributed suggestions and pulled me up on stupid mistakes, for which I am always grateful.

Special thanks to Norma Miles, to whom this book is dedicated, for all her work in helping me revise the manuscript. An author couldn't ask for a more wonderful reader.

All of you made the *Ruin Saga* that much more pleasurable to write. These books were crafted as much by your hands as mine.

# ABOUT THE AUTHOR

Harry Manners lives in Bedfordshire, England. When he's not writing, he studies science at university, reads anything he can get his hands on, and generally nerds out—for which he is staunchly unapologetic.

**Website:**

www.harrymanners.net

**Facebook page:**

www.facebook.com/OfficialHarryManners

**Twitter:**

@harry_a_manners